FOLKTALES OF *Chile*

 *Folktales*

OF THE WORLD

GENERAL EDITOR : RICHARD M. DORSON

FOLKTALES OF
Chile

EDITED BY
Yolando Pino-Saavedra

TRANSLATED BY ROCKWELL GRAY

FOREWORD BY
Richard M. Dorson

THE UNIVERSITY OF CHICAGO PRESS

Library of Congress Catalog Card Number: 67-25585
The University of Chicago Press, Chicago 60637
Routledge & Kegan Paul, Ltd., London, E.C. 4
The University of Toronto Press, Toronto 5, Canada
© 1967 by The University of Chicago
Published 1967
Printed in the United States of America

To Stith Thompson

Foreword

I. The Folk Traditions of the New World

With the appearance of *Folktales of Chile* as the initial Latin American volume in the Folktales of the World series, the question of how to define folklore in the western hemisphere comes to the fore. Oral traditions in North and South America differ in important ways from those of Europe, Asia, and Africa, and find a counterpart only in Australia. Since the history of the Americas begins in the sixteenth century, with the extension of western European power across the Atlantic sea, the culture of the Americas in the twentieth century presents a medley of imported and indigenous strands. In the Old World we can speak confidently of national folklores, knowing they are possessed by peoples who have inhabited the same land and have spoken the same tongue for many centuries. In the New World we wait with curious wonder to see whether the aboriginal Indian, the transplanted European, or the slave African tradition will dominate, or whether they will coalesce, or perhaps exterminate each other. Further, the observer wishes to know what new contributions have stemmed from the extravagant geography and revolutionary history of the western world.

These components of the New World folk traditions appear in varying strengths in one or another locality. What unites the Americas in a common folklore mixture are the great historic forces of exploration, conquest, colonization, revolution, Negro slavery, and European and Asiatic immigration, superimposed on the original Indian race. From the era of empire building in the sixteenth and seventeenth centuries derives the European tale stocks harvested in recent decades: French *contes* in northeastern Canada, English wonder tales in the southern Appalachians,

German *Sagen* and *Schwänke* in Pennsylvania, Spanish *cuentos* strewn from Mexico to Argentina, Portuguese *contos* in Brazil. The English is palest of all these tale traditions, even though the North American colonies were so thoroughly an offshoot of Britain, but beginning in the 1920's collectors struck hidden veins of Jack the Giant-Killer folktales stored among families in the southern mountains.

The transplanted ethnic repertoires of the colonizing period must be sharply distinguished from immigrant strains of the nineteenth and twentieth centuries. Although collectors are only beginning to pay them heed, these latecomers have already planted a variety of folk narratives in the Americas. From the Ukrainians of western Canada[1] to the Italians, Germans, Jews, Scotch, and Irish of Argentina and Chile, the two continents have played host to vast numbers of Europeans emigrating not to a wilderness but to established political states. Instead of confronting nomadic and erasable savages, or even the advanced societies of the Aztecs and Incas, as did the colonists, the immigrants faced modern nations with alien institutions to which they had to adjust. Yet in spite of their relatively recent appearance in the New World, the latecomers have in some places managed to introduce the festivals and folk customs which formed so integral a part of their lives in the old country. Immigrant folklore is one of the most neglected areas of collecting and research, but we have recently seen substantial collections from Detroit of Polish folksongs and Armenian folktales as evidence of the abundance that exists.[2] To what degree these hoards represent memory culture or living culture still remains an open question.

Whether transplanted in the colonial or in the national periods, the European traditions still retain their family resemblance. We cannot sharply distinguish between Iberian tale-tellers and those in Scandinavian, Central European, and Balkan countries but the

---

[1] Robert B. Klymasz, "The Case for Slavic Folklore in Canada," *Proceedings of the First Conference on Canadian Slavs at Banff, Alberta* (University of Alberta, 1966), pp. 110–20.

[2] Harriet M. Pawlowska, *Merrily We Sing, 105 Polish Folksongs* (Detroit, 1961); Susie Hoogasian-Villa, *100 Armenian Tales and Their Folkloristic Relevance* (Detroit, 1966).

contrast between the European and the Indian narrator is crystal
clear. Old World peasants related *Märchen,* wonder tales filled
with magical and violent adventures of low-born heroes winning
princesses and vanquishing ogres; *novelle,* farcical narratives of
cuckoldry and trickery; *Sagen,* legends of remarkable local
events; *Schwänke,* anecdotal jests of fools and wags. The universe of North and South American Indians, from the Eskimos
of the northern tundra to the Patagonians of Tierra del Fuego,
also displays a uniformity. This universe is peopled with wood-
land creatures who insensibly glide into human forms, with
thunderbird deities and serpent demons, with twin heroes and a
ubiquitous trickster who turns up as a coyote, a raven, a mink, or
a wandering man of magic powers. The forms of *Märchen* and
Sagen have no meaning for the Indian narrator, who does not
make believe; rather, he draws the line between immediate and
more remote realities. Tales do not simply entertain but give the
tribes their history and theology.

What happens at that dramatic historical moment when these
folktale repertoires meet? Some answers are already provided for
us in North America by Stith Thompson, who has demonstrated
the intrusion of European folktales into the story stocks of the
red man. In my own fieldwork in Michigan's Upper Peninsula, I
have heard Ojibwa, Potawatomi, and Sioux narrate occasional
Märchen, and once the teller knowingly remarked, "That's a
white man's story." But the process does not appear to operate in
reverse. Groups of white men living in close proximity to the
Peninsula Indians knew no Ojibwa narratives and the one white
raconteur celebrated for his recital of Indian traditions actually
delivered sugary romances of the Lover's Leap variety calculated
to satisfy tourists visiting Hiawathaland.[3] Longfellow's *The
Song of Hiawatha,* set in the Upper Peninsula and based on
authentic Ojibwa tales recorded by Henry Rowe Schoolcraft,
illustrates the transformation wrought on oral tribal literature
when it is adapted to the romantic stereotypes of an art literature.

Still, the historical situation of the United States differs consid-
erably from that of Canada and Latin America. The English set-

[3] Richard M. Dorson, *Bloodstoppers and Bearwalkers, Folk Traditions
of the Upper Peninsula* (Cambridge, Massachusetts, 1952).

tlers on the Atlantic coast ejected the Indian tribes, driving them ever westward and finally relegating them to reservation tracts. Hence the Indian tribal lore never penetrated into United States civilization, even though the image of the noble savage powerfully affected the imagination of his conquerors. By contrast, the Spaniards and the Frenchmen lived and mated with the subject Indians, producing a new social class, the mestizo or half-breed. We may reasonably expect the traditions too to mate.

As if the confluence of two powerful narrative streams were not enough, yet a third flowed into the New World cauldron, this time from the African continent. Negro slavery persisted in the United States until a Civil War and the thirteenth amendment to the Constitution in 1865 ended involuntary servitude, and in Brazil until peaceful legislation freed the black man in 1888. In both North and South America, enslaved West Africans chopped cotton, cut cane, and planted tobacco and coffee on the plantations of white masters. In some places escaped blacks formed independent communities deep in the bush country. Wherever they landed and in whatever conditions they found themselves, even when cruelly wrenched from their original cultures, the Africans continued to tell traditional tales. But they were not necessarily the tales of Africa.

West African storytelling bore some resemblance to American Indian storytelling, for both portrayed an animistic world, but the cast of characters differed notably. African narrators spoke and sang of jungle denizens, historical kings and chiefs provided with long genealogies, and the gods of an elaborate pantheon. There was a divine trickster but he had to share the stage with numerous other specialized deities. Africans delighted in the dilemma tale, leaving unresolved the climax of the plot—as, for instance, the question which of three suitors had done most to rescue the maiden and win her hand. When the Georgia writer Joel Chandler Harris began publishing his Uncle Remus tales in the 1880's, the general public followed the author's lead in assuming that oral fictions told by Negroes in the southern states emanated from Africa, an assumption that anthropologists came to take for granted in the twentieth century, especially Africaoriented ethnologists such as Melville J. Herskovits and his disciples. Yet in analyzing my own field collections of the 1950's from southern Negroes, I discovered that the vast majority matched European rather than African tale types.[4] This corpus of narratives belongs to the mainland sharecropper and tenant farmer cotton culture of the deep South and overlaps only at certain points with the literary tellings of Uncle Remus. The fact is that several bodies of New World Negro traditions exist; others are found along the sea islands of the Carolinas, in the Bahamas and the West Indies, in Brazil and Surinam, and these possess a much higher degree of African retentions than do the folktales of mainland Negroes in the United States. We can find in the collections of Beckwith from Jamaica and of the Herskovitses from Surinam the Anansi stories, often in the cante-fable form with little songs inserted in the plots, so characteristic of West Africa.[5] Yet the Herskovitses regard their informants from Paramibo as no more African in appearance and behavior, by comparison with the strongly African Bush Negroes of the interior, than Negroes of the Caribbean islands or the rural southern states. Ethnic repertoires may vary at different points in time as well as in different localities, and when Harris first set down the Uncle Remus stories, one generation after slavery, plantation Negroes may well have known a higher proportion of Africa-derived narratives. When collectors began probing Southern Negro traditions half a century later they encountered the Old Marster and John cycle, featuring a battle of wits between the white plantation owner and his clever slave. In all his books Harris included only one Old Marster tale. Today in the urban North, in New York's Harlem, in south Philadelphia, and in Chicago's south side, new folk forms and styles, such as the toasties and the dozens, are becoming visible in the Negro ghettoes. Since slavery

---

[4] *Negro Folktales in Michigan* (Cambridge, Massachusetts, 1956); *Negro Tales from Pine Bluff, Arkansas, and Calvin, Michigan* (Bloomington, Indiana, 1958).

[5] Martha W. Beckwith, *Jamaica Anansi Stories,* Memoirs of the American Folklore Society 17 (1924); Melville J. and Frances S. Herskovits, *Suriname Folk-Lore* (New York, 1936).

took dissimilar forms in the Americas, we can expect the folktales of Portuguese-speaking Negroes to reflect the greater harmony of the Brazilian system.

The African in the New World mated with the white and the red man to produce mulattoes, born of Negro and white parents, and zamboes, born of Indian and Negro parents. Frequently the three blood streams mingled in the same family. Sometimes whole communities of these mixed breeds emerged, living in a twilight zone between the fixed social and racial groupings of society in the Americas. The traditions of these groups should greatly intrigue the folklorist.

One synthesizing force at work among the European, Indian, and African folk culture has proved to be Christianity, in both its Roman Catholic and Protestant forms. Through the process known as reinterpretation, converted pagans identified their own deities, rites, and myths with those of Christian doctrine. A parallel process is the folk development of colorful ceremonies and dramatic legends from a shell of abstract theology. These processes yield such novelties as religious festivals sorrowing for the crucifixion of the Virgin Mary or of a colored Jesus; a cycle of miraculous cures attached to a *curandero,* whom Mexican peasants elevate to sainthood; and Negro retellings of biblical and apocryphal tales that present Moses and the Pharaoh, or Christ and the devil, as rival sorcerers. Priests and missionaries thus helped to create a religious folklore uniting in curious blends the three peoples of the New World.

Historical and geographical factors have also shaped New World folklore. By the historical element we refer to memorable episodes, heroic and picaresque personalities, and eccentric regional types attracting popular lore in the four centuries since the white man invaded the Americas. By the geographical element we allude to the giant cordillera ranges, the beckoning coastlines, majestic rivers like the Amazon and the Mississippi, the endless pampas and prairies, the jungles and rain forests, the lush bottom lands and scrubby backcountry, the treasures of underground ores, and the novel flora and fauna which have affected tradition. The character of the land influenced the character of the men who settled it, determined their occupations and livelihoods, excited their imaginations, and molded their legends. Often enough, the historical and geographical factors merged. For one instance, the traveler's tale, strewn through the writings of sixteenth and seventeenth century visitors to the New World, resulted from the historic facts of exploration and conquest and the geographic facts of the strange new hemisphere. Traveler's fables of physical and aboriginal wonders thrilled readers in London, Paris, Amsterdam, Madrid, and Lisbon, becoming a stock feature of overseas literature.[6] Such tales incorporated folk motifs from medieval bestiaries, and in a later day they glided into the hoaxing tall tale told with tongue in cheek to gull the credulous. For another example, the cattle industry bred a species of herdsman on the open range variously known as a cowboy, gaucho, and huaso, and he himself became a mythic figure, both the bearer and the subject of song and story. Conflicts between national or regional character types also generated an oral lore expressed in corridos, outlaw and hero legends, anecdotes, and witticisms. Along the Mexican-United States border wry jests pitted the greaser against the gringo, the former satirically portrayed as a swarthy, idle, thieving scapegrace and the latter as a greedy, vain, arrogant bully.[7] The folk concept of the gringo has permeated all South America.

These elements have formed the folklore of the New World. Yet each republic or dominion in the Americas reveals its own national pattern of folk materials.

II. Folk Traditions of Chile

All the ingredients combining to form New World tradition, save only the Negro, appear in Chile, the most remote and least known of the Spanish colonies.[8] A bizarre history equal to its mad geography unfolded in this sinuous sliver of a land hugging

[6] Percy G. Adams, *Travelers and Travel Liars, 1660–1800* (Berkeley and Los Angeles, 1962), discusses the travel writers' tall tales.

[7] Américo Paredes has collected and written on Texas-Mexican border lore in *"With His Pistol in His Hand": A Border Ballad and Its Hero* (Austin, Texas, 1958), and in *Buying the Wind, Regional Folklore in the United States,* ed. R. M. Dorson (Chicago, 1964), pp. 452–54.

[8] Louis Galdames, *A History of Chile,* translated and edited by Isaac Joslin Cox (Chapel Hill, North Carolina, 1941), p. 212.

two-thirds of a continent and jammed between the snow-crested Andes and the whitecaps of the Pacific. Chile falls readily into four regions which correspond to four folk traditions. In the north is the cruel Atacama desert, wrested in part from Peru and Bolivia in the war of 1879 to 1883 after nitrate had been discovered in its waterless wastes. Here has grown a lore of miners digging for nitrate, silver, and copper. The fertile Central Valley extending south from Coquimbo to Concepción, with its splendid haciendas and agricultural estates, is often called the real Chile, and here the conquistadors planted their cities and the Spanish culture with its peasant folktales. Here too the revolution of Chile against Spain was chiefly fought. The rain-soaked forests south of the Bío Bío River remained for three centuries the "Frontera" and the natural stronghold of the Araucanian Indians, who preserved their tribal institutions and oral literature in the area between the Itata and the Toltén Rivers.[9] A fourth region may be defined as the coast, extending from the port of Arica south to the Straits of Magellan, with its harbors, islands, ships, fishermen, and mariners, producing a lore of the sea. This Foreword will consider these several historical traditions, which are distinct from the fictional folktales in the body of this book.

1. The Indians

The early history of Chile is largely the chronicle of a race struggle between the Spaniards and the Araucanians. Chile first came into view as a grim footnote to Francisco Pizarro's conquest and spoliation of Peru. In 1535 Diego de Almagro, a fellow conquistador to Pizarro, led an abortive expedition southwards across mountains, deserts, and rivers in quest of gold conjured up by deceiving Peruvian Indians. The expedition ended in despair and disaster, ten thousand Indians who had been pressed into Almagro's service perishing on the way. Nevertheless in 1540 another of Pizarro's officers, Pedro de Valdivia, renewed the assault on the forbidding country, founding Santiago the following year and penetrating south to the Bío Bío, where he confronted the

[9] George McCutchen McBride, *Chile: Land and Society* (New York, 1936), pp. 17–22, describes the regions of Chile.

warlike Araucanians, a far different breed from the weak creatures whom the Spaniards had enslaved en route. The conquistadors and after them the Chileños fought the Araucanians until 1884, when a peaceful settlement was finally concluded.

A continuous literary record depicts these residents of the Arauco region that gave them their name. (They are also known as Mapuche, "people from the earth.") From the period of contact date the stirring epic *La Araucana* of Ercilla y Zuñiga and the five letters written by Valdivia to his king, Charles V. Then come the accounts of travelers and sojourners in the Frontera, and finally the field reports of modern anthropologists. The Araucanians fall somewhere between the high Inca and Aztec civilizations and the lower nomadic tribes of hunters and food-gatherers. A visitor from the United States in 1853 registered his disappointment at their appearance, which fell far short of the "gente indomable" pictured by Ercilla:

> They are generally of about the middle height, broad-chested, thick set, inclined with age to corpulency, and, as a race, far inferior in appearance to the North American Indian aborigines. The calves of their legs and their ankles are large and fleshy, and the foot, though very short, is broad and high, rising abruptly from the big-toe to the ankle with very little curve. The head, too, of the Mapuché is of a peculiar shape; it is narrow and low in front, broad and high behind, and forms almost a straight line with the back of the neck, which is massive and short.[10]

This observer, Edmond Reuel Smith, further remarked that similar characteristics of head and foot prevailed among the lower classes of the Chileans and even, where Indian blood had entered Spanish veins, among the aristocracy. Foreigners in Santiago found shoes too broad and high in the instep for their European feet.

Impressive or not, this race produced heroic and memorable leaders. The youth Lautaro, once a groom to Valdivia, led the first revolt against his master, sacked his cities, and nearly captured Santiago. His successor, Caupolicán, so enraged the Span-

[10] Edmond Reuel Smith, *The Araucanians; or, Notes of a Tour Among the Indian Tribes of Southern Chili* (New York, 1855), p. 245.

iards that upon his capture they impaled him on a stake in the plaza of Cañete while archers shot at his writhing body. In spite of the recurrent warfare, considerable intermingling and inter-marrying took place between the races. The lower Chilean classes are considered to be distinct from any other rural or urban labor-ing class in South America and one main reason is this infusion of Araucanian blood.[11] One commentator after another remarks on the difficulty in distinguishing between the Araucanians and Chilean laborers, such as the *inquilinos* who worked on the great *fundos,* or the vagrant *rotos* who roved the cities and countryside. On the one hand, the conquistadors resorted to Indian maidens in lieu of any other available women. On the other hand, all kinds of runaways from the Spanish colonies—Castilians, mestizos, mulattoes—sought refuge among the Araucanians. Each side took captives, some of whom remained permanently, others of whom returned to their own people. Nevertheless, if the races have mixed and influenced each other, Chileño and Arau-canian have retained their cultural identities. Today about a quarter of a million souls practice the Mapuche religion, per-haps a half to a fourth the number who did so in the sixteenth century.

The Araucanians, like other Indian peoples, possess a varied narrative tradition, striated now with European elements but still undeniably their own. In the *Handbook of South American In-dians,* John M. Cooper has listed a number of themes in Mapuche storytelling. These include supernatural beings called *meul·en* and *shompalwe;* grotesque monsters such as *cherufe,* a comet doubling as a cannibal giant, *waillepen,* a calf-sheep, and *piwichen,* a winged serpent; ghosts and apparitions; sorcerers; and animal characters, with the fox in the leading role. In the evening, adults of both sexes narrated stories of these figures with animation and clever mimicry.[12] Further details are added by Mischa Titiev in his field study of Araucanians in transition.

[11] McBride, p. 150.
[12] John M. Cooper, "The Araucanians," in *Handbook of South Amer-ican Indians,* ed. Julian H. Steward, vol. 2 (Smithsonian Institution, Bur-eau of American Ethnology Bulletin No. 143: Washington, D. C., 1946), pp. 752–53.

Sorcerers control the various evil spirits, collectively known as *wekufü*. Specific *wekufü*, like the vampire *piwichen* and *choñchoñ*, a winged human head, brought instant death to the beholder or even to the one who heard the sound of their passage. The term *cherufe* applied to various objects connected with heat or light, whether volcanoes, shooting stars, meteors, or will-o-the-wisps. Every witch owned a *cherufe*, usually a peculiarly shaped stone taken from a live volcano, which at her command flew to a victim and drank his blood. Graveyard corpses stolen for the use of witches formed another kind of *cherufe*, designated *witranalwe*. This ghoul could be seen only in outline, at night and on horseback, giving off a whitish hue, and seeking, like the Irish *pooka*, to lead benighted travelers astray. "Exciting encounters with *witranalwe* and narrow escapes from them are favorite subjects of stories, and such beliefs explain why parents fear to permit children to wander out of the house after dark," notes Titiev, thereby linking the Araucanians with the world-wide genre of bogeyman folklore.[13] He paraphrases one popular evening tale that illustrates several witchcraft beliefs.

> It concerns a man who was courting a girl that lived at some distance from his home. Whenever he went to see her he would hear the call of a *choñchoñ* and begin to feel violently ill. His elders advised him that the next time this happened he should plunge his knife into the ground. He followed their instructions and, to his surprise, a winged head fell to earth. He thought that it resembled his mistress, so he hurried to her house and there he found her headless body lying on its back. Thereupon, he deliberately rolled the body over, to prevent the head from reattaching itself properly. Then he went home, and the very next day he received word that his sweetheart had died.[14]

[13] Mischa Titiev, *Araucanian Culture in Transition* (Occasional Contributions from the Museum of Anthropology of the University of Michigan, No. 15: Ann Arbor, Michigan, 1951), pp. 111–12.

[14] *Ibid.*, p. 111. The *choñchoñ* falls under the class of *Malevolent or destructive fairies*, Motif F360 in Stith Thompson, *Motif-Index of Folk Literature*, 6 vols. (Bloomington, Indiana, 1955–58). Pertinent is Motif F363.3, *Sight of fairies fatal*.

This episode suggests correspondences with European and Anglo-American witchcraft. Driving a knife into a spirit is known among Lapp wizards. In England and North America a witch commonly appears in the guise of an attractive maiden and dies when her familiar is killed.

Another anthropologist recently in the field, L. C. Faron, corroborates and expands Titiev's testimony. Faron observes that the detection of malevolent night birds around the house gives rise to the "most detailed and hair-raising stories" about encounters with the supernatural which circulate from one community to another. To relieve their tension after frights the Mapuche recall these experiences in a laughing mood, secure in the warmth of their fireside circle, much as Negroes of the southern United States exchange spectral stories of ghosts and "hants" with much surface jollity to conceal an underlying dread. In their light moments the Mapuche refer to mounted Chilean policemen riding the roads at night dressed in white tunics as *witranalwe*. The following oft-told narrative, from Faron, shows the intimate relations possible between humans and a *witranalwe*.

In the environs of Pitrufquén, there lived a rather wealthy man who had many animals. He also had a *witranalwe* to guard them in his absence. Near this wealthy man lived two of his brother's sons, who were poor.

One day, the rich man visited his nephews' house. They all began to drink a lot of wine and became a little drunk by late afternoon. They began to feel hungry, but the nephews had nothing to serve the old man. They decided to steal a couple of sheep from the corral of their uncle. One said to the other that he was a rich old man and that stealing one of his sheep, perhaps even two, did not matter much. They went to the uncle's corral together, leaving the old man in their house drinking.

When they arrived, they saw a huge figure on horseback. The man wore a very large, black hat. He had a large mouth and long, sharp teeth, and a big, penetrating set of eyes. He wore a Spanish poncho, also large and black; and he had a set of silver spurs with great rowels. Upon seeing him, one of the nephews ran away, but the other, who had a

sheep under his arm, stood still before him. He fearfully
asked, "Who are you, caballero?" The answer came in a
very low and deep voice: "I am the partner of the owner of
these sheep." The nephew then said that the owner of the
sheep was his uncle and, therefore, "Señor, we are like kins-
men."

After this, the young man took a little more courage and
spoke further to the *witranalwe:* "Señor, why not let me
take this sheep for the fiesta in my house? My uncle is a very
wealthy man, and the loss of one little lamb, which he himself will eat part of, will not matter to him." The *witranalwe*
answered in a very deep voice, "All right, but I want a bowl
of *ñachi* [blood] when you kill the animal."

The young man assented to this demand, at the same time
asking the *witranalwe* to help him carry the sheep back to
the house. As soon as they arrived at the young man's house,
he told the *witranalwe* to return in a little while for the
blood. He set both the bowl and a pitcher of wine outside
the house for the *witranalwe.* The *witranalwe* approached at
a gallop, drank the *ñachi* at one gulp, and then tossed off the
wine. When he finished, he galloped off to the uncle's corral
to keep watch over his master's sheep. He never revealed the
secret to his master.[15]

In spite of the presence of a supernatural being, this belief tale
realistically mirrors the culture. The *witranalwe* wears a Spanish
poncho and spurs of the kind customarily seen on *huasos*. Like a
good Mapuche, he requests *ñachi,* a favorite dish prepared by
stringing up a sheep by its forelegs and slitting its throat, then
turning the main artery into its windpipe, while salting and pep-
pering the bloodstream. The sheep rapidly suffocates and from
its intestines is drawn a highly relished blood pudding. Envy of
their rich paternal uncle by the two brothers, and the desire to
acquire his animals, are emotions fitting the social realities of the
Mapuche and leading to the wish fulfillment fantasy of the plot,
in which the youths conspire with the *witranalwe* to flout the un-

---

[15] L. C. Faron, *Hawks of the Sun, Mapuche Morality and Its Ritual At-
tributes* (Pittsburgh, 1964), pp. 72–73. The *witranalwe* belongs to the class
of Motif F470, *Night-spirits.*

cle's authority. In its firm structure, the narrative reveals a transition from the spectral experience of an individual to the well-knit pattern of a fictional folktale.

Other narrations simply report the presence of demons. A young woman of the Liumalla region made her way to a remote mountain stream to leave an offering for the *shompalwe,* who inhabits streams and lakes, as a means of ensuring her luck fishing. Mapuche in the area found her foot by the stream and believed that the *shompalwe* had abducted her to live with him, leaving only her foot.[16]

Along with these relations of contemporary incidents involving demons, the Mapuche recount mythical stories in another vein linking themselves with founders of their race and with ancestor gods. One popular myth, found in the Central Valley and along the coast in the Toltén area, pits Tren Tren, a protective mountain spirit, against Kai Kai, an evil tree serpent or sea bird who endeavored to wipe out the Mapuche by flooding the land. The people climbed Tren Tren with their animals and the mountain kept rising to escape the flood, until Kai Kai's power was used up. So Tren Tren saved the Mapuche who now live in his vicinity. In some variants Kai Kai is pictured as having the head of a great ox, three trees for arms, and a tail rooted in the ground, which people would hit with sticks until one day the vexed Kai Kai led all the animals into the air. There they remain as spirit guardians of living animals. This opposition between protective spirits in the sky and obnoxious serpents underground, often coupled with a flood myth, permeates the oral literature of North and South American Indians.

Another long myth accounts for the origin of the *ñillatun* ceremony, the most elaborate and important Mapuche ritual combining sacrifice, dance, and prayer. According to the myth, the *ñillatun* will protect the Indians from floods and droughts by propitiating two birds who once saved the people from the spell of a *kalku,* an evil spirit. A separate myth associates offerings at the *ñillatun* with Manquián, a sea deity. Once, while shellfishing,

[16] *Ibid.,* pp. 73–74. The *shompalwe* can be grouped with other *Waterspirits* under Motif F420. Also relevant are Motifs C41, *Tabu: Offending water-spirits,* and F301.3, *Girl goes to fairyland and marries fairy.*

his feet became stuck to rocks. People came and burned offerings to him, but he gradually turned to stone and became a *ñenechen,* a god of the Mapuche. Comparable myths connect Mapuche in the mountains, coast, and valleys with local ancestral deities.[17]

One wonders whether Araucanian storytellers have added historical traditions of the Spaniards to their repertoire since the coming of the white man. Ethnographers usually slight such traditions, but the traveler Edmond Reuel Smith did pose this question directly to his Indian hosts. He discovered that they retained no recollections of Spanish conquest and did not even know the names of generals and battles in the South American wars for independence. Smith may not, however, be the most reliable of reporters, since he also states that the Mapuche possessed no origin or deluge myths. He did report a traveler's tale in reverse, presenting an Araucanian view of the outside world. An aged chief, Mañin-Hueno (The Grass of Heaven) asked Smith about the lands of pigmies, giants, and the place where people carried their heads under their arms, lands that passing travelers had described to him; yet curiously he had never heard of the fabled Patagonians close by. In particular he asked about the Country of Glass Beads. "Is it true," he queried, "that the beads grow upon trees in the land of the setting sun, and that they who gather them ride into the country at night on swift horses, and return laden before the rising of the sun, whose first rays would burn them to death?" Smith's interpreter, in answering, was reluctant to pierce the illusion.[18] Araucanians who visited the zoological gardens in Santiago came away believing the zoo keepers, and hence Chileans in general, were powerful witches, since sorcerers among the Mapuche used strange animals as their familiars.[19]

Yet there may also exist a sly comic tradition that demonstrates how well the Araucanians know the foibles of the European invaders. One example is provided in an anecdote of an Englishman visiting Valparaiso for the first time and doffing his hat in admiration at the beauty of the snow-capped Andes. His Indian

[17] *Ibid.,* pp. 75–79. Motifs are A1015.1.1, *Flood from conflict of monsters* and A974, *Rocks from transformation of people to stone.*
[18] Smith, pp. 252–59.
[19] Titiev, p. 110.

carriage-driver thereupon remarked, "Señor, do not imagine that
that is silver. It is only snow." [20]

2. Spaniards and Chileans

"Near the city [of Concepción] Valdivia fought a desperate
battle with the Indians, and some fantastic stories about it have
survived the years." [21] So wrote the eminent United States historian and ambassador to Chile, Claude G. Bowers, testifying in
1958 to the tenacity of wondrous historical traditions transmitted
in speech and print since the Spaniards first encountered the
Araucanians in 1541. Writers on Chile keep referring to these
marvels beheld apparently by warriors of both races when the
Araucanians unaccountably paused in their march. Valdivia
himself recounted this tradition, replete with folk motifs, in one
of his letters to His Catholic Majesty Charles V.

> For, according to the words of the Indian natives, on the
> day they fell upon this fort of ours, when the mounted men
> rode on to them, an old man on a white horse fell into the
> midst of their squadrons, saying: "Flee, all of ye; for these
> Christians will kill you"; and the fear they felt was so great
> that they fled. They said furthermore that three days earlier,
> when they were crossing the Biubiu river to come against us,
> a comet fell among them one Saturday at midday (and from
> this fort where we were many Christians saw it go that way
> with a brightness far beyond that of other comets), and that
> when it had fallen a very beautiful lady came forth from it
> clad in white too, and that she said to them: "Obey the
> Christians, and do not strive against them, for they are very
> brave and will kill you all."
> And when she had gone from their midst, the devil their
> master came and put himself at their head, telling them
> "that a great multitude of men were to gather together, and
> that he would come with them, for when we (Christians)

[20] George Pendle, *The Land and People of Chile* (London and New
York, 1964), p. 18. This genre is presented in R. M. Dorson, "Comic Indian Anecdotes," *Southern Folklore Quarterly*, X (1946), 113–28.

[21] Claude G. Bowers, *Chile Through Embassy Windows: 1939–1953*
(New York, 1958), p. 195.

saw so many together, we should fall dead out of fear;" and
so they went on with their march.[22]

Elsewhere the old man on the white horse is identified as St.
James, for whom Santiago is named, and the beautiful lady as
the Holy Virgin, for whom Concepción is named.[23] The miraculous interposition of saints and the Virgin Mary in behalf of Soldiers of Christ, and the blandishments of the devil to the infidel,
recur throughout the wars of the Lord.[24] In North America too
the European invaders regarded Indians as minions of Satan and
believed God was providentially directing their battles. Valdivia's
inclusion of this miracle is of greater interest since his letters are
otherwise practical and matter–of–fact, leading one to surmise
that these stories must have stirred up much excitement among
the rival forces, each with their own set of supernatural concepts.
We remember that the Araucanians regarded comets and shooting stars as especially potent monsters.

Another marvelous explanation for the success of the conquistadors during their dark hour has set in motion another en-
during legend. Some said that an army helmeted and equipped
like the legions of Caesar suddenly emerged from the forest
depths behind the Araucanians and put them to flight, then
melted back into the woods of Lake Llanquihue. Then in 1563
two Spanish soldiers limped into Concepción claiming they had
come from the City of the Caesars, built deep in the interior from
shipwrecked survivors of vessels dispatched by the Bishop of
Plasencia. An official document of the times reports this state-
ment and even locates seven Spanish-Indian settlements dotting a
lake at 47½ degrees latitude. The fabled riches of this lost City of
the Caesars enticed expeditions into the forests which never did
find their target.[25] In the mid-nineteenth century Edmond

[22] Letter III from Pedro de Valdivia to Charles V, from the city of Concepción, dated 15 October 1550, in R. B. Cunninghame Graham, *Pedro de
Valdivia, Conqueror of Chile* (London, 1926), p. 196.

[23] Smith, pp. 313–14; Bowers, p. 195.

[24] Many miraculous motifs are grouped under V250, *The Virgin Mary.*
Other motifs present are V222.1, *Marvelous light accompanying saint* and
G303.9.96, *Devil leads and misguides people.*

[25] Bowers, pp. 195–96; Benjamin Subercaseaux, *Chile, A Geographic
Extravaganza,* translated by Angel Flores (New York, 1943), pp. 187–89.

Reuel Smith heard of a race of white Indians with golden hair
and light-blue eyes, whom the Chileños called the Boroaché.
Smith attributed the legend to the crop of babies resulting from
capture of Spanish women by the Araucanians from Valdivia's
first settlements.[26]

The author of *La Araucana,* Ercilla, shared Valdivia's view of
the Indians as savages lacking religion and unaware of God, and
so was the more ready to credit them with diabolical feats. In one
verse of his epic, the soldier–poet describes the remarkable sleep
of an Araucanian chief returned from the wars.

> Deep buried in a slumber so profound,
>   As though a thousand years he had been dead,
> Until the sun three times had journeyed round
>   The earth, when, rising from his bed—
> 'What ho, ye slaves! bring forth my garments,'
>   said he,
> 'And tell me, is the meal I ordered ready?'
> The servant answered—'If I may be so bold,
>   Sir,
> Your dinner after cooking has got cold, Sir!
> For you have slept, without as much as winking,
>   Full fifty hours, forgetful of your toils,
> Taking no care for eating or for drinking.' [27]

On learning that he has slept three nights consecutively, the renowned chief explains that this is to compensate for his having
fought fifteen days in a row without shutting his eyes. This su-
perman conception of the Araucanian suggests a tradition widely
spread throughout the hemisphere which has the white man
marveling at the unnatural powers of the red man.

During the lax administration of Spain's American colonies in
the seventeenth century, members of the aristocracy indulged in
cruel and violent acts that went unpunished in the courts but lin-
gered on in folk memory. The ugliest of these legends concerns
"La Quintrala," as Catalina de los Ríos was called. She came

---

[26] Smith, pp. 293–94.

[27] Quoted in Smith, p. 24. Recognizable motifs are F564.3.2, *Person
sleeps for three days and nights* and F564.2, *Semi-supernatural person
sleeps little.*

from the wealthy Lisperguer family which had emigrated to
Chile from Worms in 1557 and attained power and eminence in
the colony. Some of the Lisperguers became judges and turned a
deaf ear to complaints about the many murders La Quintrala
committed. Historians of Chile refer to the "hateful and legendary memory of a vampirish monster" and Claude Bowers set
down a detailed account of her atrocities as he heard the litany of
horrors from a wedding guest at a *fundo* outside Santiago.[28] The
chapel bell where the ceremony took place had actually been do-
nated by La Quintrala. The name Quintrala came from parasitic
scarlet berries which embraced and destroyed whole forests.

Catherine's mother died in giving birth and the child was
raised by a slave sorceress who muttered spells over the babe. One
of Catherine's ancestresses was supposedly a concubine of Valdivia who murdered her sleeping husband by pouring quicksilver
into his ear. Catherine herself killed her father by feeding him a
poisoned chicken after he sent her slave nurse away. She grew up
into a beauty of devilish allure, combining Indian, Spanish and
German features. "Her little chin was pointed, her eyebrows
slanted, her hair a flaming red, her skin of a copper color,"
Bowers was told. She loved like an animal. One day she invited a
lover, Enrique Enríquez, to her town house in Santiago, dallied
with him, then demanded as the price of a kiss the symbol of his
knighthood, the Order of St. John. When he protested, she ordered her Negro slaves to beat him to death, administering the
coup de grace with her own dagger. The trial lasted a year and
ended with La Quintrala's being sentenced to a year of exile on
her country estate. There she attempted to seduce her padre and
flogged her slaves for sadistic pleasure. Once she appeared naked
before the celebrated image of the crucified Christ, which had
miraculously survived the earthquake of 1647, save that the
crown of thorns was pressed down over its neck; the image
turned disapprovingly toward her, whereupon she ordered it removed from her presence.

This image may still be seen in the old church of St. Augus-
tine. In her will La Quintrala left money for an annual festival to
display the crucified Christ through the streets of Santiago. Since

[28] Galdames, p. 115; Bowers, pp. 132–37.

her death La Quintrala has become a favorite subject for poems, plays, novels, and histories, which help perpetuate her infamy in oral legend.[29]

The struggle for independence from Spain, lasting from 1810 to 1818, gave luster to Chilean patriots and martial traditions. In the years 1816 and 1817 the daring activities of Manuel Rodríguez in plotting against the Spanish governor inspired the populace, for whom he became the hero of a hundred exploits and stratagems. The governor, Marcó del Pont, put a price of a thousand pesos on his head and scattered his troops in a vain effort to intercept Rodríguez' bands. A graceful young lawyer, Rodríguez employed his wiliness to throw the authorities continually off balance; he stormed into cities in full daylight with a few horsemen, seized the garrison and the public funds, and withdrew as quickly as he had come. In taking San Fernando, he had animal skins filled with stones dragged by horses during the night to imitate the sound of artillery and dismay the defending garrison. He turned up everywhere, in all manner of disguises—as a Franciscan friar, a poncho-clad rustic, a pack-carrying servant of a merchant—gathering information, inciting soldiers to desert, and discrediting their officers. Once, according to popular story, he placed himself at the palace entrance and submissively opened the door of the coach for Marcó del Pont. His death by assassination in May, 1818, when he was a prisoner under guard, enhanced his legend.[30] One recalls the tricks played by Robin Hood on the sheriff of Nottingham.

Following the crucial battle of Chacabuco, fought before the northern gate of Santiago on February 12, 1817, there arose a persistent cycle of buried treasure stories. This battle ensured the defeat of the royalists under General Rafael Maroto and the victory of the Chileans led by the famed liberators José de san Martín and Bernardo O'Higgins. After Governor Marcó del Pont abandoned the capital during the night, royalist merchants left at the

---

[29] Carleton Beals, *The Long Land: Chile* (New York, 1949), p. 11. Motifs appearing in the legends of La Quintrala are the general category S100, *Revolting murders or mutilations;* S115.1, *Murder by stabbing in ear;* S22, *Parricide;* S122, *Flogging to death;* K2214.1, *Treacherous daughter;* V128, *Motions of various kinds attributed to images.*

[30] Galdames, pp. 190–91.

mercies of the populace and the invaders hastened to conceal their wealth. When the United States travel author Erna Fergusson visited Chacabuco in 1942, she found the hacienda there owned by a Yugoslav who had continually to deal with treasure seekers. One Chilean lady appeared with a safari of six laborers and five burros to carry away the gold, plus a gentleman companion whom she hypnotized and then followed, expecting him to lead her to the charmed spot that, alas, never materialized. The owner of the *fundo* tolerated these intrusions on the remote chance that, according to agreement, he would reap fifty per cent of the recovered treasure, but only once were his expectations seriously aroused. This was when an old man from Argentina showed up with a chart of a spring, a tree, and a cross nearby marking the site where a Spanish soldier had deposited fifteen mule loads of royalist gold after the battle of Chacabuco. This soldier, so the legend went, had ordered the muleteers to bury the gold near the spring, then killed them all and fled to Argentina. Before he died, he entrusted the map and the information to his son, the present treasure hunter. But his quest too failed.[31]

The Chacabuco traditions closely resemble the buried treasure tales and hunts of Negroes in the southern United States, who dig for silver and heirlooms supposedly hidden by Confederate families from plundering Yankees during the Civil War.[32]

3. *The Desert*

Rain never falls on the Atacama desert, and that is one reason why this empty hell has proved to be the world's only source of nitrate, a mineral indispensable for gunpowder and invaluable as fertilizer, as well as being a source of iodine. Ironically, the Spaniards in their feverish search for gold skirted by sea or mountain pass the desert that contained its own form of gold. This treasure too bore its curse. Discovery of the nitrate bearing *caliche* rock precipitated a boundary dispute between Chile and her northern neighbors that flamed into the most serious war between Latin

[31] Erna Fergusson, *Chile* (New York, 1943), pp. 203–5.

[32] Common motifs here are N550.1, *Continual failure to find or unearth hidden treasure;* N595, *Helper in hiding treasure killed in order that nobody may ever find it.*

American nations. In 1879 a Chilean fleet occupied the key port of Antofagasta, then held by Bolivia, destroyed the Peruvian navy, and entered all the desert ports up to Arica, adding them to her territory by the peace treaty of 1883. A headland known as the Morro overlooks Arica's harbor, and when Chilean attackers captured this position, the defending Peruvian general spurred his mount over the precipice and into the ocean depths below.

After the peace treaty the desert region blossomed, with foreign capital and labor pouring in to develop the nitrate industry. Market prices soared and dropped according to the world's state of war or peace; competition from synthetic nitrates depressed the industry. Entrepreneurs like the Englishman John Thomas North, "the Nitrate King," made their fortunes in Atacama; North became reputedly the richest man on the globe. United States corporations built model towns in the wasteland. From this checkered history came a scattering of legends.

One popular tradition of the discovery of nitrate follows a general theme of lucky accidental strikes of rich ores. Three centuries after the coming of the conquistadors, a *roto* camping in the desert noticed that his fire gave off a sputtering blue flame. He carried back to his village a chunk of the white substance on the ground and showed it to his priest. After examining the *caliche,* the priest threw the lump into his garden. Later in the year he noticed to his surprise that the plants where the *caliche* had fallen were blooming more luxuriantly than in any other part. A more elaborate variant concerns two wandering Indians who dug a hole in which to sleep and there lit a fire that emitted blue sparks. Thinking they had dug up the devil, they raced all night back to the hamlet of Camina seeking a priest to exorcise the devil. He returned to the spot with them, carrying a prayer book and a bottle of holy water, but the fire had died out. The priest took home some specimens of the earth from the hole, analyzed them and discovered that they contained saltpeter, and then threw them out of his window into his flower bed in the poorest corner of his garden, which shortly developed into the most fertile.[33]

[33] Pendle, p. 40; Hakon Mielche, *Land of the Condor* (London, Edinburgh, Glasgow, 1947), pp. 209–10. The motif of this tradition is N596.2, *Rich mine discovered by accidental breaking off of rock.*

History upsets this legend, for the properties of *caliche* were first investigated by a Bohemian scientist, Thadeus Haenke, in 1788. Two decades later Haenke planned a series of manufacturing centers to extract saltpeter from *caliche*.

Life and death in the desert mines gave rise to grim and harrowing recitals. "The stories the saltpeter desert has to tell are no nursery tales," wrote a Danish visitor, Hakon Mielche.[34] He described a macabre game played by the miners in the early days to show their contempt of the death that faced them daily. They would arrange themselves in a circle and pass around a dynamite cartridge with a lit fuse slowly burning. The one who held it when the cartridge exploded lost the game as well as his life.[35] Edward B. Tylor, the noted English anthropologist, refers in his *Primitive Culture* to a children's game, "Le Petit Bonhomme" in which boys in a circle toss about a doll until one drops it, and suggests this is a survival of a game played by savages who would throw a live baby to each other until the baby died, the final holder then possessing special power.

With boom times in the mining towns, fortune hunters and bandits drifted into Atacama and left in their wake some familiar outlaw legends. The bandit chief "El Colorado" preyed on the mining districts and with bands as large as fifty armed men held up trains laden with silver ore. One time the manager of the silver mine at Caracoles, Peter Wessel, was riding on horse from Valparaiso to the mine with his payroll of one hundred thousand dollars in his saddlebag, accompanied by just one servant. At a wayside inn he met a sporting young man with two shiny revolvers in his belt and a long dagger in his right boot. Taking him for a well-to-do Argentine rancher, Wessel shared accommodations with him and enjoyed his companionship on the road to Caracoles. Finally coming to a crossroads, the stranger reined in, idly twirled a revolver, and asked for a little money. Seeing Wessel blanch, he said with a smile that he knew all about the payroll in the saddlebag, but since Wessel had proved so companionable, he would rest content with a mere hundred dollars. And pocketing the comparative trifle, he bowed low and rode away.

[34] Mielche, p. 190.
[35] *Ibid.*, p. 217.

This was El Colorado.[36] We have heard similar tales about Jesse
James and other good badmen.

4. *The Sea*

Although lacking the superlative harbors of the indented Atlantic coast, Chile still possesses a major port in Valparaiso as
well as over forty smaller ports strung along her coastline. Where
necessary, as at Antofagasta, her outlet for nitrate shipments,
Chileans improvised artificial harbors with breakwaters. Ob-
servers have declared the Chilean the best seaman in all South
America.[37] When in 1865 and 1866 Chile fought Spain for a second time, a Chilean vessel, the *Esmeralda,* won a stunning victory, leading to the suicide of the Spanish admiral, in capturing
the *Covadonga,* part of the blockading Spanish fleet, by flying a
distress signal and the British flag as a ruse. But the *Esmeralda*
recalled earlier glories, for this was also the name of the famous
flagship of Lord Thomas Cochrane, who commanded the first
navy of Chile from 1819 to 1822. In the so-called Nitrate War of
1879–1883 the Chilean navy outfought the Peruvian naval
fleet. Meanwhile the merchant marine of Chile developed in
the nineteenth century a brisk trade with Europe and the United
States. All this traffic on the high seas and coastal waters was
bound to form sea traditions, hinted at in this salty reminiscence
of a bartender in Concepción musing about sea dogs of the past.

> "In the old days," he said, "wooden ships came here with
> iron sailors. Now we see nothing but iron ships with
> wooden sailors. In my young days the men of the sailing
> ships used to come in here. They would sit down at the bar,
> take out their pipe, pluck a hair from their chest to clean it
> with and then they would drink a bottle of rum to clear
> their voices so that they could start ordering their drinks.
> Nowadays they go to the cinema and drink lemonade." [38]

These oldtime sailors suggest the tall-talking breed of ring-
tailed roarers on the old southwestern frontier of the United
States.

[36] *Ibid.,* pp. 240–41.
[37] *Ibid.,* p. 19.
[38] *Ibid.,* pp. 108–9.

The offshore islands of Chile have entered into lore and legend. It was on the islet of Más à Tierra in the Juan Fernández group, four hundred miles west of Valparaiso, that an irate captain deposited a Scottish sailor named Alexander Selkirk, who fended for himself for five years and learned to outrun goats before he was rescued and brought back to Britain to give Daniel Defoe the idea for *Robinson Crusoe.* This, however, is fact, and for legend one must glance south to the vast, forbidding island of Chiloé, which hugs the coast below Valdivia. Dutch pirates may have bequeathed their vision of the *Flying Dutchman* to the Chilotes, who live in dread of the *Caleuche,* a luminous white vessel sighted in the path of storm-tossed ships as a portent of their doom. Fishermen on Chiloé flee when they see the *Caleuche* glide toward shore on moonlit nights. Men who sleep and dream when the *Caleuche* approaches are the prey of its spectral crew.[39] Gabriela Mistral, the sensitive Chilean poetess who won a Nobel prize in literature, has given this impression of the spectral craft.

> "The *Caleuche* is a pirate ship—a noble outlaw of the seas, which . . . runs miles and miles under it, so well hidden that for weeks and months all trace of it is lost, and it seems to have . . . left the sea of the Chilotes for some other. . . . But suddenly on the loneliest of those southern nights, the *Caleuche* emerges . . . and runs a long course in full view, navigating at full steam, almost flying, without permitting herself to be overtaken by any whaleboat or poor fishing launch which might try to follow her. The fleeing thing, in the sight of fear-crazed fishermen, is a phosphorescent mass . . . whose deck swarms with sea devils and a tribe of witches very like them. . . .
>
> "Let its pursuers approach their illuminated prey and before they glimpse or catch the secret, the burning palace of the *Caleuche* simply stops, goes out like a great firebrand, and leaves a dead hulk, dark cinders which drift with the waves. . . ."[40]

[39] Subercaseaux, p. 202.

[40] Quoted in Fergusson, pp. 61–62. Beliefs about the *caleuche* are presented by Evaristo Molina Herrera, "Mitología chilota," *Archivos del*

Mistral considers the *Caleuche* to be neither a whale nor a ship, although it navigates and can overturn fishing boats. Its demon crew is easily identifiable because their heads face backwards and their left feet are twisted, causing them to hop crazily. Eternally young, they sleep by day and frolic at night. Almost every Chilote has seen the *Caleuche* at one time or another and believes that she carries enchanted fishermen to treasures at the bottom of the sea.

The *Caleuche* is no solitary phenomenon, but belongs with a fleet of phantom craft sighted on the seven seas and well ensconced in oceanic folklore.[41]

Yet another island with a unique body of traditions belongs to Chile—the mysterious Easter Island, twenty-three hundred miles out in the Pacific and the only colonial possession of any South American republic. Chile acquired crater–pocked Easter Island from the Dutch in 1888, and at the same time annexed the host of speculations and oral legends hovering about the giant stone statues with pendulous ears that adorn the island. A whole archaeological and ethnological literature has grown around the few hundred natives and greater number of statues of Easter Island, including books by such well known authorities as Alfred Metraux and Thor Heyderdahl, but the republic of Chile can now claim the extant legends as her folklore property, and the distinguished Chilean diplomat and journalist Agustin Edwards includes a chapter on them in his *My Native Land*. There he recounts a historical tradition widely told by the natives of a deadly fight between the Big Ears, who formerly lived on the eastern side of the island and built great statues inside the crater of the volcano Rano Raraku, and the Little Ears, who occupied the western side and practiced peaceful agricultural pursuits. A dispute arose over the desire of the Big Ears to bury ritually one of

---

Folklore Chileno, fasc. 2, pp. 37–68, reprinted in part in Félix Coluccio, *Antología Ibérica y Americana del Folklore* (Buenos Aires, 1953), pp. 109–13.

[41] Wilbur Bassett, *Wander-Ships, Folk-Stories of the Sea* (Chicago, 1917), discusses giant ships, the "Flying Dutchman" and punishment ships, phantom ships, and devil ships. The general motifs are D1123, *Magic ship* and F485, *Ship-spirits.*

their number who had died in Little Ears territory, and when the Little Ears objected, the Big Ears dug a long trench in which to roast their enemies alive. But the Big Ears workman in charge of the operation was married to a Little Ears woman, Ánguneru, who revealed the plot to her people, with the result that they turned the trap on the Big Ears. All but two of them fell into the trench to be roasted alive and eaten at a victory banquet held by the peace–loving Little Ears.

Other traditions also depict the mortal and cannibalistic combat between two tribes, who may represent a Melanesian and a Polynesian race. One orally preserved history relates a war between the armies of King Poie and King Kainga which lasted so long that one of Kainga's sons, Huru Avaid, was able to take part, killing an opponent in single combat with a well directed stone after his foe had given the deadly insult of sticking out his tongue at Huru Avaid. Another of Kainga's sons possessed two faces, of which only the front was vulnerable, but in the course of flight curiosity compelled him to turn his front face to the rear to sight the enemy, who promptly dispatched him. Over the fray presided a bony goddess of war, Huri Huri, egging on the combatants on whose corpses she would feast, chanting the while

> To eat men
> Be astir betimes.

Curiously, this flourishing oral tradition throws no light on the gigantic stone statues with their oversized ears.[42]

5. Europeans and Africans

European immigration has certainly played its part in shaping the Chilean character, as one observer after another has remarked. Bowers observed that "Chile is not so much a Spanish country as some of its neighbors. This is because of the mixture of races, which makes for beauty. The very large German, English, Scotch, Irish, Dutch, and Scandinavian elements . . . have

[42] Agustin Edwards, *My Native Land: Panorama, Reminiscences, Writers and Folklore* (London, 1928), pp. 286–90. Motifs in these traditions are G21, *Female eater of corpses;* G11.18, *Cannibal tribe;* G94, *Cannibal's gigantic meal;* and F511.0.2.1, *Two-headed person.*

made a race of women distinctly Chilean." [48] Oddly, few Spaniards migrated to the new republic. A large colony of Germans
settled in Valdivia following the abortive liberal revolution of
1848, lured by advertisements of fertile and cheap farmlands. The
advertisements neglected to say that the land still lay under forests and was drenched in rain most of the year. Nevertheless, the
energetic Germans fell to work diligently, and a century later
travelers commented on the Nazi atmosphere of the city. These
Germans, and other immigrants, came not, as in the United
States, from a desperately poor peasantry induced to supply cheap
labor for a rapidly growing industrial economy; rather they represented men of means and education looking for agricultural
and mercantile properties. Accordingly, while they contributed to
Chilean intellectual and economic life, it is doubtful if they have
contributed to Chilean folklore.

Few African slaves were brought to Chile, since under the
encomienda system the conquistadors received from Charles V
not only grants of land but also the right to use Indians on the
land as slave labor. Further, the trip from the African Gold Coast
around Cape Horn was long, and often fatal to the slaves in the
holds. Yet the few Negroes who came to Chile may have left a
permanent mark on Chilean folk tradition in the national dance
known as the *cueca*. One theory claims it originated in Guinea
and was carried into Chilean dives from Peru by a Negro bat-
talion. The *cueca* mirrors all Chilean history in the topical songs
sung to the dance and symbolizes the race conflict between
Castilian and Araucanian. The gay and erotic style is considered
Spanish, but the blatant sexuality of the courtship unfolded in
the formless, fast-moving dance is low class Chilean. [44]

[43] Bowers, p. 206.

[44] Fergusson, pp. 183–89. Yolando Pino-Saavedra gives 51 song texts in
his study, "La cueca en los campos de Llanquihue," *Archivos del Folklore
Chileno*, fasc. 2, pp. 23–71. Eugenio Pereira Salas, *Los orígenes del arte
musical en Chile* (Santiago de Chile, 1941), pp. 268–83, rejects theories of
Araucanian and African origins for a Spanish origin, traceable after 1824
through the Peruvian aristocracy.

The present selection of Chilean folktales and the Introduction by Yolando Pino-Saavedra, the leading folklore scholar in Chile today, directly contradict the ideas advanced in this Foreword. Pino-Saavedra sees the corpus of Chilean tales as homogeneous and derived from the Iberian peninsula. These positions are not so opposed as they appear to be. Yolando Pino has his eye on the fictional folktales of the European peasantry and, as the following collection proves, such tales do flourish among Chileans today. My emphasis is on collateral folk traditions produced by New World conditions, and on believed legendary narratives.

Yolando Pino-Saavedra is both an assiduous field collector and a sophisticated comparative folklorist. The three volumes of his *Cuentos Folklóricos de Chile* (1960–63), from which the present work is drawn, represent a high–water mark in South American folklore publications. Pino thoroughly annotates his texts, identifying them according to the Aarne–Thompson system and the Spanish American index of Terrence Hansen, comparing them with standard collections from thirty countries, and describing his forty informants who come from sixteen of the twenty-five provinces of Chile. He considers the functions of the *cuentos:* to entertain people during long funerals, at community work such as shelling corn, at social gatherings, or even to assist suitors in fixing the minds of their sweethearts on amorous adventures. The high proportion of magical tales caught in his net reflects western European storytelling of the nineteenth rather than the twentieth century, as he recognizes.

Unlike many national collectors, Pino knows the international scene. He belongs to the tradition of Germanic folklore scholarship introduced into Chile by Rudolf Lenz, a German linguist who came to Chile in 1890 and began collecting oral narratives in the Spanish and Araucanian languages as an aid to his linguistic studies. Pino himself studied in Germany at the University of Hamburg from 1925 to 1931, taking his doctorate there. He has reported in the German folktale journal *Fabula* on the work of his predecessors such as Lenz and another outstanding collector, Ramón A. Laval, who from 1910 to 1925 published four volumes of Chilean oral tales. The folklore research institute at the University of Chile, Santiago, which is directed by Yolando Pino, carries the name of Ramón A. Laval. A German translation of thirty-eight tales from Pino's collections, *Chilenische Volks-märchen,* appeared in 1964 in the series *Märchen der Weltlitera-tur.* On his part, Pino has translated into Spanish an essay, "The Folktale from the Ethnic Point of View," by the eminent Swedish folklorist, Carl von Sydow, who conceived the theory of the "oikotype," or regional subforms of international tales.[45]

In these activities Yolando Pino-Saavedra has played a key role in bringing South American and European folklorists in touch with each other. In the present volume he is helping to strengthen relations between North and South American folklorists.

RICHARD M. DORSON

[45] The journal articles by Yolando Pino-Saavedra alluded to are "El cuento folklórico desde el punto de vista étnico" (translation from C. W. von Sydow), *Archivos del Folklore Chileno,* fasc. 3 (1951), pp. 7–22; "Volksmärchen in Chile, Sammlung und Forschung," *Fabula,* II (1958), 173–75. I am indebted to Mildred Merino de Zela for preparing for me an annotated bibliography of Chilean folklore publications.

Introduction

Early in the year 1894, the German philologist Rudolf Lenz, a professor at the University of Chile, called attention to the importance of studying the popular dialects, customs, songs, proverbs, and sayings of the people in the young and unknown countries of the Americas. These were all branches of a new science, called in English "folklore." On the basis of the material which he had been compiling on various loose pages since 1890, Lenz completed a work on popular poetry which was printed in Santiago de Chile. He published the first chapter in Germany in 1895, and much later, in 1919, the complete text in Spanish. Motivated by his conviction that the vast field of folklore needed a greater number of scholars, Lenz published in 1905 a program for the study of Chilean folklore, the guiding principles of which came from the work of R. F. Kaindl, *Die Volkskunde, ihre Bedeutung, ihre Ziele und ihre Methode* (1903). Thus he began to prepare the way for the founding of The Society of Chilean Folklore, the first meeting of which he convoked on July 18, 1909. This act initiated the most intensive compilation and research in folklore that has ever been known in Chile. The quality of work of certain members of the society was a guarantee of scientific reliability and augured well for the future. Besides some of Lenz's own disciples, Julio Vicuña Cifuentes and Ramón A. Laval joined the group and became outstanding members. The Society of Chilean Folklore, the first to be founded in Spanish America, had four years of independent life between 1909 and 1913. Fifty-two sessions took place during Lenz's presidency. In the meetings various works were read and discussed, after which they appeared in the *Revista de Folklore Chileno* (1911–1916), in the *Anales de la Universidad de Chile,* and in the *Revista Chilena de Historia y Geografía.*

The most valuable works published as a result of this movement were the studies and compilations of certain genres of Chilean folk literature by Lenz, Vicuña Cifuentes, Laval, and Mrs. Sperata R. de Saunière. In 1910, Vicuña Cifuentes published his *Mitos y supersticiones* (*Myths and Superstitions*) and in 1912, his *Romances populares y vulgares* (*Popular and Vulgar Ballads*). These works were characterized by scientific rigor and the use of the comparative method. Laval and Mrs. Saunière produced distinguished collections of stories (for references, see Bibliography, pp. 287–91). Lenz published in 1912 the most complete study in Spanish up to that time on a small number of popular stories (types 403, *The Black and the White Bride;* 706, *The Maiden Without Hands;* and 707, *The Three Golden Sons*). In this essay the author complained that the term *cuentos populares* ("popular tales") was vague and proposed a substitution:

> . . . the fairy tale, often called "mythical tale," [is] full of miracles and devoid of relations with a definite place and time. These stories have the name *Märchen* in German. In other languages a special name is lacking; but the old Spanish word *conseja* [story, fairy tale] could well be used exclusively to designate them.[1]

Although Lenz was quite right, the proposed name was never firmly established, and he himself had to use both terms conjointly.

A little later, this same scholar studied and classified twenty-five riddle tales:

We have classified the materials in the following groups:

    I. Stories which contain various riddles that are more or less accessory; that is, the story has a somewhat general character without depending exclusively on the formation and solution of the riddles.

    II. Stories of riddles as such. The whole story is no more than the narration of the special circumstances which

[1] Rodolfo Lenz, "Un grupo de consejas chilenas," *Revista de Folklore Chileno*, III (1912), 1.

      lead to the formulation of the riddles, which are un-
      solvable for one who does not know the antecedents.
III. Stories in which certain communications are given in
      enigmatic form so that persons unconnected with them
      will not understand.
IV. Riddles with paradoxes that can be clarified only by
      more or less long explanations, although these are not
      always complete stories.
 V. Riddles which are solved only by taking some word as
      a proper name.
VI. Arithmetic riddles, which are similar to some of those
      in group V.
VII. Riddles which are in part related to the arithmetic ones
      and in part contain artificial words. The explanation
      is a short story.[2]

Agustín Cannobio, Eliodoro Flores, and Manuel Guzmán Maturana also belong to this generation. Cannobio published a collection of proverbs; Flores, one of riddles; and Guzmán Maturana, one of stories.

A second and less important stage in the study of Chilean folklore occurred between the years 1925 and 1930. When he held a chair in Chilean literature in the Pedagogical Institute of the University of Chile, Vicuña Cifuentes promoted the collection of folklore miscellanies from different parts of the country. Some of these appeared in the *Revista Chilena de Historia y Geografía;* the greatest number were published in the *Anales de la Facultad de Filosofía y Educación* (1943).

Separate mention should be made of the work of the historian Eugenio Pereira Salas, *Orígenes del Arte Musical en Chile* (*The Origins of the Art of Music in Chile*). Chapter 16 of this notable piece of research is of great significance for the folklorist. Here Pereira Salas discusses the origins, persistence, and disappearance of certain kinds of music, dances, and songs among the Chilean people.

I myself gave the first courses in general folklore in the decade 1940–1950 in the summer school of the University of Chile, in

---

[2] Rodolfo Lenz, "Cuentos de adivinanzas corrientes en Chile," *Revista de Folklore Chileno*, II (1912), 340–41.

Santiago as well as in cities of the provinces. I also brought about the creation of a university center for folklore studies, with the principal aim of promoting research in the field of popular Chilean literature, customs, and beliefs. With very small financial resources this institute has been able to publish eight fascicles of the *Archivos del Folklore Chileno* (1950–1957) and my *Cuentos folklóricos de Chile* (*Folktales of Chile*) in three volumes (1960–1963).

In the area of recent folk literature mention should also be made of the works of Juan Uribe Echeverría, *Contrapunto de Alféreces en la Provincia de Valparaíso* (*Folk Poetry of Valparaíso*, 1958) and *Cantos a lo divino y a lo humano en Aculeo* (*Songs on Religious and Human Themes*, 1962).

We will conclude this brief history of folklore studies in Chile with the words of Eugenio Pereira Salas:

> As can be observed . . . , there now exists in Chile a well-founded tradition of folklore study. . . . The University of Chile, through its specialized scientific organizations, The Ramón A. Laval Institute for Folklore Research and The Institute of Musical Research, headed by the active musicologist Vicente Salas Viú, has squarely approached this important task.[3]

From subsequent study of popular Chilean tales, it is clear to me that all of them proceed from the old Spanish peninsular tradition. The strength with which this tradition persists is so marked that our narrators relate stories which have not been recorded in Spain but which undoubtedly existed there in the sixteenth, seventeenth, and eighteenth centuries. This is a cultural phenomenon which has generally been observed in the migration of popular traditions, and which in Chile seems to be more accentuated than in other Spanish American areas. This persistence is largely a consequence of the special character of the conquest and colonization of Chile. Despite constant fighting during three centuries, the Araucanian Indians were not put down, and the Spanish government was forced to send successive legions of sol-

[3] Eugenio Pereira Salas, *Guía bibliográfica para el estudio del Folklore chileno* (Universidad de Chile, 1952).

diers in greater quantity than to any other part of America. This struggle resulted in intimate contact between Spaniards and Araucanians, and produced a racial mixture that characterizes the Chilean population of the lower and middle classes. Because of its homogeneity, this mixed population accepted and faithfully kept alive the narrative and other popular Spanish literary genres without contamination by aboriginal elements. The Araucanian Indians possessed myths and animal tales but upon receiving the impact of a superior culture they superimposed the Spanish stories upon their own weak narrative tradition and adapted them to their beliefs and customs. Nor has there been any appreciable influence from other European countries on the popular Chilean narrative. The social and economic differences between German, Swiss, and French colonists in the south of the country and the Chilean population in general have been such as to produce weak cultural contacts, not close enough to permit oral transmission of stories between the groups.

The popular Chilean stories show a notable homogeneity that has been weakened neither in the course of time nor by the 3,500 kilometer length of this narrow land. On the contrary, this homogeneity is accentuated by migrations of the inhabitants. The mining establishments of the north have attracted thousands of workers from all the provinces. The inhabitants of the island of Chiloé move periodically to the southern zone of Magallanes and to the neighboring provinces to the north. In this way there is a permanent circulation of people who bring their own customs and narrations with them and keep the tradition alive and vigorous.[4] The uniformity of the stories is altered only externally by the local surroundings. Typical regional scenes and characters are mentioned in accord with the localizing characteristic of the international tales. In the northern zone, the Andes range serves as a backdrop for the action, and some heroes are miners. In the central part of the country, the narrator alludes to the Andes and the plain in which the typical Chilean *roto* [member of the humblest class] lives. In the south the setting is the forest, and men who gather coal or work with a shovel are principal characters.

[4] See Yolando Pino-Saavedra, *Chilenische Märchen* (Düsseldorf-Köln, 1964), p. 264.

But local color does not keep the Chilean stories from conserving their original character. Thus, for example, the story of "The Little Stick-Figure" (No. 20) corresponds essentially to the development of Type B 1, "Maria Intaulata," established by Birgitta Rooth, *The Cinderella Cycle,* pp. 19–20. Neither has the influence of Catholicism, which is found at every step in the Chilean and Spanish stories, caused the tales to lose their original essence. Directly or parenthetically the narrator says that the old man is Our Lord; that the kind old lady is the Virgin Mary; and that the eagle, the dog, the cat, the horse, and the sword, etc. are angels from heaven sent by Our Lord to save the hero from the giant's ferocity or from the wickedness of the witch or devil. St. Peter is the favorite saint in our stories. He serves as a mediator between God and men and is the custodian of the gates of heaven. He knows the good qualities and the defects of people, and he himself even participates in some of them. He is more often deceived than obeyed and appears in comic stories and jokes together with the very familiar and widely known character, Pedro Urdemales.

The two hundred and seventy versions which I have chosen will indicate for the time being what kind of narrations are preferred by the imagination and taste of the Chilean people. The tales of magic, the religious tales, and the romantic tales comprise 69.25 per cent of the total; the tales of the stupid ogre and the jokes and anecdotes, 23.33 per cent; the animal tales, 5.92 per cent; and the cumulative tales, 1.48 per cent. In the villages and country districts, all kinds of stories are told among adults and in the presence of the children. In the provincial cities it is still common for nurses and maids to entertain the children of the middle and upper classes with stories of magic. The comic tales, especially those in which Pedro Urdemales figures as protagonist, are generally known by all the social classes. The smaller number of types of jokes and anecdotes is compensated for by their greater profusion and intensity in relation to the magic stories.

In my folklore travels through different regions of Chile I have been able to observe the role played by popular stories in the life of the humble and unlettered people of the villages and country areas. These stories usually serve for entertainment during domestic chores and generally at twilight or in the evening when the family gathers together. There are, however, two especially important occasions on which the narrators display their talent. Throughout most of the country it is customary for the relatives and neighbors of a family in mourning to gather for the wake and watch beside the deceased person through the night. For fortification during the vigil, they often suggest the solution of riddles and tell all kinds of stories and little jokes. One of my informants has assured me that actual contests are sometimes carried out by the narrators during the wake. The winner, the one who neither repeats nor exhausts his repertoire, enjoys a fame and admiration among the peasants much as does a renowned writer in the higher levels of society. The other important occasion for storytelling is the *mingaco,* a community work project at the end of or during which food and drink is passed out. This kind of work is disappearing, but can still be found in some rural areas of the near north in central Chile, and in the island of Chiloé. The Chilean narrators, along with their fellow popular poets, play the role once held by the ancient minstrels.

In summary, we can affirm that popular tales in Chile are still very much in use and vogue. They show an extraordinary vitality, and their disappearance in the near future is not foreseeable. The economic and cultural development of Chile, as of almost all of Latin America, proceeds so slowly that the illiteracy and cultural isolation of many communities will continue to exist for an indefinite time. This fact contributes, of course, to the maintenance of the old traditions of Spanish origin.

This book is made up of versions of folktales taken from my above-mentioned work. For its publication in English, I wish to thank Professor Richard M. Dorson, who has shown great interest in its completion, and Mr. Rockwell Gray, who has made this translation with a sense of linguistic responsibility.

YOLANDO PINO-SAAVEDRA

Contents

Part I
Animal Tales

·1· *The Vixen*

• THERE WAS ONCE upon a certain road a monkey, who was walking along with a saddle on his shoulder when he met an old vixen, a she fox.

"Why do you walk with the saddle on your shoulder, my good friend?" asked the vixen.

"Because my horse just died out from under me, dear friend," answered the monkey.

"Well, look here," said the vixen, "why don't you saddle me up? I'm gentle as can be under the reins." So the monkey saddled her and rode her down a long hill.

"What do you think? Aren't I easy to master after all?" called the vixen over her shoulder. All the while, she was thinking of how she could find a way to throw off the monkey, so she could eat up the saddle.

They stopped on a slope and the vixen spied a flock of goats. "Those don't look like goats to me," she barked.

"Right, they look like dogs, old friend," said the monkey fearfully.

"Let's get a move on, old boy!" said the vixen to the monkey.

Down below, there was a man out fox hunting. His friend shouted to him, "Hey, look, there goes a vixen with a monkey mounted on her back!"

"Loose the dogs on them—they're very close by," called the other.

"Don't you see?" squealed the monkey as the vixen bounded away, "I told you those were dogs, old companion."

"Hold on, my good fellow, and let's hightail it!" barked the vixen. When the dogs had almost reached his harried mount, the monkey tossed his lariat around a tree trunk, upon which the vixen was abruptly pulled up short and fell on her back. Away went the monkey into the hills crying, "Let my 'old friend' go to hell." And the dogs were upon the vixen in short order.

•2• *The Tarbaby*

• THERE WAS an old man named Felix who had a fig tree that yielded the same amount of fruit every year. The people of the town went to him to buy figs, but he never sold any. Then they tried to rob him, but every night he stood guard with a shotgun. Since it was absolutely impossible to steal the figs, two men said to each other one night, "Let's pretend to be dead men, as if we were spirits, and that way we can get some figs."

"But how are we going to rob him while he's guarding the fig tree?" asked one.

"Look," answered the other, "that's very easily arranged. We're simply going to turn into ghosts."

When night fell, the two met near the old man's house and advanced upon the coveted fig tree. From some distance, they could make out old Felix seated with the shotgun in his hands. One of them whispered to his companion, "We've just got to take the risk, if we want to eat those juicy figs." Then the first one boomed in a very loud voice, "When we were still living, figs were our favorite dish."

"Now that we're dead and gone, we're looking for old one-eyed Felix," answered the other in a quavering, hollow voice.

"You're looking for me?" cried the old man, who jumped up without waiting to find out any more, leaving his shotgun where he dropped it at the foot of his precious tree. The two robbers ran into the orchard with peals of laughter, filling their pockets and eating until they were ready to burst.

The next day, when dawn came, Felix went to look for his shotgun. Since they had been dead men who robbed him, they'd paid no attention to weapons. Then the old man went straight off to the house of a neighbor woman and told her everything that had happened, asking her how he could protect his fig tree so the spirits wouldn't rob him again.

"Look here, neighbor," she said, "since I'm a potter by trade, I'm going to make you a little figure." With that, she set to work molding a figure at the very place where the thieves might get in to rob Felix of his fruit. They placed a basket almost full to the brim with figs in the little figure's hands. When the thieves came in the night, they ran across this little man. "Good evening, friend," they said, "What are you up to here in the garden at such a late hour?" Not a word from him. "This fellow must be in a bad humor," they thought. "Offer us one of your figs, my friend." Not a blessed word. "Why the devil don't you say something?" they asked, gradually getting more and more put out with the taciturn little man. Finally, one thief said to the other, "I'm going to give him a smack, and that'll put an end to this business."

"But he's all alone, and there are two of us," protested the other. "Let's just take his figs and nothing more." The first thief, however, raised his fist and gave the mysterious little man a resounding wallop. There he stuck! "Get me loose," he begged the other, butting the little figure frantically with his head but merely sticking all the tighter. Since the silent figure seemed to be a roly-poly fellow, the robber kneed him in the belly and stuck there with his leg hung up in the air. "Well, come on, help me, man! He's winning!" shouted the helpless prisoner to his companion.

"You give it to him, old boy!" answered the other in his timidity. Soon the first one was hung up on all sides, quite helpless. Then his companion entered the battle, taking care to keep his right arm free so he could arrange to get away. Finally they limped off, dragging the insistent little man behind them. Passing by a neighboring house, they called for help, yelling that a goblin was eating them alive. The neighbors rushed out, only to find that a little tarbaby had the two men bound fast.

"There's no such goblin as this," chuckled one of the neighbors.

"We're the sons of Uncle Felix," cried one of the prisoners. So Uncle Felix was notified, and it was time to mete out some punishment. There was only one way to get them free. Felix covered the two thieves with grease and, after administering a sound thrashing, loosened the tarbaby from his prisoners.

"Did you pay me for the figs?" asked the old man, giving them a sound blow for each fig stolen from his tree. Eventually, Felix lost count and exacted double pay from them before his hand got tired. They were branded with the mark of the grease forever after.

Part II
Wonder Tales

· 3 · The Three Stolen Princesses

• THERE WAS ONCE upon a time a king and a queen who had a baby girl. The king was so disgusted at having a daughter that he wanted to kill her. The following year they had another child, a daughter also. When the king heard this news, he went off roaming through the city and forgot all about his home. The queen stayed home to bring up her daughters. The following year, they had a third child, again a daughter. The king, upon hearing this, flew into a boiling rage and even wished to forsake the city. Finally he said, "I'm going to raise these girls," whereupon he sat down to figure out how he could keep his daughters there without anybody seeing them.

Now in this same city there lived an old hag whom he sent for so that she might give him an idea about what he could do with his girls. She told him to turn them into oranges, and added that, if he wished, she herself would do the job. The king promptly agreed. The old crone changed the three lovely daughters into oranges by her enchantments and told the king to station a caretaker so that nobody would touch them. The king paid a young man to guard his precious fruit, under penalty of having his head chopped off if he were to lose even one. The youth was constantly on guard there, for the oranges were exceedingly beautiful.

Now in this same land there were three giants, who knew perfectly well that those oranges were really three girls. One day one of them said to another, "Nobody can take care of these girls better than we can." So he prepared to go and steal an orange. One of the giants was called "Shameless," the second, "Terrible," and the third, "Hairy Dog." It was Hairy Dog who resolved to get an orange from the king's tree. Late at night, he flew into the garden in the form of a great bird with steel wings and headed straight for the orange. The watchman, greatly startled at seeing this awful monster, took up his sword to kill it. But the bird struck him a fatal blow with its wing and flew over the wall with the largest orange, taking it home to his older brother.

As day was breaking the next morning, the king looked out at his oranges and saw only two. The watchman couldn't be found anywhere, for the bird had killed him with a slash of its vicious wings.

The next night, Hairy Dog announced to his brothers, "I'm going for another orange." By now, the king had a second watchman guarding the girls under the same penalty of death. Once again, Hairy Dog swooped down in the form of a ferocious bird. Spotting the creature, the youth seized his sword to attack the bird, which rushed upon him with its wings and knocked him down. Hairy Dog easily plucked the second orange and carried it away in his beak to the middle brother. When the king arose, he glanced into the garden and saw one lonely orange hanging on the tree. The guard was lying dead and bloody in the corner. Immediately they searched for another caretaker to protect the one orange left. No one would take the job, until finally they came upon a gallant, handsome lad of eighteen named Manuel. He considered himself a good fighter and said he had the heart to care for the king's orange.

"I'll give you the job," said the king, "but if my last orange is lost, I'll have your head."

"It's a bargain," Manuel answered. "Will you grant me permission to order a sword made in your workshop?"

"That," answered the king, "will be the least of your problems."

The boy ordered a tempered sword made of the purest steel, with a blade so strong that nothing could nick it. In the night, the bird came for the last orange. Manuel, when he saw the great creature, asked it what it was up to. The bird screeched that it had come for the remaining orange and that its job was to care for the fruit. They battled in the garden for a long time, but the bird could not catch Manuel, for he kept springing aside, pushing on the tip of his sword. Suddenly the bird landed a blow with his wing and threw the young caretaker a great way off, where he lay as if in a deep sleep. When Manuel came to in the morning before dawn, he looked everywhere for the orange. Seeing that it was gone, he thought to himself, "It's better to go in search of the bird, even if it kills me, than to have the king chop off my head." So he set out following the trail of blood that had dripped from the wounds he had given the bird the night before. Manuel followed the signs a long way until he came to a pinnacle of rock and lost the trail. He tried to lift the rock to see if the bird was there, but his wounds had weakened him too much. Glancing to one side, he noticed some smoke and headed over to see what it was. Two men were sitting by a fire roasting meat from an ox they had just quartered. They thought themselves very bold fellows at this adventure and wanted to know if Manuel was one of their kind. He assured them that even if he were better than they, they were certainly all going to be companions. They stayed there together for several days, their only food being the oxen of a certain king.

One day Manuel told his friends about the bird he was after and invited them to help him in his hunt. The three set out, and came eventually to the great pinnacle. He told one of the men, named Pedro, to turn the rock over. Pedro grasped the pointed rock with all his might but couldn't budge it. Manuel told the other, called Diego, to take a turn. He strained and strained and moved the rock a tiny bit.

"Good Lord, what a fine pair of friends I have!" exclaimed the youth in disgust. With that, he gripped the rock with both hands and tossed it far aside, revealing a hole which was very dark at the bottom. "Here," continued Manuel, "we're going to make some knots and loops from the hides of all the oxen you have killed." Believing that the hole was very deep indeed, they slaughtered some more oxen until they had gathered about twenty skins. With these, they made a little basket and took it to the hole. The first to go down was Pedro.

"If you see any light," Manuel told him, "jerk on the cord." Pedro had gone down about thirty yards when he became very fearful and started to jerk the cord furiously. The others pulled him up, and Manuel asked, "Well, what did you see, man? Tell us!"

"Not a thing. Just plain darkness," answered Pedro trembling. Next, Diego was sent to go down until he hit the bottom. When he had descended about fifty yards, he too became very frightened and pulled the cord. Then Manuel announced, "I'm going down myself now, and you two are going to stay here. If the cord doesn't reach, you must hold on and pull me out." So they let him down into the pit with his sword. Down and down and down he went into the gloom. Just as there was no more slack left in the rope, Manuel glimpsed daylight at the bottom. When his helpers pulled him back up, he ordered them to kill more oxen in order to add skins to the rope. "After you let me down," he continued, "I want you to come here at twelve o'clock noon and wait for me until one. If I don't give a signal by then you can go home, but you must come to check every day without fail." Down went Manuel into the gaping pit once again. With just a bit of cord left at the top, he reached the bottom and set out to explore the land, coming eventually to a beautiful palace where the oldest princess was being watched over by the giant named Terrible. When she saw Manuel, she was frightened out of her wits and gasped, "Boy, what are you doing here? This giant is very daring and fierce." When he had told her how he had come from up above, and seeing that it was very late, she added, "Terrible isn't coming home today. He should be back about twelve o'clock tomorrow." So the princess invited him in and served him everything he needed, building up his strength to resist the giant.

The next day, after arising and washing, Manuel took his sword and went to the large patio to exercise. He practiced running and jumping about, so the giant wouldn't be able to catch him. He tried out his sword and found it without fault. Then the princess called him in for breakfast, which was so large that twelve o'clock came before they knew it. The princess pointed out the way from which the giant was sure to come, and Manuel went out to await him. Very soon, he heard the thundering tread of the giant's approach, for Terrible came in a rage whenever he smelled the odor of human flesh.

"Little worm," raged the giant as he came into view, "what are you doing here on my property? Today's the day I'll drink your blood!"

"We'll see who's going to drink it," answered Manuel. With that, the giant rushed at him to tear him to pieces, but the boy pivoted on his sword and sprang aside, managing to wound Terrible in one arm. Manuel used his sword, and the fight was so vicious that both were soon exhausted. Suddenly the boy gathered his strength and slashed the giant's arm completely off. With that, he leaped upon the giant and killed him. Throwing the little pieces away, Manuel returned to the palace. The princess, who had been watching all the while from the balcony, was overjoyed. When the boy announced that they were leaving, she said, "First you have to look for my other sister, who is watched over by the giant Shameless."

"I'll go in a moment," he answered.

"Ah, no! It's far away, and you would arrive very late," protested the princess. "You're so exhausted now that you should just stay here tomorrow and go the day after." So Manuel stayed on that day and all the next, nourishing himself to build up his forces.

When he got to Shameless' palace, the second princess saw him and was also greatly frightened. "Ay, my lad," she cried, "what are you doing in these parts, when the giant doesn't even let a bird in?"

"I have come in search of him," declared Manuel fearlessly. She told the boy that the giant wouldn't be back until the next day around noontime, for he had gone off on a long trip. So Manuel spent the day with the second sister. In the evening she gave him a fine soft bed. The next morning, he took up his trusty sword and began his exercises again. If he had been light on his feet in the first fight, now he felt like a bird. After a delicious breakfast and lunch, Manuel went out to await the giant. About twelve o'clock, he heard a great noise, and began to prepare himself on the field where the giant played. When Shameless arrived, he sneered down at the boy, "Little worm, what are you up to here? Today is the day of your death."

"We'll see who's going to die first," answered Manuel. Immediately they jumped on each other and battled furiously, neither one able to catch the other. After a long struggle, the boy landed a telling blow with his sword and slew the giant. Breathless and weak, Manuel stretched out in the shade of a tree, for this giant had been far more daring and fierce than the other. When he had recuperated, Manuel returned to the palace and told the princess to make ready to leave. But she told him of her other sister who was captive nearby. The second princess would not go without her. So Manuel bade her good-bye and set out that same afternoon on the search for the remaining princess. When he came to the third palace, the princess cried out, "Ay, my boy, for god's sake, what are you doing here? The giant who guards me is so strong!"

"I'll take care of him in short order," he answered.

"But this giant is very good," she said. "He's surely going to ask you whether you come for good or for ill. Then you must say that you have good intentions. He'll tell you that you have to fight a bit, and you must agree to that. He's going to be eager for a lot of conversations, for he's a great talker."

Since the giant was to return the next day around eight or ten, Manuel lodged at the palace and was served with good victuals. He and the princess talked way into the night and fell in love with each other. When it was time to rest, she gave him a lovely soft little bed.

The next morning, they sat down to a fine breakfast in the dining room, and were in the midst of eating when they heard a rumbling noise.

"There he comes," said Manuel, dashing out with sword in hand. But when the owner of the castle saw the boy coming, he simply said, "Good morning, friend. What are you doing around here?"

"Good day to you," returned Manuel. "I've come to battle you for the princess that you robbed from me."

"And how do you want it, boy?" asked the giant. "Shall we fight it fair or dirty?"

"As you wish. We'll fight it clean or for keeps."

"All right," said the giant. "We'll fight it fair and square." Off they trooped to the giant's field, all the way conversing like old friends.

"Here's the spot," said the third giant when they arrived. "How do you want to start, face to face or back to back?"

"We're going to come at it rump first," decided Manuel. He went to one corner of the field and the giant to another, and they slowly advanced backwards toward each other. When they bumped, Manuel pivoted on his sword and jumped on top of the

giant, who didn't even see him. They fought on in this way
without either one's getting hold of the other. Finally the giant
struck the lad on the arm with one of his wings. The agile youth
leaped far aside, and as the giant tried again to get him with a
wing, Manuel dealt him a fierce blow which left one of his arms
hanging. From then on, Manuel had the upper hand, until finally
he wounded the giant deeply. When the boy had him helpless on
his back and was about to give the death blow, the giant cried,
"Don't kill me. Grant me my life, and I will be your bosom
friend. Take the princess you have come for. I know you killed
my two brothers, and I promise to help you in every way I can."

"You won't betray me later if I give you your life?" asked
Manuel. The giant promised that he wouldn't, and that he would
aid the boy in any tight spot. Manuel had only to think of Hairy
Dog, and the giant would come running. When they returned
together to the palace, Hairy Dog insisted that Manuel stay until
the next day. The princess waited on them in the dining room
while the giant talked about the trips he had made to look for
the oranges, and how the first watchmen had been helpless
against him. "The only one who stood up to me was you, Manuel," he mused. "If I had managed to whack you soundly with
my wing, your sleep would have been longer."

"But now you've got what you deserved," answered the boy.
"You caught me the other time because I was out of shape."

That night, they enjoyed themselves and all went peacefully to
sleep, for the giant had told them to rest at ease. After breakfast
the next morning, Hairy Dog delivered the princess to Manuel
and reminded him that if anything happened, he should always
remember Hairy Dog. Manuel bade him good-bye happily and
went to fetch the remaining sisters. They were dancing with joy
at being reunited again, for it had been years since they had seen
each other.

When the party arrived at the hole with the rope, Manuel told
the oldest princess to get into the little basket first. The two men
up above had begun to arrange a winch, and when they saw that
Manuel was jerking the cord, they began to wind it furiously until the first princess emerged at the top. But as soon as she was
up, the two helpers started to quarrel over her. "She's mine," said

one. "She's mine," yelled the other. And on it went until she screamed, "Stop it, both of you! There are three of us in all." So they let the basket down again, with Pedro remaining in possession of the first princess. When the second one was pulled to the top, Diego claimed her. Once more they tossed the little basket down. This time, Manuel told the youngest princess to get in, but she begged him to go up first, for his companions might betray him. But he was sure that his friends were very good men and would do no such thing.

"Look here," she said finally, "take this ring in case they use foul play and you are stuck down here below. If you say to the ring 'seven stations upward,' it will take you out of here." Then she climbed into the little basket with her baggage, and was hauled to the top. When the basket came down a fourth time, Manuel thought to himself, "I'll bet those two are up to no good!" He found a rock about his weight and stuck it in the basket. When he tugged the cord, the two helpers wound it up as fast as could be. The basket had gone up a good part of the way, when Pedro and Diego stealthily slipped out their knives and cut the rope.

"My friends betrayed me, just as I thought," said the lad as he heard the hum of the falling basket.

The princesses left for the palace with the others, and Manuel was stuck in his hole. When Pedro and Diego arrived at the king's palace, they passed themselves off as the ones who had saved his daughters. Naturally, the king was overcome with joy to see the girls, whom he had long ago given up for lost. Very soon after, the oldest daughter married Pedro, and the second one, Diego. The youngest sister had spoken at the beginning when she greeted her parents, but after that they couldn't get another word out of her.

Meanwhile, Manuel was in the pit for three days. After crying all this time, he stuck out his hand and hit the finger with the ring the princess had left him. He remembered instantly what she had told him. "Ring," he said, "by the power that God has given you, seven stations under the earth." The ring took him to a place where he stayed a long while, not knowing what to do. This land was owned by the King of the Pigmies, who put Manuel to work as a shepherd. One day he was lying sobbing in the shade of a tree and wondering where he was, when he heard a voice above him. He looked on every side and didn't see anybody, until the voice spoke again. Manuel looked above him and spied an eagle. "Is it you, little eagle, who speaks to me?"

"What are you up to?" asked the bird.

"Well, I'm just stuck here, eagle, and I can't find any way out," replied Manuel tearfully.

"Listen," said the bird, "tell your boss to make you some batches of dough and to give you seven lambs to eat, and then come right back. I'm going to get you out of here."

When Manuel had been granted all that he needed, he returned to the eagle, which picked him up in its claws and flew into the sky. It soared way up, almost beyond where the eye can see, and screamed, "Hungry, Manuel!" Immediately the boy whipped out a batch of bread and fed it to the bird. They had flown on up some distance more when the eagle called to him, "Hungry, Manuel!" At that point, Manuel passed it a whole lamb. Flying on, the eagle had devoured the lamb when it spoke again, "Hungry, Manuel!" Now the lad passed it a batch of dough and a lamb. After a while, the eagle had eaten all seven batches and all seven lambs, and there was still some flying left to do. "Hungry, Manuel!" it screeched again.

"Now I don't have a thing to give you," answered the boy desperately.

"Pull off one of your own calves," was the answer. So Manuel pulled off his calf and gave it to the eagle, which gobbled it up in one bite. Just at this point, the boy managed to see light above them. The eagle had flown some distance toward this light when again it screeched, "Hungry, Manuel!"

"What on earth can I give you now?" he asked.

"Pull off your other calf," commanded he bird. Manuel tugged eat his other leg and passed it to the eagle. With this last meal, the great bird just managed to flutter up to the top, where it dropped Manuel. The boy wanted to stand up, but of course he couldn't. The eagle wheeled away into the sky to take some air. When it flew back, it screeched to Manuel, "Stand up straight, my boy."

"I can't do it, little eagle," answered Manuel, floundering on the ground. Then the bird spit up one of the calves, and Manuel fitted it on to his leg just as it had been before. They did the same with the second calf, and he could walk again.

"All right, Manuel," said the eagle. "Now that I've taken you out, be on your way." The boy thanked the great bird and set off, coming out on a road very far from where he had first approached the hole. Night soon overtook him, but he continued plodding along in light and darkness. One day, after having walked for so long, he was lying under the shade of a tree when he remembered the giant Hairy Dog, and said to himself, "Even if he comes to kill me, let's see what happens! I want Hairy Dog to appear before me here!" Suddenly Manuel heard a rush, and the closer it came, the more it sped on. He hid behind a tree, and Hairy Dog flew by like a bullet. Failing to catch sight of the lad, the giant retraced his footsteps. Leaping about, he saw that the youth was hidden and called out, "By my soul, man, what are you doing here of all places?"

"Here's where I'm stuck, old boy," said Manuel. "I can't tell where to turn, and I want you to take me on the way."

"I'm all yours," said the giant. "Mount up on me and hold on for dear life, because I see you're still weak." The boy climbed on Hairy Dog's back, and the great creature went along as slowly as a giant can. Once he wanted to let loose and run, but Manuel fell off behind.

"Good God!" exclaimed Hairy Dog, "if we keep on this way, we're never going to get the princess. She's about to be married. There are only three days left, and you're so weak that I can't make good time." They traveled on, Hairy Dog holding himself at half speed, until nightfall. After dark, he left Manuel in a safe place and went out to raid a sheep pen. The giant brought back a skinned and quartered sheep, from which Manuel was to eat. They took the leftovers for the road. Now that the boy was a little stronger, Hairy Dog was able to travel faster. The next night, the giant brought another sheep, while Manuel prepared the fire. Once Manuel was well fed, the giant could run for all he was worth. He didn't take any turns, but hit out as the crow flies toward the palace.

The next morning, when Manuel had breakfasted, Hairy Dog said, "We have to arrive at the castle today, for tonight is the wedding feast, with the marriage tomorrow. If you can only get there in time, my boy, the groom will be shunted aside." That day, they sped through the little towns, or so it is told, for no one was able really to tell what was going by with such a rush. The bystanders had barely looked at the boy and the giant when they had already disappeared at the other end of town. Just as twilight was thickening, they arrived at the palace and hid in a dense clump of trees in a nearby orchard.

"Now, you're to stay here," said Hairy Dog to Manuel, "while I filch everything from the palace dining room so we can serve ourselves." The giant took away everything that was on the table without being seen by anybody. The guests were flabbergasted— all the food seemed to have disappeared. When the second course was served, the same thing happened, while Hairy Dog and Manuel gaily served themselves in the orchard.

Meanwhile, Hairy Dog said to Manuel, "I'm going to tell the princess that you're out here in the orchard, and ask her to invite the king, the queen, and the other guests to take a little stroll over this way." Hairy Dog trotted off and got to the princess' side without anybody's seeing him except her. He told her the news, and she announced to one and all, "I wish, with your consent, that we might go out to the orchard for a little air and to see the night." The king and his guests thought it an excellent idea. The princess led the way straight toward where Hairy Dog had told her to go. When they saw the great beast, everyone was terrified by such a ferocious looking animal. But the princess ran up to embrace him, while Manuel came out of the shadows and told the party not to be afraid. Then she called the king and queen and told them that Manuel was her husband, for he had saved her from captivity. The king pronounced, "If it is true, then take this man in marriage." They all trooped merrily into the palace and began the celebrations all over again. Manuel was washed, shaved, and dressed befitting his new position. The priest, his assistant, and even the bishop himself were called to wed the young couple. Even to this day, they are surely living happily together at the palace.

· ONCE UPON A TIME there was a fisherman who had to give fish to the king every day. On the day he failed to do so, his head would be cut off. He lived with his wife, a little pup, and a baby two months old. When he returned home in the evening, his wife never came out to meet him, but his dog was always at the door barking a welcome.

One night the fisherman couldn't for the life of him make a catch. Suddenly a mermaid appeared and said, "Listen to me, fisherman, if you give me the first creature who comes out to greet you at your door, I will give you fish." He thought to himself, "My wife never comes to meet me, and neither does my baby boy. My dog is the only one who's always there." So he made the deal with the mermaid, and tossing out his net, he drew it in heavy with fish. Now there were fish for the king and enough left over to sell in the city.

When the fisherman got home that night, out came his little boy as fast as he could creep and hugged his father about the legs. Then the fisherman said in his heart, "My son, my son, I have to give you to the mermaid." Without a word, he went off to the king's to deliver his fish and sell the rest to the townsfolk. That evening, he brought home everything he needed for his humble cottage, but never mentioned a word of what had happened with the mermaid.

This man went on fishing every night. The bargain he had made with the mermaid was to deliver to her, at the age of sixteen, whoever came to the doorway. Gradually the fisherman became richer than a king, and meanwhile his son grew up by leaps and bounds. The boy came to be a handsome lad, and when he was coming of age, his father grew very sad, for he knew that the deadline of his fateful bargain was drawing near. Although his wife served him faithfully, he would not take a bite to eat. One day she said to him, "Eat, my love. I have done you no wrong." But the fisherman answered nothing, until finally his son asked him, "Why won't you serve yourself, father? Maybe it seems wrong to you that I am here."

"No, my son," he answered, "it's not that at all. You see, I was once a poor fisherman and one night I couldn't catch a thing. Then a mermaid made a bargain with me to trade fish for whoever should come to greet me at my door. As I thought it would surely be my little dog, I agreed. When I came home on that evening so long ago, you scrambled out and hugged my legs. Now the time is up, and I have to deliver you to the mermaid. That, you see, is the cause of my sadness."

"Ah," answered his son, "is that the only problem you've got? Go on and give me to her. But first you must go and buy a colored saddle." The poor man shambled off to the store to buy some colored blankets, with which he made his son a saddle.

"Now, papa," continued the boy, "we're going to round up the animals." Since the following day was the time for delivering the lad to the mermaid, the father and his son left the horses corralled and ready that night. Early the next morning, the boy got up and saddled the most cantankerous mare in the herd. His mother was fixing breakfast and crying for her son. He bade her good-bye and went outside with his father. They mounted up and rode away toward the sea.

The mermaid was waiting at the water's edge, and when she caught sight of the lad, she exclaimed, "How lovely he is, and what a beautiful saddle! You must give me the boy and the horse, all together." At that, the father threw his lasso into the middle of the sea, where the mermaid caught it. Then the father rode to his house at breakneck speed, not turning once to look back. The mermaid stood with her eyes glued on the youth on horseback. "How lovely he is, and what a beautiful saddle!" Then she began to tug the horse into the sea, but the beast tugged back, and the more it pulled, the more the sea fell back around the mermaid. The horse pulled and strained until the mermaid, tired of being dragged from the water, dropped the lasso. The valiant animal galloped off toward the most tremendous mountains on earth, with the boy clinging tight to its neck.

The young man became lost in the great mountains. After traveling a long while, he came to a place where there were flocks of birds and beasts guarding a dead cow.

"Why aren't you fellows eating?" asked the young horseman as he rode up.

"Because," answered the Lion of Africa, "we're all of different sizes; some would eat more and others, less."

"I'll divide the victuals for you," volunteered the boy. He dismounted, tossed off his poncho, and began to parcel out pieces of the dead cow to all the animals, from the biggest beast on down. All the animals were very content with this new arrangement. Once the shares were all doled out, the boy leaped upon his horse again and rode away. He had gone about a quarter of a mile when the Lion of Africa sent a falcon to fetch him. Immediately it occurred to the lad that the animals weren't full and that they were planning to eat him as well. But, having little choice, he returned to the beasts' encampment and presented himself before the lion.

"I've called you back," purred the lion, "because we've agreed to give you a magic charm. My boy, when you're in a tight spot, you need only say, 'In the name of the fiercest lion in all the world.'" The youth thanked the great beast warmly. Then up stepped the greyhound and addressed him, saying, "When you get in a jam, just say, 'In the name of the most light-footed greyhound in the world.'" After this, the falcon added, "When you find yourself in hard times, say, 'In the name of the most light-winged falcon in the world.'" Finally the dove said "My friend, when the going is rough, you must say, 'In the name of the swiftest dove in the whole world.'"

Now that the fisherman's son was blessed with charms, he continued on his travels. A short way along the road, he dismounted, turned himself into a lion, and chased his own horse. The poor thing had run about thirty yards, when he caught it. "Now, why do I need a horse after all?" the boy thought to himself, and away he dashed, transformed into a lion. He traveled for two days and two nights without stopping. Next, to try out his other charms, he turned himself into a greyhound and traveled on for two more days and nights. Following this, he made himself a falcon and flew as long and as far as he could. Still there was no house to be seen anywhere. He lit in a tree and said, "In the name of the swiftest dove in the whole world." Catching sight of a house, he swooped down, turned himself back into a young man, and approached the house to ask for work. A gentleman appeared and hired him to shepherd his flocks.

Now, the man of the house was very rich and had a single daughter. Early the next day, she got up to make breakfast for the wandering lad. After eating, he went out with the master of the house to see the flock, all counted to the last head.

"Never take the sheep and cows to that lake yonder," cautioned the rich man, "for there's a wild boar that always eats my livestock." But no sooner had the man gone inside than the young shepherd led his animals off to that very same lake. He had just arrived when the boar rushed out ferociously and snatched a sheep in his fangs.

"In the name of the African lion, the fiercest in the world," said the young shepherd. Immediately he turned into a lion and began wrestling with the boar. They struggled the livelong day, but neither could gain the upper hand. Finally the boar roared, "By the mud of my lake, I'll make short work of you."

"By the kiss of a virgin maid and a sheep's head cooked in a virgin pot with vintage wine," returned the lion, "I'll gobble you up in a twinkling." At last they broke off. The boar scurried away to his lair by the lake, and the boy returned home with his flock. When the owner came out to count his stock, he saw that only one sheep was missing. Now how they waited on the boy's every wish! Afterwards, the master said to his daughter, "Listen, my dear, this must be a daring young fellow we have here, for he lost only one sheep from the whole flock. You, my sweet, are going to keep an eye on this chap."

Even earlier the next day, the daughter rose up to make the morning meal. And a tasty affair it was! Three glasses of old vintage wine, the very best in the house. After breakfast, the lad trotted off with his flock to the same lake. Sure enough, out roared the boar like mad in pursuit of the sheep. The shepherd boy made himself into a lion again, and the fight was on. When they had battled a great while, the boar said, "By a little mud from my lake, I'll make pieces of you." The lion replied, "By the kiss of a virgin maid and a sheep's head cooked in a virgin pot with vintage wine, I'll be done with you in no time." The daughter overheard every word of this and went to tell her father.

"And how are you, my daughter?" he asked.

"As pure as the day I was born," she answered.

"Good enough, my dear. Now you're going to cook this fellow a sheep's head in vintage wine with a virgin pot." Very soon after, the youth came in with his flock and corralled them for the night. The master went out to count the animals and found not one missing. He lassoed the oldest sheep and cut off its head to toss into the virgin pot. They gave the shepherd boy his supper, and if they had pampered him before, this night he was treated like a king. Meanwhile, the sheep's head boiled on the whole night through.

Very early the following day, the daughter and the shepherd awoke. The boy breakfasted richly on sheep's head, and set off for the lake. The wild boar hove into view once more, and they began to fight fiercely. This time the shepherd beat the beast down with a few blows. He dragged it away from the lake and began to open it, whereupon a fox popped out of the boar's belly. Immediately the youth turned himself into a greyhound, the most light-footed in the world, and lit out after the fox. He caught it at the very threshold of the house of a neighboring giant, and carried it back to the same lake to open it. Out of the fox came a dove, which flew away straight toward the giant's palace. Then the boy said to his charm, "In the name of the falcon, the most light-winged in the world," and he caught the dove at the sill of the giant's balcony. He carried the bird away to the lake and sliced it open. Finding an egg inside the dove, he seized it and headed back for the palace, where he found the giant deathly ill and stretched out on his bed.

"Give me the egg, boy," moaned the giant, "and I'll grant you all my treasures."

"First hand over your keys," answered the shepherd, "every last one." When the ailing giant had done this, the boy grasped the egg tight and said, "Open your mouth wide, because I'm going to toss this inside." With all his strength he hurled the egg, which broke to smithereens on the giant's forehead and killed him on the spot! Now the young shepherd began to open all the doors of the palace. In one room he found a little princess locked up. And what a lovely girl she was! He opened a second door and found another little princess, even more beautiful than the first. Opening a third door, he found a third princess, lovely without equal. This one the boy married.

After his wedding to the third princess, he returned to visit his master and to see how things were at the ranch.

"My son, don't go," implored the rich man. "Marry my daughter, for she's the only one I have, and I'm a man of great wealth."

"It's not out of scorn that I don't marry her," answered the boy, "it's just that I have another." So his master paid him, and he set off for home, telling his wife the story of how he had been married to the mermaid and run away from her and had then become a shepherd.

"Well," she said upon hearing the tale, "see that you never go to the seashore any more, for she could nab you again with no trouble at all."

The days passed in this new life, and the youth became a hunter of birds. Bit by bit, he forgot about the danger of the sea's edge. One day when he strayed there by chance, the mermaid spied him and pulled him in. He didn't come home anymore, and his wife was sure that he had finally fallen into the mermaid's power. She bustled off to a jeweler's and ordered three golden apples. When these strange fruits were ready, she want to hide in a wood near the mermaid's haunt. Rummaging around, the young wife took out one of the golden apples and began to juggle it from hand to hand. When the mermaid spied the gleam of the golden fruit, she called, "sell me your apple, princess."

"If you will show me your husband down to his shoulders," she answered, "the apple shall be yours. Not otherwise." So the mermaid grabbed the young man and raised him out of the water to his shoulders. When the princess recognized him as her husband, she threw the apple to the sea maiden. Then she entered the little wood again and took out another apple even more beautiful than the first. When the mermaid saw this one, she cried, "Oh, princess, sell me your lovely apple."

"Of course. Simply show me your husband to the waist, and

you shall have it." The mermaid seized her captive husband and lifted him out up to his waist, whereupon the princess tossed her the apple. Once again she returned to the grove to get the third and most beautiful apple. When the mermaid asked for that one as well, the princess replied, "Certainly I'll sell it to you if you'll lift up your husband in the palm of your hand." When the mermaid did this, the young man turned into a dove and flew far away into the clouds. The princess hurled the apple to the sea maiden and returned to shore in her little boat. When she got home, her husband was sitting there awaiting her. They were married again, and this time the princess insisted, "Never go hunting again, my love, for now there's no need. If the mermaid should trap you another time, she would never let you out of her clutches." And that is the story of the mermaid and the poor fisherman.

• 5 • *The Fisherman*

• ONCE UPON A TIME there was a very poor fisherman who was childless and who lived with his wife, a dog, and a mare. As he was fishing at dusk one night, he made a cast which netted him a great load of fish. In the catch there was an especially lovely colored fish. At this moment, a voice from above spoke to him, "Heed well, fisherman. You must eat that colored fish you have netted. The first water you clean it in must be given to your mare, the second water to your dog, and the final water in a cup to your wife." The man took his fish home and instructed his wife not to do anything with the colored one until he had come back from delivering the other fish to the king. Returning from the palace, the man began to wash the lovely fish. The first water he gave to the mare, the second to his dog, and the third to his wife. Then they ate the fish itself for dinner. The fisherman found two little swords inside and buried them in the garden. Soon after, his wife became pregnant, and the dog and the mare as well. First the bitch gave birth to twin puppies which were the spit and image of each other. When her turn came, the fisherman's wife bore two little boys. A few days later, the mare bore two rose-colored colts which no one could tell apart.

Now, the fisherman's sons grew by leaps and bounds. When they were ten, each one planted a sprig of an olive tree. The sprigs took root, and very soon the trees themselves were sprouting. When the boys were fifteen, they trained the two colts and dogs. One dog was named "Iron Breaker," and the other, "Chain Breaker." When the two lads became eighteen, the first-born said to his father, "Give me your blessing, papa, for I want to go a-wandering." The old man gave his consent, and early the next day the first son saddled his horse. His father went to the garden and brought him one of the swords. What a beautiful weapon it was! His son grasped it well and told his brother that if the olive tree which he had planted should wither, it would mean that he had found work in his wanderings. Then he departed and came upon a road which he followed until, quite late, he came to the palace of a king.

"Good evening, my fine young man," called the king. "Tell me, where are you going?"

"Your majesty," answered the boy, "I'm wandering about in the world."

"Get down, my good man, and come inside," said the king, who immediately set two servant lads to guard the boy's horse and dog with great care.

Now it chanced that this king had two daughters. He went to fetch them and told the boy to choose the one who most pleased him. Straightway the young man chose the older, and was married to her. The months passed after the wedding, and one day the young man sat down before a window and noticed a green meadow in the distance. When he asked his wife what it was, she answered, "That's where you go and never come back."

"I'm going to go, and I'm going to come back," he said resolutely.

"Please don't, my love," she begged, "for you'll surely never return." But the boy insisted, and sending for his horse, he rode away to the green meadow. What a fair smell he found there in the sweetness of the grass! He was riding toward a house in the meadow, when out came an old crone with twelve strands of hair.

"Good day, my son," she croaked. "Get down and take these twelve strands of hair to tie up your dog and your horse. I don't want to be bitten or trampled!" The boy tied his animals and was invited to come in. The old dame was bustling about with her pots, roasting pork sausages. In the midst of this hustle she opened a little box, grabbed a fistful of dust, and threw it at the youth. In a twinkling, he turned to stone. Then she threw dust at his dog and his horse, which became two more stones. The strands of hair were turned into tremendous chains to bind them.

Early the next day, the brother who had stayed at home got up and went out to see his olive tree. He found it withered. "Now my brother has found work," he said to himself. "Father," he called, "give me your blessing, for I'm off to look for my brother." His father bestowed his benediction on the boy and went to bring the other sword from the garden. The second brother took the same road as the first, and came to the very same palace. The little princess rushed out, overjoyed that her husband had come, "Get down, my welcome love, and come inside!" The servants came to take care of his horse and dog. The young man realized in his heart that his brother was married to this lovely girl. They sat down to chat, and the "wife" fed supper to her "husband." All the while, he was puzzling over how he could possibly consent to sleep with his sister-in-law. When it was bedtime, they undressed and lay down together. The brother placed his sword between himself and the princess, with the guard toward her and the point beside himself.

"What are you doing, my dear?" she asked, astounded.

"It's a vow I made, and I must fulfill it."

"If that is your vow, then I wish you good fortune, my love," said the princess as they settled into bed. The young brother didn't move a muscle the whole night through, for he was full of curiosity about what had become of his older brother.

When the day broke, he arose and went to sit by the window, where he saw the green meadow. "Look there, sweet," he called to the princess, "what is that place?"

"Didn't I tell you before that that's where you go and never come back?"

"But how come I went, and am here again?" he asked, thinking all the while to himself, "That is where my brother is." Then he turned to the princess and said, "I'm going again, and I shall return again. Now get me some breakfast in a hurry, so I can be gone to the meadow." She brought him his breakfast immediately, while the stableboy saddled his horse. The brother rode off into the prairie, and as he drew near, he was struck by the odor of pork sausages being cooked by the old crone of the meadows. Arriving at her little cottage, he glanced at the two stones outside and recognized them right away. The old woman shambled out and cackled, "Get down, my son, and take these two strands of hair to tie up your horse and dog." The youth was no fool, so he merely put the strands on the back of the necks of his trusty animals. As soon as he entered the house he spotted the other stone; and recognized his brother.

"Chain Breaker," he called to his dog, "grab this old girl and kill her!" The dog leaped on the old woman and began to maul her, until finally she cried, "Call off your dog, boy!"

"Down Chain Breaker!" he shouted. "Now, old lady, bring this stone back to life." The crone snatched a fistful of dust and tossed it on the stone, whereupon the other brother immediately rose up. "Now give life to the other two stones outside," ordered the younger brother. The horse and the dog were liberated also. Then he shouted to the two dogs to tear the old dame to pieces. They jumped on the woman and quickly made mincemeat of her. The younger brother opened her magic box, grabbed a load of dust, and scattered it all around the yard outside the house. Immediately an army of people began to stir and come to life. When this task was done, he said to his older brother, "Let's be off to your place, for I have come to get you."

"Right, brother," answered the other. "But what a deep sleep I had!"

As they were about halfway along the road to the palace, and were chatting together, the younger brother said, "There's something I'd like to tell you and not like to tell you."

"Speak up, my brother."

"Last night I slept with your wife," said the younger one. In a flash the older brother lifted his sword and killed the younger one. He left him lying dead on the roadside and rode off for the palace. When his wife ran out to greet him, he said, "Don't you see, I went *and* I came back." As night was falling quickly, they supped and went to bed. This time the young man didn't put any sword between them, so of course his wife asked, "Now have you fulfilled your vow, my darling? Didn't you place the sword here last night?"

"Yes," he answered, "the vow has been performed." But in his heart, he thought, "I have slain my brother unjustly." He couldn't sleep all that night, thinking of the great wrong he had done.

Early the following morning, he sent for his horse to be saddled, buckled on his sword, and set off to search for his brother. On the way, he came upon a little old woman in the road.

"Good morning, my boy," she said, "Won't you tell me why you're so pained? Don't you know that the little old ones give wise counsel?"

"Yes, mother," he said. "Yesterday I killed my brother unjustly. Now I'm trying to find a way to bring him back to life."

"Look, my child, do you see that boulder up there on the hill? A green lizard is there. Now give the spurs and the whip to your horse to get there at twelve noon sharp. The lizard will be panting with its mouth open, and you must give it a stroke of the sword and cut it in two. Be careful not to make any mistakes." The boy found the lizard just as she had said, and axed it in half. Then he pierced it on the tip of his sword and rode to where his brother lay. He crossed the wounds with the lizard, and the dead brother jumped up in one leap.

"Mount up on my horse," said the elder. "I've come to get you."

"What a sleep I've had," mumbled the other.

As they rode up to the palace, the princess was very embarrassed at not being able to tell which of the two was her husband. The elder brother, seeing her so confused, said, "I am your man." She threw out her arms and hugged him to her. "This," he added, "is my brother, whom I now introduce." The princess raced off, happy as a lark, to tell her father that a charming brother-in-law had arrived. The king came out stumbling and hopping with joy at the news. Losing no time, he fetched his remaining daughter and delivered her to the younger brother in marriage. As the two daughters were his only offspring, the king divided his kingdom between them. So it was that the two youths became rich and powerful men and lived on together in the same palace.

·6· *The Prince of the Sword*

• THERE WAS ONCE a youth who lived with his mother and sister. Nearby was a prince who lived enchanted in the middle of the sea. One day the prince passed by the house where the three lived. He saw the young girl, fell in love with her, and went straight to her door. When the elderly woman came out with her daughter, the prince was so pleased that he took the girl by the hand, drew her up behind him on his horse, and rode away. No sooner had he arrived at the center of the sea than he leaped in with the maiden, who didn't even wet the tips of her fingers.

When her brother came home and discovered that his sister had been carried away, he was greatly puzzled, for the prince had not even said where he was from. The youth rose early the next day, and set out to follow the trail of the mysterious prince. Eventually he came to the sea, and there he lost the trail. "Here is surely where they threw themselves into the water," the boy thought to himself. Immediately he continued in the same direction and came upon the most beautiful street in the sea, which led him to the prince's castle. His sister was there, walking to and fro in the yard. Seeing her brother, she rushed out to speak with him.

"Where is your husband?" he asked.

"He is off to the wars," answered the girl, "but he returns promptly every afternoon." The brother and sister strolled through the orchards of the palace, surveying all the prince's riches. She showed him a spring where gold was flowing like water. When the young man had seen how great the prince's wealth was, he exclaimed, "My sister is well-established here!"

Dusk was falling, and the hour of the prince's arrival had come, so the girl hid her brother away in a back room. The prince rode in and told his wife that the battle was almost won.

"And now," she asked, "what will you do with your war?"

"Either I shall conquer or I shall die," proclaimed the prince.

"Listen, my sweet," said his wife, "I want to tell you something. But please don't be angry. You see, my brother has come."

"Well, where is he?" said the prince, peering around.

"I have him hidden here, because I thought you'd be vexed." Right away, she ran to fetch her brother and introduced him to her husband. The prince found him very charming and invited him outside to see the treasures. When they had seen all the wealth of the palace, the prince pointed to the spring where gold was flowing like water, and warned the young man never to touch the gold where it bubbled out. Of course the boy promised that he would not.

Early in the morning, the prince left his bed and went again to the wars. His brother-in-law wandered about, observing all the riches once more. The running spring of gold pleased him so much that he drew near it, thinking, "Why does the prince forbid me to touch this?" He thrust his finger halfway into the gold liquid, and drew it forth turned into pure gold. "Now they'll catch me for sure," he thought. "But as long as it's for so little, I might as well be caught for more." So he undressed and washed himself in the spring, whereupon he turned completely into gold. Next, he took a sword and thrust it into the spring also. Then the boy took a beautiful rose-colored horse which the prince kept at the palace, and rode for the battlefield where his brother-in-law was at war. At this moment, the prince and his forces were in deep trouble. The youth rode up, drew his sword, and flew into the thick of the battle. He beheaded the enemy as a man would behead chickens, making them all retreat far to the rear.

"What a valiant youth has come to aid me in battle!" exclaimed the prince, astounded at the prowess of the mysterious rider. He commanded his soldiers to capture the man with utmost care, but they were unable to get near the great swordsman.

The youth galloped away and returned to the palace. When the prince rode up close behind him, the young wife rushed out and asked, "How has it gone today, my dear?"

"Excellent, my little one," answered the prince. "A young man on a rose-colored horse came to help me in battle. He was a handsome, well-dressed fellow and his horse was shod with gold." Meanwhile, the young brother-in-law was nowhere to be seen.

The next day, the prince returned to the war. As soon as he had gone, the youth left his room to eat breakfast. His sister was shocked to see her brother wrapped in gold. Again he saddled the horse and rode toward the scene of battle. The prince's soldiers were not fighting. The youth alone began to fight, beheading the enemy like chickens. The prince again ordered his men to capture this strange man, but once more it was impossible. This time, it happened that they pricked him on his left leg. By four in the afternoon, the young horseman had won the battle.

"What a brave warrior!" gasped the prince. "To think that he has single-handedly gained us the victory. There I was with my troops, and the enemy had me almost beaten. I have won by the grace of God and the strength of this strange youth."

The young man rode home to the palace with the slight wound in his left leg and shut himself in his room. Moments after, the prince arrived and said to his wife, "Today was better than ever, for I have triumphed. I won the war, my darling. The young horseman returned again to help. He must be an angel from heaven, for he has the power of God. As soon as he arrived, my soldiers fought no more, for he was capable of conquering the enemy army by himself, shining and dazzling with his gold sword. He cut off their heads like chickens."

The boy, who had been listening to everything his brother-in-law said, stepped out of his room. The prince, immediately recognizing him as the same horseman, threw open his arms and embraced him with great joy.

"I had power," said the young brother, "because I had found a good horse and felt a great force within me. If I hadn't gone to the war, my prince, they would have defeated you. You had forbidden me to touch the golden spring, but I was curious to see why. First I touched the gold with my finger. Seeing that I had gone that far, I washed myself in it, and my whole body became gold."

Thereupon the sea was disenchanted and disappeared, leaving only a great city. The prince himself had not known that if one bathed in the spring the city would be freed from its spell. Since the boy had washed in the golden liquid in all ignorance, he had broken the enchantment.

The prince has remained there to this day, living happily together with his brother-in-law. Both became very rich and powerful.

• 7 • *Seven Colors*

• THERE WAS ONCE a very poor couple who lived in the country and had one little boy. At the age of seven, the boy's adventures began. He made his father fix him a little saddle, with which he mounted the old man's kids and tamed them as if they were horses. He did this until he was fifteen or sixteen. One day he found a newborn sheep and raised it in his flock. It grew and grew until it was enormously big. The boy broke it to saddle so he could ride it as he wished. When his "horse" was ready, he announced to his parents that he was going out riding. It frightened the poor old people to see him mounted on a sheep and determined to go away like that. His mother was so startled that she became confused in preparing his clothes and patched his pants with more than seven colors.

The boy rode to the nearest city and began to ask for work at the king's palace. Seeing this lad mounted on a sheep, the guards were astounded, especially by the haughtiness with which he asked for the king. But his majesty advised them to let the boy in.

"I've come looking for work, your majesty," announced the boy boldly, "and I believe that you will give it to me." The king, amazed to see the boy on the sheep, stammered, "What work can I give you?"

"I'm a countryman," he answered, "and I can do almost any job."

"Young man," continued the king, regaining his wits, "by chance I have a ranch with a whole herd of livestock. Every cowboy I have put in charge there has failed to bring me even one cow, and none of them has ever returned from the job."

"Well," said the youth, "I'll bring you cattle any time you wish." Although his saddle was fitted with every kind of trapping, his only weapon was a little knife that he had once brought to his mother.

"You can go to my ranch to work," continued the king. "I give you permission to kill a cow for meat."

They prepared the boy, and he rode off into the country on his sheep. As he galloped into the king's ranch, he looked far and wide and was very surprised to see so many animals. "What can the reason be," he thought, "that nobody brings cattle to the king?" He took out his lasso and tied a cow to a vetch tree at what seemed to him a good place for a camp. The lad was busy skinning the animal when a giant appeared on an enormous horse.

"What are you doing here, young feller?" roared the giant. "Why, I could cut off your head with one blow."

"The king sent me," answered the boy, "and ordered me to kill this cow for food."

"I don't give a damn for any king. Now come out here, so I can cut off your head."

"Just wait a half a minute," answered the boy. "Let me get on my horse." He mounted the sheep and rode toward the giant. As the monstrous man slashed out with his sword, the boy passed underneath his horse's belly and reached up to stab him. The giant toppled lifeless to the ground. The youth had a terrible struggle to drag the body away from his camp. The only thing he noticed was a diamond ring the giant was wearing. He removed it from the giant's huge finger and fastened it on his belt. Then he returned to finish skinning his cow.

The young cowherd enjoyed himself on the ranch until Saturday, which was the day he had promised to return. He saddled his sheep early and rounded up the livestock, picking out the biggest and fattest animal for the king. As the boy led the animal into the palace, the king was full of wonder. Even the most famous horsemen and cowboys had never brought him a single cow. He received the boy warmly and sent him to rest and to be served the best in the palace.

Knowing that the king had three daughters, the young cow-puncher said, "Your majesty, send me your three girls so I can lunch with them." The king looked at him and laughed, "What else can I do? I have to tolerate him, because he may be a great man." At this same time, the king gave him the name of "Seven Colors." For a laugh, the girls went to while away some time with the cowhand while he ate lunch. But before they arrived, Seven Colors took the diamond ring from his pocket and placed it on the hand with which he took the spoon. When the oldest daughter breezed in, she exclaimed, "What a beautiful diamond, Seven Colors!"

"Here it is, all yours, Miss."

Soon after, they prepared him again and sent him out to the fields to do the same job. He had lassoed another cow and was busy skinning it when a second giant appeared and grumbled, "What are you up to here, you young whippersnapper? Come out so I can send your head flying."

"Watch out that you don't come to the same end as the other," cautioned the boy.

"Come out here on the double!" roared the giant, getting red in the face. "I don't want any more palaver with you."

"Just let me get on my horse," said the lad calmly. The giant gaped at the youth's "horse." The lad mounted his sheep and rode it toward the great man. When the giant took a swing at Seven Colors, the youth went under the horse's belly just as before and knifed his enemy, who crashed stone dead to the ground. Seven Colors tugged the body over to the same place where he had left the other. The second giant was wearing a diamond even bigger than the first one's. Seven Colors took this ring as well, and hung it on his belt.

He spent the week happily, without being bothered by anyone. On Saturday, he rounded up the animals, chose the fattest, and led it into the palace. As soon as the king has risen that morning, he had gone out with his binoculars to see if his cowboy was

anywhere in sight. The princesses were waiting anxiously to see
if he would bring another diamond. Suddenly they all caught
sight of the cloud of dust where he was coming with his cow in
tow. When the boy came riding in triumphantly, the king didn't
know how he could honor him for having at last provided the
palace with the meat they had lacked for so many years.

"This fellow is nothing less than a servant of God," thought
the king. Once more he sent the boy to eat lunch, and once more
Seven Colors asked for his daughters to keep him company. The
princesses could hardly wait to hear these words. They were at
his side in a flash. Just as before, he had placed the diamond on
his right hand before they arrived.

"What a beautiful, shining diamond, Seven Colors!" gasped
the second princess, her eyes bulging in their sockets.

"Here it is for you, my lady," he said, slipping it off his finger.

After this, they gave him provisions and sent him off to the
ranch a third time. He was busy skinning a cow for dinner when
yet another giant loomed over him. This one was even more furious than the others, and headed straight to attack Seven Colors.

"Just a minute!" shouted the cowhand, holding up his hand.
"Let me at least get on my horse." The giant looked about everywhere and saw neither hide nor hair of a horse, but only that little sheep. This merely made him all the more sure of the fight,
for he thought he would slice up both the boy and his animal
with one stroke of his sword. Seven Colors galloped out on his
sheep and, as before, ducked under the belly of the other's horse,
reaching up and stabbing the giant quite dead. As he struggled
to haul the body away, he saw that this giant was wearing a diamond even more exquisite than the other two. Seven Colors
placed it on his belt and returned to work until Saturday, when
he saddled his horse and chose the best animal from the herd for
the palace table.

The king was observing as usual with his binoculars. When he
spotted the column of dust, he shouted gleefully, "Here comes
Seven Colors." As soon as the boy had reined up at the gate, the
king sent him to rest and have lunch. This time the princesses
didn't wait to be invited, but appeared at his side as soon as he
began to eat. He had to put on the diamond before their very eyes.

"What a lovely diamond, Seven Colors," sighed the youngest daughter.

"Here, you may have it," said he, offering it to the princess.

As before, he soon left for the ranch and set himself to skinning his cow. He put it on the spit to roast, but no giant appeared. Seven Colors wondered about this, and waited about four days to see if one would come. When there was no sign of another giant, he set off to see where they could possibly have come from. Arriving at a palace, the valiant cowboy called out in vain, but no one answered. Then he walked from door to door of the silent palace and found everything shut tight. Finally he spied a ferocious frog through a crack in the window.

"What are you doing here?" asked the frog. "Get out before the giants come and eat you alive!"

"What giants?" he asked, not at all frightened.

"The same ones who have enchanted me here where nobody can enter."

"Those must be the three giants I killed," said Seven Colors. The frog saw that he was very little and could hardly believe that he was telling the truth.

"You aren't fooling me, are you?"

"I don't have any reason to, for I killed all three of them and have come to see if there are any more."

"If that's the case," said the frog, "then I don't have to stay in the palace a day longer. You must be the man who can free me from the enchantment. Look for the keys in the corridor. You'll have to open seven doors to get here, for they've locked me in with seven different keys." Seven Colors took the key ring from the hall and opened all the doors, with his knife ready, until he came to the beautiful frog and asked how he could disenchant her.

"I'm the queen of the palace," she answered, "and the man who frees me will be the king here. Take me by the legs and throw me on the floor as hard as you can." The cowboy, shaking with fear at seeing such a gigantic creature, took her and threw her on the floor just as she had ordered. In the same instant, a princess more beautiful than any of the king's daughters stood where the frog had fallen. Then the queen rang a bell, where-

upon all the servants and slaves of the palace instantly appeared.
She ordered them to open the boxes that were scattered about.
Immediately they brought the new prince the finest clothes there
were so he could change. She made him shave and wash up (because I don't think he had shaved since he was born). He threw
away his pants of seven colors and was almost unrecognizable as
the same person, for he wasn't, after all, so bad looking.

"Tomorrow," said the princess, "we must have the marriage
ceremony." The cowboy thought, "I'll just have to take her on
my sheep's rump," for he could think of no other way to carry
her. They spent the day together happily and arose early the next
morning. While everybody was changing clothes and preparing
for the trip, Seven Colors was thinking about saddling his sheep.
All at once, he heard the hoofbeats of a carriage approaching.
Going to the door, he saw outside a crystal chariot plated with
silver and gold, with coachmen better dressed than his master the
king. Since this was Saturday, the day the king was awaiting
him, Seven Colors climbed into the chariot and rode off with the
horses sparking fire.

When the carriage was within sight of the other palace, the
king spotted, instead of the usual dust cloud, a radiance as if the
sun were coming over the earth. Greatly excited, he called the
princesses and asked them to tell him what was coming, for he
couldn't make out a thing.

"It looks like a carriage drawn by horses," they chorused.

"It must be a king and queen coming to make us a visit," said
the king, scrambling about and beginning to make the proper arrangements for a reception. When the chariot rolled into the
town, all the inhabitants, who had never seen such a beautiful
vehicle, rushed toward the palace gate admiring the great coach.
The king was waiting in the doorway with the three princesses.
The carriage door opened and the new prince climbed down. He
began to speak flatteringly to the king as if he had known him
for a long time. All the while, neither the bewildered king nor
the princesses could tell who it was. Only the youngest daughter,
who had perhaps looked upon him more carefully, recognized
the prince.

"I believe it's Seven Colors," she whispered in the king's ear.

"Hush! What nonsense!" hissed the king. "How can you imagine such a thing?" Then the prince spoke up, "Don't you know me, my king?"

"No, my fine majesty, I can't say that I do," answered the king, still quite baffled.

"Why, I'm Seven Colors, the cowpoke you had on your ranch." With this the poor flabbergasted king almost fainted, and then fell to his knees to beg the prince's pardon for the name he had given him. Seven Colors told his story and concluded, "I have suffered all of this. Now you can send whoever you wish to the ranch, for he will run no risks with giants. But now I've come to ask you for a favor, your Majesty, for I wish you to be my godfather. I'm going to marry the princess I freed from enchantment."

"I am at your beck and call, your majesty," answered the king.

So Seven Colors and the princess were married in his godfather's palace. By the groom's orders, the whole town was invited to the wedding, rich and poor alike, and everyone was waited on lavishly. After the celebration, the young couple bade the king good-bye and rode off to their new palace, where, I believe, they are living happily even today.

.8. *The Faithless Sister*

• ONCE UPON A TIME there was an old couple who had a little boy and a little girl about four or five years old. The old people died in bed one night. The following morning, the children awoke and began to play on top of them. When the boy and girl tired of this and saw that the old folks would not awake, they jumped off the bed and kindled the fire, putting some potatoes on to roast. After gobbling up their little breakfast, they returned to the bed, lay down together with their mother and father, and soon fell asleep again. The next day they also arose and made a fire. After breakfasting on potatoes, they ran outside to play. But they quickly tired of their games, and went inside to wake up their parents. The old people would of course never wake up again. About this time, two men arrived and asked the children where their mother and father were. When the little boy answered that they were still sleeping, the men entered the house, only to find the old couple stark dead in bed. The two men were full of pity and carried the old man and his wife away to the cemetery for a decent burial. Passing by the house on their way back, they called to the children, "Come on to our house. What will ever become of you two here alone?" But the little boy refused and said that they wouldn't budge. So the two little ones stayed on, living there by themselves.

One day the boy got up very early and went out into the fields. As he was wandering about, he met a tiny old man who said, "What are you up to, my son?"

"I'm searching for food, old father," the child answered.

The man gave him a shotgun and said, "Take this, little one, so you can hunt birds and at least keep alive." The lad thanked the old fellow over and over, and just as he had set off on his way, the man called to him again, "Take this pair of puppies, my child, and raise them to keep you company."

As the boy walked through the fields with his puppies and his shotgun, he surprised a flock of pigeons and fired at them, felling almost every one. He and his dogs picked up the birds and carried them home to the little sister. The two of them set about dressing the birds. When they had cleaned a few, they roasted them and had a delicious supper. Later, the little brother went to the fields again with his dogs and came home as before, loaded with birds. Now nothing was lacking in the children's household.

In time, the lad became a man. One day, while hunting in the mountains, he got lost. He had walked so far that he had become separated from his faithful dogs. Suddenly he heard them barking far in the distance. He followed the sound of the yelping and came upon them battling with a giant. The boy's arrival gave spirit to the dogs, which summoned up all their courage and knocked the giant to the ground.

"Don't let these animals kill me!" he shouted to the boy. The lad called his dogs to leave the giant, who added, gasping for breath, "Listen, boy, I'll give you all my riches if only you keep these beasts away."

"Toss me your keys," returned the youth. The giant quickly

handed over the keys and took the boy with him to deliver up his palace and all his wealth. Once the lad had taken possession of the palace, he closed the giant in the most secure room and set out for his own house. When he arrived home, he said to his sister, "Over yonder, I've had a little fun, and I've come to take you, for I'm now a very rich man."

"Let's take all our possessions with us," she replied joyfully.

"No," answered her brother, "what do we want with them now? I have more than enough. Let the first poor man who passes by benefit from what is here." So they both left the little house and came to the palace quite late that night. The boy put the key to the giant's room in his pocket and handed the rest to his sister. "You, who are now the lady of the house, will take these keys. But never, never, never open this door, my sister," he said, pointing to the giant's room.

With the dawn the next morning, the young man went hunting. No sooner had he left, than his sister determined to open that very room which he had warned her about. Since he had forgotten to take out his key after changing his clothes, she rummaged in the pockets of his vest and found it. Immediately she ran to open the door. The great giant emerged and, with a few tender words, he ensnared her heart. She was greatly pleased by this monstrous fellow and soon accepted him as her lover. Now the girl did not lock the room. When her brother returned in the afternoon, he poked around in his pockets and, finding the key, put it safely in the vest he was wearing.

When he left to hunt the following morning, the girl ran straight to the giant to chat with him.

"Look here," he said in his great, rumbling voice, "why don't we kill your brother so the two of us can live peacefully together. He's not so courageous; it's those dogs that are the brave ones. You get sick," he continued to the girl, "and tell him you can be cured only by eating a *nalca* plant which is in such and such a place. Then I'll go there and kill him. Take these two strands of hair and tell him to leave you the dogs to chase the chickens, since you're here all alone."

When the brother arrived in the afternoon, he found his sister ill and asked her what the matter was.

"Oh, brother dear, I'm ailing a bit," she moaned.

"And what will make you better, sister?"

"If only I could eat a piece of the *nalca* which is found in such and such a place, my dear brother."

"So be it," declared the boy. "Tomorrow early I shall go to search for it."

Bright and early, the boy got up and put on the teakettle.

"Ay, my little brother, leave me the dogs so they can chase the chickens. I'm ailing so that I can't move."

As soon as he left, the girl leaped up with great haste, tied the dogs with the strands of hair, and returned straight to bed. The dogs, noticing that their master had gone, began to leap against the strands, which had become chains for them.

Soon the boy found the special plant and was busy picking it, when suddenly the giant loomed up and said, "Now I have you in my clutches."

"So you do," observed the boy. "But I'm going to ask you for one favor."

"As long as it's not for your life, why not?"

"I'm just going to climb this tree to bid good-bye to the world." So the young man scrambled up into the branches, crying all the while for his lost life. He climbed to the very peak of the tree and shouted lustily, "Break Iron, Break Chain," at the top of his lungs. The two dogs perked up their ears and sprang against the strands. Immediately they broke into pieces and the dogs raced full speed toward their master's voice. At his last shout, the dogs dashed onto the scene and leaped five yards up into the tree.

"Kill that giant for me, boys," he shouted jubilantly. The giant bellowed for the boy to call off the beasts, but he was merciless and refused. In a few savage bounds, the dogs had killed the giant. The lad headed home with his trusty companions to take the plant to his sister. She was better after the first bite, and her brother suspected no foul play.

Again the following day, he went abroad to the fields and came upon a little road. Following it, he eventually came to the house of a very rich gentleman, who cordially invited him in to rest and chat a while. The youth told of his sufferings while the rich man listened attentively. After some time, he said, "Listen, my fellow, you have suffered a great deal and shouldn't have to bear any more. Marry my daughter."

"This seems like a good idea, since it is your pleasure," the boy returned. "I shall receive her gladly."

"Tomorrow you will marry," said the gentleman.

"Quite so, my lord, but first I must go to find my sister, for the two of us are all alone."

Meanwhile, the boy's sister had gone to the place where the giant lay dead and had taken his right eyetooth to hide in her pocket. Just as she returned, her brother drove up and took her away in the carriage. The young man introduced his sister to the nobleman, who received her with open arms. Then he sent for the minister, the bishop, and the archbishop to celebrate the wedding. When the joyous day drew to a close, the master of the house said, "Now is the time to prepare the beds for the newly-weds." The boy's sister offered to fix the bed for her brother and his bride. Where her brother was going to sleep she placed the giant's eyetooth in such a way that it would be near his lungs. The young man and his wife went merrily off to their bed, un-dressed, and lay down together. As soon as he turned on his back, the eyetooth pierced his lungs and killed him. His beloved shook her husband, but to no avail. When she put on the light and saw that he was indeed dead, a great wail burst from her throat. Her mother and father heard and came running to the bedroom.

"Lord in heaven, my daughter, what on earth is the matter?" asked the rich man frantically.

"My husband has died," she sobbed.

"How can he have possibly died so soon?" asked her father. They took the boy out of bed and placed him in the parlor to keep their vigil. After they had watched the wake over him, they mournfully carried the young husband away to be buried. His dogs trailed behind all the people in the procession. Searching in vain for their master, the dogs began tracing the trail where the dead man had been borne. When the dogs came to the cemetery, they stationed themselves one at each end of the tomb, and began to scratch the earth and throw dirt on all sides. Digging and digging, they finally reached the coffin. Each dog seized one end of it and lifted it from the grave. They unnailed the box, took out their master, and placed him face down on the ground. When they had located the wound, they began to lick it tenderly until they found the giant's eyetooth and removed it from the body. They licked and licked until the wound closed and the young man came back to life.

In the meantime, the widowed wife was walking up and down in the hall, sobbing for the brevity of her beloved's life. In the midst of her bitter tears, she happened to look toward the cemetery and caught sight of the boy returning with his dogs.

"It appears to be my husband!" she gasped, unable to believe her eyes. As he drew closer, she recognized him clearly, and a strange cry escaped her lips. "My husband is coming yonder!" Her mother and father heard this and rushed out of the house, following their daughter and seeing her in the arms of the young man. What exceeding joy! The mother and father ran to meet their son-in-law, falling upon him and embracing him. Once they were all in the house, the marriage was celebrated over again. If there had been happiness at the first wedding, now there was twice the joy. The young man's dogs told him they were going to round up all his livestock. For three days, the dogs labored at the roundup and filled some eight corrals with animals. Afterwards they returned and said, "Good master, your stock is penned. Go see it and count it." Upon hearing this, he asked his father-in-law to take him there in the carriage. Arriving at his palace, the youth began to show all his riches to his mother- and father-in-law, who exclaimed that now he was richer than they.

"Master," barked the dogs, "here ends our companionship. We are not dogs after all, but really angels from heaven sent down to leave you with these riches. Today we shall go to the church, and tomorrow you must invite your whole court to go to mass. We two shall be turned into doves on the high altar."

The next day, the young man went to mass as they had commanded although he didn't listen to a word, for he had eyes only for the doves. When the priest had taken the host, the doves took flight and circled up into heaven. The youth left the church, following them as high as his eye could go until they were lost in the clouds.

•9• *The Lost Prince*

• THERE WAS ONCE a king who had three sons. They decided one day to go hunting in the forest. One took the left-hand path, another went to the right, and the youngest chose the middle trail. When it was time to return home, the two older brothers emerged from the forest, but the youngest was nowhere to be seen. The two waited a long time for him, but finally concluded that he must have gone on ahead. Meanwhile, the youngest son went deeper and deeper into the woods until, having no notion of where he was, he became totally confused and lost. Night fell upon him, and the gloom of the forest closed about.

The next day he continued wandering in the forest until he was almost limp from hunger. As night came on again, he glimpsed a little light among the trees and headed for it, but the more he walked, the farther he found himself from the light. Finally day broke, and he was still on the same path where he had seen the light the night before. About noontime, he saw that there was a palace in the forest, and approached, hoping to find work and earn something to eat.

In the palace lived a king with his daughter, probably the most wicked woman who ever was. The ruler gave the wandering youth the job of gardener, under the condition that every day he had to bring him a bouquet of the very best flowers. The boy took very good care of the garden, and overnight it was flourishing and blooming. Every day he took his king a garland of the loveliest flowers. The daughter was so envious of the flowers for her father that she asked the gardener why he didn't bring her some as well. But, as the king had given him no order for this, he took the daughter no flowers. The princess could see no way of getting the boy in trouble with her father. Finally one day, she told the king that the gardener claimed to be a very brave man, even capable of bringing back the three-colored mare with bells of gold which the king had lost in the land of the pirates. So his majesty called the young man and asked him if it was indeed true that he had let slip this boast. The gardener swore that he had never said such a thing.

"No," said the king, "my daughter cannot be deceiving me. You said it, and there is no help for you but to go and bring me my horse. Tomorrow you will make the journey." The boy went away to his room to cry over his misfortune, for the king had threatened to cut off his head if he didn't bring the precious mare back. As he was weeping, an old crone appeared and asked, "Why do you sob so, my son?"

"How should I help it, grandmother, when I am commanded to bring back the three-colored mare with the bells of gold?"

"Ah, that's no matter," she said. "The first thing is for you to summon up all your courage and take this little wand. With it, nothing can happen to you. You ought to speak with your king and tell him you'll do the job, but that first you're going to bring him the soothsayer parrot which the pirates have. Ask the king for bread and wine, for the bird is a great tippler, and if he sees that you bring him wine, there will be no squawking." Thus it was done. The gardener spoke with the king the next day, and was given bread and wine in order to tempt the prophetic parrot, for now the king had become more interested in the bird than in the mare.

"With this wand," the crone told the boy, "you will be able to break the parrot's cage to bits, for he has a steel cell which nobody can open. Then you should begin to chat with the bird and to offer him bread and wine so that he'll lose his tongue. The tough part will be getting over the boundary, but once you're past the line, no one will follow you."

The boy did just what the old woman had said. The parrot, upon seeing him, began to squawk, "My masters, I'm being stolen." But the gardener rushed up with the wine and whispered to the bird, "Quiet, my little parrot, I've come to give you bread and wine." The bird, much taken with this idea, calmed himself, and the young man fed him until he was reeling and tipsy. Then the youth put the wand on the cage, which immediately flew wide open. He snatched the drunken parrot out and darted away. Very soon, the bird came to and began to screech, "They've come to bag me, my masters. Now they're making off with me. Help!" With all the hullabaloo of the bird, the guards awoke and went in hot pursuit of the lad. As he reached the boundary, the guards were right on his tail. But the squawking of the parrot was all in vain, for the boy arrived safely at the palace with his catch.

The king was overjoyed that the parrot had been returned to the palace, but the princess would not cease pestering her father about the three-colored mare with the golden bells. So one day, he told his gardener that it was high time he brought home the mare. The youth, already advised by the old hag that the capture of the parrot would be the hardest test, set out the next day with his magic wand. She had told him, "When the mare begins to whinny, threaten her with the wand and she will be still." That was just how he did it. The boy arrived at the corral about midnight, and the mare started to whinny in order to sound the alarm. The boy raised the wand as if to beat the animal, and dropped it on the gate. The gate at once broke into pieces. He grabbed the mare's bridle and leaped upon her, dropping the wand. She galloped off as if to fly. By the time the guards awoke, he had already sped across the boundary, and so arrived safely at the palace.

The next day, when the lad was back at work in the garden, taking the best bouquets to the king, the princess was as envious as ever. All of this was because she had fallen in love with this adopted prince, for he was a handsome, gallant lad. She begrudged his paying her no heed, but could find no way to put him in the king's bad graces. One day it occurred to her to tell her father that the prince would bring home the snake which lived in the forest. This was the most terrible creature on earth, and she was certain that the young prince would die there. The serpent could gobble up a Christian man from a block away. How could he possibly save himself from this fate! So, the king called for his gardener and asked him if it were true that he had indeed boasted of bringing in this serpent which did such great evil in the forest. The youth answered flatly that such a thing was not so.

"Can my princess be lying?" asked the king. "It can't be, for my daughter would not deceive me. You have no resort but to go tomorrow and bring me the serpent." Again the young man went away to his room to weep in solitude.

"Now the jig is up," he thought. "I'll be the snake's victim for certain."

"What is it, my child?" asked the tiny old crone, popping out from nowhere.

"Imagine this," answered the gardener, "The king has ordered me to bring him the snake which haunts the woods."

"Ay," she gasped, "that *is* risky, my lad! But I'll do what I can for you. It's going to be a nasty task, but it will allow you to finish once and for all with this roguery." The boy didn't understand this. "Look here," she continued, busily scratching her head, "you must ask the king for an enormous wagon with two teams of oxen, a quarter-cask of sweet wine, and also a tub big enough for the wine. Then get some bran and a load of leather thongs. After that, you must station yourself in the middle of the forest, taking great care to arrive there about one in the afternoon, so the serpent will be sleeping. In the wagon, you must empty the wine into the tub to make a hodgepodge with the bran. Finally, unhitch the oxen and hide yourself far off. That way the creature, smelling the tub, will come on his own. Once he has eaten all this, he will be drunk and will fall asleep."

The boy went to the forest with his wagonload and followed the instructions of the old hag precisely. While the snake was sleeping, the odor of the wine reached him, and he began to dream, letting out hisses loud enough to deafen the young prince even where he was hidden among the trees. Eventually, the wine odor woke the snake, who followed his nose to the wagon and coiled down on top of it. Although the gardener prince had sought the biggest tub in the kingdom, the serpent could hardly fit in it. He gobbled up everything the youth had left there, and lay so groggy and full that he couldn't even uncoil himself. The prince seized the chance and bound the snake with all the thongs. He pulled them so tight that the creature couldn't budge an inch. The great serpent woke up just as they were entering town, and loosed a hiss that made the whole village shake. The people, frightened out of their wits, could find no place to hide. When the wagon had come within a block of the palace, the snake spoke up and said, "Tell the king's daughter to come out." The princess appeared on the first floor of the palace, where the snake saw her. Immediately, he threw his horrible breath and brought her to him like a fly.

"Now you're going to be my victim," hissed the snake as he gobbled her up on the spot. Seeing all this, the king ordered the prince to return with his snake and leave it in the woods, for he couldn't stand even the sight of it. When the boy drove back to the forest, the snake said, "Let me go and leave me be, because nobody's going to bother you any longer."

The prince thought that surely the king was going to kill him. But it wasn't so after all, for the king realized that his daughter had been at the root of the troubles, and had even driven the snake to the point of speaking. The prince came home in his wagon, trembling with fear.

"Now, at last, I understand what was going on," declared the king. And you, instead of my daughter, will remain as my companion in the palace, for I have no heir."

So it is that if the old king is now dead, the gardener prince is the ruler of that palace.

· *10* · *The Wandering Soldier*

• ONCE THERE WAS a princess who proclaimed that whosoever could hide himself so that she could not find him would be her husband. But, if she saw him, she would kill him. She would always have to say first, "Where are you hiding?" Men began to arrive for the pledge. One young man came, made his vow, and went off to the mountains to hide himself inside a hollow tree. There was a time limit of three days, and at the end of this time, the princess went to her door, took her binoculars, and began to scan the countryside. Sure enough, she spied him in the middle of the mountain inside the hollow tree. At the time of the deadline, the young man returned to the palace.

"Did you see me?" he asked anxiously.

"Yes I did," she answered abruptly. "You were in the middle of the mountain inside a hollow log."

"By God! I was indeed," he admitted. Without further ado, she sent him away to be beheaded. Soon after, another lad arrived and also made the bet. This fellow mounted an eagle and rose away into the clouds, hiding himself behind the sun. Out came the princess and began to search, but wherever she looked, she could see neither hide nor hair of him. Little time was left before the deadline when she chanced to glance up at the sun. She glimpsed the poor boy hidden behind it, mounted on his eagle's back. Soon the lad arrived, full of hope, at the palace of the princess and asked her, "Well, did you spot me?"

"Yes, I saw you, all right. You were behind the sun sitting on your eagle." In a jiffy he, too, was dispatched to lose his head.

Very soon after, another young hopeful came on the scene. This chap turned himself into a fish and went to the sea, hiding himself behind a rock. The princess came to her doorstep and looked first to the mountains, and then into the clouds. She could see him nowhere, but at last she hit upon it and looked toward the sea. She spotted the youth behind a rock, made into a fish. When the young fellow returned, she notified him that she had seen his hiding place.

"And where was I?" he asked, still incredulous.

"Behind a rock, turned into a fish," she replied laconically.

"It's quite true," he moaned as they carried him off to the chopping block. In succession, another man appeared to take up the bet. This one ran off to a craggy cliff which had a great cave in the face. He slipped inside to hide. Early the following day, the princess stepped out on her doorsill and began the search. He was not to be seen. She looked to the clouds. She peered into the middle of the sea. He seemed to have vanished, until finally she happened to spy the cliff and saw him crouched inside the cave. When the boy came confidently back to the palace, she simply said, "I saw you."

"Where was I then?" he asked hopefully.

"You were on the cliff inside the cave."

"Yes, I was there, all right." He, too, was hustled off to the axe.

Now, there was in this land a little drunken soldier. One day
he too went to take the vow with the princess to see if he could
marry her. After he vowed, he went to hide behind a tree. When
the princess took a look, she saw him easily. "Why should I get
out my binoculars to look for this fellow?" she thought with a
chuckle. Next, the little soldier strolled down a street, where he
met a vixen who was shaking turkeys out of a tree. The vixen
nabbed one and trotted off with it to her den. The little soldier
observed all the while, but kept his lip tightly buttoned. Soon she
returned and carried off another turkey. All this time, the little
soldier was as quiet as you please. The vixen came back a third
time, shook down another turkey, and scurried away. This time,
admiring the soldier as a gentleman who knew how to keep silence, she invited him to her den. The foxes invited him inside
and served him an exquisite stew. The vixen spoke to her companions about finding a place to hide the young soldier, for the
princess would surely be on the lookout. All the foxes began to
think about this and draft all the necessary papers for their
different plans. But the whole project came to nothing, for mother fox, who had stolen the turkeys, tore the plans into little
shreds. Then she sent the soldier to have two gloves of iron
made. After securing these at the blacksmith's, the little soldier
brought them back to the den. The vixen fitted them on her
paws and began to dig a cave near the princess's palace.

"Just you stick right behind me," she told the soldier. Then she
pushed ahead, scratching away at her tunnel. She dug until she
had left the soldier at the very threshold of the palace.

Now the deadline of three days was drawing near. The fox
finished her task and left the little soldier standing right under
the doorsill. The princess came out to search and first looked into
the clouds, then toward the great mountain ranges, and then into
the center of the sea, but she caught not the slightest glimpse of
the little drunken soldier. Finally she was so bored with peering
and staring that she declared to herself, "I must keep my promise, just as it is pledged. The tipsy little soldier will be my husband."

The next day, the soldier popped out and rang the palace bell.

"Good morning, my good princess," he said cheerily. "Did you see me?"

"I couldn't see you anywhere," she answered. "And where can you have been hidden all this time, that I couldn't spy you out?"

"I was standing right under your feet," he chuckled.

"How can such a thing be? No matter where I looked, I didn't catch even a glimpse of you."

"I was right under your nose," he insisted gleefully.

"You must be right, for I never looked down once," she admitted. "My word must be fulfilled." So they sent for the priest and the bishop, and were married with great celebrations. After all this merrymaking, the vixen came to the new prince and said, "Good day, my fine little soldier. Now that you're a married man and you are the one who wears the pants, I hope you will grant us foxes the favor of having the right to wander wherever we wish." Thus ends the tale of the vixen and the soldier boy.

· 11 · *Pedro the Blacksmith*

· THERE WAS ONCE a blacksmith named Pedro who wished to be the best blacksmith in the world. Therefore he made a deal with the Devil that nobody would be able to do better work than he. At the end of a fixed time, the smith would deliver his soul to the Devil in exchange.

Now it happened that God's keys to heaven were in bad repair, and he sent St. Peter to the blacksmith to have them fixed. Later God went with the saint to pick up the repaired keys, and said to Pedro the blacksmith, "Ask for whatever you wish." Saint Peter told the smith that he should ask for glory. But instead, Pedro requested a chair in which whoever might seat himself could not get up until the blacksmith gave the word. He also asked for a fig tree dark with fruit such that anyone who climbed it could not come down without his permission. Finally he requested a lambskin pouch such that anyone who entered it would never get out. God granted him these three wishes

Finally, the day arrived when the diabolical pact was up, and the old Devil came in search of Pedro. The blacksmith invited the Devil to sit down and rest his weary feet. After a bit, Pedro said, "Let's be off!" But the Devil couldn't budge an inch. He pushed and tugged and pulled, but there was no help for him. Pedro grabbed the red-hot tongs and singed him with them until he tired of the sport. The old boy left in great haste.

A little later, two new devils came to look for Pedro. They spotted the loaded fig tree and climbed up to eat some of the juicy fruit which hung so thick on the branches. After the feast, they wanted to get down. But now they were going to skip! Pedro snatched a red-hot brand from the fire and burned the new devils with it until he was bored with his game. These devils left, hopping for their lives, without a word about the pact.

The next day, the old Devil returned to seek Pedro once more. This time, he took the blacksmith over his shoulder and carried him away. But Pedro had the lambskin pouch with him, and slyly asked the Devil if he thought he was capable of getting into the bag. The Devil proudly answered that of course he was capable, and jumped deftly inside. Once he was safely in, Pedro drew the strings and went to his own house, where he pounded Old Nick on the anvil as long as he could. Finally the Devil escaped and scurried away.

Not long after, Pedro died. He knocked at the gates of heaven, but St. Peter didn't want to open them for him, because the blacksmith had not asked God for glory.

"Go on," said St. Peter to the smith, "go over there to the colored doors." Meanwhile, the devils had riveted these doors shut, not wanting to see hide nor hair of the blacksmith. So God personally took Pedro to leave him at the devils' entrance. On the way, the blacksmith found a horseshoe and took it along with him. When the devils spied him coming, they bolted the doors even tighter. The blacksmith returned to St. Peter and called out, "Namesake, open the door so I can at least see what I have lost." St. Peter opened the door a crack, and then another little bit. Then the smith gave a mighty shove and entered into glory, sitting himself firmly in a chair. And from that spot he didn't budge, because the Lord had granted him the wish that wherever

he sat, he would not be moved. God had to send to have another
chair made for St. Peter.

· 12 ·   *Pedro Urdimale Gets into Heaven*

• A GENTLEMAN named Pedro went wandering in the world and
came upon a magic charm. Continuing on his way with the little
charm, he became very sick, and then remembered his magic
power.

"Look here, charm," he said, "I ask you to make me better." In
a twinkling he was cured. As he went along again, the road
passed through some mountains, and Pedro got lost. After much
wandering about and getting even more confused, he remembered his special gift.

"Come on, charm. Take me out into my own land, for I can't
tell east from west." Immediately the charm transported him out.
But soon Pedro set off again and once more lost his way. As he
approached some towering mountain peaks, practically dead
from hunger, he spied an animal. He was a shrewd man, and
managed to catch the beast and kill it, after which he built a fire
and roasted a chunk of meat. Even in those distant parts, Pedro
somehow managed to keep himself alive. But when his animal
was all eaten, he was in great need once again, and remembered
his charm. It took him back to his own land a second time, and
Pedro was very content with his magic power.

One day, he took a stroll through glory and came to the doors
watched over by St. Peter. Immediately Pedro began to clamor
for the saint to open the doors a tiny bit, so he could see inside.
St. Peter heard him and opened them just a crack.

"Just a touch more, Namesake," begged Pedro Urdimale.
"How lovely it is inside. Just a little bit more. It's beautiful!"
With so many "tiny bits," he managed to squeeze in up to his
shoulders, and kept calling all the while to St. Peter to open the
doors just a little more. When Pedro was in up to his chest, he said,
"An inch more, my namesake. How marvellous it looks inside."
Just at that moment, he butted the door with all his might, and

pushed in up to his waist. Now St. Peter slammed the door on him and cut him clean in two, the trunk of his body remaining outside.

"It doesn't matter, anyway," said Pedro, "that a piece of me is outside. That's the part with all the sins." At this point, God passed by and asked him why half of his body was sitting outside glory.

"Because that's the wicked part, my Lord," he answered. Then God grabbed the tip of Pedro's foot and stuck the two halves together. He was saved, and continued to live on in glory for centuries without end.

· *13* · *José Guerné*

• THERE WAS ONCE a poor mule driver named José Guerné, who was married. One day he ran out of matches and paper for his cigarettes. He rode up to a general store and began pounding on the counter for service. Finally a woman emerged from the back room.

"Ma'm," said José, "I'm looking for a box of matches and a wad of tobacco leaves." They cost him fifteen cents. Now there happened to be a little doll with a green dress on top of a cabinet in the store.

"Buy me, José Guerné," she called out as he was paying the woman.

"I'm going to, I'm going to," he answered, looking up fascinated toward the little voice. He purchased the little doll and stuck it in his saddlebags. When he had ridden just a little way down the road, he felt a tug on his belt. Looking behind, he saw a princess seated on his mule's rump. "Now, this is just what I want," he thought to himself.

José Guerné arrived home at sunset, about the time of prayers, and said to his wife, "I'm going to sleep in the other room, because I have to get up before dawn tomorrow."

"And since when is this?" asked the old lady suspiciously.

"You see, I have to make a quick trip over yonder tomorrow," explained her husband. "Do you think I've got another woman or something?"

At bedtime he went to his room and was turning down the bed when suddenly the princess appeared before him. They began to chat in the night, while the old woman was outside listening and trying to figure out what was going on.

"José Guerné," she called, beating on the door, "Have you got another woman in there?"

"What woman? I'm all alone," he replied. Immediately the princess turned herself into a little parrot and flew up into the rafters. José's wife entered three times to check, but each time she found him without another soul.

"Go on to bed, old woman," he said. "Let me sleep in peace." His wife scooted out before he could take a smack at her. Then the princess flew down and said, "Don't you see, you're already married!"

"Not at all," he answered.

"Tomorrow," she insisted, "you must open the door early to let me go. I know I'm yours and that I've cost you your hard earned money."

"Fifteen cents is nothing for a woman," thought José to himself. Then he gathered together all the money he had and gave it to the princess.

"Watch carefully where I go," she said. "You'll wear out shoes of iron and never arrive."

The next day, José Guerné set out to follow the little parrot. He wandered for a year through the mountains, even speaking with tree trunks and sticks in his long search. One day he was lying on his side under a big *quillay* tree on the last woolly hide he had. Suddenly he heard a voice in the tree above him say, "How are you doing?"

"Ah, little parrot," called José, looking up into the tree. "Why don't you come down?"

"No, José," she answered, "but if you'll take down your pants so I can light on your rump, then I'll fly down."

"Of course I will," he answered. So down she swooped, leaving two claw marks on his backside and flying up into the tree again.

"There you are, José Guerné. Now, good-bye to you. Watch

closely the way I'm going. You have to search for me at the city
of Three Aces to the Roundness of the World. You'll wear out
shoes of iron and never arrive." José just stood there watching
her, and then set off in pursuit once again.

One day he came to a low place in the hills and found there
two sisters blacker than a frying pan. They had been squabbling
for ten years over which one was more beautiful.

"Look sister!" cried one upon spotting José, "there goes a
young fellow who can settle our argument." They called him to
serve as judge in the beauty contest.

"Well, girls," said José after thinking a minute, "if I were to
marry one of you, I'd think you both equal. Listen, I'll tell you
the truth: one of you is like the sun, the other like the moon. I'd
choose either one with my eyes closed." And they were both
blacker than an old teakettle!

"We're so happy, young man," they shrieked. "Thank you ever
so much! We're never going to fight again." But no sooner had
José Guerné set out on his road again than they called him back.

"What can these pesky women want," he grumbled, "especially
when I'm in such a hurry?" They were so thankful that one of
them said, "We're never going to quarrel again. Look here, sister,
this young fellow is on a long trip, and we haven't even given
him a magic charm."

"Do you know the city of The Three Aces of the Roundness of
the World?" asked José.

"No," they answered, "we've never heard of it." Then one sister
gave him a magic shawl and a little magic cap. When he put
them on, he would become invisible. The shawl would give him
food whenever he said, "Little shawl, by the power that God has
given you, bring me the dishes of kings."

"I'm going to give you this pair of boots," continued the other
sister. "Whenever you want to transport yourself, they'll take you
if you say, 'Little boots, by the power that God has given you.'"

José Guerné left them and walked for seven days with his
magic charms. One day he was bored and thought to himself,
"Enough of this! Here I've got these charms. I'm going to ask
for something and see if what the women told me is true." He
put on the cap and shawl and noticed a man on horseback com-

ing from the other direction. When the rider passed by, José gave him two sound whacks from behind.

"Who the devil's hitting me?" shouted the mystified horseman.

"It works," said José gleefully to himself. "Now, I've only to try the other. Good Lord, I've been all this time without testing it!" He put on the boots. "Little boots, by the power that God has given you, to the regions of the world!" He didn't ask for any place at all. Suddenly he found himself lost in the heights and called, "Down to earth!" José fell immediately back to the same spot where he had taken off.

In the meantime, the little parrot had arrived at her father's palace. He locked her up with seven keys, for she was very beautiful. Whenever they took her anything, they closed all the doors upon entering so that nobody could see her. Now it happened that a consul from another land fell in love with the parrot princess just from hearing her name. He presented himself to her father, and soon there were only three days left before the marriage. At this point, José Guerné put on his boots and remembered the city the princess had told him about.

"Little boots," said he, "take me at dawn to the city of The Three Aces of the Roundness of the World." He took off at daylight, and flew in almost nude from his great trip in the winds. José landed at the house of a poor man near the castle and asked him, "What's new in these parts?"

"What's new!" exclaimed the old fellow. "Why there's a princess locked up with seven keys. She's going to marry a consul the day after tomorrow at the first hour of dawn. She's called 'Little Parrot.' "

"That's who I'm looking for," declared José Guerné.

"I'm deeply sorry I can't even offer you a cup of hot water," said the poor old man, shuffling about his cottage. The poor man had eighteen children, and the king kept them all in hunger.

"Don't worry about it, my friend," said José. "Tomorrow we'll have plenty." Then José whipped out his shawl and uttered the magic words, "By the power God has given you, set a table here with the richest dishes for this man, and let it never be empty." When the banquet was all set out, the odor drifted on the breeze up to the king's palace. Then José went, dressed in rags, to the

door of the palace to ask a servant girl for a pair of pants to give
to the other poor fellow.

"Get out, you old swine!" was the only reply from the king's
personal maid. Presently, a lady-in-waiting came by. Her job was
to take care of the princess, to comb her hair and bring her the
slop from the kitchen for dinner.

"Listen, Lady, can you come here for a moment? Just hear me
out," hissed José from beyond the gate.

"Why, of course, old grandfather."

"I want you to give me an answer," he continued. "Where can
I find the city of The Three Aces to the Roundness of the
World?"

"Have you come for a princess who is called 'Little Parrot'?"
asked the lady.

"She's the one I'm following," said José. "Can I go into the
kitchen?"

"How can I possibly let you?" she said. "The king is a very
mean man."

"I've got a little cap which I can put on to be invisible."

"Then put it on, old fellow," she said. He placed the magic cap
on his head. "Where on earth are you?" called out the lady,
dumbfounded.

"Right here," piped up José as she led him into the kitchen
where the servants prepared a stuffed chicken and other tidbits
for the invisible guest.

"What time do you have to take the princess her lunch?" asked
José when the meal was over.

"At twelve o'clock on the dot," answered the lady-in-waiting.

"Then go ask her if I can send her up a letter. Tell her José
Guerné has arrived." When the lady went to the princess's room
at lunchtime, she hid the letter and said to the princess, "Do you
know what, my princess? A man has come in search of you. He
calls himself José Guerné."

"I don't believe it!" she cried. "He'll wear out shoes of iron and
never arrive."

"But didn't I tell you so?" insisted the servant. "And he has a
magic charm which makes him invisible." She returned to José
in the kitchen and said. "The princess told me to tell you go up

so she can see if you are really the one after all." José was still invisible when the lady-in-waiting led him into the princess' room.

"Are you here, grandpa?" the maid called out. José told her he was and decided to remain invisible until nightfall. When dusk had gathered and the princess lay down to sleep, José was there inside the room. He took off his magic cap and went over to her bed.

"Oh, papa!" she called, startled to death. "There's someone here." The king came running with his gun loaded and, looking over the whole room twice, didn't find a trace of anyone. By the second check, he was thoroughly angry. "Listen, daughter," he roared, "if you shout again, on my word as king, I'll cut off your head."

"Now I'm really in a spot," thought José to himself, crouching invisibly in the corner. When the king had gone out, fuming, the princess waited in suspense to see if the man, who had now disappeared, would touch her again. When she felt him, she cried, "Are you from this life or the other?"

"From this one," answered the voice.

"And who are you?" she gasped, shaking all over with fear.

"José Guerné," said the mysterious voice.

"José Guerné, listen to me. It happens that I'm engaged to be married, and you don't exist any more."

"Then I don't believe that you do either."

"José Guerné, take down your pants," she commanded. When he had done so, she saw the marks her claws had left the other time. "Now I believe you. How did you ever get here? I'm to be married tomorrow, but it doesn't matter, José. Come to bed here." He slept with the princess for three days and received all kinds of money and delicious food.

"What a hearty eater my little girl is," exclaimed the king as all the delicacies were sent up from the kitchen. Finally the princess said to her lover, "José Guerné, with all the marriage ceremonies under way, we have to make up some excuse."

Now the princess had a very beautiful coffer made of precious metal. It was a sort of music box which was going to be played at the table before the wedding.

"Listen, José," she said, "you're going to accompany me to the ceremonies and stand behind the back of my chair, and then I'm going to say, 'When I came to the palace, I had a coffer with a gold key, which I lost. Arriving at the palace, I found a silver key, and now the gold one has appeared.' "

After he had received the instructions, José went out with the servants to get a new suit made so he could appear with the princess at the banquet. When she arrived at the great ceremony, her husband-to-be saw her and was astounded by her beauty. Everyone sat down to dinner, but first the princess announced, "I'm going to ask everyone here to tell a little story." As it was her turn first, she began, "My love, soon you will be mine. I had a coffer of gold and lost the key, after which I had a silver key. And now the gold one has appeared." Then she turned directly to her fiancé, "My darling, which key suits the coffer better, the silver or the gold?"

"Why, the silver one, my little love," he answered. Then out popped José Guerné from behind the princess's chair and said, "Here is the gold key which appeared, and not the silver one." And thus began the wedding of José Guerné with his princess.

> So they looked for priest and bishop,
> Fresh potatoes, corn, and peas.
> Those who didn't come by wagon,
> Made the trip in burlap bags.

· 14 · The Little Frog

• Now WE'RE GOING to spin a little tale called "The Little Frog." There was in a certain time a king with three sons, Pedro, Diego, and Juan. This king was so stingy that he didn't want any servants, so he put his sons to work, one as foreman, one as keeper of the keys, and the third as administrator. They quickly had to become jacks-of-all-trades.

"Brothers," one of them said, "we work like dogs, and this father of ours—why doesn't he find a man to do these jobs for us?

We're going to ask for permission to work outside. We won't have to mess around as pig herders, cowhands, and what have you. If this rich one has so much wealth, why doesn't he pay?" So the three brothers shook on the deal. That night, after they had stabled their horses, they went to the dining room where the king was seated.

"Papa," said one, "we wish you to grant us a favor."

"What can it be, my son?"

"We wish your permission to see the world, to learn about the life of the peasants and the poor people."

"Is that so, my good fellows!" answered the king. "What need have you of that, seeing that you have everything here?" But they insisted firmly until the king gave in. "So be it," he said, "if that is your wish. But within a year's time, you must return to me, each one with a decaliter of silver."

"Very well, if all goes well with us. If not, we'll bring no silver."

The oldest son left home first, as is still the custom today. He was given his father's blessing before he galloped off on his horse. After riding for a long time he came about midday to a humble little cottage. Suddenly he heard a lovely voice and the song of a young woman from within the house.

"Ah, if that girl is pretty, I'll marry her," he declared. Her voice was so wonderful that the birds above the house fluttered and twittered as she sang. Presently, her father came to the door.

"Good morning, father," said the young prince cheerfully, "I've stopped because I heard that beautiful voice. If she is single, I would marry her."

"Ah, yes?" returned the old man. "My daughter is not for marriage. She belongs here in the house.'

"We'll see about that. Can't I at least see her?"

"Come on out, child," called the old man. The girl was a little frog inside an earthen jug with a tiny bit of water. "Hop out, daughter," continued her father. "The gentleman here wants to see you." Out jumped the little frog.

"And this is your daughter?" said the prince, aghast.

"That she is," answered the old man gruffly.

"There'll be no wedding with this thing!" exploded the prince, kicking the creature off to one side. The frog hopped back into her water and sat tight inside. Away rode proud mister prince.

The next day, the second brother, Diego, set off on the same road. The very same thing happened: he passed the little house at about noontime, just as his brother had done, while the girl was singing and the birds were fluttering about in joy.

"I have to marry this girl who sings so beautifully," declared the second prince. He saw the father in the doorway and called out, "Good morning to you, father."

"Good morning to you, sir."

"Is this girl who sings unmarried? If so, I would marry her. Is she your daughter?"

"Yes, she is my child," answered the old fellow, "but she is not to be wed."

"Make her come out," ordered the prince. If she had been ugly the day before, now she was a horror. Ugh! She was all covered with warts and wrinkles.

"And you call this your daughter?" gasped Diego. The second prince's kick was even rougher than his brother's. "To think I was going to marry this filthy thing!" he roared, riding off posthaste.

"Don't you see, papa?" mourned the little frog. "You're provoking them into beating me. Do you think it doesn't hurt me?"

The following day, Juanito, the youngest son, set out on the very same road, and at the same hour he, too, passed the little cottage, where he heard the precious voice.

"With this maiden I must marry, no two ways about it," he declared to himself. "And this voice! If the girl is single, she will be mine." Her father came to the door and the young prince greeted him, "Good morning, father."

"Good morning, sir. I suppose you come on the same errand."

"Listen, old father, is this girl who sings here single?"

"Yes, she is."

"I wish to see her in order to marry her," said the prince.

"My daughter, sir, cannot wed," insisted the old man.

"But I will marry her for her lovely song, for the beautiful sound of her voice." When the old man continued to refuse, the prince grasped his hand and declared, "Word of a king, I intend to marry her however she be, ugly or not, so long as she is single."

"All right," he said finally, "for single she surely is! Come out, my child." The little frog appeared, frowning and very pretty.

"This is she?" asked the prince.

"Yes it is," said her father, all the while expecting a violent kick from the young prince. But not at all, for they went to find the priest and the bishop and were married right there in the little cottage. After the wedding, it grieved the youth to see that his wife was a frog.

"Hmmm, you're sorrowful," she said to her husband. "Go to bed, and I will sing you a lullaby." He lay down, and presently she sang him to sleep.

Soon the year set by the king was up. The youth's brothers rode by the humble cottage on their way home, and looked in.

"I'll bet this fool has married the frog! The filthy fellow!" said one in disgust.

"You boys go on ahead," said the youngest prince, coming out. "I'll come along behind and catch up as best I can." Then he ran to the little frog and said, "Listen, today is the deadline for returning to my father's house. And how can I possibly go?"

"Go along," answered the froglet. "Why not? You have your horse and your saddle. Just be off with you."

"But I agreed to bring my father a decaliter of silver. Where on earth am I going to get it if I haven't worked?"

"That's no matter," she said. "Look there in the corner for a bag and some coal." Her husband began rummaging about in the dark corner of the little house. "Go on with it now," she called, "But mind you, don't untie the sack. And here in the other corner there is a pile of wood chips. Take one of the little ones and put it in the sack along with the coal." The young prince, sobbing and grieving all the while, took the sack and the decaliter and measured out the coal. Next, he threw in the chip of wood and tied the bag tight.

"That sack you will take to your father," she said, "and you must wear your own clothes." Originally the little frog had taken his old clothes to hang up and had given him clean ones. Now he was to return home dressed from head to toe just as he had left.

The other brothers arrived triumphantly at the palace with their decaliters of silver. They had earned a good fortune on their travels. A little later, Juanito, the youngest of the three, came home full of heaviness and sorrow.

"My boy seems in such bad straits," said the queen. "But it really doesn't matter after all." The two older brothers were bustling about emptying out their silver before the contented king. Juanito went up to his father to pour out his coal [the narrator laughs.] "Tinkle-tinkle" went the whole load of silver which flowed from his humble sack. Then he pulled out the little chip and placed it to one side, emptying the rest of his coal sack until the scale was overflowing with silver.

"Here, this is for you, papa," he said, as astounded as the rest. "And here, so you can admire yourself in its reflection, is a little chip of pure gold."

"Good lord, my boy!" gasped the wide-eyed king. "This lad has indeed worked more than you others, who are even older than he. Look here at the beauty he brings me. And the rest of you, nothing!"

As the sons all had to leave the following day, they went that night to the king's party with all the celebrations and trimmings. Upon setting out in the morning, the two older brothers said, "Papa, we'll come back on Sunday, but we wanted to get married first."

"So that's it, eh?" said the king. "Very well then, get married, but you must, at all events, return to the palace. Do all three of you want a wedding?"

"All three," they answered. "But Juanito is already married." So the older brothers were wedded and returned the following Sunday for a gay party without their wives.

"Ah, mama," boasted one, "my wife knows how to embroider so well."

"*My* wife can weave so wonderfully," added the other. "If you could only see how she does it."

"Now then," announced the queen, "each one of you three

must take a cloth so your wives can make me an embroidered tablecloth for my dining room." She cut a bolt of cloth for each of the brothers.

"For God's sake," thought the youngest, "what can I do? What is my little frog going to make of this?" But, nevertheless, he wrapped up the queen's cloth in his bundle and took it home. The older brothers set out first, with Juanito following behind, for he always gave them the first place. They jeered back, insulting and scolding him, "You fool! Husband of the frog! By God, what a filthy scoundrel! You little pig!" But he just kept his pace, jogging along on his horse.

When he brought his bundle to the little tub where his wife was sitting in the water, he said, "Listen, my love, my mother has sent this for you to make her a tablecloth."

"Bring it here," she said, grabbing the linen and ripping it to shreds. "That's for your precious embroidered cloth!" How the young prince cried and sobbed! "Go on to bed," said the froglet, "and I will sing to you. Look at all this carrying on and bawling. Get straight under the covers!" Sobbing like a baby, the prince climbed into bed and was sung softly to sleep.

Sunday came, and the other brothers rode by the house, calling to Juanito, "Come on, old boy, the time is up. Let's be off."

"Go on ahead," he answered. "I'll catch up." They galloped off with their beautiful embroidered tablecloths. "Now I must go to my mother's again, my dear," said Juanito to the frog. "What in the world am I to do?"

"What indeed are you going to do!" she exclaimed. "You'll just take this little box with a key, but you must not open it on the way. It is to be delivered straight to your mama."

When Juanito rode off for the palace, the others were already far ahead, as happy as larks and joking about their foolish little brother. They had arrived and delivered their embroidery to their mother when the youngest rode into the courtyard.

"Good morning, my son," called the king and queen, thinking meanwhile, "Surely he hasn't married at all, and that's why he's worse off than his brothers, who have such fine wives."

"I've brought this little box for you," said Juanito, gathering himself together. When the queen opened the lid, she unfolded a thing more beautiful than had ever before been in her hands. What an exquisite tablecloth!

"These other cloths will be for my servants," she declared, pushing aside the gifts of the older brothers, "and this fine one from Juanito will be for my table."

Now it happened that the queen had a funny little dog which had just given birth to three puppies. When the older brothers were about to leave the next morning, they said, "Ah, our wives really know how to train dogs. Can't each of us take a puppy home to be raised?" When the queen gave her consent, Juanito thought, "What will my poor wife ever do with this puppy?" But he took the little dog anyway and wrapped it in his bundle. The other two set off ahead, calling back as usual, "You dirty pig! What does your stupid woman do? What does your frog do, for Christ's sake?" But Juanito simply trotted along as silent as you wish with his puppy.

"Listen my sweet," said Juanito sadly to his wife, "my mother sent you a puppy dog for training. My brothers say that their wives know so well how to teach dogs to sit, to walk, and all that."

"Oh, is that so? Bring it here." She took the little dog and smashed it against the tub. "There's your lovely dog for you." How Juanito took on and cried!

"This is a nice kettle of fish!" he sobbed. "What can I possibly do now?"

"Get right into bed and I'll sing to you," answered the little frog. When he had eaten supper and snuggled under the blankets, she sat on the edge of the bed and sang as never before. Very soon, Juanito stopped crying and was soothed to sleep.

Sure enough, the Sunday deadline came again, and along rode the two brothers brimming over with merriment and laughing little Juanito to scorn. Each brought his little trained dog and called out, "Come on, brother boy. Hop to it, stupid!"

"Go on ahead, my dear brothers. I'll catch up later, since I haven't saddled my horse yet." When he had saddled and scrubbed the animal, he said dejectedly to the little frog, "I have to be off to my mother's, for my brothers have already gone by."

"Then go on along, Juanito. What are you waiting for?"

"Well, after all, what am I going to take her?" he asked, very puzzled.

"Let's see," mused his wife. "Ah, take this little box with a key. But, remember, I forbid you to open it on the way."

"Yes, my dear. What have I got to do with this anyway?"

Of course, the older brothers arrived first with their jubilant greetings and their little trained dogs as nice as could be. The queen gave the commands, and the pups performed just as they were told. When Juanito rode in, he handed the little box to the queen. She opened it to find a little puppy which danced out on his hind legs, a dove fluttering on each side.

"How delightful!" she cried, clapping her hands with glee. "This is really fine! Juanito's pup is much better taught than his brothers'. This is what I call an enchanting little gift!" The puppy strutted about on its hind legs, skipping and dancing with the doves on both sides. Finally he leaped onto the queen's shoulder, and from there to the table.

"These other dogs will be for my servants," she declared, "and this one for me." She tucked the little pup under her arm, much to the bewilderment of the two dumbfounded brothers.

"Now then," added the king in a solemn voice, "the queen and I know the work of our daughters-in-law. I wish to see the three of them here before us. On Sunday, I shall await you all here at the palace."

"Good enough," clamored the other two. "This little fool is going to come with his frog."

The older brothers rode off posthaste to prepare their wives for the great day of the reception. When Juanito got home, he said to the frog, "My love, both of us have to go to the palace on Sunday. How in the world can I go with you?"

"How will we go?" she croaked. "Why, we'll just pick up and go, of course. Why shouldn't we?"

On Saturday the frog-girl told her father to fetch the best team of oxen in the pasture, clean a special tub for her trip, and get a long twig for a switch. On Sunday morning they yoked the oxen and put the girl, along with a little box, in the tub inside the wagon. The father goaded the oxen while the frog sat behind with Juanito, who was crying bitterly with shame. Eventually, he and the old gentleman fell asleep with the jogging of the wagon. When Juanito awoke, he saw the frog's father leaning back, trying to hold the reins to a team of horses which were pulling a most beautiful coach all fringed with gold. The frog had become a princess lovelier than any in all the kingdoms of the world. With her, she carried a little guitar and its case.

By this time, the older brothers were already waiting with the king and queen to see how Juanito was going to arrive with his little frog. Suddenly, they glimpsed a great coach rolling in to the castle.

"Ay! And who might this gentleman be who is approaching?" they all asked, staring wide-eyed at the splendor of the vehicle.

"Juanito!" gasped the queen, "It's my little Juanito!" She ran out immediately to greet him. The family and servants all carried the youngest prince and his wife back into the palace on their shoulders. The older brothers were pushed aside, while the young couple was served richly and well. How lovely was the dress of Juanito's wife!

"Of all my daughters-in-law," exclaimed the king, "the most beautiful is surely Juanito's wife. God bless this charming girl." Then the enchanted princess presented a pot of flowers to the king, and another to his wife.

After the banquet was served, the king and queen were the first to dance. Meanwhile, the frog-princess took all the bones from her plate and began sticking them on her husband's chest. The other brothers' wives were all agog at this, and immediately did the same.

"Do you all know how to sing?" asked the king after the first dance.

"Of course our wives know how. They have charming voices," clamored the first two brothers.

"So does mine," piped up Juanito finally, for he always came in a little behind.

"Now then," said the king, "the wife of my oldest son must play and sing so that my youngest daughter-in-law may dance." The frog-princess took the floor to dance with her husband. On each graceful turn of their whirling waltz, she strewed pearls and diamonds and flowers on every side.

"Wondrous, simply charming!" cried the king. "This is beauty, if I've ever seen it. The real thing!" He bubbled on enthusiastically until the dance was finished. "Now, the wife of my second son will sing, and my oldest son will dance with his wife." The dance began, but with every turn and whirl, the couple dropped horse turds all over the ballroom, for the bones from their meal had turned to dung.

"Oh, Jesus, Jesus!" roared the king frantically. "Take them out! Servant, scrape this up and sweep it clean!" By my soul, the two wives were ashamed.

When the palace had been swept clean, the king announced, "I wish the youngest girl to sing so the middle one can dance." The very same mess flew off her on every step. How was anyone to know what the meaning behind this was? Again, the servants had to clean everything, shake out the carpets and scrape the floor.

"Now, that's more like it," sighed the king with relief. "This is what I call a fine and fragrant ballroom once again. This time, my oldest daughter-in-law must sing while Juanito dances with his wife." The young couple took the floor again. With each step of their delicate dance, they cast pearls and diamonds on every side. Once more, the entire palace marveled at them.

"Ave Maria!" cried the king, clapping his hands. "What beauty!"

Meanwhile, one of the brothers sulked in the corner, mumbling, "Why didn't I marry the frog?"

"I, too, saw her and should have wed her," grumbled the other. "But I didn't take the chance. And to think that this damn fool brother of ours went and did it. She's very beautiful and very unusual, that wife of his."

All through the celebrations, the father of the frog-princess was standing by, watching intently. Now he knew at last what he had. He had never known before that she was really his daughter, for she had been born in the form of a frog.

The king's celebration lasted for three days. When everyone was exhausted, he announced, "I'm going with Juanito to leave him at his house. The rest of you go along ahead, for I wish to ride in his coach with his family." Very downcast and deeply ashamed, the older brothers saddled their horses, hauled their wives up behind them, and departed. When the king arrived at the little cottage which had been so ugly, not even his own palace could compare with what it had become. The house was transformed into a jewel of beauty.

"If this is my son's house," marveled the king, "I'll no longer return to my own." And with the lovely song of the princess, who would think of leaving anyway? The old man loosed the oxen and put them out to pasture. As for the princess, she was freed from enchantment and remained a lady forever after. She lives happily together with her husband, the king, and the queen to this very day.

> This story will have to do,
> For it went through a broken shoe,
> And came out in a little bean stalk
> So Hugo can take up the talk.

·15· *Delgadina and the Snake*

• ONCE UPON A TIME, in a country village, there lived an old woman with her daughter, whose name was Delgadina. She was a lovely little girl about five years old. She grew and grew, and before long she was a young woman of fifteen. One day her mother sent her to a rivulet with a bit of *mote* [stewed wheat] to wash. Being as poor as church mice, the girl and her mother lived on this *mote,* and managed to gather together a few other odds and ends. On her way back from the stream, Delgadina met a pretty little yellow snake about six inches long. She picked it up tenderly and carried it home to her mother.

"For God's sake, child," cried the old woman, "throw that creature out!"

"No, I won't. It's so pretty that I'm going to bring it up." So Delgadina continued to care for the snake. Every day she went to see it in its little clay pot, like those they use in the country. Often she took it crumbs of bread and the little bit of milk she could pick up here and there. And, as the neighbor women fed the snake flies, it ate a touch of everything. As three or four years went by, the snake kept growing bigger. Delgadina, too, was growing up. Eventually, the snake had gotten so big that he no longer fit in the tiny pot, so she put him in a much larger one. But he outgrew this one in six months' time, whereupon Delgadina put him in one of those big casks they use for storing wine. The creature kept on growing, until he turned into a gigantic snake, tremendously long and fat. When Delgadina took him out to play, she would often make a sign, at which he went all by himself and slithered back into the cask.

One day when she was eighteen and was about to give the snake his meal, he said, "Listen to me, Delgadina. I'm going to go away because I don't fit here any longer, and you have no way to feed me, what with all the expense. I know how poor you are, and you and your mother don't have the means to keep all three of us alive."

Delgadina was heartbroken, for she had brought him up, just as when you bring up a little pig and get used to him. Then the snake added, "Don't worry, Delgadina, I'm going to leave you a fortune. Now pass your hands and fingers several times over my eyes. Then rub your hands with the tears from your serpent. This is the charm I'm going to leave you: when you wash your hands and then shake them, gold coins of all sizes and values will drop from you. With this, you will be able to live as another person." When they had done this, he crawled out of the barrel and said, "God be with you. Good-bye, Delgadina."

"Good-bye," she answered faintly. The serpent went off to the sea as a crocodile would. Poor Delgadina just stood there confused. Since the only washbowl she had was nothing but a little piece of a barrel lid, she put her hands in this water and shook them. All of a sudden an immense load of gold coins both big and small fell to the ground.

"Here at last is a stroke of luck," she said joyfully to herself. "Mama, come here. Go to the market to buy everything we need. Bring cheese, pork, meat roll, bread, sugar, and whatever you can think of. At last we can eat something here."

Several days passed, and all the while Delgadina hid her secret charm. Nobody knew a thing about it. After a bit, she built a little cottage with all the gold. Nearby, there was a king who had heard from someone that an old lady in a country village had a very charming daughter who shook gold coins from her hands after washing them.

"Hmmm," thought the king, "I would like to marry this girl. If I'm rich now, I'd be all the richer." In the neighborhood of the palace, there was an old witch who had one daughter. The king called for the crone and asked her if she knew about the girl from whose hands flowed all the gold.

"Yes, sir I've heard the rumors," she told the king.

"Look here," he said, "why don't you bring her to me. I'll pay you a pretty fee."

The old dame, who happened to be very friendly with Delgadina's mother, accepted the offer enthusiastically. She scurried off to the little cottage where the girl lived with her mother and said, "Listen, my old friend, I've come for Delgadina. The king wishes to speak to her."

"How can this be? It's not possible," cried Delgadina's mother, very frightened by this news. But the witch knew how to handle this business and said to herself, "Here's where I get my cut." Now, it just happened that the witch's daughter was the same age as Delgadina. The crone took both girls and set out for the palace. On the way, she grabbed Delgadina by surprise, plucked out her eyes, and threw her into the sea, proceeding from there to the palace with her own daughter. This girl was an ugly sight, but the witch convinced the king that she was the girl of the golden coins.

"The old dame can't be deceiving me," thought the king. "The girl simply must be this way. All right, old one," he said to the witch, "take her away, and tomorrow bring her back for the wedding. And be quick about it, won't you?"

Meanwhile, Delgadina was floating around in the sea, and it chanced that some fishermen who were at work noticed her swimming over the waves. They drew alongside in their boats and fished Delgadina out. She was dressed beautifully, and they thought her an angel fallen from heaven, despite the blood still on her face. As these fishermen lived in some rocks and coves on the shore, they took Delgadina to their homes and furnished her with every kind of comfort. They even gave her eyes some treatments. Delgadina lived there a long time and became their idol.

The king had married the witch's daughter at such a lively wedding that the guests still had bottles in hand the following morning. The day after the ceremony, the king kept watching and wondering when his bride would go to wash her hands. Finally she went to scrub her hands, and not a thing fell from them. The king began to smell something fishy. After she had washed up, combed her hair, and gone back to her room, he called to her sternly, "Look here, why didn't any gold coins flow from your hands just now?"

"Because, by sleeping with you last night, I lost my charm. It was all your fault," she said, looking him steadily in the eye. The king swallowed this tale and went on living with her, for after all, there was very little he could do.

All this time, Delgadina was living with the fishermen. One morning after they had gone to their work, she was in a cave by the shore and heard the voice of an enormous creature at the entrance.

"Delgadina, what are you doing here?" it boomed. Immediately she recognized the voice of her friend, the giant snake.

"Do you know me?" he asked.

"Yes," she gasped, trembling with joy. "You're the little snake I raised."

"Well, tell me then, how did you ever get here in this cave?"

"How in the world!" she exclaimed. "The witch put out my eyes and threw me into the sea, where the fishermen rescued me and brought me here where they live."

The serpent began to weep bitterly, and said, "Delgadina, my poor little Delgadina, pass your hands over my eyes." She stroked the snake's eyes thoroughly. "Do it again," he continued. "Now rub very hard. Put your hands right in my eye sockets. Once more." When she had obeyed, the snake said, "Let's see now. Open your eyes." She opened them wide. Delgadina had always been a pretty girl, but now she was a lovely young woman with deep, sea-green eyes.

"Can you see me, my little friend?" asked the snake.

"Yes, I can, I can!" she cried joyously, skipping about the

cave. "Are you happy?" she asked, hugging the serpent tight.

"Very happy, my dear. Now, where are your clothes? Get dressed, for we've got a long way to go."

"How can we go?" she asked. "I haven't any idea where I am."

"Just mount up on my back," said the snake, "and hold tight around my neck." She mounted her great friend and off he went, slithering and swimming. When they came to the very spot where the witch had thrown Delgadina in, the snake hissed, "Get down, my child. Here we are." Delgadina climbed out onto the beach, and the giant serpent added, "Take great care, little one. Go straight home." Delgadina ran off obediently, calling back happily, "Good-bye, good-bye, my little snake."

After the serpent had slipped back under the waves, the girl recognized the place and skipped off to her house. The poor little old woman was sitting in her rocking chair, sobbing bitterly and thinking of her daughter who had disappeared so long ago. Delgadina dashed into the cottage and told her the whole story about the witch, the kindly fishermen, the cave where she had lived, and especially about the great snake that had restored her sight and brought her home.

"Well, my little lost darling," laughed the old woman as she wiped away her tears, "sit down and let's drink a bit of *mate* [a kind of South American tea]. There's cheese, too, and a bit of everything else."

The days passed, and the king heard rumors that the girl of the golden coins had returned.

"This is a fine pickle," he thought. "I'm stuck with the wrong wife. But, wait a minute! I'll just fix up a delicious little meal, eh? And then I'll call all the people of the province, old and young alike, to come to the palace for a banquet." So he prepared his enormous dining room and filled it with everyone in his land. There was no distinction, rich and poor, wise and foolish, all were helping themselves at the king's table. When everyone had been served, grapes were brought on. Some people who didn't know any better ate them stem and all. But the more intelligent ones, like Delgadina, picked the grapes off before eating them. After this came the finger bowls. The ignorant people stuck their entire hands in the bowls, but Delgadina was better brought up

and merely dipped her fingers. As soon as she took them out—
presto!—some drops fell on the table and became coins of gold.
All this time, the king had kept an eye peeled. When he saw the
money dripping from her fingers, he left his observation post and
scurried over to the girl.

"Aha! Pray tell, why did these coins fall from your hands?"
asked the king. She confessed the reason, and he examined the
coins eagerly, finding them all genuine stamped gold. "This is
my woman," he announced. "Let the great men of the court
come hither. And grab that old witch and my former wife. We'll
heat up the ovens for them." In a flash, the nobles of the court
had caught the old crone and her daughter just as they were finishing their grapes. They tied them as you would a hog for
slaughter, and when the oven was piping hot, threw them in.
They were turned to ashes even before hitting the flames. Then
the king turned to Delgadina's mother and asked for the girl's
hand in marriage. Both mother and daughter consented happily.

"I may have been rich before," said he, "but now I'll be rolling
in gold."

The king let Delgadina spend a few days at home in the little
cottage, and then called her back to his kingdom for the wedding. The guests made merry for about eight days. There was
every imaginable kind of food and drink in the great palace banquet hall. In fact, a little bit is still left over, a bitter old swig of
wine somewhere here on the table. Shall we finish it off?

·16· Sleeping Beauty

• ONCE UPON A TIME there was a city in which there was a palace belonging to a certain king. In the palace lived a man rolling
in riches, equalled in wealth only by the king. The rich man had
one daughter, and he pampered her greatly, for she was the apple
of his eye. She was about fifteen when one day she was helping
her mother comb some wool. In the process, she pricked her finger, turned very pale, and died soon after. Upon her death, her
father ordered that several acres be cleared in the forest and that

a house be built there. Then he carried his daughter to the house, along with provisions for a year's time, and left her sleeping there as if she had been in her own bed.

A year later, the king went out with a manservant to look over the woods. After traveling some way, they got lost. After wandering for three days, they came upon the little house. It was locked up tight, so they peered through the glass windows. The king saw the girl lying on a bed. They tried to enter, but couldn't, until finally they kicked in the door with their boots. The king softly approached the maiden and pulled back the covers, but she was lying as if asleep. Noticing that one of her fingers was swollen, he lifted it and pulled out a splinter. Immediately, the maid opened her eyes and saw the handsome king. Then she told him her story, as much as she could remember. Since the king and his servant were very hungry from their wanderings, they rummaged around amongst all her provisions and victuals and began to cook a meal. They had a great celebration, and the upshot was that the king took the maiden to bed after the feasting.

They were in the little house for a long, long time. After one year, they had a baby boy, and later a little girl. But now they had been there so long that the supplies were running out. The king announced that he and his man would return to the palace, and would be sure to send the girl something to eat every day. Before departing, he gave the young woman a dress with little bells, and told her that if by any chance she were in need, she should put it on and take three steps. Then the bells would sound, and he would go wherever she was.

When the queen saw the king arriving from the forest after so long an absence, she was furious, for she suspected that he had another woman. After a time, the king was faced with a war and marched off with all his army on the day the battle was to begin. But he had left a boy who went secretly every day to take food to the girl in the little cottage. One day while the queen was taking the sun on her balcony, she spotted the lad headed off with a little pot. She called him over to find out just what was going on. He answered that he was just going yonder to leave some food for a worker, but of course the queen didn't believe him and told him abruptly that he would die if he refused to tell her the truth. Placed in such a spot, the youth was very afraid, and confessed that the king had commanded him to take food to a young girl in the little house in the woods. The queen ordered him to go along and tell the girl to send the older child to be put in school, for the king thought it was about time for his education to begin.

The boy trotted off to the forest and gave the young mother the news. She thought for a minute and said, "If I don't send my son, it may displease the king. I guess I'd better obey." She dressed and arranged her son in his Sunday best, and sent him off with the messenger boy. At the palace, the queen promptly handed the little child over to the cook, with instructions that he be beheaded and served up as supper for the king.

"How can I possibly cut off his lovely head?" said the cook to herself, admiring the handsome little boy. She took him away from the castle to a shepherd and said, "Take this boy and give me a lamb in exchange. You must keep the lad safely until someone claims him." With that, she carried the lamb back to the palace and put it in the king's stew. When he arrived, the queen served him merrily and strolled behind his chair, mumbling, "Eat, eat, for you're eating your own flesh and blood."

"What are you talking about there?" he asked, busily spooning up the delicious stew.

"Oh, it's just a manner of speaking that I have."

Quite early the next day, the king went off again to the wars. He came home only at night. As soon as he was out of sight, the queen said to the servant lad, "Now you're going to bring me the other child from the forest, for it's just about time for school." Away he went and brought the little girl, who was also handed over to the cook for beheading and the stew.

"I can't possibly kill this little lass," said the kindly cook, admiring the lovely child. She took this one to the shepherd, also, and left her in exchange for a lamb. That night when the king came home, the table was set and his supper was brought in steaming hot. Once again the queen slipped past and mumbled, "Eat, for you're eating your own flesh and blood." The king was puzzled by all this, but she insisted that it was merely her way of saying things.

The next day, the king marched off again, this being the last day he was going to fight in the war. Immediately the queen sent for the girl in the forest as if it were the king summoning her. She was to come in to see her children, who were very well and getting on splendidly at school. Upon hearing the news, the young woman was filled with joy and dressed herself for the trip, taking the bell covered dress with her in a package. As they approached the palace, the queen came out, boiling in black rage.

"Ah, you thankless wretch, it's because of you that the king has cast me off. Commend yourself to God, because you're going to die." The queen seized a knife to behead her, but the girl asked for permission to put on a special dress, since it was after all the last time she could wear it. Then she wished just a few minutes to take a stroll in the hall. On her first turn in the corridor, all the little bells jingled. The king, who was three leagues away at his war, heard the sound and said to himself, "The girl is in danger!" He ordered his captains to carry on, and turned his horse toward the palace with his sword in hand. As he galloped nearer, the bells jangled once more. The king spurred his horse on even swifter than before. Entering the palace gate, he spied the wicked queen with the girl's hair in one hand and a knife in the other, about to slice off her head. He screamed and made her drop the knife. Then he grasped the wicked queen and ran her through on the spot with his sword. Thus was the girl of the forest saved.

After the king had found out the whole sad story about the queen's treachery, he told the girl he had never called for the children and knew nothing of the affair. Asking the boy who had carried food to the forest to explain things, the king realized that the children had been given to the cook. Then he questioned the cook and commanded that they search for the shepherd who had the children. The king was so overjoyed at finding his little son and daughter once again that he appointed the shepherd to be his counselor and the cook to be a special nurse for the children. When order and peace were restored to the palace, he sent for the priest and married the girl of the sounding bells. The children were baptized, and they are all living happily together there until this very day.

· THERE WAS ONCE a married couple who worked faithfully their whole lives as coal gatherers for a very wealthy rancher who lived in the mountains. This couple had a single daughter and a dog. The wife died one day, and with the years, the husband followed her, charging his daughter to bury him behind the ranch beside his wife's body. He warned her not to tell anyone that she was left alone so that people would continue to respect her.

About a year had passed, and finally the nearest neighbors, who were a mother and two daughters, realized that the girl was all alone. Meanwhile, a voice surprised her in the house one afternoon.

"Leave a washbowl of water just inside your door, for I wish to keep you company." She looked all about and saw only a little bird perched on the branch of a tree in the dooryard. She agreed gladly and left a bowl of water. That evening when she lay down to sleep, the girl heard a little bird bathing himself in the bowl, and at the very same moment a young man sat down on the bed to talk to her. He offered to visit her the following night as well, and immediately disappeared. At the same hour the next evening, she placed the bowl of water by her door and went to bed to wait. The youth came again, and soon they were intimate friends. He filled her life with all she had lacked.

Meanwhile the neighbor women were discussing the idea of offering the girl some company and seeing, incidentally, what she did all by herself in that lonely little cottage. They had nicknamed her *"La Guacha"* [Little Orphan]. One afternoon the older daughter from next door strolled over to pay a visit. Although the little orphan refused to let her stay, her efforts were in vain, for her neighbor simply climbed into bed for the night. The girl didn't place the bowl by the door. Later she felt the desperation of the bird as it fluttered down into the room. The lodger slept very well, and in the morning went home to report to her mother, *"La Guacha* sleeps alone."

"The trouble is that you surely fell asleep," answered the old lady.

"Well, of course, I couldn't help it," protested her daughter.

"Then tonight your sister will go. Let's see how she makes out."

It was just like the first time. The younger sister forced herself upon the poor orphan and stayed the night. The girl didn't place the water this time either. When the sister returned home the following day, she declared, *"La Guacha* sleeps alone." But her mother, not at all satisfied, ordered her not to shut her eyes the next time.

The second time, the visitor changed the hour of her arrival. Since the girl had not set the water out for two nights in a row, she had left the bowl this time in hopes of seeing her friend and telling him what was happening. Now, before the neighboring sister left for the orphan's house, her mother gave her three razor-sharp knives and said, "If you see water in the room, you must get up and say that you need to go outside. Then put the knives on the bowl with the water."

The orphan and her unwelcome guest went to sleep as usual that evening. About the time dawn was breaking, the neighbor girl heard the bird fluttering with great difficulty. She got up and saw that the room and the bowl itself were covered with blood. With that, she picked up her knives and went home to tell her mother what had happened.

When the little orphan awoke some time after, she saw the same horrible sight. Everything was smeared with blood. She vowed then and there to wander over the whole world until she found him whom she had lost. Leaving her dog alone and putting on her father's clothes, she disguised herself as a hermit and set off on the lonely road. For a weapon, she carried an ancient sword which had belonged to her father. Night came upon her as she was descending the hills, so she searched out some *patagua* shrubs and climbed into one for refuge. Nearby was a pond with some ashes on the bank.

"God only knows who's camping there," she thought, fearing that there must be some bad men about. Great was her surprise when at midnight three ducks arrived and began to wallow in the ashes. The orphan recognized them as the three neighbor women. They had kindled a fire and sat down to talk.

"What do you suppose *La Guacha* will say now that her little bird must be dead?" piped up the younger daughter.

"Today I was in the palace," answered the mother, "and the queen has issued a proclamation, that she will permit anyone to enter the palace who can bring the sick prince a remedy. But nobody will succeed in this."

"Mama," spoke up the older daughter, "you must know what is needed to heal the prince and cure those wounds of his."

"You've got your nose out for news," retorted her mother. "But I'm going to tell you, even though I ought not to. The prince can rise hale and hearty only if he is cured by a feather dipped in our blood. And when, pray tell, is he going to get that?"

"Let's be off to sleep," chorused the three ducks. "Day is about to break now." And letting themselves slide into the water, they swam quacking away.

Immediately the orphan girl climbed out of her bush and ran, with her heart full of vengeance, all the way to her house. A new day had already begun when she went to her room and took a very thick earthenware bottle. Then she headed straight for the house of the three neighboring witches, who always slept in one bed. She sliced off the three sleeping heads with her sword and took their blood until the bottle was filled. Following her footsteps toward home, she sat down about three in the afternoon to rest on a little log. Out of nowhere an old man approached her and asked, "Where are you going, my child?"

"My father is sick, and I'm in search of some remedy."

"He could never be sicker than the prince," answered the old man. "You should see how the king and queen are carrying on and mourning. The palace is all dark with their sadness. The prince lay dying this very morning, and there is free passage for whoever wishes to give him a remedy."

Upon hearing that, she jumped up sharply and set off at a run. From everyone she met on the road, she inquired breathlessly, "Is it true that the prince is gravely ill?" She always received the same reply, "Terribly grave. He won't live through the day." She met a boy on the road and asked him for the location of the palace.

"Do you have some medicine for him?" he asked.

"Yes, yes," she gasped, exhausted from her race.

"Then let's run faster," he replied. "You might be able to arrive while the prince is still alive."

When the girl got to the palace gate at last, everyone who saw her disguised in her father's clothes let out a shout of gladness. "There's an old man at the door who has come with a remedy for the prince." They notified the queen, who said mournfully, "It seems like a lost cause, for now he can hardly breathe. But since this is the last person and he is so old, let him come in."

Coming to the prince's bedside, the girl said in a gruff, manly voice, "Everyone go out of the room. Leave me alone with the prince." When they had all obeyed in order to see this prodigy, she took the bottle out of her jacket and dipped a feather in the blood. She began to cure the prince's wounds, especially a gaping one in his throat which practically separated his head from his trunk. As soon as the remedy was applied, his flesh drew together. The miracle was done, and the prince was healed. He sat up in bed, and looking straight at the old fellow, said, "You have saved me, old man. I shall give you whatever you ask."

"That's not important," said she. "I only ask you for the ring you have on your hand as a remembrance."

Then the prince rang a bell beside the bed. The queen and all the court came running, for the bell was rung only when the prince needed to be together with everybody. Thronged in the doorway, they found him dressed and healed of his wounds. Just at this moment, the little old man slipped unobtrusively away through the crowd. The only one to see him was the queen, who said, "You must never leave my side, for I believe that you have healed my son."

"You may pay me, madam, with that ring you are wearing on your right hand." This ring carried a portrait of the prince. The queen immediately took it off and passed it to the old man. Then she dashed off in great excitement to see her son. The queen thought that the old hermit would wait for her, but the disguised orphan girl slipped away and returned to her own cottage.

Several days passed, and she fulfilled her vow by placing the bowl of water night after night. The bird didn't come. Finally she said sadly, "He's angered with me, and the whole thing is unfair." It was a great and joyous surprise for her when she heard the fluttering of wings one night. She was sleeping with her hands resting on her breast and the two rings placed on her fingers. But this time the young man had come with his sword unsheathed and the intention of killing her in vengeance for the knives. Hearing the noise, she started up in bed, and the sparkle of jewels caught the prince's eye. He recognized his own ring and remembered the gift he had presented to the old man. Immediately he fell on his knees to beg her pardon, and she told him the whole story of the witches, whose corpses were still to be found in bed at the neighboring house.

When her innocence was proved, the prince took her up and carried her to the palace to be his wife with the king and queen's consent. The newlyweds received the crowns of the kingdom, while the old royal couple stayed on as guests at the palace. The little orphan and her prince lived happily for many years after this.

· 18 ·   The Four Little Dwarfs

• THERE WAS ONCE a little woodcutter who had such a poor family that he had to go hunting for bits of bread to keep them all alive. He depended as well on the meager pieces of wood he could cut. But in spite of his poverty, he had four little burros with which he patiently carried the sticks to town in order to buy odds and ends of food for his children. One day he said to his wife. "Listen, my love, I'm bored with all this woodchopping, and besides, I have cut all the trees down to nothing. If I chop any more, the landlord will have a fit."

"But, my dear, they haven't said a thing to us yet," she protested. "We're so poor that we have no choice. The wood keeps us alive."

"I suppose you're right," he sighed. "I'm going to go for the last time, and we're going to become rich, my love." The woodcutter trundled off to the forest with love for his family swelling in his breast. While he was chopping busily in the woods and loading his burros, four little dwarfs popped out from among the trees and began to recite:

> "Monday and Tuesday, Wednesday three,
> Monday and Tuesday, Wednesday three,
> Monday and Tuesday, Wednesday three."

The woodcutter knew the verse by heart and continued:

> "Thursday and Friday, Saturday six,
> Thursday and Friday, Saturday six,
> Thursday and Friday, Saturday six."

"What a lovely little song the woodcutter is singing!" exclaimed the dwarfs. "Let's go listen." They ran up as fast, you might say, as a little black man. "Good morning, Mr. Woodcutter. How does that beautiful song go?"

"Why it's what you already know, little dwarfs. How do you begin it?" Then he who was the head of the little men spoke up, "It's like this:

> Monday and Tuesday, Wednesday three,
> Monday and Tuesday, Wednesday three,
> Monday and Tuesday, Wednesday three.

But we don't know any more of it."

So the woodcutter continued:

> "Thursday and Friday, Saturday six,
> Thursday and Friday, Saturday six,
> Thursday and Friday, Saturday six.

Don't you see?" he said. "It has the days of the week. The whole thing goes like this, my little friends:

> Monday and Tuesday, Wednesday three,
> Thursday and Friday, Saturday six.

The six days of the week. Now say it, little dwarfs."

The four little men sang the verse over and then called merrily, "Good-bye, woodcutter, until we meet again." And away they ran, skipping with glee. But suddenly the head dwarf remembered and said to the others, "A fine thing this is, what with the woodcutter so poor and all! We didn't even give him a magic charm. Each one of us has to give him something so he can live in peace and not have to scratch about with his burros working himself to death. I have it! We'll each give him a foot." With that, each dwarf promptly cut off one of his tiny feet. "Don't cut any more, Mr. Woodcutter," they called, running back into the clearing. "Each of us has brought you a charm. You must ask our feet for all kinds of things—good stuff and big, food, clothes, money. You have one wish with each foot, and then it disappears."

Having heeded the instructions carefully, the woodcutter returned to his humble little house and found his poor wife suffering pangs of hunger.

"A fine kettle of fish," she said "you didn't bring me a thing, not even a few sticks of wood."

"No, my little love, for we're going to have all we can eat in a jiffy," he cried, dancing about the kitchen.

"Mama, I want a piece of bread," whined one of the thin little children.

"There's nothing not even a crumb in the cupboard, my child," she said, feeling her own hunger gnawing in her belly. At this moment, the woodcutter took one of the dwarf's feet and said, "Little foot, by the power that God has given you, put money here and food, and granaries filled to the brim, loads of fowl and eggs, and tasty meals all cooked for me and my children."

Quick as a flash his wife was flooded with treasures of every imaginable kind. Since it was late, they sat right down to the most delicious meal which had ever been eaten in that cottage. Then the woodcutter took the second foot and said, "Set me out the wardrobe of a king with palaces of the best sort all filled with money, and with a roof of silver and another of gold so that I can bless myself and my family. And let those who are owners come to me as servants, although I'll always let them keep their own property, of course."

One day, some time after these miraculous events, the woodcutter's rich brother stopped by and asked him, "How have you had such extraordinary luck, my brother? You are so rich and powerful now, and before you were nothing but a grubber for sticks in the forest."

"I went to the mountain," he answered, "and was cutting wood to feed my starving children, when four little dwarfs came; each one gave me a foot which was a charm. That's how it all came about."

"Aha!" thought the other, scheming, "I'm going to act like a poor man in order to get more." (Don't you see that greed, as they say, breaks the bag?)

The rich brother hurried away to dress himself in rags. Then he went with a team of four burros and a spindly old rope to start chopping trees. Very soon, the four dwarfs appeared and began to sing:

> "Monday and Tuesday, Wednesday three,
> Thursday and Friday, Saturday six."

They leaped and danced about while they sang, just as the woodcutter had taught them to do.

"And Sunday seven," added the rich brother three times in a row.

"Let's go see the woodcutter," squealed the dwarfs excitedly. "Good morning. What are you doing here, sir?"

"Good morning to you. Can't you see? I'm chopping up some sticks, for I'm a very poor man. Just look at my rags. Say, why don't you fellows give me a magic charm?" He came right out with it.

"Why, of course. We have some right here with us. Let's give a little something to the woodcutter." Saying that, they each handed him a foot. "Ask any of these feet for what you wish, and you will get it." But they didn't mention a word about asking for big and beautiful things. That advice had been reserved for the first brother.

"Fare thee well," called the dwarfs, disappearing into the forest depths.

The rich man went home as happy as could be and announced gleefully to his wife, "Now we're really going to be richer than my brother, and we'll have an even finer palace."

Now, this couple had been married only a year and had a little boy of about three months. The young wife, being one of those women who love any kind of novelty, grabbed one of the feet and said, "Little foot, by the power God has given you, give my baby a beard." And what a hairy growth sprouted on the child's chin! The baby cried bitterly to feel the whiskers on his soft little face. When his mother went to give him milk, he pricked and tickled her so that she couldn't get near the poor child, who continued to wail from hunger.

When her husband arrived at lunch time, she said, "Little foot, take off my baby's beard." The beard was gone in a flash, and the foot also disappeared. Then the rich brother came in to ask for livestock and money. He immediately missed the two feet and was greatly vexed to hear what his wife had done with them. (With your permission, my friends, something embarrassing is coming up.)

"Look what you've done," he roared, red-faced with rage, "when I was going to be richer than my brother! Little foot," he screamed to the third charm, "stick yourself up my woman's ass!" And so it was done. By God, she was in a tizzy and suffering from the pain.

"She's surely going to die!" thought the husband as he saw his wife writhing on the ground. "Little foot, by the power of God, take the other foot out of my wife's ass." Presto! Away went the foot.

This is what happens to the envious. To the rich man, everything he had seemed very little. The poor little woodcutter was the innocent one. There you have the tale of the four dwarfs and their magic feet.

•19• *Maria Cinderella*

• THERE WAS in a certain place a little old gentleman who was a widower and lived with his only daughter. They were very happy together. One day in the winter, the little girl saw the fire dying out.

"Papa, papa," she called, running to the old man, "the fire has just gone out, and we don't have any more matches."

"My child, go over and ask the neighbor woman for some," he replied, meaning a widow who lived nearby. "Ask for a few hot coals and bring them back for our fire." The little girl ran out in the freezing cold to the neighbor's house across the way.

"Don't let your dogs bite me, mama," she called anxiously as she drew near. "Don't let those ferocious things bite."

"Don't worry, child," said the woman, appearing in the door. "They don't bite. My, what a chill there is in the air! Why are you going about in this weather?"

"Our fire went out, mama, so I've come to ask you for a few coals."

"But of course, my little one. First sit down and warm up a bit. I'm going to make you a touch of honey soup before you run along." The little girl spooned up the soup with great relish and ran home to her father.

"Light the fire, daughter, and be quick about it," said the old man through his chattering teeth.

The next morning, the girl got up even earlier than usual and promptly put out the fire that was still smouldering.

"Papa," she called once again, "the fire went out and there are no matches in the house." The old man told her to go next door again. She scurried off and found the widow already up and puttering in her kitchen.

"Oh, my dear," she exclaimed, "is it the fire again? Surely you're putting in thin sticks instead of the hard kind."

"Yes, mama, that's it," she said distractedly, sniffing the aromas in the kitchen.

"Well, at any rate, sit down and warm your little feet. I'll make you another bowl of honey soup."

After this, the old man's daughter kept up the little routine of putting out the fire early in the morning and running to the widow's for coals. One day the old woman said to her, "Tell your papa, my sweet, that he should marry me so he won't be bothering me all the time. My fire never goes out on me. I always take care to put in a thick, hard log, and you people don't look for one."

The little girl dashed off home to serve her father his breakfast. As he was wiping the last of the egg off his chin, she said, "Papa, do you know what?"

"What is it, my little girl?"

"My friend next door says you should marry her so I won't

keep pestering her every day for hot coals. She's so good, and you can't imagine how generous she is."

"Is that so?" said the old man skeptically. "Is she so very good?"

"Very, very. Every time I go she gives me honey soup."

"Ah, my daughter, now she may give you soup with honey. It will be soup with bile, if I marry her."

"No," she insisted, and kept pestering the old man until he gave in.

"All right. You're a stubborn one. But mind you don't regret it!"

Her father married the widow, who continued as good as before. He had a daughter by her and named her Maria after his own little girl. As the stepdaughter grew up, she became naughtier and meaner every day. One day she looked at her half sister and said, "This girl spends the whole day just eating. She doesn't even know how to work. We're going to put her out into the fields as a shepherdess."

"So, you're tired of her already, eh?" asked the old man as he sent his daughter off to care for his animals.

Soon after, one of the cows in the herd bore a calf and died while the calf was very little. Maria the shepherdess began to feed it *chaicancito* [toasted flour mixed with boiling water] and milk from the sheep.

"This lazy girl is always hanging around with her calf," whined the stepdaughter. "She hasn't done a stitch of work. Why don't we set her some task?"

"What can we possibly give her?" asked the stepmother.

"Let her spin."

The stepmother and her daughter brought Maria a lock of wool and said, "Look here, you take this wool and bring it to us twisted and spun. And if you don't, you'll pay with your head."

The poor little shepherdess left the house with her spindle and wool, crying and sobbing bitterly as she walked into the fields. All of a sudden, the little calf spoke to her, "Listen to me, Maria. You arrange the wool, and I'll spin it. Just put the spindle over my horns." They looked for a little grove of trees and sat down in the shade. She put the spindle on the calf's horns, and it began to spin out the loveliest thread, using its little hooves to turn the spindle. When they had spun the whole lock of wool, she returned with her work done as nicely as you could wish. Then Maria fetched some bran and straw and gave it to the calf, which hadn't had a bite of grazing all day. How he ate after working so hard!

The next day she was given another lock of wool, and every day thereafter. The other daughter was shrewder than her mother and suspected something fishy.

"Mama, this Maria can't possibly do all the work we give her. Why, the two of us together can't do what she manages to get done in one day. I'm going to punish her for this." The following day the stepdaughter followed Maria into the fields, hiding and spying from under the trees. The girl and her calf went into a grove of thorny bushes and arranged the spindle for the day's work. When the stepdaughter observed this, she ran home in a frenzy and said, "Mama, it's not Maria who spins so beautifully. It's that calf of hers!"

"How in the world?" asked her mother, astounded.

"She fixes the wool and puts the spindle over its horns. The calf twists it with its hooves, and that's how they spend the whole day."

"What are we going to do with this animal?" puzzled the stepmother.

"I'm going to play sick, mama, and when the old man arrives, we'll tell him I'm sick from desire to eat the meat of Maria's calf. They'll have to kill it then."

The daughter was lying in bed with the old lady bustling about her when the old gentleman arrived.

"Ay," called the mother, "my daughter is ailing so. She says she has a fancy to eat roast meat from Maria's calf."

"My daughter is certainly more important than a calf," thought the old man. "We can always get another animal." He took up his axe and went out to slay the calf. Then his wife brought a tray and put all the intestines on it cut into even slices. She sent the heartbroken shepherd girl to wash them in a nearby stream and told her that if one little piece was missing, even a smidgen, she would beat the daylights out of her.

"Oh, what can I do now?" sobbed Maria to herself. "My mother will surely break my head with a stick." She cried for her calf as much as for the beating she feared to receive.

While she was at the stream washing the last pieces, an eagle swooped down and stole one, flying off with it in his beak.

"Oh, Lord of my soul," she cried in despair, "now I'm surely done for!" She calmed herself and thought, "I'll just have to hide everything." Then she turned the tray over and buried all the remaining intestines under some rocks by the stream's edge. All this time, the eagle was swooping up and down above her, hoping to seize another piece. Maria trudged off dejectedly and came to a big house surrounded by some tall trees called *peumos*. The eagle roosted in the treetops. Then a woman appeared in the doorway and said, "Good day, my child. What are you up to, and why so many tears?"

"Good morning, ma'am," Maria answered. "Why shouldn't I cry? My stepmother sent me to wash intestines all counted and measured. She told me she'd beat me if I lost one little piece. That eagle over there came and robbed me of one by the stream."

"Come, come, my dear," soothed the woman. "If I weren't in such a hurry to go to mass, I could get it back for you. But anyway, I have three daughters, and I'm going to put you in charge here while I'm at church. Give the children a good sound whack if they're bad, and beat the mattresses and clean out the oven for me."

Maria agreed and the lady hurried off to mass. Then the girl grabbed the children and began to work, combing and scrubbing and dressing them up in their very best clothes. She sat them all down in their chairs while she aired the mattresses and shook out the beds. After this she swept out the oven, filled it with fresh wood, and lit the fire. When the lady returned from mass, she found everything spick and span and all in order.

"How fine!" she exclaimed. "Now I'm going to give you some intestines I happen to have here in the house. And I'll add this little magic wand. Whenever you're in trouble, just say, 'Magic wand, by the grace that God has given you, grant me such and such a thing.' But be careful never to show this to anybody. As you're on the road home, about halfway along, a burro is going to bray. When he does, you must look down to the ground. And when the cock crows, look up to heaven. Now run along with you."

"All right, mama, I'll do just as you say," answered Maria as she hastened away to wash the new intestines. She placed the washed meat on a tray, put it on her head, and set off on the road home. Halfway along the road, a burro let out a bray and she bent over to look at the ground. Further along, the cock crowed. Maria looked up to heaven, and down fell a gold star on her forehead. What a lovely star it was! But she didn't realize what was happening to her, and just kept on walking and walking.

Meanwhile, the stepdaughter had eaten the calf's meat and was feeling better. She was looking out the window and called, "Mama, mama, here comes Maria. You should see what she's bringing on her forehead! It covers her eyes. Do you see?"

"What on earth can it be?" said the old woman, running to the window to peer out. "Maria," she called, "what have you got there? Why, you filthy girl! You little pig!" she cried, seeing the gold star. Just look at the way you dare to come home! Get a cloth and cover that filthy mess on your head." They wrapped her head with a dirty old rag. "Look at this dirty creature!" screeched the mother and her daughter.

"Ay, mama," whined the stepdaughter enviously after Maria had gone off to the corner in disgrace, "how prettily Maria really came home. Why don't you do the same thing again? This time you get sick and say you have to eat my calf."

"Good enough. I'll do it," cackled her mother.

When the old man came home from work in the afternoon, his wife was moaning and in pain.

"What have you got, old woman?"

"How should I know, old man?" she answered. "I think I'm going to die, and I have such a desire to eat a roast from my daughter's calf." Well, they were at it again. Just imagine how they carried on with their fussing! So the old man went out to look for his other daughter's calf, which he promptly killed, skinned, and roasted. Then the stepmother called her own daughter and gave her the same tray full of intestines cut up just as before, and the same instructions and threat.

The second Maria left the house crying and full of the fear of her mother's blows. As she was washing this batch of intestines, an eagle swooped down and seized a chunk of the meat, for the other eagle had told this one how it had stolen a delicious dinner at the stream. Then the stepdaughter frantically turned the tray over and dumped the rest of the meat under the rocks. A little later, she arrived at the same house where her sister had gone before.

"Good day, ma'm," she said as the lady came out to see what all the wailing and carrying on was about. "My mother sent me to wash meat, and that nasty eagle over there stole some from me. How can I ever get the intestines back?"

"Well," answered the lady, "I can't get it back now, for I'm on my way to mass. You just stay here and take care of the house. Spank my children, beat the beds, and fill the oven with all the junk around the house."

"Very well, ma'm." As soon as the lady was out of sight, she set about giving the children a good beating, pulling their hair and smacking their rumps. She aired out the mattresses and beat them with a cleaver. Finally she gathered all the junk to burn in the oven, but didn't light the fire.

"Did you do everything I asked?" said the woman upon returning.

"Yes, ma'm, it's all done."

The mother looked over the children, who were all red where they had been thrashed. "Very well," she said. "Now here are some intestines for you. When you're halfway down the road, the cock will crow, and you must look down at the ground. Then when the burrow brays, look up to heaven."

The second Maria took her meat on the tray and went along listening intently and waiting for the cock to crow. When it did, she looked obediently down at the ground. Soon after, the burro brayed, and the girl looked up to heaven. Down fell a big hunk of burro dung smack on her head. She kept right on walking.

At home, her mother had gobbled up the roast and was now much better. She was out taking some air when she saw her daughter and gasped, "For heaven's sake, child, what have you got there? Now you've really been into it. Just look at yourself in the mirror." Maria looked and saw that she was splattered all over with the burro dung. Her mother dashed off for the prettiest silk kerchief they had and put it over her daughter's forehead. All this time, the other Maria sat by the fire, her head wrapped in the old greasy rag.

One day the old man, always patient, said to his first daughter, "Don't you see? Didn't I tell you it was honey soup first and bile afterwards? Now what do you think of your new mother?"

"It doesn't really matter, papa," she answered sadly, all the while feeling the little magic wand hidden under her dress.

The stepmother was a faithful churchgoer and never missed a mass. She and her daughter, who wore the lovely silk kerchief on her forehead, dressed up and went together. One Sunday when she couldn't stand it any longer, the older Maria jumped up from her place beside the brazier and said, "Why are they the only ones who go to mass? I'm going to go too." With that, she took the magic wand from her belt. "Little wand, by the grace God has given you, give me the finest coach, a horse that will shake the ground where he trods, and a coachman too." In the wink of an eye it all appeared, and she was instantly dressed in clothes more lovely than the queen's. Then Maria rode off to mass, leaving the coach and coachman at the church door while she went in to kneel down near her mother and sister.

"Mama, mama," whispered the wicked sister to the old lady, "isn't that Maria over there?"

"Hush, silly girl," hissed her mother. "What do you mean, 'Maria'? She's sitting in the ashes by the fire."

"But it looks just like her."

"No, it's impossible. Now don't bother me with this nonsense any longer."

The mass was barely finished and the holy cross elevated, when Maria rode away in her elegant coach. Of course, she arrived home ahead of the others and asked the wand to take everything away and leave her sitting beside the coals as usual.

"Don't you see that the little fool is right here?" said the stepmother as the two women came in from mass. "Does this look like the same girl who was in church this morning? Now don't be so foolish and scatterbrained."

The following Sunday the two women left for mass early, and the same thing happened.

"It *is* Maria," insisted the other daughter this time.

"Nonsense, not at all," answered her mother. "How could you imagine such poppycock?"

As before, when the mass was over Maria rode away in her great coach. And what do you suppose? A prince noticed this lovely girl as she was leaving the church.

"I'm going to come good and early next Sunday," he thought, "to find out where that girl is from. She's so pretty and graceful in her wondrous coach."

After the two women had gone off to mass the next Sunday, Maria asked the wand for her coach all decked out in gold, some golden slippers, and an exquisite dress. Off she went in all her splendor. In church, the prince was watching and sought to sit by her side. When he saw Maria, he knelt down next to her to pray and then whispered to his guards, "One of you over there and another here; I'll guard the middle." As the mysterious girl left the church, she saw the two guards waiting near her coach.

"Hallo!" called one, "here she is." But she skipped away, and instead of grabbing her, they managed to get just her foot and pull off one of the golden slippers. Maria Cinderella hopped into the coach and sped away.

"A fine thing," moaned the guards. "How are we going to confess to the prince that we've failed?" They combed the whole town without any luck, for the slipper would fit nobody.

"She must not be in town," suggested one of the nobles of the court. "She has to be a woman among the peasants."

So the prince and his retinue set out for the country, one of their horses saddled with a sidesaddle such as women use, for in those days they had no ordinary saddles. The prince rode with the golden slipper to show. Lo and behold, they drew up eventually before the house of the old stepmother. The old lady and her daughter, dressed in their finery, came out to greet the young prince while Maria Cinderella was off hidden in the corner. Her stepmother had told her she was in no condition to receive a fine gentleman and that she should get inside the oven until the visitors had gone.

"Miss," announced the prince to the stepdaughter, "I've come to see who can be the owner of this slipper. I'll marry whoever it fits."

"It's mine," she said without hesitating. "Bring it here." It happened that her foot was equal to that of Maria Cinderella. She slipped on the little golden slipper as nicely as could be, an exact fit.

"You," announced the prince, "are surely the owner of my slipper and shall be my wife." They sat her in the sidesaddle reserved for the right lady. But just as she was bidding her mother good-bye, a bitch appeared and began to bark:

> "Wow, wow,
> Burro dung sits up now.
> Golden star without a bow,
> Wow."

A servant lad pricked up his ears. "Hark, master. Listen."

"Go on, get out of here you bitch," yelled the exasperated stepmother to the cur.

"Wait a moment. What is the little dog barking about?" asked the prince.

"She's just a pesky animal, sir," the old lady answered hastily. But the young prince dismounted and went through all the house, searching in every corner. He didn't find a thing until he uncovered the oven, and there was poor Maria Cinderella in a terrible state, the old greasy rag tied on her head.

"Oh, miss! What, pray tell, are you doing here?" asked the wide-eyed prince.

"Well, here I am, just sitting, your Highness."

"So I see. I'm searching for a girl who lost her slipper at last Sunday's mass. Whoever it fits shall be my wife."

"The slipper is surely mine," she said timidly.

"How then did it fit the other girl?"

"You can see that her foot is identical to mine," said Cinderella, "but can she produce the companion slipper? Let's see if she can."

"Oh," gasped the stepmother, "where did you get that idea?

Where on earth do you think you have it? This is absolutely impossible."

"But I have the other slipper," said Cinderella as she went out to wash up. She asked the magic wand to dress her in the clothes she had worn to church, and to bring her the coach and coachman along with the other slipper.

"Don't you see?" she said as she came back in. "Here is my slipper, and the prince has the other one."

"This at last is my wife," declared the happy prince. Then his men seized the other Maria from the saddle, gave her a smack, and knocked her down in the dust. They kicked her soundly a couple of times, and that was the end of that.

"Get up in the saddle, my dear," said the prince to Cinderella.

"No, where the burro dung was mounted, I'll not climb up," she replied.

So the prince carried her and her father away on other horses for a beautiful wedding with priest and bishop and all the trimmings. There was great rejoicing at the castle that day.

> That's the end of the tale.
> It went down deep in the ground
> And sprouted up in a beanstalk,
> So Benedicto can tell us one more.

•20• *The Little Stick Figure*

• THERE WAS ONCE a woman who had a little girl by a certain gentleman. When this man returned some time later, he didn't recognize the girl as his daughter, and as she grew up, he fell in love with her. Her mother had let her know that the man was her father, so she respected him as her father. But as they had never said a word to him, he followed the lovely girl day and night, leaving her no peace. Finally she went to see a priest to ask how she could free herself of her suitor. He advised her to make some requests of the gentleman.

The girl went to her father and made three requests, which he

accepted. Her first desire was that he bring her the dress of the
sun. Away he went wandering and walking until he found this
beautiful dress. After that, she sent him to look for the dress of
the moon. He brought that to her also. Finally she sent him in
search of the dress of the walking sea and the dancing fishes.
When he brought the third dress, she knew not what to do, and
ordered a disguise of a stick figure made for herself. She put on
this wooden clothing and fled from her insistent suitor.

The little stick figure arrived looking for work at the house of
a certain man who lived with his mother. They gave her a job
taking care of the turkeys, but the other servants at the farm de-
tested her and threw her into the hen coop. There sat the girl,
who was really a princess and had magic power.

The following day was Sunday, and the young landlord bade
his mother good-bye and set out to go to the races. The stick figure drew near and asked him in a soft little voice, "Why don't
you take me, good master?"

"You think I'm going to take *you* riding, you stick figure?"
With that, he snatched his whip, gave her a few lashes, and galloped away. She returned sadly to her turkeys. A few minutes
later she left the fowls scratching about on a little hill and asked
her magic charm for a coach with fine horses and two Negro
footmen. Then she put on her dress of the sun and rode off to the
races. The beautiful coach rolled up to the track, carrying the
young lady and her two servants. The young landlord went over
to introduce himself and ask the lady where she was from, for
she had never been seen before in those parts. She answered that
she came from a city far away, a place he surely didn't know. As
he insisted on finding out more, she finally said, "Sir, I come
from the city of Whiplash."

"And where in the world is that?" asked the mystified gentleman.

"Very far away," she answered.

In the afternoon, about five o'clock, she took leave of him in
her coach, after having made a date to meet him again the following Sunday. The stick figure returned to her turkeys and
made all her elegant things disappear. The next day the lord of

the house arrived and told his mother of the lovely lady from Whiplash, hoping perhaps that the old lady might have heard of that city. But it was no use; the name was a mystery to her as well.

The next Sunday, the young gallant decked himself out in his best clothes and went to the races to await the lady's arrival. As he was riding away from his ranch, the stick figure came running out and asked, "Why don't you take me, master?"

"How do you think I'm going to take a mere stick figure to the races with me?" he retorted, giving her a stinging blow with his *chamanto* [a poncho-style blanket]. Away she fled with her flock of turkeys. But as soon as the master had disappeared in the dust down the road, she prettied herself up again, climbed into the coach, and put on the dress of the moon. When she rode into the square near the races, the landlord failed to recognize her and introduced himself to this new lady.

"Miss, where do you come from?" he asked.

"Sir, I am from the distant city of Blanketblow."

"But this is certainly strange. Last Sunday a lady came from the city of Whiplash, and now you come from Blanketblow. Where are these places, anyway?"

"They're very, very far away," she answered mysteriously.

At five o'clock in the afternoon, they bade each other good-bye, promising to meet again the following week. The stick figure rode home, made all her things disappear, and returned to her little flock of turkeys.

The next Sunday, the young gentleman dressed once more to meet the mysterious lady at the races. As before, the stick figure approached him and asked, "Why don't you take me, my lord?" His only reply was to strut over and give her a kick with his spur. She scurried off with her birds to wait until he had gone away. This time, she called for the dress of the walking sea and the dancing fishes. When she arrived at the races, the gentleman was waiting but didn't recognize her in this new dress.

"Where, pray tell, do you come from, my lady?"

"Kind sir, I'm from the city of Kickspur."

"The first Sunday, there was a lady from Whiplash, the next

one from Blanketblow, and now you from Kickspur. Where *are*
these places from which three such lovely ladies have come?"
There was no answer.

At five o'clock the gentleman took his leave of the lady and
gave her a ring with his name as a remembrance. Once more she
returned home to her turkeys. This time the young lord came
home the following day and fell into his bed deathly ill, because
he did not know where the three ladies had come from. He was
so ailing that he asked his mother to please make him some of
his favorite *tortillas* [a kind of round bread cooked in hot ashes].
The little stick figure overheard and begged the lady of the house
to let her make them for the young man. At first his mother
would hear nothing of it, for the girl was exceedingly dirty. But
she promised to scrub her hands with hot water, and finally the
old lady was persuaded to accept the kind offer. As the stick
figure bustled about in the kitchen, she placed the young man's
ring inside the *tortilla* and sent the piping hot bread to the lord.
When he broke it open, he found the ring and called to his
mother, "Mama, tell me who made these *tortillas*."

"Why I did of course, my son."

"Mama, you can't have made them," he insisted.

"But I tell you I did."

"Don't deny it, mama. You didn't make them at all. And if
you don't tell me the truth, I'll die."

"My son," she admitted, "the little stick figure prepared them
for you."

"Then she is my wife," exclaimed the prince, sitting upright in
bed.

"It can't be!" gasped his mother. "She, your wife!"

"Yes, mama, it has to be so. If it's otherwise, I'll die here and
now."

They called the stick figure and sent her to wash up and tidy
herself. She ran to her room, where she jumped out of the
wooden disguise in which she had been dressed so long, and put
on the dress of the sun. When she returned to the lord's bedside,
everyone in the household begged her pardon for having abused
her so and for having tossed her into the hen coop. They sent for
the priest, his assistant, and even the archbishop. The little lady

was married to the young lord, and they lived happily forever
after.

• 21 • *Florinda*

• THERE WAS ONCE a married couple who had a daughter and
named her Florinda. When she was just a baby, her father
brought her a crucifix and placed it in her cradle. She always
looked at it, and when she was old enough for school, she even
took it to class with her. The other students called her "the little
fool of the crucifix," until finally she was so ashamed that she began to leave her cross at home.

Florinda was about ten years old when her mother died. Her
father was left all alone in the world, but he was a very rich gentleman with great possessions. He began to live wildly and
wander all over town from party to party, looking for a woman
to marry but finding none. Eventually he fell into poverty, and
one day he thought, "This carrying on is nonsense. Why don't I
just marry my daughter, Florinda." Upon arriving home, he told
her of his plan.

"No, of course not, father," she said, clutching her cross. "May
God and the Consecrated Queen keep me from such a thing!"

"Now what can I do?" grumbled the old man. "I've lost every
chance I had. How can it be that I'm not going to get married?"
He went off dejectedly to drink and revel with the little money
he had left. When he returned from his spree, he announced to
Florinda, "You simply have to marry me, no two ways about it."
Just as he was about to throw his arms around her, she ran to the
altar where the crucifix was and disappeared. "She's a witch, she's
a witch!" screamed her father. "Why did she hide like that?"

The next day, the girl said to her godmother, "Look, mother, I
must go away from this place."

"What on earth for, child?"

"Because I just have to. You'll see. Now cut my hair short." So
the kindly old woman clipped off her lovely tresses. Then
Florinda took a horse from her father's herd, saddled it, dressed

herself all in his clothes, and rode away to see the world. She hadn't the slightest notion where she was going, for she had never left the house before.

When her father stormed in that evening, he noticed that the saddle was gone along with one of the horses from the pasture. Right off, he lassoed another horse and galloped away on the same road taken by Florinda. When he rode alongside the girl disguised as a man he called, "Good day, friend. Have you seen a girl riding nicely on horseback hereabouts?"

"No. I haven't seen her in these parts."

The old man galloped away, but was soon bored with the chase and returned, only to meet the other man once more. "Are you absolutely certain you haven't seen a girl?" asked her father a second time.

"Yes, quite sure."

Florinda had three copper coins in her pocket (for in those days there was copper money, which we don't have any more). She was suddenly very hungry, and as she was riding by the palace of a king, she went up to the gate. One of the servant ladies saw her and asked, "Now what do you suppose this young fellow wants?"

"Good morning, miss," called Florinda in her deepest voice. "Do you think you could do me the favor of selling three copper coins' worth of broth?"

"We'll have to speak with the king to see if there is any."

When the king heard about the visitor, he called Florinda into the palace and asked the disguised girl what she had requested.

"Your majesty," she said, "I've a terrible hunger, and need to buy a little broth."

The king agreed cordially and set a table for this youth, all the time admiring him intently and thinking how handsome he was. It happened that this same king had a daughter. Thinking of this, he summoned one of the nobles of the court and said, "Man, take this young fellow's horse and put it in the stable. Then serve him with the best of everything we have."

After the meal, Florinda took out her coppers to pay. But the king intervened. "No payment here, my friend. Just enjoy the meal." When she had made ready to continue her journey, he added, "Surely, you aren't going now. Postpone it until tomorrow and stay here to chat a bit with a lonely old man." Florinda consented, and they arranged her a room and a bed for the night.

Right after breakfast the next morning, she prepared to ride on again.

"Don't mention such a thing," said the king. "Tomorrow is surely time enough. Rest yourself and your horse."

"Well, I suppose," she said hesitantly.

The following morning the king told Florinda that she was not to go away any more, for he had a daughter that she could marry.

"How is the princess going to marry me sight unseen?" protested Florinda, searching desperately for an excuse.

"No," answered the king stubbornly, "the word of a king cannot fail. What I say is done, for I'm still the one who gives orders around here." This was a fine kettle of fish! Lord above, how was a girl going to marry a princess? Nevertheless, a fine wedding was celebrated with the priest and all the trimmings.

At bedtime that night, Florinda whispered to the princess, "Listen, my dear, I want you to keep a little secret for me."

"Of course, my love. Why not? Just whisper it in my ear."

"I'm a girl, a woman just like you," blurted Florinda.

"All the better then," said the princess happily. "We'll live together like two doves in the world."

"All right, but you must promise to keep the secret just as if I were a man."

Whenever they took Florinda out to a party, she always picked up men's things, admiring knives, revolvers, and what not. The princess was always given gifts for ladies. And when they took her to the garden, Florinda picked a carnation or a jasmine, which are men's flowers, while the princess picked roses.

One day the princess' father said to the queen, "My dear, we've never told the godfather that his goddaughter was going to marry. And she has such a handsome husband now, so fine and shapely. Why don't we write the old boy to come and meet our son-in-law?" The queen agreed that it was a fine idea, so they sent out the letter with news of the wedding and especially of the young husband's beauty.

When the godfather, who was also a king, received the message, he called his court fortune-teller and asked him, "Is it really true that my goddaughter is married?"

"Yes," answered the prophet, "she's married all right, but to a woman, just like she is. The husband is no man, if I know what I'm talking about."

"Can it be true, man?" gasped the other king as his jaw dropped open.

"True enough, I'm afraid, sir," answered the fortune-teller.

"I'm going to make a little bet with my friend," thought the second king. "We'll just see if the old prophet is right." He and his queen loaded the royal ship and set sail for the other palace. The only boats to anchor on the beach of that sea were those of the two neighboring kings, so when the first king saw the sail of his friend's boat approaching, he called his queen and ran down to the beach to meet the visitors. Florinda and the princess ran ahead with the old folks behind them, the king all the while noticing what a beautiful body his son-in-law had. He was virtually under the spell of the young husband's charm.

"What do you think of my new son-in-law?" asked the king when his friend had disembarked. "After all, he's your godson now."

"Very pretty, very, very fine," answered the second king. "But, my friend, your 'son-in-law' is a woman, for heaven's sake. Two women have married each other!"

"Don't tell me!" exclaimed the first king, dropping behind the others. "How can that possibly be? He's got to be a man."

"No. I'm telling you, old friend, I'd bet all my money and my palace and goods in the bargain."

"It's a deal," said the princess' father, still incredulous. The two kings shook on their bet and decided on the next day to hunt wild pigeons for a bit of stewed meat. That way, they could see how the new husband handled a gun.

Florinda overheard this conversation and whispered to the princess, "Now we're really sunk. How are we going to pull this one off?"

"I'll tell you my plan," answered the princess. "But, God knows, if we have to die, we'll die."

The next morning, they all ate breakfast together and then each one gathered up his provisions, gun, and ammunition. Florinda rode out ahead of the others at a gallop, brooding to herself all the while. Meanwhile, the visiting king walked along behind with his friend saying that the husband was a woman and all the rest of it.

"I still don't see what you mean," said the first king. "After all, he has the body of a man, doesn't he? This is all poppycock."

Riding along well ahead, Florinda came upon a tree heavy with wild pigeons. She stationed herself below and carefully took a shot. Down fell a whole cloud of pigeons. She was busily stuffing them in her game bag when the others arrived.

"Don't you see, old boy?" said the first king triumphantly to his friend. "If she were a woman, she wouldn't shoot like that, would she now?"

"Well, what of it?" answered the other. "For the love of God, if I've told you once I've told you a thousand times—she's a woman. Now, let's make another test. This time we'll all go bathing in the river."

The king went over to Florinda and said, "Very good shooting, my son. By the way, tomorrow we're going to get up early and take a little swim in the river." Florinda bravely answered that it seemed a fine idea.

In the night, she was talking secretly with the princess and said, "Lord, tomorrow they're going to take us bathing!" The poor girl was very confused at this news and hardly knew what to say.

Early the next morning, they breakfasted and set out. Everyone had to bathe himself bare-bottom, without a stitch of clothes. Again Florinda rode off well ahead at a gallop. In great consternation, she undressed and leapt into the river, scrubbing herself busily.

"Come on out, Florinda," called the two kings as they rode up. "After all, you're a man like the rest of us." Just at that point, her crucifix came flying over the waters. With that, Florinda stood up in the river and found herself turned into a man. Instead of trying to hide herself, she faced the others boldly and merrily scrubbed herself all over [the narrator laughs] so they could see full well she was a man. The king gleefully slapped his friend on the back in triumph.

After Florinda had ridden back to the palace alone, she found her wife sick in bed from fear that they were both going to die.

"Listen, my dear," said Florinda joyfully, "we're safe. I've become a man by the grace of God." She proceeded to tell the marveling princess all about the crucifix her father had brought her as a child. "It turned me into a man. I can still see it now flying across the waters."

The other king, who had made such an enthusiastic bet in great certainty, was much grieved and in a great rush to leave for his own palace. That very night, he loaded his boat and set out to kill his accursed fortune-teller. The first king had promised to let him stay on at his palace, paying as he could, and not to run him down in public.

When the second king arrived home and was disembarking in a white heat of fury, the old prophet came out affectionately to greet his master.

"Step aside!" roared the chagrined king. "Didn't you tell me that my goddaughter's husband was a woman? What do you say now?"

"Of course I did, your majesty. She was a woman."

"He was as much a man as any I've ever seen," wheezed the king, getting redder and redder in the face.

"That's because the Lord turned her into one. But of course I couldn't foresee that he was going to pull a trick like that. She was a woman in her first form."

"Humph, I'm simply going to kill you, and that's all there is to it," steamed the king, totally exasperated.

"As you wish, your highness. But what I say is the gospel truth. It was all the Lord's work."

> And now the story is done.
> It went down deep in the earth,
> In a beanstalk then popped forth,
> So another can be begun.

.22. The Moorish Prince and the Christian Prince

• ONCE THERE WERE two brothers who loved each other very much. One day the first one, who was called Christian Prince, heard tell of The Beauty of the World. He asked the other brother, named Moorish Prince, to accompany him in search of this beauty. Moorish Prince agreed and went to tell their father of the plans.

"Son, for God's sake," protested the old man, "when will you ever get there? She's so awfully far away."

"But going with my brother, I'm sure to find her."

Finally the king gave his consent, and early the following day the two brothers set out on their search for The Beauty of the World. They walked the livelong day. That night, Moorish Prince found a camp site, unsaddled the horses, and made a bed for his brother. As soon as they had supped, Christian Prince fell asleep in the wink of an eye. But Moorish Prince just lay there listening. Soon he heard two *traras* [mythical birds] light in the tree under which they were camped.

"Good evening, old friend," said one *trara* to the other. "What's new over your way?"

"Nothing much except that Moorish Prince and Christian Prince are going in search of The Beauty of the World. If Moorish Prince were to hear these words, he would be able to bring her back. If he doesn't, he won't be able to."

Early the following day, the two birds bade each other goodbye and flew off. Moorish Prince had heard everything they had said. When the other brother awoke, the two of them traveled on for the second day. At night they came to another big tree, where they made their camp once more. After Moorish Prince had made up their beds, they ate supper. Then both brothers slid into bed. Christian Prince fell asleep at once, but Moorish Prince stayed awake again, listening carefully. Once more the *traras* flew into the tree.

"Good evening, *comadre*," croaked one. "What news over your way?".

"Just that Christian Prince is on his way with Moorish Prince in search of The Beauty of the World."

"Will they get there, *comadre?*"

"Yes, because they're already close. Now, if the Moorish Prince were to hear these words about three golden hairs on Christian Prince's back, and if he were to pull them out, they would serve him for company."

Moorish Prince heard the whole conversation. He turned his brother face down, pulled out the three hairs the birds had described, and stored them away very carefully. When dawn broke, the two birds said good-bye to each other and disappeared into the clouds. As the sun began to climb higher, Moorish Prince got up, saddled the horses, and fixed breakfast as usual. The two brothers traveled the whole day through, and late in the afternoon they set up camp at another big tree. After supper, Christian Prince immediately fell asleep again. Moorish Prince kept his usual vigil until he heard the *traras* flutter down into the tree.

"Good evening, *comadre*. What's the news tonight?" asked the first.

"Oh, not much, except that the two brothers are still in search of The Beauty of the World."

"And will they fetch her, *comadre?*"

"Yes, if Moorish Prince, who has his brother's hairs, hears these words. He's going to arrive at twelve o'clock on the dot where The Beauty of the World is. Then he's going to pick her up and carry her on his shoulder."

It happened just as the *traras* had predicted. As Moorish Prince was carrying The Beauty over his shoulder, she looked back and spotted three giant snakes chasing them.

"Faster, Moorish Prince," she screamed, "three of the fiercest serpents are right behind us."

Moorish Prince grabbed the three golden hairs and threw them out behind him. Immediately they turned into the three fiercest and roughest giants in the world. The giants tackled the snakes and killed them all in no time. Moorish Prince continued with The Beauty on his shoulder, although now she was bent and

twisted from looking behind. When he arrived at the encampment, he found his brother in a deep sleep. Moorish Prince tiptoed in very softly and put The Beauty of the World to bed beside his brother. Soon after, Christian Prince awoke with great
joy to see her at his side.

As day came, the *traras* returned again to the tree.

"Good morning, *comadre*. What's happening?"

"Nothing more than the news that Moorish Prince brought
The Beauty and has her at his brother's side." With that, the two
birds flew away. When day broke in earnest, both brothers set
out for home. They spent that night under the same tree where
they had camped on their second night out. Once more the *traras*
returned to this tree.

"Good evening, *comadre*. Do you bring any news?"

"Very little except that the two princes are bringing home The
Beauty of the World all bent over."

"Could she be straightened up, *comadre*?"

"Yes, it's possible. If Moorish Prince were to hear these words,
she would be straightened. Soon they're going to ford a stream,
and if Moorish Prince were to hear this and they were to wash in
the stream, with The Beauty washing upstream and the brothers
downstream, she would become straight as an arrow."

Thus it was that Moorish Prince took his brother and The
Beauty to wash in the stream. Afterwards, they found that she
was upright once more. What a joy for Christian Prince to see
his wife standing nice and straight!

The next afternoon they arrived at the camp where they had
slept the first night. The *traras* appeared as usual.

"Good evening, *comadre*. What do you say this time?"

"Not much, except that they're bringing The Beauty with
them and they're very close by. He who hears and tells these
words will turn to stone and sea. He who hears and tells these
words will turn to stone and sea. He who hears and tells these
words will turn to stone and sea."

Bright and early the next day, the brothers continued toward
their palace. How glad the king was to see his sons arrive with
The Beauty of the World! Christian Prince and Moorish Prince
lived on together at the palace for a long time. As the months

passed, Christian Prince became angered with his brother and jealous of him.

"Look here, brother," said Moorish Prince one day, "why are you treating me this way after all I've done for you. I went all alone to get The Beauty for you. When we spent the second night under that tree on the road back, the Beauty of the World was all bent over. I heard from the *traras* that we had to wash her in the stream. And wasn't it true, brother, that she stood up straight as a ramrod on the spot?"

"Yes, so it was."

"The next night," continued Moorish Prince, "we camped under the first tree we had used on the journey out. When the first *trara* asked if we were bringing The Beauty, the other answered yes and said 'He who hears and tells these words will turn to stone and sea.'" At this, Moorish Prince turned to stone up to his knees, and continued, "'He who hears and tells these words will turn to stone and sea.'" Then Moorish Prince turned to stone up to his waist.

"Ay, brother," cried Christian Prince, "tell no more!"

"No," he said, "I have to tell it all. The *trara* said a third time, 'He who hears and tells these words will turn to stone and sea.'" With that, Moorish Prince turned completely to stone.

Christian Prince lived on with his Beauty of the World. In time they had a healthy little baby, who became the apple of their eye. One day a *trara* flew by and croaked, "Christian Prince didn't know how to thank his brother. After bringing him The Beauty, poor Moorish Prince turned to stone. If Christian Prince were a man, he would behead his baby and rub the stone with that blood. Then he would bring Moorish Prince back to life."

Upon hearing these terrible words, Christian Prince spoke with his wife.

"Why don't you do it?" said The Beauty. "Look at what your brother suffered to go and get me."

Then and there, Christian Prince grabbed his baby and cut off his little head. He stopped the blood to catch it and rubbed the stone where his brother had been petrified. Moorish Prince sprang back to life and Christian Prince rubbed the rest of the blood on the child's body, reviving him as well. Now he and his wife were glad beyond words, for both the brother and the child had been restored to them.

After this event, Moorish Prince harbored a certain rancor that he had been turned to stone for his brother's sake. One day he went out to walk on the beach and found the three golden hairs in his pocket. When he tossed them on the sand, the three fiercest giants in the world sprang up before his eyes. Moorish Prince told them to go and tear the palace to pieces. That of course was the end of Christian Prince and The Beauty of the World. Once Moorish Prince had taken his revenge, he picked up the three little hairs and stuck them carefully away in his pocket.

•23• *The Golden-Haired Beauty*

• THERE WAS ONCE a woman with three sons, Pedro, Diego, and Manuelito. One day Pedro and Diego set off walking. Shortly after, Manuelito took a sack full of cornbread and went in search of them. After a long trip, he came upon three girls high in a pear tree squabbling over their looks. Each wanted to be more beautiful than the next.

"Here comes Manuelito," called one excitedly. "We'll call him to judge which one of us is the most beautiful. Hey, boy! Come over here a minute."

"Now I'm in for it," he thought. "These girls are going to pelt me to death with pears."

"Come on! What are you waiting for?" they cried.

"If they really beat me, I'm going to get out of here on the double," thought the boy, timidly approaching the pear tree full of sisters.

"Son," said one of them, "we've called you to judge here. We're fighting because each one of us claims to be more beautiful than the next. We're almost dead from hitting each other with pears."

Manuel saw that he was in a real pickle. There seemed no way to satisfy all three of them. Finally he said, "So that you'll be at peace, one of you is like the sun, the other like the moon, and the third like Venus, and I bid you all good-bye, ladies." As he was scurrying off, the girls called from the tree. "Now," he thought, "the jig is really up. They're not satisfied."

"Young man," they called after him, "we're so content that each of us is going to grant you a magic charm." Then one gave him a cap which would render him invisible when he wore it. The second gave him a magic wand, and the third a magic shoe which would enable the wearer to cover great distances.

Soon after the boy had set off, he came upon some animals eating a cow. There were tigers, lions, elephants, buzzards, vultures, ants—all the animals in the world. The bigger ones were cuffing the smaller ones and not letting them eat. It was a mess.

"Go and fetch that fellow over there so he can divide the cow," roared the lion.

"Good Lord, they're going to devour me on the spot!" thought the lad, unable to see any way of satisfying all of them. Nevertheless, he bravely took out his knife and parceled out the cow, giving the biggest chunk to the biggest animals, and the smallest to the smallest. To the ants went some tiny bits and crumbs from the boy's cornbread. The animals were all content and gobbled away, each at his own portion. When Manuelito had gone, the lion suggested that they all grant him a charm, and sent the falcon to get the lad.

"Boy," screeched the bird, "the lion has called for you."

"This is surely the end," he thought. "Now they're going to swallow me in one bite." But like it or not, he had to return.

"We've all agreed to grant you a charm," purred the lion. "So, whenever you're up against it, say, 'May God and the animals save me from this danger.'"

As Manuelito went on his way, he saw a burning hawthorn tree. Next to it was a snake which was unable to get free of the fire. The boy ran up with his magic wand and pulled the snake out of the flames.

"When you're in trouble, lad," hissed the snake gratefully, "just say, 'May God and the serpent favor me in these hard times.'"

A bit later, Manuelito came to the house of a king for whom his brothers were working. There was also in the house a black woman who was a great teller of tales and terribly envious. The king became very fond of Manuelito and put him in charge of all his workers. They, too, loved the youth well, but all the while, his brothers were plotting enviously with the wicked black woman.

One afternoon, two doves were sitting in an orange tree. The cock had come with a hair from The Golden-Haired Beauty and placed it on the back of his mate's neck. She didn't want to receive it, and Manuelito, in hiding, laughed at this little game. Immediately the black woman, who had observed everything, said to the two older brothers, "Let's tell the king that the boy has claimed to be brave enough to go in search of the king's seven-colored horse and the harness with golden bells which were stolen by the enchanted *laras*."

The brothers promptly announced this lie to the king, who summoned Manuelito before him.

"Look, my boy, they've told me you're of a mind to go to the enchanted *laras* to search for my horse and harness."

"No, my king, I've said no such thing, for I know very well that they would kill me."

"Nevertheless," declared the king sternly, "you're going to have to go, or I shall cut off your head."

The boy left the room crying. As he was wandering outside, a parrot in an orange tree squawked, "Why are you sobbing so, Manuelito?"

"Why shouldn't I cry, little parrot? The king has ordered me to look for the seven-colored horse and the harness with golden bells."

"That's terrible! Surely the *laras* are going to kill you for that. They have the horse locked up with seven keys, and the harness is hung up on the post of a cot."

After this, Manuelito went to the edge of the sea and struck the waters with his magic wand. The sea opened immediately, and he passed through to the other shore. There he came to the kingdom of the *laras* and put on his magic cap in order to be invisible. As he stood puzzling over how to open the doors, he glimpsed an ant crawling up and down on them.

"Here's just what I need," he thought. "May God and the ant help me in this tight spot." Right away the little ant went scurrying through the lock and opened the doors for him. The boy took the horse out as cautiously as could be and then returned to get the harness. "May God and the little birds help me in this hard moment," said Manuelito. Just then a falcon swooped in and carried the precious harness outside. Manuelito took the horse and harness and rode for all he was worth. The *laras* came roaring after him in hot pursuit. Coming to the sea's edge, Manuelito struck the water again with his wand. The sea opened wide and he went safely through to the other shore, the *laras* remaining on their side of the water.

When the youth delivered the horse and harness to the king, he was so pleased that he could think of no way to reward such service. The black woman and the brothers were more envious than ever, for the boy was obviously the favorite of the court.

"Now," cackled the black woman to the brothers, "we're going to inform the king that Manuelito has claimed to be prepared to search for The Golden-Haired Beauty, who is also a prisoner of the bewitched *laras*. Surely they'll kill him this time, as they've killed everybody who has ever gone there."

When the king was informed of this, he of course summoned the lad and said, "I hear you are ready to go for The Golden-Haired Beauty."

"No, my king. How could I have said such a thing? This time, they'll finish with me for good."

But the king was not in a mood for "no," and he told Manuel to go or forfeit his head. When the boy went out weeping, he encountered the little parrot roosting in a peach tree. It asked him what the matter was.

"There's nothing to do but cry, my parrot, for now the king has sent me after The Golden-Haired Beauty in the kingdom of the *laras*."

"That will be the end," squawked the raucous bird. "They'll make short work of you this time around."

As before, Manuel arrived at the seashore and passed through the sea with the help of his magic wand. As he approached the *laras'* place, they came out to head him off. When he told them his mission, they replied, "You must do three jobs if you want The Golden-Haired Beauty. If you complete them successfully, you may take her away. If not, your head will stay here."

In the night, they put him inside a granary. The wheat was

mostly chaff with very little grain. The *laras* gave him the stub of a candle, by the light of which he had to thresh all the wheat in the granary. Manuelito entered the building crying. The candle stub would not last long enough even for half a peck of wheat. In the midst of his despair, he spied an ant crawling in the wheat and remembered his charm. "May God and the ants save me from this tight spot," he said. Immediately a whole swarm of ants appeared and began to clean the wheat, carrying the chaff outside. When dawn broke the next morning, they had left the wheat spanking clean, as bright as gold on the granary floor. The *laras* came in, their plans all made for killing the little upstart.

"Here it is, ladies," he declared proudly, "the whole granary of wheat as clean as a whistle."

"You've got a hand for chores," they admitted, looking about wide-eyed. "But there's another little job coming up tonight."

That night the *laras* put him in a room filled with tubs of fat. He had to wash them sparkling clean by the light of another candle stub. Sobbing away, Manuelito remembered the animals. "May God and the beasts save me from this sorrow." In the twinkling of an eye, the animals tumbled in one over the other, lions, tigers, and every manner of beast, and began licking the tubs furiously. Lord, how they did lick! Before the candle stub could burn down, they had the tubs as clean as new. When the *laras* came in the morning, they found everything shining.

"What a man you are for a task! But there's yet another before we hand over The Golden-Haired Beauty."

The following day, they called him and gave him a flask of water and put a kerchief in his hand. He had to climb a great tall pole with the flask and the kerchief in one hand, and if he spilled one drop, his head would come off. Manuelito thought immediately of his friend the snake. "May God and the serpent smile on me on this dark day," he cried. The snake appeared and propped up his arm so it wouldn't shake while he shinnied up the pole. Manuelito went up and down without losing a drop.

When he went to the *laras,* the boy found that there were three princesses, The Golden-Haired Beauty and two more. They had all been put to bed and covered up tight, and only the heels of their shoes could be seen.

"Choose your Beauty and pull her out by one foot," said the wicked *laras*.

Manuelito pondered and then remembered. "May God and the serpent help me again in this woe," he said. In that very moment, a little snake popped out from one of the heels and disappeared. He grabbed hold of that shoe and pulled out The Golden-Haired Beauty.

Of course, the king was so overjoyed when Manuelito returned with the girl that he could think of no fit payment for such a deed. Finally he gave The Beauty to Manuelito as his wife. They were married happily, and the king handed his crown over to the brave youth, naming him the new ruler of the kingdom. As for the wicked black woman and the two brothers, the king ordered that they be burned in an oven and their ashes cast to the wind.

Manuelito lived on happily with The Golden-Haired Beauty. Since that time, there have been many girls with golden blond hair in this neighborhood. They all came from the lovely lady with the golden locks.

•24• *The Magic Coconut*

• ONCE UPON A TIME there lived a spinning woman who spun fourteen strips of cloth every day. One day she sent for her son, a foolish boy, to sell a strip of cloth in the town. He went on the errand and promptly sold the cloth for one *peso*. On the way back the boy met three bandits who were killing a little kitten. He felt such pity for the cat that he bought it with his only *peso*. Away went the robbers, and the lad just stood there looking at his new possession. As he reached down to pick it up, the little cat ran off to a hill and climbed a tree. The lad shook it down, but immediately it leaped up into a second tree. Trying to get it down, he failed again, and the cat disappeared into the distance.

Eventually the foolish boy wandered home. When his mother asked him for the money, he told her he had bought a cat with it. When she heard that, she grabbed him and beat the living daylights out of the poor simple fellow. The following day he was sent to sell another strip in town. He received his *peso* in the market and headed home, meeting the bandits in the same place. This time they were killing a dog, which the boy quickly asked them for.

"How much will you give for the pup, simple boy?" they asked.

"One *peso*. I don't have any more."

The laughing bandits took the *peso* and made off, while the simple youth stood looking at his new pet. No sooner had the men disappeared than the puppy ran off into the hills and out of sight. The boy chased the dog a while, but was soon tired and turned toward home without a cent. When his mother asked him for the money, he confessed the sad tale. She thrashed him a second time for his nonsense.

The next day, he set off to sell yet a third strip of cloth, for his mother was determined that he learn how to be responsible in this business. Sure enough, on the road home he came upon the bandits killing a gigantic snake. With every blow of their sticks, they would hurl it down and then lift it up for more. The lad took pity on the creature and bought it from them as well. The serpent lay there for a while, just quivering. Then as soon as the crooks were a good distance off, it slithered away from the boy under a big rock. He was a husky lad and turned the boulder over, but the snake slipped out and immediately shot under another one. The boy turned this rock over, and the whole game was played again. Just as he was turning over the third rock, the foolish lad found a coconut. Studying it in his hand, he thought, "If I eat it, I won't be full. But if I take it to my mama, she won't believe that I've paid a *peso*. It's better to take my beating and eat the coconut right here." But he couldn't break it open, so he turned it over and over until he found a key which opened the coconut. Suddenly, a black man popped out and said, "What is your wish, my first master?"

"What indeed are you going to offer me!" exclaimed the boy. "I want a table covered with every kind of good victuals, and intelligence for myself."

When this wish was immediately granted, the boy sat down to eat until he was popping full. Then he grabbed his coconut again and said to the genie, "All of what is laid out here must go up in smoke." And so it was done. Then the lad began to calculate. "I'm an educated young man now and have my magic charm. Since my mother is poor, I won't return to her house ever again."

The simple lad skipped off to romp around, and late in the evening came to the house of a little old woman. He asked for lodging, but she answered that she couldn't help him, for she was too poor even to offer him a bit of supper.

"Pay no mind to that, old mother," he answered. "I just want a place to lay my head for the night." He bedded down on the old lady's floor, and late at night he seized his coconut and located the key again.

"What would you have, my first master?" asked the genie, popping out.

"You can well imagine what I want. A table stocked with the best delicacies and silverware in the world." Before he could even finish the words the loaded table appeared. Then the boy woke the little old lady and told her to help herself. She tasted all the things she had never eaten before in her life. When they had both eaten their fill, the boy told her to keep everything for herself, the dishes, silver, and the whole elegant setting.

"What news is there in these parts, old mother?" He asked when they had finished eating.

"No news," she said, "except that the king can't find anybody to make him a palace of gold without and silver within."

The boy resolved to do this job, and all that night the old woman couldn't sleep for thinking of the reward the king was surely going to give her for finding this boy. As soon as dawn broke, she scurried off to the palace and told the king the great news. Without a moment's delay the king paid the old lady a generous reward and sent five soldiers home with her to fetch the youth as a prisoner. The boy was still sleeping when the little group arrived. The old lady shook him awake and told him the king had summoned him. The poor foolish lad was puzzled at this, for he had committed no crime, but nevertheless he followed the soldiers obediently to the palace.

"Good morning, lad," bellowed the king from his high throne.

"Is it true that you have promised to build me a palace of gold without and silver within?"

"Yes, I'm prepared, your majesty. But you must give me eighty thousand carpenters, one hundred thousand jewellers, and fifty thousand furniture makers.'

At the royal command these people were gathered, and the king accompanied the foolish boy to the site of the future palace. The youth was given a deadline of three days to do all the work. If he couldn't accomplish it in this time, his head would be promptly chopped off. When the king had gone, the simple lad took off his poncho and stretched out on the ground where the palace was to be built. His laborers stood around wondering why their boss hadn't given them some working orders. At eight o'clock in the morning the boy jumped up to take breakfast with his men, for the king also supplied them with meals. After eating, he returned to the work site to lie down again. At twelve o'clock he took lunch with the men and then went back for a nap. At four-thirty, they all had tea, after which the boss returned calmly to sleep.

"Why isn't the boss working?" mumbled the puzzled workers. "Shouldn't we do something to end this nonsense?"

At suppertime the boy rose to take the night meal with his men. When they returned to the site, the king had the area surrounded by soldiers so that the foolish boy couldn't run off. Everyone went home to bed, calling it one day lost.

The following morning he continued sleeping while the soldiers kept watch against his escape. As dawn came his workers began to appear, but the young boss made no sign of working and just lay there at his ease. The same thing happened on the second day. The lad took breakfast, lunch, tea, and supper with his men, and each time returned to his customary nap. The king was totally exasperated and went about mumbling that two full days had now passed. There remained one more before the time ran out.

Early on the third day the workers arrived eager to begin, but the foolish lad was slumbering peacefully. Just as on the other two days, he took his meals and his naps. Then the king declared that none of his officials should leave the site, for all of them had to be there with the youth on the morning of the deadline. The ranks of the guards were swelled with troops of additional soldiers. At midnight, the boy stood up on the very site where the palace was supposed to be and turned the key in the lock of his coconut.

"What is your pleasure, my first master?" boomed the genie.

"What do you suppose it will be! I want a great palace to appear here on the spot, gold without and silver within, with different bells of all sounds and the corrals full of all the animals that God has made in the world."

No sooner had he let out the words than all was as he had asked. The boy entered the marvelous new palace and began to roll up little balls of paper which he threw up toward the attic. Wherever the balls hit, a gold star was formed. Soon the attic and all the rooms were full of brilliant gold stars. Then the boy lay down in a bed more beautiful even than that of the king. As day came on, the pealing of the bells began, each bell with its own sound. All the animals in the new corrals began to bellow; the horses neighing, the burros braying, the sheep and goats bleating and baaing, the cocks crowing, and the turkeys gobbling about in the dooryard. When the king heard this racket he scrambled out of bed to see what could possibly be going on. He ran pell-mell and smacked his royal head on a crossbeam, falling flat on his face. Jumping up, he looked out the window and gawked to see the marvelous new palace outside, rising high and shining. What a joy for the king! As he stood there for a long while just gaping in disbelief, the day dawned fully. In the bright morning light he went down to touch the palace. A servant woman told him that the young master was still asleep. The king paced up and down the corridor until the master builder came out of his bedroom, whereupon the king took him by the hand and led him around the palace to examine every lovely detail.

Now it happened that this king had three daughters. He sent for them immediately and told the boy to choose one for his wife. The simple lad looked them over carefully and chose the oldest. The wedding was the same day, and the newly wed couple went to live in the great palace the youth had built.

One day the young husband went strolling in the town and

forgot the coconut in his other pants. He met some new friends and became so fascinated with them that he stayed to take a few glasses of wine in town. Meanwhile, a Negro servant entered the boy's palace to ask his wife for a little bread. The princess told him there was neither bread nor the money to buy it with, whereupon the Negro seized his master's pants off the hook and found the magic coconut. When he turned the key in the little lock, the black genie flew out as usual.

"What is your pleasure, my namesake?" he said to the Negro.

"What do you think it will be! Move this palace with all its riches to the other side of the sea, and see that my master wakes up tomorrow as bare as the day he was born."

The following morning, the king heard neither pealing of bells nor bleating of animals. He couldn't understand what was going on, and as soon as light came, he went to look out his window. Lo and behold, the palace had disappeared in the night! He glimpsed only his young son-in-law sleeping with open arms on the ground. Immediately the king commanded that the boy be taken prisoner. His head would come off if he could not produce the palace again in three days' time. After the young palace builder was locked away, the dog and the cat he had saved so long before came and began to scratch on the cell door. The jailor felt sorry for them and ordered the door opened. They ran in to find out why their master was a prisoner. He told them the whole sad tale.

"We're going to go in search of the palace," they said. "But if we don't return by tomorrow, all of us are doomed."

The two animals ran off to the seashore.

"Let's say you will be the horse here," purred the cat to the dog. "After all, you're much bigger than I." With this the cat leaped on the dog's back and they crossed the sea together. On the other shore they walked through the mountains until they found a house, and asked for news of that region. The owner wasn't really sure if anything was going on in those parts, but he volunteered to call somebody who could tell them. Then he piped on a little whistle. Suddenly birds began to swoop down in great flocks, as well as every kind of animal in the world. None of them, however, could say what was new in his part of the world. A mouse and an eagle were missing, so the gentleman blew again and again until they too sped into the gathering. When he asked them where they had been all this time, the eagle said he had become fascinated with eating some intestines in a palace of gold they had found.

"And you," the gentleman asked the mouse, "what have you been fooling around with?"

"I was completely taken with eating some candle stubs," squeaked the mouse excitedly.

"What else did you see?"

"I saw a princess sleeping in the arms of a black man."

"And what else?"

"I saw that the Negro had a coconut in his belly."

"That's just what we want," cried the cat and the dog.

"All right, little mouse," said the gentleman, "take these two fellows and show them the palace." The mouse had hidden himself among the grasses so the cat wouldn't chase him, but the cat and the dog both reassured him that they had no evil intentions.

When the three of them arrived at the palace, the dog said to the cat, "You, being such a good hunter, are going to sneak in and station yourself at the Negro's backside. And you," he said to the mouse," being such a light-foot, will hop on the head of the bed and put your tail up the Negro's nose."

The Negro sneezed violently from the tickling of the mouse's tail. In his convulsion, he farted and blew the coconut way out behind him. The cat snatched it up and made for the door.

"Who's going to carry the coconut?" said the dog, once they were safely outside.

"I'll carry it," said the cat, "for I was the one who nabbed it."

They delivered the little mouse back to the gentleman with the whistle, thanked him kindly, and dashed off to the sea's edge.

"Give me the coconut," said the dog, "and I'll cross over." But the cat refused and said he would make the crossing. "Then get up pickaback," continued the dog. The cat jumped on and they swam out to sea. Suddenly the dog took a great dive, and the cat, trying to hold on, dropped the coconut, which was gobbled up by a fish. When they got to the other shore, the dog naturally asked the cat for the precious nut.

"Ay, my dear," moaned the cat, "back there where you dove, I dropped it while trying to hold on."

"All right, then you must wait for me right here." In his rage, he gave the cat a couple of sound kicks. The poor cat began to sob bitterly. "If I don't arrive by twelve o'clock on the dot," growled the dog, "we're all done for, and our master as well."

The dog swam out to where they had lost the coconut and plunged down as deep as he could. After a very long and futile search, he came out exhausted on the beach where some fishermen were at work with their nets. One of them felt sorry for the bedraggled animal and tossed him a fish. The dog tore open the fish's belly, and after a few gulping bites, he found the coconut and sped back to the sea. The fishermen stood there astounded at the curious sight. Exactly at twelve o'clock, the waterlogged dog got to the tree where the cat was sitting patiently waiting for him.

"Take the coconut, pussy," he barked.

"You take it, my dear. I'm so clumsy I'm afraid I'll drop it again."

They dashed off to the jail and presented the nut to their anxious master. With the coconut in hand, he returned to the site where the palace had been just a few days before. When he turned the key, the black genie zipped out and said, "What is your desire, my first master?"

"I want my palace back with all its riches, and I want the princess to be sleeping in the arms of the black man."

He had hardly uttered these words, when the entire palace appeared just where it had been. The youth went in and sure enough, there was his wife asleep in the black man's arms. He ran to fetch the king. When the old ruler saw how things stood, he said, "You're the husband here. Take the justice that you wish."

Straightway the lad commanded some of his servants to shut up the horses, and others to make two great heaps of wood. Then they lashed the black man hand and foot, tied him to a pole stuck in the middle of the stacks of wood, and set the fire. Dust and ashes were all that remained. After this punishment, the palace builder ordered the two wildest colts in the pasture to be lassoed. They tied a thong to each of the princess's feet and strung her between the colts. The wild creatures were loosed and quickly made two princesses out of one. When the boy had taken his revenge he went to inform his father-in-law. The king answered that it had been well done, after which he sent for his two remaining daughters and told the boy to choose one. The simple lad married the youngest daughter that very day.

Once he was living together with his new wife in the restored palace, the cat and the dog said, "Master, we're not what you think, but really angels from heaven who have come to grant you these riches. From now on you'll have a carefree life, because your new wife is spotless, not a traitor like the first one. Furthermore, on Sunday you must invite your whole court to go to mass. We'll be in the church that day. When the priest takes the host, you will see two little doves on the main altar. We will be those birds, ready to fly into the sky."

It happened just as they had predicted. When the priest consumed the host on the following Sunday, the two doves flew high into heaven. And that's the tale of the magic coconut.

•25• *The Foolish Boy*

• ONCE UPON A TIME there was a fool who walked through the streets selling his apronful of *tortillas,* eating most of them and tossing the rest to the dogs to see them scrap. A princess happened to see him from her window and laughed at the simple boy. Upon hearing the laughter, the lad said, "May God make this princess pregnant by me." He had no sooner said this than she felt herself with child. The princess was up in a tower where she saw no one other than the ladies who came to feed her. One day her mother went to visit her and found her daughter suspiciously fat. She ran downstairs to tell her husband, and when the father saw his daughter, he knew immediately that she was indeed pregnant. Seeing this, the king ordered one hundred of his men to load a ship with supplies. After a month the ship was ready. The princess was taken down from her tower and put aboard, to be left on an island in the middle of the sea on which there was a gigantic rock.

When the boat sailed into the cove of the island, the crew went ashore to turn over the enormous rock. Then they unloaded the boat into the hole, throwing the princess in last of all. The boulder was rolled back into place by the hundred men, and she remained in the dark pit as a prisoner. The months came and went, and in due time she had her little baby boy under the boulder. He began to grow by leaps and bounds. When the boy was ten years old, he started to push and struggle to see if he could lift the great rock and glimpse the light of day, about which his mother had so often told him. The boy got up early every day to strain and sweat with the boulder, until finally his mother told him not to hope, for the stone was lifted before only by a hundred hearty souls. But the intrepid boy persisted, and one day he managed to budge it ever so little, enough to see a crack of daylight. After this, he struggled in earnest with the rock and succeeded in turning it over. As he walked out into the light, he picked some fibrous reeds along the beach and wove a sling out of them. At this point, the boy and his mother had very few provisions left, so the young son went hunting for birds to keep the two of them alive on the lonely island. Very soon, he took to swimming in the sea. One day he took a notion to swim to the opposite shore. He had barely come out on the other side of the sea when a giant stomped up and shouted down to him, "What are you doing here, little earthworm, where not even the birds live?"

"I've come to battle with you," he answered bravely. He leaped upon the giant and fought furiously, bringing him down to the ground.

"If you let me live, all my riches shall be yours," wailed the monstrous man. The boy stripped off his enemy's key ring and went to the giant's palace. He shut the conquered giant in the strongest room there was and locked the door, after which he swam back to the island to get his mother.

"How will you ever get me across the sea?" she asked anxiously.

"I'll carry you pickaback," answered the lad, leaping into the water with the frightened woman.

Once they were safely on the mainland, he took her to the giant's palace and gave her the key ring, taking care to remove the ring to the giant's room and telling his mother never to go near that door. She promised solemnly not to. During these days, the boy kept very busy hunting. While he was out his mother tried every day to see if she could open the forbidden room, but none of the keys she had would fit it. One fine morning, her son changed his clothes and forgot the key in his vest pocket. She rummaged about after he had gone to the fields and found the key she had been hunting for. Opening the special door, she saw the giant looming before her, and almost collapsed to see the great man at the point of death from starvation.

"Don't be afraid, ma'm," groaned the giant, "I'm a man like everybody else. Your son is very brave and has me locked in here."

After she had brought him a meal, the mother returned the key to the same pocket in the boy's vest. He came home that afternoon and found it just as he had left it. Meanwhile his mother kept bringing food to the starving giant whenever her son was out. After a bit she became very intimate with the prisoner. As they were together one day, he asked her how they could possibly kill the boy, for he was very fearless. "Aha," he shouted suddenly, "I have it! You pretend to be sick and tell him that you can be cured only by bacon from the wild boar. Once he goes there, he'll never return, for those are the fiercest beasts in the world. They'll make short work of this chap."

That afternoon the boy arrived to find his mother moaning in bed. "Oh, my son, I feel so terribly sick. I need the bacon from the wild boar."

"Well, how can it possibly be where I can't find it?" he said.

Early the next day, the lad saddled his horse and set out on the hunt. He took a road which led him to the palace of a blind king. A princess came out and received the young man, ushering him in to the king's presence.

"Whither are you bound, young fellow?" asked the blind king. When the boy told of his mission, the king called to his daughter, "Listen, my child, go fetch me such and such a horse and sword. And as for you," he added to the boy, "how little he loves you who sent you on this chase. But at all events, you will go and return. Do you see those green mountains in the distance? There is the haunt of the wild boars. If you arrive when their eyes are open, give it to them with your axe. Then cut out a piece of bacon and pierce it on the tip of your sword, getting as far away as possible by spurring your horse, for if they ever catch you, they'll eat you up in a couple of bites."

The boy did just as he had been told and returned to the king's with his piece of bacon, which he left on the table at the entrance to the palace. Immediately the princess changed the bacon for a piece from an ordinary pig and stored away that of the wild boar. After a visit with the king, the boy received his things from the princess and rode off to his mother. With one chew of the meat, she was immediately better.

When the boy had gone hunting the next day, the giant said to his mother, "Ah, my love, what a brave man your son is. But you're going to make yourself sick again and say that you can recover your health only with the Water of Life."

The boy returned the next afternoon, and exclaimed, "Ave Maria, mama! Sick again? What on earth will bring you health?"

"Yes, I'm ailing, my child. But the Water of Life will cure me for certain."

"How can this water be where I can't find it?" he said.

The following morning he rode off in search of the precious liquid and headed straight for the king's palace.

"Where are you going this time, my good young fellow?" asked the king as the boy rode in.

"I'm looking for the Water of Life, for my mother is very ill."

"Ah, my friend," sighed the king, "how little he loves you who sends you. But, after all, you will go and come back. My daughter," he called to the princess, "bring me such and such a horse and sword for the young gentleman." Then he turned back to the boy. "At twelve o'clock sharp, you're going to arrive where there are some ferocious serpents. If their eyes are open, take the flasks of the Water of Life. If not, leave the water there."

Just as the king had said, the youth arrived at noontime to find the serpents lying about with their eyes open. He immediately seized the precious flasks and ran for it, whipping and spurring his horse in earnest. When the snakes awoke, they rushed fiercely in pursuit, but the young horseman was already far in the distance. He rode into the king's castle with his horse all in a lather and put the flasks of water on the same table. The princess slipped in and changed them for others. After they had served him lunch and changed his horse, he rode away to his mother, who was better with one swig of the water.

When the lad set off hunting once more the following day the giant said to his mother, "Your son is a daring one, all right. How the devil can we kill him? I've got one last idea. You play sick again, and this time you can get better only with three colored apples guarded by my brother, who is stronger and braver than anyone. From this trip the youngster will never return."

The boy found his mother sick a third time and set off for the colored apples, riding first to the king's palace.

"Ay, my lad," said the king sadly, "how little you're loved by the one who sends you. This is a very fierce giant. He keeps me in darkness, for it was he who put out my eyes. But you're going to go, and if you win the battle, ask him for my eyes before you do away with him." Then the king ordered his daughter to bring another horse and sword. This sword weighed seven *quintals* [a little over 700 pounds]. When he was armed and saddled, the youth bade the king and his daughter good-bye and rode off to meet the giant.

"Arrrrh," roared the giant. "What are you doing around here, little earthworm, where not even birds live?"

"I've come to do battle with you," was the answer.

"Good enough, but let's have a bite to eat first." The giant got out his spit and planted it in the ground. Then the boy took his sword and cut off half the cow they were to roast. He ate voraciously and beat the giant in finishing his half of the cow. After dinner, the giant took a little nap. When he arose, he brought two barrels of wine, a little drink for each one. Eventually the time came for the great battle.

"Will it be on foot or horseback?" asked the giant.

"As you wish," answered the boy. "The terms are yours."

They began with swords, taking great strokes at each other until the sparks flew from the steel. With one astute blow the young warrior cut off the giant's right ear, and in a moment more he had knocked the monstrous man to the ground.

"Where are you keeping the king's eyes?" asked the boy.

"I have them in the sole of my right shoe."

The lad hacked open the giant's shoe with his sword. Sure enough, there were the king's two eyes, which he wrapped up and placed carefully in his pocket. After this, he beat the giant with his axe until he killed him. The boy took the three colored apples from the orchard and returned to the king's. Once more the princess took what he had brought and substituted some similar apples on the table. When the boy had presented the overjoyed king with his eyes, the ruler called to his daughter, "Bring this young fellow his horse and keep the one he went to fight on."

The boy's mother was cured with one bite of an apple and the next day her son returned to his hunting as usual.

"What a valiant fellow your son is!" said the giant, unable to believe that the young man had returned unharmed. "But now, you must fake sickness once more and tell him you can be cured only with the black cow's milk."

Finding his mother sick when he came home, the brave young man rode off in search of the black cow's milk, going first to visit the king.

"Ah, my poor boy," moaned the king when he heard of the new mission, "how very little you are loved by whoever sends you. But, anyway, you will go and come back. Do you see that green mountain high up over yonder? There's where the black cow is. Now my daughter will bring you the horse and the sword and a fresh flask so you can milk the cow."

At twelve o'clock sharp, he came to the pasture of the dreaded black cow. He remembered the king's words: "If the cow's eyes are open, you're to take the calf very carefully from the teat he is sucking and fill your flask from that same teat. Then cover the flask, put it in your pocket, and flee for your life."

When the boy had followed these instructions, the cow awoke and stormed after him, shaking the earth with each of her bellows. The daring fellow spurred and whipped his horse on and eventually the monstrous cow tired of the chase and returned to her mountain pasture.

At the palace, the young man handed over the horse and sword, and as before the princess secretly changed the remedy he had brought. He chatted a while with the king and then rode home to cure his mother.

Now the giant was in despair. "I've never seen such a bold one as he is," he moaned to the mother. "But there's one last resort: a very ferocious lioness. If we don't get rid of him on this trip, we never will."

This time the ailing mother told her son that only the milk of the lioness would cure her. He accepted the mission and galloped posthaste to the king for advice. Once more the wise old ruler said, "My boy, my boy, how badly they love you to send you for that. Can you manage to see that bare mountain range over there? That is where the great lioness has her den." The king told his daughter to bring the sword and continued, "You're going to arrive just at noon. If the lioness has her eyes open, put the cub to one side and start milking the mother."

The lad followed the instructions carefully and put the flask of milk in his pocket. He rode away, drawing blood with his spurs, and with the lioness in full pursuit, roaring so as to shake the earth. But she too tired after a long chase, and finding herself far from the mountains, returned to her den.

When the boy had arrived at the castle and the princess had quietly changed the flask of milk for another, the king declared, "This is the last of your trials and sufferings. You have been saved from all the beasts, but now you will not be saved. They're going to kill you when they have you strung up from your hands and feet in the top of an apple tree."

When the boy rode up to his own house, the giant lurched out from the orchard and bellowed, "Now I'm going to make mincemeat out of you."

"Very well, then," replied the boy, "but first I wish to ask one favor of you. I simply want you to behead me without losing a drop of blood. Then cut me in pieces, throw me in a sack, blood and all, and tie me to the tail of my horse, which will carry me away outside the city gates."

The giant did just as the boy requested, and the horse galloped away with his tail straight out so as not to smash the flesh. The faithful steed headed straight for the king's palace. Meanwhile the king had sent his daughter to prepare a bed with virgin linen, bedclothes which had never known sin. When the horse galloped up, the king and the princess rushed out and untied the sack with the greatest of care. They took it to the bedroom and arranged the body piece by piece just as it had been in life. Next they brought the bacon of the wild boar and rubbed it over the wounds. Secondly they sprinkled the black cow's milk over the whole body, adding the lioness's milk as well. Finally they squeezed the three colored apples and put the juice on the wounds, which immediately closed and healed. As a final step, they sprinkled the Water of Life all over the boy. He opened his eyes and was alive.

One sunny morning after the princess had been nursing him for a month and he was now up and about, the king came in.

"Good morning, young man. How are you feeling?"

"I'm very well, your Majesty."

"If that's so, then you can get up for good. But I want to try a little test first. Daughter, bring me the sword that weighs twelve *quintals*" [about 1212 pounds].

When the youth began to swish the sword with the ease of a man flicking a cigarette ash, the king added, "Let's see, my good fellow. Go over to that big rock and give it a whack." The boy couldn't even raise a bit of dust from the rock. "You're still lacking strength," observed the king. "Back to bed with you."

They fed him and cared for him for another month. When he felt ready to get up again, the king told his daughter to bring the sword weighing fourteen *quintals* [about 1414 pounds]. The boy hefted the weapon and went over to the same rock. This time he split it into tiny pieces with only one stroke.

"Now," said the king when he saw this feat, "you can go home without any worries. I'm going to give you this sword and you needn't be afraid of the giant for any reason."

When the giant saw the daring lad coming in the distance, he called to the boy's mother, "Look, woman, there comes that son of yours."

"What do you mean!" she gasped. "You cut him up into tiny pieces and tied him to the horse's tail. Whatever gives you the idea he could possibly come back?"

When they recognized him for sure, it was a dark day for both of them. The boy wanted to attack and finish off his gigantic enemy with a few blows, but the giant fought back fiercely. The youth conquered and killed his foe only after a long and bloody battle. Very soon after, the brother of the first giant appeared and tried to carry off the body, but the young warrior did away with him as well. Now the lad's mother came trembling and kneeled before her son, begging for pardon. Without a moment's hesitation the boy lifted his enormous sword and brought it down, parting the woman in two halves.

After he had ridden back and reported to the king, the old ruler declared, "Now, since you have been saved and because you restored my eyes to me, I'm going to make you my son-in-law." He sent for the priest and bishop, and the princess was married to the brave young warrior. After the ceremonies the king announced, "My son, you are going to be the new king and I will be nothing more than a gentleman of the court."

The young couple became very rich and powerful with all the treasures that the giants had possessed. That is the tale of the fool's son who became a giant killer.

•26• *The Five Brothers*

• THERE WAS ONCE, my dear gentleman, a certain landlord who had five sons. Their names were Pedro, Diego, José, Juan, and Manuel. These boys were so brotherly that if they found even a tiny loaf of bread, they would split it among all five of them. They had two hundred acres of grazing land, animals, nice little houses—everything they needed. But that wasn't enough for these lads. They always wanted to have just a little bit more. One day, Pedro, being the oldest, asked Diego if he would like to make a little trip. It seemed like a good idea and very soon all five brothers had agreed to set out together. Even little Manuel was to go. His brothers loved him very dearly, for he was a brave and manly lad. They were all boys with good manners and a nice way about them. When the plans were made, they went to confer with their father.

"Listen, *taitita*" [affectionate diminutive of "father"], they said (for in those days you called your father by that name), "we'd like very much to make a little trip for a year to see if we can't perhaps bring home a charm that might please you."

"All right, my lads," said their father, "I'll give you my permission." Then he called to Anita, the boys' pretty little sister. "Daughter, make your brothers something to take with them on their journey."

The following day, the old gentleman gave them his blessing. At the end of a year's time they had to return to their father's house alive and well. He wouldn't have any dead men on his hands! But God will help them, for with the parents' blessing, the young ones make out well. The five brothers set out on the way and came about noontime to a fork of five roads, just like the fingers on your hand. Pedro assigned a road to each of the five of them and said, "We're going to take a little snack before we part. After one year, we'll all meet here to return to our parents' house with something for our sister, who will surely be praying for us." Each of the brothers set out on his own road.

Pedro came to the house of a man who was, by profession, an excellent thief. This man hired him for a companion, for he noticed that the boy had just the right kind of build for slick robberies. The thief began to teach the boy all his trade, boasting that he had no equal and had never been caught. After six months Pedro knew three times what his master did, for he would go and take something right from under your nose. When you looked, he didn't have a blessed thing. Imagine how light-fingered he must have been!

The second brother, Diego, arrived at the cabin of a great hunter. This man took him in as a companion to hunt birds in the forest. After five days, Diego had become a better hunter than his master. What an eye he had for that business! After six months, he knew so much that he didn't even have to look before he aimed. Diego, king of the hunters!

Meanwhile the third brother, José, came to the house of an old bone-setter. People came to this man all broken and falling apart to get treatment. José stopped there and learned from this true master. After six months he too was better than the teacher himself. A man would come in with fractured bones and José would leave him like new, as if he'd never had a break in his life. What hands the boy had!

Juan arrived at the dwelling of an old man who raised the dead. The cadavers came in every day, and after little Juan had been at this job for three months, he raised them better than the old resuscitator himself. Now there was nothing more to teach him of this art.

Manuel, the youngest brother, ended up at the house of a fortune-teller, who taught the boy his trade. Manuel learned to know where his father, his family, and his brothers were and what profession they had. He soon did all this even better than the master, for Manuel felt it as a gift in his head. When a year was up, he said, "My brother Pedro is on his way to the little tree where the five roads part." Can you imagine? He knew even then that his brothers were headed home. He bade good-bye to the old man, and went to join them.

They all arrived at the junction, each one with his suitcase full of money and dressed to the teeth. When Manuel shuffled in, he asked, "Tell me, what professions do you bring, brothers? If you wish, I'll tell you myself. You, Pedro, are an excellent thief. Diego has become a great hunter, José a fine bone-setter, and Juanito an expert at raising the dead. In case you haven't guessed, I'm a furtune-teller. Now then, in this tree there's a partridge. Kill it, my good hunter." Diego took aim and shot down the bird with ease. "All right, José," added Manuel, "now arrange the bird." As José was busy taking the bird to pieces and dressing it, Pedro slipped over and stole one of the wings. The partridge was all dressed except for the one missing wing. Manuel turned to Pedro and said, "Give it over now, brother."

"It's true enough that you're a professional at this," answered Pedro, for he realized that Manuel could divine just about anything. When the partridge was whole again, with its wing restored, Manuel continued, "Come on, Juan, bring this bird to life." And there on the spot Juan did it. "Pi-pi-pi! Pi-pi-pi!," squawked the bird as it flew into the brush. Now that each of the brothers had made a test of his gift, they all went to present themselves before their father.

"Here they come!" shouted the rest of the family from the front door. The five brothers were received in fitting style, each one coming in well groomed and carrying his great suitcase full of belongings.

"Well, well, my lads," said their father, "Let's see what professions you have brought home."

"I," spoke up Pedro proudly, "I am a fine thief."

"Then be off with you," roared the father. "I want no thieves in my house."

"But Our Lord died between two thieves," said the others, "and the good thief is our brother, Pedro."

"What's your profession, Diego?" continued the old man.

"I'm a great hunter."

"And you, José?"

"I'm a bone-setter."

"Ah, very fine," said their father. "It just happens that I want my leg set, and you're the one to do it." When the father had asked Juan, he turned to Manuel, who had been standing by watching quietly.

"And you, little Manuel, what have you brought home to me?"

"Why, I'm a fortune-teller," answered the boy calmly.

"A fortune-teller?"

"Yes, I was just foreseeing the things you were going to say to my brothers."

"How did you know?" asked his father, gaping at his youngest son.

"Each one has his profession, and you should be thankful," answered Manuel.

Now it so happened that there was a king who lived nearby and had heard that the sons of such and such a gentleman had come home with some exceptional gifts and great riches. Someone had stolen a princess from this king five years ago and he had no idea where she was to be found. He knew that one of the brothers was reputed to have become a fortune-teller and it occurred to him that this might be the solution to his problem.

At the same time, Manuel was divining and announced to his

brothers, "The king is thinking, boys, and a voyage is going to befall us soon."

"Why is that?" they all chorused, astounded.

"Because the one who has this princess is Old Long Arms, who lives in the sea's current on the other side of the Island of Ivories. This tremendous giant is guarding her there, and we've got to go to search for her. The king will arrive to get us at ten o'clock."

"I'll believe that when I see it," scoffed the father in a huff.

When the king did arrive, it was two minutes before ten.

"Good day, my good man," he called to the boys' father. "Are these five fellows your sons? I want to know which one is the fortune-teller."

"I'm the one," spoke up Manuel. "Are you he that comes in search of his daughter?"

The king marveled at the boy's foresight and asked if the brothers dared to look for his girl.

"Why not? Of course, your Highness," they all answered. "We shall go to the Island of Ivories."

"As soon as you bring her home, the one of you who works the most on this task shall be her husband." The king offered to give them a crew for the long trip, but the five brothers preferred to go alone, for they knew well enough how to work together and manage a boat. Without losing a moment, they set out for the Island of Ivories, sailing straight as an arrow on their course. Those boys were no fools!

"Look, Pedro," said Manuel as they sailed up to the island, "you'll be the one to steal the princess from Old Long Arms. I'll tell you where she is hidden. Diego can take a shot at the giant if necessary."

So Pedro slipped into the castle and grabbed the princess so fast that she didn't know what was happening until they had her in the boat. They were all sailing away from the island when Manuel cried out, "Take aim, Diego, Old Long Arms is about to fall upon us!" The giant was following them, planning to crush the little boat, which was still just off shore. As the giant loomed into view, Diego took a quick shot and broke one of his arms. The brothers sailed on in peace. Soon Manuel began to relax with the rolling of the waves and forgot all about his duty. Suddenly Old Long Arms dropped his good arm on the little boat and smashed it to splinters. But José, the bone-setter, reconstructed the ship in a few minutes, leaving it as good as new. The brothers climbed back aboard with the princess and were sailing on, when the girl fainted and died on the floor of the little craft. Right away, Juan, who had learned to raise the dead, came and revived her. As they sailed on, Old Long Arms came into sight once more, but this time Diego took careful aim and shot the giant down for good. There were no more misadventures, and they landed with the true princess of the realm. It had been five years since she was carried away by the wicked giant from the Island of Ivories. The king was leaping with joy at the arrival of his long-lost daughter. When she told her father all the adventures of the trip, it appeared that all five brothers claimed to have worked the hardest and to have gained her hand in marriage.

"She's mine, she's mine," shouted Manuel. "I knew where she was."

"And what about the boat which I repaired?" answered José.

"And if it weren't for my killing Old Long Arms, we'd never have gotten here," put in Diego.

"Without me," added Pedro, "you never would have stolen her."

"And I, after all, brought her back to life," concluded Juan.

"Just a minute. Hold your horses," intervened the king, "Each of you is going to shoot an arrow so that you can realize your folly. Five men can hardly marry one woman."

The deal was on. Pedro took up the bow first and shot the arrow fifty yards. Diego came for his turn and shot it sixty yards, José a few inches more, and Juan just a step further.

"Let's see mine," shouted Manuel as he shot. "There it goes beyond the others. The lady is mine!" Manuel had won by a good twenty-five yards.

"I have five daughters," announced the king, "and each of them is going to marry one of you boys."

That was the end of the squabble. The king himself married them all, baptized them, and gave the five true men his blessing. Manuel became their king, and all lived happily together as true Christians in this life.

· Now you're going to hear the tale of the Jewel Stone. There were two brothers, one very rich and the other very poor. The poor one gained his livelihood selling wood in the village to maintain his little children. One day he was out scratching around with his burros. He was picking up *relvun* [a Chilean herb] from around a *litre* bush, one of those with the open branches which droop to the ground thick and big. Along about sunset, when dusk was already gathering, the old fellow heard a voice say, "Open Jewel Stone." At the same moment a big stone rolled away on a nearby cliff that was very beautiful and seemed like the wall of a house. Out from the gaping hole rode fourteen bandits. The woodcutter stayed silent as a mouse, counting those fourteen souls all mounted on their horses. The captain of the band began to assign everybody his part, one, two, three, where they were to stage their holdups.

About an hour after they had ridden away, the poor man crept as silently as could be out of the *litre* plant, where he had been hidden in the branches, and said with the same voice, "Open Jewel Stone." Immediately the stone rolled back, revealing a most precious thing in the form of a palace with all manner of riches, money, clothes, spurs, lassos for the robberies, and what not. They were very accomplished bandits and naturally their cave had to be a treasure house. In a few minutes he had taken all he could, loaded his burros with gold and silver, and set out for home. He told his wife about the great find and warned her not to go spreading the news.

After this stroke of good fortune, the man began to arrange his house bit by bit, for it was a ramshackle affair. In a year's time he had fixed it up and built a little inn where people could lodge, especially the drivers with their animals. He was going up rapidly in the world. Eventually his rich brother came to visit him. As the richer you are the more you want, this brother was astounded and curious to find out how his brother had become so wealthy.

"Good afternoon, my brother," he called cordially.

"Good afternoon. Ah, and now I see that I'm 'brother,' when before I was always just 'old burro driver.'"

"Yes, that's how it goes," said the other. "But what luck have you had to have become richer than I, with such a pretty little house and all that you have here?"

"Aha, I'm going to tell you a secret. In such and such a place where the *litre* bush is, there is a lovely rock that's called The Jewel Stone. Fourteen bandits came out of it, and inside I found silver, gold, and everything beautiful and precious."

"Well, for heaven's sake, let's go there without wasting any time," said the other.

When the plans were made, each one took his four burros and went to hide in the branches of the *litre* bush. As darkness fell, the poor brother whispered, "This is about the time." In a few moments more, they heard a noise and then a voice which said, "Open Jewel Stone." The great stone rumbled back. As quietly as could be the fourteen bandits rode out on horseback. The captain gave each one his orders, and they galloped away for a night of robbery. The old woodcutter calculated about an hour of time after they had gone. Then he sneaked over to the stone and said bravely, "Open Jewel Stone." Straightway it fell aside, and he saw all the riches stored inside. The two brothers loaded their burros and sped away with the treasure, saying as they left, "Close tight, Jewel Stone." The great stone returned just as it had been before.

The next day the rich man urged his poor brother to return for more, but the other cautioned him that it was not wise to try again so soon. Nevertheless, the second brother was so full of greed that he went alone to the *litre* bush. The bandits appeared as usual and rode away into the country. After waiting the necessary time, the rich brother approached the stone and repeated the magic words. After the stone had rolled away, he filled his saddlebags with the best gold in the cave. When he was set to leave, he realized that he had completely forgotten the name of the stone. "Open Long Stone," he called. "Open Lovely Stone." But the stone wouldn't budge. Much later, as dawn was breaking, he heard the hoofbeats of the band returning to the cave. What in the devil was he to do? Since there was a big cask nearby, he slipped inside. The captain of the bandits came in with a light and spotted the stuffed saddlebags.

"Who's robbing us? We're going to search the place from top to bottom," he yelled in a rage. The other bandits rushed in and began to jab at everything they saw. One was leaning on the very cask where the man was hidden.

"Hey, captain," he said, "we haven't turned over this cask yet."

They all set to pushing and tugging until they found the poor fellow inside. They stripped him of his clothes on the spot and sliced him open, just as you would a pig. They washed him down and left him cut open on the top of a dining table to see if by chance there were two men or only one.

When the rich brother didn't return home the next day, his wife went to the other brother and told him.

"What can we do about it?" said the poor brother's wife. "We haven't seen hide nor hair of him."

"He has to show up, he simply has to," wailed the other's wife.

"But he didn't go out with me," added the poor brother. "No sir, not at all! Why should I have to look for him? For heaven's sake! I told him a thousand times that it was too early to go again. But I'll go have a look, just in case he's at the cave."

In the afternoon the poor brother set off with his four burros and waited under the *litre* bush for the bandits to ride out. When they were gone, he slipped into the cave. The first sight his eyes beheld was his brother cut wide open on top of the table. "Just as I thought he would be," said the poor fellow to himself. He put his brother tenderly in a sack, all wrapped in a sheet, and loaded him on a burro, just as he had done before with the sacks of gold.

When the bandits arrived after daybreak, they didn't find the corpse, and thought the *lola* [a mythological monster] had taken it.

"What can we do?" said the captain. "I knew there were two at this game. It has to be the old woodcutter who's in on this, because the other looked like his brother, the rich man. Now here's my plan: each of us is going to spread out through the town to see if we can pick up some news. Let's get going."

After breakfast the next morning, each of the bandits set off for a given spot in search of the old woodcutter. It so happened that the poor man lived near a shoemaker, whom he had hired to come to the cemetery and bury his brother's corpse. Of course, the old shoemaker was blindfolded first so he wouldn't know whom he was burying. Since the pay was good, he had done the job gladly. By chance, one of the bandits passed through the part of town where this shoemaker had his shop and asked him to repair one of his heels. When the repairs were promptly finished, the bandit paid the little man.

"Why, I have some of this same money here," said the cobbler, looking wide-eyed at the bandit's coins, for it was not a coin well known in those parts. "They called me several days back," he continued, "to go and bury a corpse, but I didn't know who it was. They paid me with the same coins you are carrying." This was enough for the bandit, who hurried back to report to his captain.

"That's that," said the chief bandit, "we'll be off to the wood-cutter's little inn, for he's the culprit behind this mess. I'll load up with olive oil which I'll pretend to sell at the inn. You," he said to his companions, "will be inside the barrels. Once I lodge at the inn for the night, you can come out and massacre the poor man and his family."

The captain took seven casks in his load, one with olive oil and the others with his men inside. He presented himself at the inn as a mule driver. The wife of the poor brother bought a bottle of the oil and found it delicious. She and her husband took care of the inn with the help of a very clever little girl whom they had brought up.

"I'm just going to try the mule driver's oil," said this girl to herself as she picked up a big jar to get a sample. When she passed one of the barrels, a bandit called out, "Is it time yet?" for he thought the captain was coming to check.

"No," she answered, not at all taken aback, "not yet. I've come to make sure you're not sleeping." She was not at all afraid and passed by all the casks, noticing that all but one were full of men. She ran to the hostess, calling, "Come quickly, mama, you'd better see how the stew is cooking." The old lady excused herself from the table where the bandit captain was taking a few drinks.

"Don't you realize," whispered the girl, "that the barrels are full of people?"

"These are the bandits, all right, the bandits of the Jewel Stone unless I miss my guess," said the poor man's wife. "Listen, I'm going to call on you to sing me a *cueca* [Chilean folk dance] while I dance. We're going to make a big catch right here."

Meanwhile, her husband, having no idea of what was up, continued chatting with the mule driver.

"My good fellow," said the woman, approaching the driver, "why don't we dance a little *cueca*. My feet are simply freezing." He accepted, and on the first pass of the dance, the hostess pulled a long hook from under the bed and stuck it secretly in her belt. On the second pass, she let the driver have it in the belly and spilled his guts all over the floor.

"What in the world have you done, my love?" gasped her husband.

"Arm yourself," she shouted, "the whole inn is full of bandits!"

The woodcutter grabbed an old saber he had, the young girl took her potato-peeling knife, and the three of them knocked on the first barrel.

"Is it time?" called the muffled voice from inside. When the hostess said yes, they cut off the first bandit's head as he emerged, and proceeded to do the same with all the rest. When the whole bunch lay dead and headless, they notified the town, the police, and the criminal judge. Everybody realized immediately that these were the bandits of the Jewel Stone, but nobody knew where it was.

"I can tell you all about it," spoke up the woodcutter.

When the judge came to examine the goods, he said, "Why, this harness is mine." Someone else spoke up, "And that mule is mine." It turned out that everything the thieves had belonged to somebody in the town. Then the robbers were carried out of town in a cart. There was a cemetery nearby, but the populace preferred to simply dump them in a ravine. After this, the whole town followed the little woodcutter to the Jewel Stone. He commanded it to open, whereupon the biggest treasure trove anybody had ever seen gleamed before them all. There was simply everything inside, even fruit.

With this great discovery, the judge declared that the towns-people would get half the money and that the rest would go to the woodcutter's daughter, for she had done the real work. That was how the poor brother became rich. Everybody found his own goods in the cave and returned happily to town. Thus ends the little tale of the famous Jewel Stone.

·28· *Blanca Rosa and the Forty Thieves*

• A CERTAIN WIDOWER had a beautiful daughter called Blanca Rosa who was the living image of her mother. The mother, upon dying, had left the girl a little magic mirror and had told her daughter that if she ever wanted to see her, she need only take out her looking glass and it would give her her desire. After some time, the widower married again, this time to a very envious woman. When the stepmother saw the daughter talking all day with her mirror, she took it away from her. This lady considered herself the most beautiful woman in the world. She asked the mirror, "Who is the most lovely of all women?" The mirror answered, "Your daughter." As the little glass didn't flatter her with the right answer, she became furiously envious and ordered her daughter killed. The men who were supposed to do the job abandoned the girl, and a little old man helped her.

Meanwhile the stepmother asked the mirror once again who was the most beautiful woman in the world. "Your daughter, who is still alive," was the answer. In a rage, she called for the little old man who had helped the girl and sentenced him to death if he didn't bring her the tongue and the eyes of her daughter. Now, the old fellow had a pet dog with blue eyes. Seeing that he couldn't defend the poor girl, he decided to kill the dog and convince the stepmother that he had followed orders. After this, he left Blanca Rosa to God's care in the forest. The stepmother was very pleased when he brought her the blue eyes and the tongue on a silver platter.

For a long while the life of Blanca Rosa was sad and full of pain until one day she came upon the hideout of forty thieves.

One morning when she had perched high in the crown of a tree, she observed a band of men leaving the forest. The girl climbed down to the den from which they had emerged and was dazzled and amazed to see all manner of jewels and delicious dishes. The good food was what she most wished for so she crept in and ate to her heart's content, returning afterward to the tree top and falling into a deep sleep.

When the thieves returned to their lair, they found everything strewn about and suspected that somebody had found them out. The leader, however, didn't think so, but left a guard at the entrance just to make sure. When they had all gone off on their forays the next day, Blanca Rosa came down again. The guard saw her and was fascinated with such great beauty. He believed that she was a being descended from heaven and dashed off pell-mell to give the rest the news. But when they returned to the camp, nobody put much stock in what he said. After this, the chief ordered five men to stand guard to see about this strange apparition. All of them saw Blanca Rosa and reported the same news, believing that it was the Virgin of Heaven come to punish them. Meanwhile Blanca Rosa took her pleasure in the hideout while the thieves were away. On their return, they found nobody. The chief himself decided to stand guard, for he couldn't be convinced of all these goings-on. Great was his surprise when he saw Blanca Rosa descend from the tree. Never before had he seen such a beautiful woman. He begged her pardon, thinking that she was surely the mother of God, and called his companions to repent and adore her. But Blanca Rosa, full of anguish, protested that she was not the Virgin, but rather only a poor orphan cast out of her stepmother's house. The only thing she wished was shelter so as not to die of hunger in her solitude. The thieves refused to believe this and continued to worship her as the Virgin. They built her a throne of gold, dressed her with the most lovely dresses, and adorned her with the most precious jewels. From that day on, Blanca Rosa lived happy and content among her robber "relatives."

It was rumored in the city that there was in the forest a den of thieves who adored a beautiful woman. When the stepmother got wind of this, she refused to believe it, and insisted that she was the only beautiful one in the world.

"Little mirror," she asked the charm, "by the power God has given you, tell me who is the most beautiful of all."

"Blanca Rosa is the most beautiful woman," answered the little glass.

In desperation, the stepmother sought out a sorceress and offered her a great sum of money if she would only kill the lovely stepdaughter. The old witch searched through the forest until she found the hideout and, with lies, cajoleries, and flatteries, was able to see Blanca Rosa. When the old charmer was sure it was the right girl, she pretended to be a poor woman who wished to show her gratitude for some gold that the girl had once given her. She handed the girl a basket of fruit, but Blanca Rosa told the old woman to keep it, for she already had a great deal.

"If you won't accept this bit of fruit," croaked the old lady, "at least let me touch your dress and run my hand over your silky hair." She stroked Blanca Rosa's head and jabbed her with a magic needle. Instantly the girl dropped into a deep, deep sleep. The old hag slipped out in a wink and went to the stepmother to tell her that her daughter would trouble her no longer.

When the thieves arrived at the forest lair, they found their precious queen sleeping. As she didn't stir for many days, they believed her dead. After great weeping and many efforts to revive her, they resigned themselves to the task of the burial. Her outlaw friends placed her in a casket made of pure gold and silver, dressing her beautifully and adorning her with the most exquisite necklaces and pearls. They sealed her in against the least little drop of water and threw the casket into the sea.

Now there was in a certain city a prince who lived with his two old maid sisters and was very fond of fishing. One day he was out in his launch pulling in some nets when he saw in the waves something that sparkled and shone over the waters. Anxious to find out about this mystery, he called some fishermen to help him land the beautiful floating casket. They loaded it into his boat and he took it home, shutting himself in his own room. The casket was riveted so tight that he couldn't open it until he brought his whole tool kit to the task. After seven days and seven nights of labor, he removed the lid and found the girl dressed with such lovely garments and jewels. He tenderly removed the body and placed it on his bed, where he stripped it of its clothes and removed the jewels one by one, puzzling over the mystery of this person. When he found nothing, it occurred to him to comb her silken hair. The comb got snarled on a little bump, which the prince removed with a pair of tweezers. Immediately the fair girl sprang to life, and he realized that she had been bewitched all the time.

"Where are my thieves?" cried Blanca Rosa, seeing herself alone with this man she had never met, and totally nude. To console the distraught girl, the prince began to tell her the tale of how he had found her floating over the waves, assuring her that he was a good man and that there was nothing to fear. She would not be calmed and insisted on leaving, so the prince drove the needle back into her head and walked out to think what he could possibly do with the lovely maiden. Meanwhile the two old maid sisters were at their wit's end to see what their brother was doing locked in his room day and night. He hadn't even appeared to eat. They began to keep watch through the keyhole. Great was their shock when they spied a golden casket and heaps of jewels.

The prince returned to his room after long thought and removed the needle once again from Blanca Rosa's head. He told her he had not been able to find the forty thieves and asked her to remain in his house under his protection, as his wife. If she didn't wish to go into the street, she could remain in her room and nobody would know the secret.

One fine morning when the prince had gone off to fish and had left the sad and melancholy Blanca Rosa in her room, the two sisters were seized with curiosity and opened the door. They were very indignant at seeing such a pretty girl seated on the bed. Immediately they stripped her of her fine clothing and necklaces and threw her nude into the street. Blanca Rosa frantically tried to hide and eventually arrived, breathless, at the house of an old cobbler. She was crying so bitterly that the old man took her in and hid her. The prince arrived home and found her room empty with the clothes strewn on the floor. Disconsolate, he wandered aimlessly in search of the lovely girl until someone told him of a beautiful young woman at the cobbler's house. Sure enough, he found Blanca Rosa there and took her joyfully back to his own place, where he began the preparations for the wedding. As a punishment for his sisters, the prince sent for two wild horses and had the old maids bound to them head and foot. The bucking broncos tore them into a thousand pieces. Immediately after this, the wedding was celebrated with great pomp. The forty thieves attended at Blanca Rosa's request and brought the bride many marvelous gifts. She and the prince lived very happily for all the rest of their lives.

•29• *Juanita*

• THERE WAS ONCE a young housemaid who had a baby girl. The child's godmother asked for the baby, for the girl hardly had the means to care for her. The lady brought the child up and later delivered her to the Virgin Mary. The little girl grew up to become the nursemaid of the little angels up above. One day, when she was well grown, the Virgin said to her, "Juanita, I'm going out and will be a while. I want you to stay here in the house and take care of these children. See that they don't fall out of heaven. I'll give you the keys and you can open all the doors except this one, which you must never touch."

The girl agreed, but spent three days thinking, "Why doesn't my mother want me to open that special door? What can she possibly have in there?" Finally she gave in and opened it just a little crack. Seeing how beautiful it was inside, she opened the door just a bit more. Of course glory is beautiful. It has to be! When Juanita had taken a good look, she closed the door carefully, but the key was already stained. A little later, the Virgin arrived and looked over the household.

"Look here, Juanita, did you open that door?"

"No, mother, I didn't."

"No, Juanita?"

"No, I tell you I didn't touch it," she insisted firmly.

"Bah," said the Virgin, "I'm going to take you a long way from here for you to die, for the dogs and birds to eat you."

She didn't throw Juanita out, but rather set her on top of a thorn bush and abandoned her. Nearby there happened to be a palace. The prince was out for a walk when he found the girl. How lovely she must have been, what with such a strict upbringing in glory!

"Ah, young miss, what are you doing in this thorn bush?" he asked.

"Here my mother left me, and here I have stayed," answered Juanita sorrowfully.

"Well, it's time enough now," said the prince, lifting her down and carrying her away to the palace, where shortly after he married her.

This same prince had a ranch far off which he had to visit to check on his workers. When his wife was expecting a child, the prince said to his mother, "Mama, I've got to ride out to the ranch for a few days. I want you to care for my wife as you would the loveliest flower."

"Go along, son. You know how I esteem her. Don't have so little trust in your old mother."

"When the day of birth comes," continued the prince, "find her the best midwife in town."

His mother assured him that all would be well, and the young husband rode off peacefully to his ranch. When his wife was ready to bear the child, the midwife came and a beautiful little baby boy was born. The prince's mother and the midwife stayed nearby to care for the child. One day Juanita fell asleep, and the Virgin came to steal the baby, leaving the poor mother covered with blood. When she awoke she looked frantically about, wondering where her child had gone.

The mother-in-law got wind of this and flew into the room screaming, "You shameless bitch! You swine! You ate him up." When her son arrived home, she was still ranting. "Listen, my son, your woman had a beautiful boy, but she devoured him before you got back."

"She devoured him, mother?" he asked, astounded. "How could she possibly do that?"

"She ate him up," insisted the old woman. "He just disappeared and nobody knew a thing about it. You have to kill her."

The prince refused, saying he had not the heart to slay his own wife, whatever she had done. Some time later she was expecting another baby, and the prince once again announced that he had to visit the ranch. This time, he instructed his mother to bring two midwives and to be especially careful. But a few days after the birth, the young mother fell asleep again and lost her child. When she awoke she began groping anxiously for her baby, remembering with terror how she had lost the first one. Once more the mother-in-law dashed into the room in a fit.

"Now you've gone and eaten it! Look how the blood is all over the blankets! We've got to kill you for sure this time."

The poor distraught mother was left all alone without even a midwife to care for her. When the prince returned, the queen declared, "Don't you realize now? She did the same thing again. She gobbled the child up whole."

"But, mama," he protested, "how is she going to eat up a baby?"

The prince insisted that it was impossible, and after much struggle succeeded in calming his mother. By the time his wife was expecting a third child, he had to visit the ranch again. He cautioned his mother to take great care and find out just what was going on. This time the old lady brought three midwives. They made the mother very comfortable and took excellent care of her. Nevertheless, Juanita was once again heavy with sleep, and when she dropped off, the Virgin came and stole the third baby as well, leaving the poor mother spotted with drops of blood.

"Madam, for the love of God," screamed Juanita to her mother-in-law, "where is the child?"

"You've eaten him alive," shrieked the queen. "This must surely be your end."

"But how can you imagine that I would eat him? I fell asleep and haven't any idea what happened. Or have you hidden the baby from me?"

"No, you ate him and you'll die for this," said the queen menacingly. But the king opposed her until the prince got home.

"Ay, my son," wailed his mother, "look what your bitch has done! She gobbled up the child alive." When the prince again refused to believe this, the queen was all the more furious. "Death is the only path for this woman," she raged. The prince was heavily grieved.

Finally the king intervened and called to the great men of the court, "Bring seven cartloads of wood and make a castle of logs here." They built the wood up in a great pile, lifted the prince's wife to the top, and kindled the fire. They had stuck in branches, dry leaves, and what not, but the flames wouldn't catch. There was nothing but a little smoke.

"What's going on?" said the king. "Haven't you lit the logs yet?"

"It doesn't want to light, your highness," protested his men.

He ordered them to blow harder, and finally the flames caught and roared hungrily at the logs. Just at this moment a woman appeared with two children walking beside her and a third in her arms. When Juanita looked down from the top of the bonfire, she cried out, "My mother!"

"Aha, am I your mother?" asked the woman. "Didn't you open the forbidden door when I left you?" Juanita was silent. "I'm going to ask you three times," said the woman, "and if you don't answer, I'll let you burn alive. Did you open that door or not?"

"Yes, mother," answered Juanita shyly.

"Well, why did you deny it to me?"

"Because you had said you would be angry with me."

"Ah, don't you see everything you've had to suffer for that?" said the Virgin. "Now come down from there."

"But I can't get down," wailed Juanita as the flames licked closer.

"Just come right on down," said the Virgin, lifting up her hands. Juanita fell into her arms from the top of the great crackling pile of logs. "Well, well, let's be off home now," soothed the Virgin, tenderly holding the girl.

In the palace, the prince was weeping bitterly for his wife. All of a sudden, there she was before him! The Virgin greeted the young husband and asked him, "Do you know these three children?"

"No," answered the prince, "I can't say that I do."

"They are yours," she answered, "and your mother and father

believed they had been eaten by your wife. It was really a punishment I was administering. I brought up your wife and I carried away the children because of a lie she once told me. But now you two are going to be together, not here in this palace, but in another place. I'll take you there immediately."

The prince picked up one of the children, his wife another, and the Virgin the third, and they all set off together. The Virgin left them a couple of blocks from the palace and said, "Now, Juanita, look back at the house of your mother-in-law." Juanita looked and saw that the whole palace was being consumed in flames. "Do you see," continued the virgin, "that the mother and father condemned themselves for what they were up to, and you have been saved. Now, when it is time, I will come for you."

> That is the end of the tale,
> Which sprouted in a bean stalk
> And came out through a broken shoe

Part III
Religious Tales

Food for the Crucifix

· THERE WAS ONCE A poor man who had one little boy whom he granted as godson to a rich gentleman. Such was the lad's ill fortune that one Friday his mother died. A few days later his father followed her to the grave. Then the rich man and his wife took the little boy in to bring him up. As he grew he became very conceited and remained quite ignorant. When he was about fourteen years old, both his godparents died, leaving him an orphan without any resources. Finding himself all alone, he was quite lost and finally decided to go in search of work. Eventually he came to a large house full of men and women. It seemed like a logical place to find a job, so the lad presented himself to a priest who was nearby.

"This is no work," answered the father, "this is the mass. But I'm going to give you the job of sacristan, passing out books and so on."

One day when he was in the church, the boy saw a very thin, wounded man. "Who can this man be," he thought, "that they don't give him anything to eat? I've never seen anyone so skinny before. He's going to be my friend." He walked over to the man and said, "Help yourself to some food from this plate, my friend." In a flash the food disappeared, and the boy was astounded. "Thanks be to God that he has now eaten," he said.

The priest came a little later to seek his young helper, because a sick man was waiting to confess. When he saw the man, the lad began to cry and paid no attention to his job, which was to hold the candle for the priest. The next day, they came to get the priest to confess a young girl. While he was assisting, the boy began to clap his hands and laugh happily.

"Why don't you take care of your duties?" scolded the priest. On the way home, he asked the boy why he had cried the first time and laughed the second.

"You didn't see anything, sir," he answered. "Yesterday the buzzards were eating that poor sick man alive. They were plucking out his eyes and tongue. I cried to see such a sad sight. And this young girl today—there were doves of every color flying about her head. I laughed from my joy at seeing the birds and some angels that came to meet her."

"Well, well," replied the priest, "let's go home and have some lunch."

This boy continued to take his thin friend meals at all hours. It always seemed to him that the man ate the food. One day the priest was asked to marry a couple. He invited his assistant to go along too, telling him that this looked like a great celebration. The boy ran to find his friend and invited him to the wedding too. The three of them all went to the festivities together. When they arrived at the house, the priest asked the host to give the boy some of his best liquor. But the lad immediately gave his glass to his friend, who drank it down in one swig. The hours flew by, and everybody got tipsy. The liquor went to the priest's head so fast that he began flirting with the maid and finally went to bed with one of the girls at the party.

"Take the priest home now," the boy's friend said to him. "It's high time for him to go."

"Come on, master," called the boy to the priest, "it's getting very late."

"Yes, yes, all right," called back the priest, disengaging himself reluctantly from the ladies. They returned to the church, and the boy went to see his friend home.

When the young sacristan came to serve the thin man breakfast the next morning, the friend spoke for the first time. "Look here, you know your master is condemned, don't you?"

"Why do you say that? How can it be?"

"Because he was playing around with the maid and was also coupled with one of the girls at the wedding."

The lad returned to the priest and said, "Master, you are condemned."

"What! Who ever told you that?"

"The friend I have there inside the big house," said the boy, pointing to the church.

"Well, who on earth is this friend?"

"That man all flesh and bones who is standing there so bruised and hurt. He was the one with whom we went to the wedding."

"You go in and ask your friend how I am to be saved. Now run along about it," urged the priest, nervously wiping his brow.

The lad trotted in obediently to the thin man. "Friend, save my master for me."

"No, he cannot be saved."

"How can that be?" cried the sad little sacristan.

"Go tell your master that he has to study all over again to be a priest. The day he can sing the Gloria will be the day in which he is saved."

From that moment the priest began to study in earnest to be ordained anew. The day he sang the Gloria he was saved, and the maid and the other girl were condemned. Then the Lord Jesus told the boy that they were going to leave together. When they got to heaven, the lad exclaimed, "Good Lord, friend, here you don't even give me anything to eat! When I was with my master, I at least brought you buckets of coffee and plenty of food and drink."

The Lord Jesus went to fetch the host. The boy gobbled it up and entered into glory, where he is even to this day along with his friend.

That's the end of the little tale. It went through a broken shoe, so another one is due.

· *31* · *The Poor* Compadre

> To know and to tell
> A lie does quite well.
> I walked by a creek
> Thrashing my stick,
> I went through the corner
> Stumbling along.

· ONCE THERE WAS A MAN, not so rich and not so poor either. His wife was expecting a child. When the baby was born in the night, the man said, "It's a boy. Now, the first person to arrive tomorrow, be he rich or poor, old or young, will be the *compadre* [godfather] of my child. The next day as dawn was breaking, the new father got up and saw a poor little old man standing in the door.

"Good morning, *compadre*," said the father. "Come on in." He took the man to see his wife, announcing that the *compadre* had arrived. But the old fellow was hardly to her liking. Then the man asked for three days' time in order to bring clothes for his new godson. Sure enough, at the end of that time, he returned with all kinds of boys' clothing, even a cute little hat. Once the baby was dressed, he looked as fine as if he had just arrived from the best tailor. The parents tried some other clothes on the child, but they weren't as good as those brought by the kindly godfather. As soon as the mother was able to get up, they took the child to be christened. Afterwards the old man said, *"Compadre,* when my godchild wishes to come to me, give him your blessings."

As the boy grew up, his clothes grew along with him. The clothes his mother and father gave him didn't fit any more, but those of his godfather continued to be just right. They never tore or got dirty, but became even prettier and more sparkling clean every day. Eventually, the lad was sent to school, where he was a very studious pupil with an excellent memory. But now that he was a big boy, the other students used to tease him every day. "You little bum, if it weren't for your godfather, you wouldn't have any clothes."

One day when he was about nineteen, a good boy but ignorant, he said to his father, "Papa, I want to go to find my godfather. The clothes I have were given me by him, and those you've given me are no good."

"All right, my son, the old man told me to let you go whenever you asked."

His parents blessed him and he set off on the search. He had hardly left the house when he found himself at his godfather's, for the old fellow already knew he was coming.

"My godson, have you come at last, my little one?" cried the old man joyfully. Saying that, he took the lad up into glory, where the music of heaven began to play. The old man was very affectionate with his godson and gave him the host to consume. After the celebration, he carried the boy to a little wooden house. There was the lad's mother hung up by some strands of wire and about to fall into a roaring fire below. His father was sitting by gloomily with his head in his hands.

"Why is my mother strung up like that?" asked the puzzled boy. "If she were cut down, she would fall right into the flames. And my father, why is he so sad there in the doorway?"

"Do you really wish to know, my godson?" asked the old man. "This all began when you were born. Your papa said 'Be he rich or be he poor, be he old or be he young, the first one to arrive tomorrow will be the godfather.' Well, I heard those words and came the next morning. He took me in to see your mother, but I wasn't at all to her taste. That's the reason why my *comadre* is condemned and my *compadre* is so sad over his wife's stubbornness."

"But how can my mother be saved?" asked the boy anxiously.

"Your mother can't be saved. But if you really want to save her, you can." Upon saying that, he buckled a band very tightly about the boy's waist and locked it with a key, which he flung into the air, saying, "Now the key is at your house."

The lad went off in a great torment, for the band was pressing on his empty stomach. The old man had told him that when he arrived home and they took off the band, he must order a mass to be sung. The boy wandered on and on for two years in order to pay for his mother's guilt. When he finally arrived at his house, he was starving—a sack of skin and bones. He told his parents that his godfather had made him suffer for his mother's sin and said that the key to the band had to be somewhere about the house. The poor parents looked everywhere for the key to the terrible iron band, but it was nowhere to be found. When they sent the maid to kill a turkey for dinner, she found a key in the bird's stomach and gave it to her mistress. It fit perfectly in the great lock on the band and the boy was set free at last. By that time his stomach was shrunken and dry from his long suffering with no food. Immediately he ordered a mass sung with band accompaniment in a beautifully decorated church. When the chorus sang the Gloria, a dove rose from the church and fluttered up into heaven. It was the boy leaving earth. His mother was very happy and was saved from her fate forever after.

Part IV
Romantic Tales

· 32 · *The Simple Lad and the*
Three Little Pigs

• ONCE IN A CERTAIN KINGDOM there was a king who issued a proclamation that whoever should guess what his daughter had could marry her, be he rich or poor. Each man was allowed three guesses, and if he failed, his head would be chopped off. As soon as the edict was proclaimed, the youths began to arrive like flies. Rich and poor, all began to guess

"My royal majesty," they would say, "your daughter has eyes." The answer was no. "Your daughter has a mouth." The answer was no. "Your daughter has a nose." But the answer was also no. Things continued like this for some time, with people being beheaded left and right.

Now in this kingdom there lived a woman with a foolish son. She had three little pigs, and she sent her son to town to sell one of them. He took the little animal under his arm and went through the streets shouting, "Pig for sale. Who'll buy my little pig for sale?" By chance, the king had ordered his daughter to buy all the pigs she might see. So as the lad passed by the palace, she called out, "How much do you want for your pig, foolish boy?"

"I? All I ask is that you let me grab your ankle."

"You filthy fool," she answered, "you think you're going to come messing around my ankles?" But the servants urged her to do it, for there was no other way to get the pig and they could always wash her afterwards. The boy was told to come upstairs in the palace. When the ladies-in-waiting had removed the princess's slippers and stockings, the fool felt her ankle. Then he loosed his pig for the princess and left.

When he got home late that night, his mother asked him for the pig money, and he told her they had promised to pay him after he had brought the other pig the next day. Early the next morning, the simpleton went forth, shouting the sale of the second pig. And how the clouds of dust and ashes flew off the dirty boy!

"Here comes that fool with his pig," said the princess, catching sight of him. When he was close by, she called, "How much are you asking, simple one?"

"All I want is for you to let me grab your knee."

"Yesterday," she said, "you felt my ankle and nothing happened. I guess there's no danger. All right, go ahead."

Up came the simpleton and took the princess by the knee. By the time he was back downstairs, the servant girls were already busily at work scrubbing their mistress. The boy left his pig and returned to his mother, who asked him for the money. He told her that he would be paid upon delivery of the third pig.

Early the next day, the lad took the third pig to town. He had been grimy with ashes the day before, but this time he was loaded with them. All along the way he shouted, "Pig for sale."

"How much do you want this time, simpleton?" called the princess.

"I'll ask you to turn up your skirt to the waist, even though I don't touch you at all."

"You grabbed my ankle, and nothing came of it. The same with my knee. Well then, all right."

The sooty lad stumbled upstairs a third time, and the princess snatched her skirt up to the waist. There on the right side of her navel the lad saw a sign which said "the sun and the moon." The young simpleton was starting down the stairs when he said to himself, "Rich and poor go to try the king's riddle. Why don't I?" The princess heard him and called frantically, "Listen boy, come over here. I'm going to pay you five thousand *pesos*, but *don't* go to the king!"

"Now of course I won't go," said the fool, and down he went to leave his pig and head for home. He gave the money to his mother, who was overjoyed with her young businessman. Then he told her to order him a new suit and a golden cane, for the next day he was to get the money for the second pig. Early the following morning the fool went out to the street, shouting, "Rich and poor go to try the king's riddle. Why can't I go?" The closer he came to the palace, the more he shouted.

"Lord in heaven!" gasped the princess, "what if this simpleton should come to be my husband!" She called out the window.

"Don't go, my silly friend. I'm going to pay you ten thousand *pesos*." The boy took the money and went whistling off home to his mother.

On the third day he went to get the money for the third pig. He shouted the same thing, but much louder than before.

"Lord bless me!" cried the princess, hearing his voice in the street. "If ever this fool should marry me!" She called him over. "Come here, simple chap. I'm going to pay you twenty thousand *pesos* so you won't go."

"Now I certainly shall not go," he replied, "for you've just finished paying me for my pigs."

When he arrived home to pay his mother, she had a barber and a kettle of hot water ready. They cut his hair and cleaned him up, stripping and scrubbing him as never before. When he had dressed himself from head to toe, he was the most elegant youth in the whole city. Then he leisurely picked up his gold cane, lit his cigarette, and strolled down the street toward the palace. The princess spotted the good-looking young man and was all agog over him.

"May God and the Virgin permit this fellow to guess the riddle," she sighed. As the gentleman passed her window, the princess bowed and he bowed elegantly in return. Then the king greeted him at the palace door.

"Good day, my fine young man. Do you come to guess?"

"Yes, your majesty, that was my plan."

"You know that you have three guesses and no more. On the third failure, I'll cut off your head."

"Your daughter, my good king, has a mouth."

"No, that's not it at all."

"Your daughter has pretty little eyes."

"Wrong," said the king.

"Your daughter has a sign on the right side of her navel which says 'the sun and the moon.' "

"That's it, my good fellow!" cried the king. He took the boy by the arm and guided him inside to officially close the guessing. When he presented the youth to the princess, she breathed a sigh of relief. "Thank God that this gentleman has guessed right."

The priest and bishop were sent for and the wedding was performed with great rejoicing in the palace. Then the king handed his crown over to his son-in-law and appointed him as the new king. He has remained as ruler until this very day. That's the tale of the simpleton who had three pigs.

·33· He Who Has Money Does What He Likes

• THERE WAS in a certain time a gentleman who bought a block of land and made a square house to cover the block. At each corner he wrote, "He who has money does what he likes." When the house was done, the king found out about it and said, "Does this powerful man do what he wishes just because he has money?" He summoned the man before him and asked if it were true that he had a house with that slogan, as the rumors said.

"Of course, your majesty, I have such a house."

"Ah, I see. Then you do whatever you wish with your wealth?"

"But naturally, sir! In my house, I do as I desire."

"I have a daughter locked under seven keys," said the king. "She is guarded by seven guards. And you must get her with child within nine months, if you can do with your money whatever you wish."

"Most certainly," he replied, but he left the palace full of fears and worries about this challenge.

It so happened that there was a poor old crone who was always wandering in his neighborhood begging one thing or another. She approached the rich man and asked, "Why are you so pained, young master?"

"Go on, granny. How can I help it? I have just finished building my beautiful house a block wide and a block long. Now I go to the king and he tells me I must get the princess fat with child in nine months in order to live up to my slogan. But how can I ever get in where she is?"

"Poof! And you with all that money! Do you have any gold?"

"Yes, I can scrape it together."

"Then send to have a little wagon made and a little gold turkey with a key inside and a secret door. Then you put this turkey in the wagon, and I'll pull it along the street. The trick is that you'll be inside the bird," she cackled.

The rich gentleman scurried right off to the waggoner's to order his cart and to the jeweler's for his turkey. They made him a pretty little golden bird in which he could fit sitting down. It was loaded into the wagon, and away went the old crone, pulling it down the street. "A visit with the little turkey, fifty *pesos*. Another visit, another fifty." Finally she passed in front of the king's palace. One of the servant girls saw her and ran to tell the king that there was an adorable little turkey pulled by an old woman, something which would surely please the lonely princess locked away in her room. The king ordered the woman to be called and asked her the price for a visit to the little golden turkey.

"For an hour or two, fifty *pesos*," she answered.

"And for a night?" asked the king.

"Three hundred, and good bed and food for myself."

"It's a bargain."

They took the little turkey into the princess' room. What a pretty bird it was and how sweetly it gobbled! As night came on, the wealthy gentleman stealthily opened the door and began to chat with the girl. She gave him all he asked for, and he slept with her that very night. He arose very early in the morning, before anybody was stirring, and hopped back into his turkey. When they brought the princess her breakfast, she affectionately fed it to the bird.

The following day, she wanted the bird again for the whole day. Another three hundred *pesos* and the old woman well attended to her. In all, she was there three nights with her golden turkey. Finally the old lady said, "Now this is surely enough. I won't stay a minute longer. I'm losing money left and right. Why, I can make three hundred *pesos* in the wink of an eye outside. After all, three nights. It's quite sufficient!"

"Don't take away my pretty little bird," wailed the princess. "I have such fun with him." She ran out to grab the golden turkey, but the old woman promptly snatched it and made away with it, heading back to the rich man's house. Along the way, she was earning fifty *pesos* here and there as she went. She arrived at the house with a load of money, and the rich gentleman happily stored his bird away. He had told the princess his name was "He Who Had Money Did What He Wanted."

That's how it stood, until one fine day the nine months were up. The king was relaxing at home, when he suddenly heard a "wah," and again, "wah, wah."

"Bah!" he roared, "what's going on here. It sounds like a baby in my palace." Off he went to investigate. "What have you got, my girl? What's that in your arms?"

"This is what was left by 'He Who Has Money Does What He Likes.'"

"How strange," mumbled the king. He sent immediately for the rich gentleman, but he didn't appear, fearing that the nine months were up and nothing had happened. After three royal summonses, he finally gave in and came before the king.

"Good morning," said the king, "He who has money does what he likes, and you have done a great deal."

"Oh, yes?"

"Yes, there's a child over there which is yours. I haven't seen my daughter going out anywhere, but the baby is your work and you're going to marry the princess."

"Fair enough," he answered. "As long as it's mine, everything's all right."

They went to fetch the priest and bishop and make the arrangements for the wedding. After the ceremony, the newlyweds headed for the corner called "He Who Has Money Does What He Likes." They're likely to be living there to this very day.

· 34 · Juan, Pedro, and Diego

• THERE WAS ONCE a very poor couple with three sons by the names of Juan, Pedro, and Diego. The old man had a pear tree which was always heavy with fruit. One day Juan said, "Papa, give me permission to pick a couple of bags of pears to sell in the

city. Then I can buy something we need for the house." His father agreed, and immediately Juan climbed into the tree and began to shake it. Pedro and Diego were down below gathering the
pears into two sacks. The next morning Juan loaded his horse
with the pears and set out for the city. On the road he met an old
man who asked him what he had in the bags. Juan said they were
full of shit.

"Then shit it must be," answered the old man.

The lad entered the city hawking his pears. The servants of the
king called him over and brought out their prettiest baskets and
finest tablecloths to receive the fruit. Juan undid his sacks and
filled the baskets with shit. As soon as the king got word of what
the pear vendor was selling, he flew into a rage and had him tied
to a stake and beaten a hundred strokes. When Juan was finally
able to mount his horse, he rode home in absolute silence and fell
groaning into bed.

The following day Pedro told his father that he was going to
sell pears in town.

"You're not going to do what your brother did, are you?"
asked the old man.

"No, papa, I'm going to bring the things for sure."

Pedro climbed into the tree and shook the fruit down to Diego
on the ground. When the second son rode off to town, he met the
same little old man in the same place.

"Good day, my boy. What have you in your sacks?"

"They're full of stones."

"Then stones they must be," said the man and took his leave.

Pedro entered the city calling out his pears. When the king's
servants heard him, they said, "Your majesty, there comes that
idiot with the crap again."

"Call him," roared the king. "If he got a hundred whacks yesterday, I'll give him two hundred today."

The servant girls brought out some old baskets and called the
boy over. Pedro couldn't see why they had brought such beat-up
old things, but they told him to never mind that and just unload.
Opening his sack of pears, he filled the basket with stones.

"They're stones, plain old stones, your majesty!" cried the servants, racing into the palace. The king ordered Pedro to be taken

off and given two hundred lashes. The boy rode home in great
agony, barely able to sit on his horse, and went straight to bed.

The next day, Diego prepared to go. His father was sure he
would meet the same fate, but the youngest son pestered the old
man until he got his consent. Diego loaded his sacks of pears,
taking care to fill two extra suitcases of fruit for any poor man he
might meet on the way. And sure enough, he came upon the little man exactly where Juan and Pedro had seen him. Before the
old fellow could say a word, Diego took off his hat and greeted
him.

"And what have you there, my boy?" asked the old fellow.

"My bags are full of pears."

"Then pears they must be."

After Diego had ridden on for a good distance, he remembered
that he had forgotten to invite the old man to have some pears,
and galloped back full speed to find him.

"My Lord, grandpa!" he said, "I had forgotten to offer you
some fruit. Put your poncho down so I can give you a load."
Diego turned over his suitcase and filled the old fellow's blanket
with pears.

"Give me your right hand, my boy," said the man. He blessed
it and added, "Whatever you put your hand on is going to speak.
Also, I'm going to give you this vest which will never fail to give
you all the money you want to pull out of it."

Diego thanked the old man warmly and rode along his way.
He came to a *pellin* tree leaning over to one side. Anxious to see
how his magic charm worked, he laid his hand on the tree and
said, *"Pellin,* what are you doing all bent over?"

"Here I am," answered the tree, "because nobody has straightened me up since I was little, and I'll have to stay twisted as long
as the world exists."

Traveling on a bit more, Diego found a stone in the road. He
laid his hand on it and asked, "Stone, what are you doing here?"

"Here I am," said the stone, "and as long as the world is, I'm a
stone in the road."

Now Diego was sure that his charm was good. He rode into
the city calling out his load of pears for sale. When the servants

saw him, they said, "Here comes that nincompoop with the stones, your Majesty."

"Call him," fumed the king. "I gave him a hundred blows the first day and two hundred the second. It will be three hundred today."

The servants took the most ordinary baskets they had and called Diego over to unload his pears. He could hardly believe that they intended to receive his pears in those grubby baskets, but they told him simply to get busy and unload. He undid one sack and poured a load of the most beautiful ripe pears into the old moth-eaten baskets. The servants rushed to tell the king that this was the real thing, and returned with the finest baskets and tablecloths in the palace. Diego filled all of them and was given a hundred *pesos*. He went immediately to the nearest store and bought sugar and herbs, flour, salt, chili, and cigarettes for his parents. After this, he stocked up on meat at the butcher's and rode for home with all the provisions.

How happy the old parents were! They were overjoyed that he hadn't fallen into the same folly as his older brothers. His mother was waiting for him with the water boiling in case he brought something to eat. They all sat down to a delicious meal, and the mother carried some food in to Juan and Pedro, who were still nursing their sores in bed. Then and there the older brothers decided it was about time for them to move along, for surely their parents weren't going to look very favorably on them after this episode. Juan and Pedro soon went on their way, while Diego stayed home with his parents and thought of following his brothers.

A few days later, the youngest brother went out to look around. He bought a cow and took the meat, along with ten sacks of flour, home to his parents. Diego had become a wealthy man. After this, he brought his mother a maid and two laborers for the farm work, and a stack of gold and silver.

"Papa and mama," he said finally, "I'm going out to search for my brothers. You folks do as well as you can with the things I've left you, for I don't know whether I'll return or not."

When he had bade his home good-bye and traveled for some

days, he came to a king's palace and asked to be allowed to do something for charity in that kingdom. The king granted him permission and thought to himself, "How wealthy this boy must be! He goes about trying to give charity! Not even I, with all my riches, do that."

Diego posted a notice telling everyone in the city to come and receive his charity. That night he lodged at the palace and, early the next morning, began to distribute alms, carrying great lapfuls of money to everybody who was in need. In the afternoon, Juan wandered by. Although Juan didn't recognize his younger brother, Diego knew him immediately and gave him such a load of pure gold that he went away all bent over from the weight of it. Then the king called Diego in and told him that he had done enough for the day. The king's three daughters were sitting in the hall of the palace for the boy to choose one as his wife. This seemed all very well, but he insisted on sleeping with the girl he chose before marrying her, assuring the king that he wouldn't touch even a hair of her head in the night. He chose the oldest daughter, and right after supper they lay down together and quickly fell asleep.

In the night Diego awoke while the princess was sleeping. He laid his hand on her and spoke to it. "Little frog, *paipay,* who has been here before?" he asked.

"Don Juan the butcher," was the answer.

"I'll never marry this one," declared Diego. He didn't sleep a wink, and when God put out his lights at dawn, the boy quietly got up and slipped out of the castle. Shortly after, the king arose and went to his daughter's bedroom.

"Where's your husband?" he asked, amazed to see her alone in bed. She had no idea. "He's a fine rogue, he is," fumed the king. "When did he leave?"

Diego traveled on and on until he came to the palace of a second king. There he asked for the same permission to distribute alms in the kingdom. The king granted it, marveling at the wealth of this man, who could do what even a rich ruler could not. Late in the day, Pedro passed by without recognizing his brother. But Diego knew him immediately and also gave him a load of pure gold. That afternoon, the king led Diego home to his palace and presented three daughters waiting for the young man's choice. He picked the second one, insisting as before that he be allowed to sleep with her before marriage. In the night, Diego awoke and laid his hand on the princess.

"Little frog, *paipay,* who's been here before?"

"Don Juan the butcher."

"I won't have this one either," thought Diego. "I'll just slip out of here at dawn."

When the king came in that morning and found his daughter alone in bed, he was infuriated. "A devil of a rogue he is, going around cheating like this."

After wandering on, Diego came to a third palace, where he again got permission to post his charity signs. This time he gave less, for he had already found his brothers. In the afternoon the third king took the boy home to choose one of his three daughters, the apples of his eye. The condition was the same: He would sleep with the girl without harming a hair of her head. Diego thought of the oldest daughter the first time, and the second one at the second palace, and chose the youngest daughter of the third king. That evening the two lay down to sleep like two babies.

"Little frog, *paipay,* who's been here before?" Diego asked in the night, resting his hand on the princess.

"Nobody," was the answer. "I'm just as I was the day I was born."

"This then will be my wife," he said happily.

Early in the morning the king headed for their bedroom. "I don't want to make a racket," he thought. "Surely this poor boy is worn out from so many donations of charity." So he paced back and forth in the corridor until Diego came out.

"A very good morning to you, young man," said the king cheerily. "What do you say, will you marry or won't you?"

"I will, your majesty, with all happiness."

The king dispatched messengers to the priest and the bishop. The other two kings were invited to the feast with their daughters. Even Juan and Pedro showed up, for now they recognized their youngest brother, who had gone up so far in the world and who had been so generous with them.

"Why didn't you marry my daughter?" asked the other two kings, storming up to the groom in righteous indignation.

"With your consent," said Diego calmly, laying his hand on the oldest princess's dress, "I'll show you a little something. Little frog, *paipay,* who's been here before?" The answer came back about the roaming butcher. "Don't you see?" continued Diego, "It doesn't want me to marry your daughter." He did the same with the second daughter. But when he put his hand on her dress, the little frog didn't speak, so he changed the hand to her backside. "Little rump, little bump, why doesn't your companion speak?" he asked.

"Because it has an objection," was the answer. Diego smacked the girl and the objection flew out. He put his hand on her front once more. "Little frog, *paipay,* who's been here before?"

"Don Juan the butcher," was the shameful answer.

"How can you ask me to marry a daughter like this?" Diego asked the red-faced king. Then he laid his hand on the third and youngest princess, and the answer came back that she was pure. Diego embraced her and cried happily, "This is my true wife!"

The other kings clapped their hands in astonishment and left the palace in great shame, not even stopping to bid Diego goodbye.

That day there was a great wedding feast and much joy in the palace of the third king. After the ceremony, the king and queen passed their crowns to the newlyweds and appointed them the new rulers of the kingdom. They stayed there ever after, ruling peacefully together with their parents.

·35· King Clarion of the Island of Talagante

• THERE WAS ONCE a king called King Clarion of the Island of Talagante. He had a son and named him the same. The boy was well brought up, but as they educated him at school until he was eighteen, he knew little more than his classroom and the palace.

Eventually he left school and began to wander about the city with his friends. As he was returning to the palace one day, he spotted a little boy in the street offering for sale a picture of a beautiful princess for fifty *pesos*. The lad showed him the portrait, but the young prince was ashamed to buy it, for his friends were laughing and teasing him. Very embarrassed, he took leave of the boy, but later circled back by another way and asked again for the price of the little picture. He found out from the lad that the princess was alive, but forgot to ask where she lived. Then he bought the little portrait and took it home to his room, where he hung it at the head of his bed. Every day he would lie down there and contemplate it tirelessly for hours on end. They had to call him for meals, but he never ate more than a spoonful, always hurrying back to his room to stare enraptured at the portrait. This went on for many days, until the queen, very puzzled over her son's behavior, followed him upstairs from the table and slipped into his room before he could close the door. When she glimpsed the lovely picture, she exclaimed, "Ah, my son, and what are you up to here?"

"I'm just looking at this portrait, Mama, and thinking of how I could deserve this girl."

The queen called down to her husband, "Come up here, darling, and see what your son has. Here's the reason he eats neither day nor night."

"There's nothing for you to do but set out to find her," said the king to his son upon seeing the picture. The king had a boat equipped and stocked it with silver in order that his son might go in search of the princess.

The prince traveled a long time. He would arrive at a port, disembark, and wander through the city from one side to the other, always hoping to catch a glimpse of the mysterious princess. He sailed this way from port to port, until he finally came to a city with a great palace. The princess was there, for as he walked through the town, he spied a portrait just like the one that he was carrying. Asking where the lady of the portrait was, he was informed that she lived right across the street.

So as to be near the place, the prince rented a room and set up a little shop to sell colored threads for embroidery and other odds and ends. As he was down in his shop one morning, he noticed the girl in the upper story across the street. Quickly he constructed a rope ladder long enough to reach her window. When everyone was asleep that night, he climbed up to see the lovely princess. She was at first startled by her unannounced visitor, but then she saw that he was really a charming young prince. They chatted for a bit and eventually came to the topic of marriage. The princess accepted his offer, and that very night they slept together and promised to continue faithful to each other. The prince had thought of asking for her hand, but her father was a man about town and could hardly ever be found in the palace.

The young man stayed with the princess for several days after he had taken her (all women must be the same, you know). Then he bought a little house and hired an old lady to help him.

"Granny," he told her, "I'm going to make you the owner of this house and everything in it. Now if by chance the princess should have a boy, you are to deliver this ring and this letter to him." The ring had the prince's name engraved inside, "King Clarion of the Island of Talagante." After that, the prince took his ship and sailed home to live peacefully with his parents.

Not so long after they died, and he became the ruler of that kingdom. In this same city there was a very rich millionaire, who had almost as much as the king. The rich man and his wife had a little girl, whom they made the king's goddaughter. She was her parents' favorite and a very good student at school. After she had grown to be a beautiful young woman, they didn't want anybody to see her and kept her always locked away under seven keys. No one but her lady-in-waiting could go in. Whenever the rich man visited the king he said, "*Compadre,* your godchild is very well. She's never going to give you any reason for comments." And the king would always return, "*Compadre,* even though she's locked in with seven keys, the shrewd ones always get in."

Meanwhile, the girl with whom King Clarion had slept had a baby boy, and gave him over to the old lady to care for and raise. She brought him up well and taught him to speak. Some time later, she became deathly ill and called for the boy.

"Open that box," the old lady said from her bed, "and take out the letter and the ring you find there. You must never lose them, because I'm not long for this world and can help you no more."

When she died, the lad buried her and went out wandering. After a long journey in a boat he had bought from the sale of the old lady's house, he landed at a certain town. As he walked alone through the streets, he heard someone shouting, "Oh, Lord, now I'm truly done for. My capital is gone forever!" Searching about, the young man saw a poor old woman sobbing in the gutter. She told him her money was gone and she had no way to continue living. The boy gave her a *peso* and asked her why they couldn't work together. Since the old lady was a baker by profession, they made a deal. She was to bake and the lad would sell her products in the street. He had good luck as a vendor and the people flocked about the handsome youth to buy hot bread. He had been working for the old woman for some days when he chanced by the millionaire's palace and saw his beautiful daughter on the balcony. She sent the maid down to see what the young fellow was selling. The maid ran to tell him that the princess would buy all his bread, but the boy simply said he would wait in the entrance with his goods.

"Little lady," said the maid running back, "he's such a lovely boy. We wanted to bring him in, but he wouldn't come."

"See if you can't find some way to have him come up tomorrow," answered the princess, gazing out at the lad.

When he passed by the next day with his hot bread, he refused once again to enter the palace. But the maids simply pulled him in and shoved him upstairs, locking him into the princess's chamber. Finding themselves thus face to face, the lad and the maiden began to chat. The conversation eventually came around to marriage, for she was very bored with being closed in all this time by her tyrannical father. The boy protested that he could hardly marry her, for they were millionaires and he only a poor bread vendor. The princess insisted that she would help him with her father's money. Thereupon, she bought all his bread and filled his basket with money, telling him to use it to build her a house. So it came about that the lad went past the millionaire's on business every day from then on, until finally the two of them promised themselves in marriage, whenever it was possible. He made a rope ladder to climb up to her window at night.

All this time, the millionaire continued to boast to King

Clarion that his godchild would never give anyone a reason for gossip. And the king always replied, "Even though she's under seven keys, the sharpest ones will find a way in."

"But, *compadre*," objected the rich man, "in my palace, nobody enters."

Meanwhile, the boy continued to come innocently by selling his bread. Finally he wished to work no longer and settled his accounts with the old baker woman, leaving her his part of the business so she could live out her days in comfort. Then he found a handyman and began to construct a house across the street from the millionaire. Every night, he slipped over and slept with the imprisoned girl. The following morning, he would always leave with a pretty sum of money, until he was able to build a magnificent mansion across the street.

One fine morning the king was strolling through the city and noticed the great new house across the way from his friend's. It occurred to the king one night to prowl around there disguised as a coal peddler, to see if he couldn't find out about the owner of the grand mansion. The boy called the peddler in to see his wares, and seeing that he was a stout fellow, asked him, "What kind of a man are you, old boy?"

"Pretty damned good, young sir," answered the disguised king.

"By George, that gives me an idea!" exclaimed the lad. "Will it be just between us two?"

"Of course, fine sir," said the peddler. "Just tell me what's on your mind."

The boy told the peddler about his nightly visits across the street to get a little money, and asked him to come along as a helper. He passed the king a bottle to warm his spirits to the task and warned him not to let out a peep on this job. When the king came to the house, he immediately recognized it as his friend's. The girl tossed the rope ladder down and the two men climbed up to her bedroom. The peddler was dispatched to the kitchen for something to eat, where he began making love to the cook. All the kitchen help were having a great time with him until well into the night. Afterwards he spread out his sack and lay down under the stove. Upstairs the young man was asleep with the millionaire's daughter.

At dawn the next morning, the king tramped up to the young couple's bedroom and called, "Kind sir, is it time yet?"

"Yes," answered the youth, stretching himself awake. "Take the chamber pot and toss the 'meow-meows' out the window."

When the peddler had gingerly executed the task and the boy had dressed, they went to the millionaire's treasure pile. Both of them filled their sacks to the brim and climbed down the rope ladder to return to the youth's house in the faint dawn light. The boy slipped the peddler a bottle of wine and asked him to return the following night with a trustworthy companion to help in this work. Then he gave the old man a hundred *pesos,* cautioned him to secrecy, and bade him good-bye. The king promptly went home to bed at his palace.

When the millionaire had breakfasted that morning, he strolled over to visit the king, and found him still sleeping. He burst into his friend's bedroom to see if he was sick. The king stretched groggily and sent for a bottle of wine so they could chat.

"I'm going to invite you to something interesting, *compadre,"* said the king, "but only on the condition that whatever you see, you won't pipe up at once. If you do, I'll have your head rolling in the streets."

"But don't you realize that we're *compadres?"* protested his friend.

"Yes, *compadre,* but don't you realize that I'm the king?"

The deal was made, and that night the two of them dressed like peddlers, blacked themselves up with a bit of coal dust, and set off into the night. The king introduced his friend to the young man at the mansion. The rich man followed, sheepish and a bit ashamed, behind the king, who posed as the chief peddler. When the boy had livened their spirits with a bottle of wine, the three of them crossed the street for their night's work. The millionaire was staring wide-eyed at his own palace.

"Compadre," he whispered frantically to the king, "this is *my* house!"

"Sssh, mum's the word," hissed the king. "Remember, not a solitary word." Then he made the rich friend climb up first on the rope ladder, following close behind in case the old fellow should have a fit at the top. As soon as they were inside, they were packed off hastily to the kitchen. As before, the king began to play around with the cooks, full of flirtatiousness and coquetry. His friend just stood there tight-lipped, not uttering a word.

"Come on, *compadre,* grab hold of this little honey," laughed the king as he pointed to one of the scullery maids. But the rich man was still as a stone while the king cavorted on. When everyone had gone off to bed, the two friends were alone in the midnight kitchen.

"By heaven, *compadre,* this is a real mess!" gasped the millionaire.

"Well, didn't I tell you that even when girls are under seven keys, the tricky ones somehow get in?"

The rich man was greatly troubled with the whole matter and decided he would simply have to kill his daughter. But the king said no, and warned him again that if he said a word, his head would come off. That night they bedded down in the kitchen. Before dawn the millionaire got up nervously and said, *"Compadre,* isn't it time yet? Let's get going, for heaven's sake!"

"I'll just send my *compadre* on ahead," thought the king, "so he'll have the job of tossing out the stinky 'meow-meows' in the chamber pot."

After the millionaire had distastefully done that first task of the morning, the youth led them to the money pile. The king began filling his sack as fast as he could, tossing in heaping armfuls of silver and gold. The rich man was dejectedly dropping in small handfuls, trickling the money through his fingers coin by coin.

"Toss it in, toss it in, my friend," called the youth. "You'd think you were afraid of this job." The king filled his own sack and came over to help his friend until the other sack was stuffed.

"There now," said the king gleefully, "that's what I call a good sackful!"

They all went down the ladder and returned to the boy's house.

"Just give my friend a hundred *pesos,* kind sir," suggested the first peddler. "Enough for a little drink."

"That's a good idea," beamed the youth. "And whenever you're in the neighborhood, don't forget to stop by."

"Fine and dandy," said the king, as he and his friend hurried out the door. The rich man wanted to go straight home, but the king was against it. "If you go now, old *compadre,* you're liable to do something tactless." So he took his friend home to the palace, where they both changed into something fresh.

"On my word, I'm going to kill this girl of mine," stormed the rich man in a rage.

"The two of them are going to be killed," announced the king, "for I'm going to take care of the boy."

Immediately after breakfast they went out to make the catch. The king went for the boy, and the rich man brought his daughter down in a flash from her room. They dragged the young couple to the edge of town where there were some apple trees, and put a noose around the neck of each one. At the signal, they raised the two nooses, and then let them fall again. Once more they gave each other the signal, hung the two prisoners up a bit, and then lowered them a second time. They were bumbling around like this for some time, while the young man was struggling to get free of the rope. In the midst of the hubbub, the king noticed a ring the boy was wearing, and asked him for it. The lad passed it to his executioner, and the king read, "King Clarion of the Island of Talagante." He looked up astonished and asked the boy how he had come by this. Then the lad told him that his mother, when she was on her death bed, had delivered to him a letter and a ring with which he could find his father.

"Have you got the letter with you?" asked King Clarion excitedly. The boy passed him the tattered sheet of paper, which the king scanned with shaking hands. Then he asked about the old woman who had brought the boy up and the old king and queen of that city. The lad told him that the old woman had died, and that only a daughter of the old king and queen remained as queen of the city. Now the king was sure that this was his own son, but not letting on about it, he said to his friend, "All set, *compadre,* now we're really going to string these two up." They hoisted the young pair once again and right away let them back down.

"We just can't do it," said the king. "We can't hang this lad."

"And I haven't got the heart to hang my daughter," said the rich man.

"Nor have I to hang my son," added the king.

"What's that you said, *compadre?*"

"Just what I said," answered the king, handing the letter over to the millionaire. "This is a son of mine that I had in a distant city, because I bought a portrait of the lad's mother."

"My God! Now what will we do?" asked the rich man, totally flabbergasted.

"We're going to marry them," said the king, "but not here. It will be in the palace of this boy's mother."

The party set sail the very same day for the city where the lad's mother still lived. When they arrived, the queen was giving an audience. The king recognized the woman he had loved so long ago and ran up to embrace her. She knew him at once but didn't want to return the embrace, remembering full well how he had deserted her. Then the king announced that he had come to be married along with his son. The queen was delighted and soon the double wedding was under way with all the celebrations and festivities. The priest and even the bishop and the cardinal were there.

When both couples were married, King Clarion took his new wife home to his palace. His son remained with his queen as king of his mother's city. And there they are to this very day, if perchance they haven't died.

· *36* ·   *The Basil Plant*

• THERE WAS ONCE a woman who had three very pretty and industrious daughters. They all lived across from the king's palace, where they had a garden with the very best and finest basil plants. Now this king was accustomed to come out every day at dawn to see the daughters, for they pleased him very much. One day he called down to one of them from his balcony, "Listen, you tricky girl, how many leaves does your basil plant have?" She looked up and chanted back,

> "Shut your mouth, you king so sly.
> How many stars are there in the sky?"

The king went fuming inside, mumbling, "She'll pay for this." He hired a man and a mule and filled the saddlebags with oranges. He ordered the man to sell the fruit, being sure to go by the girls' house. Sure enough, they called him over. "Orange vendor, come back. How much are they a hundred?"

"For you, miss, I'll leave them all for a little kiss," he replied.

The oldest daughter, who had called him, was enraged and bustled into the house, slamming the door behind her. The next day the same thing happened to the second sister, who was equally enraged. "Get along, you old pig!" she yelled from the door. "Imagine offering me oranges for a kiss." She too flew into the house all flustered and hot.

"Didn't you buy any oranges?" asked the youngest daughter.

"No, of course not. Didn't you hear what he wanted for them?"

"You mean to say you didn't kiss him?" said the youngest, infuriated. "Why, we would have had all the oranges we could have eaten. If he comes again, I'm going to go out."

As soon as the man passed again, she dashed out, calling, "Come back, orange man, come back."

"How could I resist a lady as lovely as you? If you'll just give me one little kiss, the oranges are yours."

"Can it be true?" she said. "Go on and unload the fruit."

When he had finished unpacking, she gave him a kiss on the lips, and away he went.

The next morning, the king got up especially early and went out on his balcony to see the girl. "How many leaves does your basil plant have?" he called merrily. She looked up and taunted back,

> "Shut your mouth, you king so sly.
> How many stars are there in the sky?"

"Shut your own mouth, you deceiving girl," laughed the king. "How many kisses did you give the old orange vendor?"

"Well, that was a nice trick," she said to herself, "but the king isn't going to win." Immediately she got herself a black costume, a little bell, and a gentle little burro. Early the next day, she rode forth ringing the bell, "Ting-a-ling, ting-a-ling." She was dressed in the black suit with very long fingers so as to appear especially skinny. The girl rode around to the palace gate and rang the bell, but the guards wouldn't let her through, wanting to know who on earth she was. With a long face and the very black costume, she told them she was Death come to visit the king. They promptly let her in, trembling as they opened the gates. She trotted right up to the front door. "Ting-a-ling, ting-a-ling, I've come to fetch the king."

Inside the palace, the king leaped up in his nightshirt, begging her not to carry him off. "My dear little, lovely little Death, don't, oh, please don't, not yet!"

"Ting-a-ling, ting-a-ling, I've come to take my king," and she rang the bell over and over. He begged and insisted so that she finally said in a low, hollow voice, "Under one condition will I leave you: that you give the burro three kisses on his backside." The king promptly lifted the burro's tail and kissed him three times. Then Death rode away. "Ting-a-ling, ting-a-ling, now I won't take my king."

When the king had recovered from his shock the following morning, he went out to see the girl and called down, "Listen, you deceitful creature, how many leaves does the basil plant have?" She jeered up from below,

> "Shut your mouth, you king so sly.
> How many stars are there in the sky?"

"Quiet down yourself," he shouted back. "How many kisses did you give the grimy old orange vendor?"

"You pipe down," she returned. "How many times did you kiss the burro's behind?"

The king rushed into his palace, muttering to himself, "What the devil! Now I have to call for this girl and marry her." So he commanded the mother with her three daughters to appear before him. She was greatly frightened by the summons and was sure the king was going to kill all of them. But the daughters weren't very upset. "For eating so many oranges," they laughed.

"These are your three daughters, are they not?" asked the king when the old woman appeared trembling in the throne room.

"Yes, sir, that they are."

"Well, then, I'm going to ask you for the youngest."

"But how can you, sire? I'm so very poor!" sobbed the old woman.

"That doesn't matter," answered the king. "Tomorrow will be the wedding, and don't worry about its doing you any harm."

After the ceremony, the king told his new bride emphatically to keep her nose out of the justice he meted out in his kingdom. (Don't you see how he thought she was a devilish person?) The new queen agreed to this request with the reservation that the king must promise to grant her one favor before she died, whenever she should ask him for it. Soon, petitions and complaints began to come in to the king from his people. The first case was that of a man who had ridden into town on a mare followed by a newborn colt. While he was shopping in town, another man had ridden off on a stallion followed by the first man's colt. When the owner of the colt rode out to round it up, the second man had claimed that it belonged to his horse. They had argued for a long time and finally decided to bring their case before the king.

"Let's see," said the ruler, "both of you stand over there. The one whom the colt follows will be the owner." The two men joined together and set their horses to walking, but the colt, being so young, staggered unsurely behind the stallion, whereupon the king declared in favor of the owner of the stallion. The man with the mare went to seek the queen and tell her his troubles, for she was known as a merciful person. She told him to keep mum and come back in the afternoon for further instructions.

A few days later, two more men came before the king with a complaint. One had said that whenever he stayed out in the cold, he froze. The other had mocked him and said that he dared to stay out in the coldest night. The king appointed a board of judges, who asked the man who stayed out all night what he had seen. He answered that there had been a tiny little fire above him in the hills. The judges answered that he had surely warmed himself there and thus avoided being frozen. But the two were not content and continued to squabble over this question until the king ruled the same as his judges. The loser left the court in low spirits and went straight to the queen.

"Don't worry about it," she counseled. "Tomorrow I'm going to see to it that the king learns how to dispense justice."

When the man returned the next day for more advice, the queen told him to go and wait in a pasture where the king was going to ride by. He should go with a bag of barley and a big pot to cook it in. "Then," she continued, "when the king comes by, he's going to ask you what you are doing. You must tell him you're cooking the barley in order to sow it. When he asks you how in the world such a thing can be, you must answer, 'Your Majesty, since you say that stallions can bear colts, why can't this cooked barley grow?'"

When the king arose early the next day to set out on his trip, he ordered the queen to put on the pot for breakfast and throw plenty of wood on the fire. After waiting for a while, the king became impatient and noticed that the pot was sitting in the doorway.

"I thought I told you to be quick," he said to the queen. "How is that pot going to boil sitting in the doorway?" At that moment, one of the disputants came in and said, "Your Majesty, you said the other man hadn't been frozen because there was a tiny fire on the hillside; why then can't your pot boil in the doorway with such a big fire in the stove?"

The king went off to the country in a very bad humor, thinking angrily about the queen, for he knew that these tricks were of her doing. Soon he and his retinue came upon the man who was cooking barley in a field alongside the road.

"Man, what are you up to there with that pot? Why on earth are you cooking barley?" asked the king.

"To sow it, sire," he answered.

"But whatever makes you think it's going to come up?"

"Why not?" answered the man. "If stallions can bear colts, why can't this barley sprout?"

The king stormed away, fuming to himself, "This is the queen's doing and I'll make her pay for it. I warned her before not to stick her nose into my affairs." When he returned to the

castle at lunchtime, he said to his wife, "It's just about time to
settle our accounts for all this meddling around of yours." He
stamped outside and lit an enormous bonfire, but the queen said
it really didn't matter to her, for we are all born to die. She was
very calm at the prospect of being roasted. When the bonfire was
crackling high in the air, the king took her up in his coach and
said, "You must amend your ways and prepare to die."

"So be it," said she, "for I'm not afraid of death."

Arriving at the site of the burning, the royal couple got down
from the coach and strolled up and down, arm in arm, until the
hour came and the king beckoned to the executioner. Just as the
fire was piping hot to receive the queen, she cried, "Wait, all of
you!" She beckoned to the king. "Do you remember that I am
entitled to ask for a favor before dying?"

"Why, yes, I do recall something like that," answered the king.

"Then come over here." As he approached, she embraced him
and hugged tight. "There you are, my love."

"That's enough, enough," groaned the king, trying to pull
away.

"No, this is the request," replied the queen. "If you wish to
burn me, we'll burn together." Realizing that she wasn't going to
loosen her grip, the king gave in, and said, "Why should the two
of us fry together? In this case, I'll pardon you, but never try
your tricks again. Now let's be off to the house."

"I'm at your command, my dear," answered the queen smiling.

"From this day on," declared the king, "I'm not going to dispense any more justice. You're the one who has to do it." And
that was how the queen came to be judge at the royal court.

·37· *The Wager on the Wife's Chastity*

· THERE WAS ONCE a gentleman named Manuel who lived
alone in his home, where he kept a little store. One day he announced that the first girl to arrive in the morning had to be his
wife, be she one-eyed, lame, poor, or whatever else. It chanced
that a very poor girl came along. This girl was in fact so poor

that when she entered a house, she had to go out backwards, for she was dressed in front and had nothing to put on behind. But she was a pretty lass, and the young gentleman announced that her poverty didn't matter, she was to be his wife. He gave her a fine gift and told her to make herself a dress. The girl went home, hiding from her gruff old father, and told her mother to notify the old man that her suitor was coming to speak to him at twelve o'clock. Right on the dot, the young man arrived at the house and called out to see if anybody was at home. The old woman started out quite ashamed, for she, too, was dressed only in front and hadn't a stitch on behind. She came out forwards and then backed up quickly into the house, letting out three good shouts for her husband. Finally the old fellow arrived, very surprised, with his hatchet on his shoulder.

"Don't be afraid, my little old man," said the youth, "I've come to greet you and ask for your daughter's hand in marriage."

The man turned purple with rage and screamed, "Go away, sir! Get out of here, and don't come around to make fun of me!" He was so angry that he paid no attention to the stammered protests and even took a swing at the suitor with his hatchet. Then he summoned his daughter to find out just what this fellow had said to her.

"He told me he had made a promise," she said, "that the first girl who arrived at his store had to be his wife. I was the first, and I guess that's why he's here."

"But, daughter," said her father, "how are you going to marry if we're so poor?" By now the young man had pleaded so convincingly that the old man believed him. So, as the days went by, preparations were made for the wedding. The youth took the old people and their daughter to his house and dressed the father as a grand gentleman and the mother as a noble lady. Then they went to the registry and the priest and were duly married.

It came to pass that nobody saw this girl any more, for she was hidden in the house with her husband, who had put his father-in-law in charge of the store and his mother-in-law in charge of the household. The new wife had nothing to do, what with maids and everything you could wish. One fine day an envious rich man came to the house just as the husband was about to make a little trip.

"I'll make you a bet, my friend," said the rich man, "that your wife will betray you while you're out sailing in your boat."

The husband set off without saying a word to his wife about the trip or the day he would return. She was very surprised by his sudden absence. As soon as he was gone, the other man spoke with an old sorceress and asked her what she could do to help him win the bet.

"That's the easiest thing there is," she cackled. "I'll go to lodge at that house tonight and get into the bedroom by saying that I'm the aunt of the young wife." The horrid old woman managed to do just that. She embraced the girl with affection and began settling down for the night in the same room. But while the young woman wasn't watching, the old sorceress took a handful of bedbugs and scattered them in her sheets. In a jiffy, the girl was itching so she couldn't keep still. As she jumped up to shake out the bed, the old woman was watching her with great care and noticed a mole covered with sealing wax on her left leg. After the young bride had swept out all the mess in the bed, she fell into a deep sleep. There on her bedside table was her ring along with her nightgown and the seal which covered her mole. The old trickster tiptoed over, pocketed the articles, and skipped out of the house in the middle of the night.

The next day, the rich man had a rendezvous with the old woman and received the three articles. So it was that when the boat came in, he was waiting triumphantly at the dock for his friend. Each one had bet his whole ranch and fortune.

"Good morning, friend," called the man when the husband docked. "How is everything? Ahem, I won the little bet, and here are the proofs." He produced the ring, the nightgown, and the seal from the girl's mole. "If you wish to know more, I can tell you that your wife has a brown mole on her leg."

The husband spoke not a word, but merely set off for his house, stooping with grief as he walked. He said a formal "good day" to his wife and not a peep more came out of him. Very surprised and hurt, she thought, "What on earth can be wrong with my husband? He has never been like this before."

The next morning he asked his wife to take a little stroll with him. He didn't mention where they were going, but told it only to a shoemaker he employed. When they came to the river bank, the husband got into a boat and told his wife to follow him. Then he said to the shoemaker, who was waiting nearby, "Kill this treacherous woman and bring me her eyes as proof." The shoemaker rowed away with the poor woman across the river.

"Ma'm," he said when they had reached the other bank, "the boss told me to pluck your eyes out, but I'm not going to do it. Instead I'll kill my dog and take her eyes to your husband."

"Oh, how can I thank you!" she cried. "Now, I want you to loan me your clothes, and you are to take mine."

The shoemaker returned to his employer and gave him the two eyes from his dog. Meanwhile the young wife had gone in search of work, dressed as a man and with her hair clipped short. She worked for a couple of days with a man who sold coal, but soon went on, always wandering and walking in her loneliness. Finally she drew near the palace of a certain king. The prince saw her and ran in to his father.

"Papa, a young man near the palace is looking for work, and he's very lovely and fine to look at."

"Give him a job," ordered the king. "Tomorrow, my son, you can take him to the mountains to round up some wild bulls and see if he's suited for work on horseback."

When dawn broke the next day, the prince went to the stables with the disguised girl. She saddled the best horse there was and tossed one rein over the edge of a fence, setting the horse right down on his backside.

"Good heavens!" exclaimed the prince, "it looks like this chap is more of a horseman than I am."

They rode away in search of the bulls. With the first toss, the new cowhand lassoed a bull and pulled it down on its snout to the ground. The young prince was astounded by the ability of this young stranger. That night, back at the palace, he said to the king, "Papa, the young man is better than I with a lasso. But I swear he acts just like a woman."

"Go on, you silly boy," said the king. "How can a woman be so handy with a rope? Now, tomorrow you will invite him to go looking for some of the wildest colts we've got."

What do you suppose! The new cowhand had no sooner arrived at the pasture than she lassoed the wildest colt and brought it down on the spot. The prince reported this to his father, but still insisted that the youth made him think of a woman.

"You're on the wrong track, my lad," scoffed the king. "Take him to a dance tomorrow at that house where there are plenty of girls."

The next night, the mysterious youth went with the prince, drank until he had covered the table with empty bottles, and took one of the girls to dance. When it was late, he carried her off to bed. Immediately after they were out of sight of the prince, the girl revealed herself to the prostitute and gave her all the money in her pockets so she would keep the secret.

"How did it all go last night?" the king asked his son the next morning.

"How did it go! Lord, he was the first dancer on the floor. He drank everybody else under the table and took a girl to bed with him!"

The king could find no more proofs with which to test the cowhand, so he called him in and said, "Look here, young fellow, since you've been very useful in my house, I'm going to give you a palace as a reward." Saying that, he crowned the young girl and made her a king like himself.

Very soon after she became king, she sent her police out to search for a certain man named Manuel. When he arrived, the king said, "Good day, sir. I've sent for you because they told me you were married, and I want to know what you've done with your wife."

"Yes, sire," he answered, "I was married, but my woman did me wrong. That's why I sent her to be killed."

"Are you quite sure of that?" asked the king.

"Yes, I am, your Majesty."

"And how was it? I mean, how did she betray you?"

He told the king the whole story, after which she sent her police with instructions to bring in the envious rich man at all costs. When he appeared, the king said, "Tell me a little something about this bet you made with the other gentleman."

"Yes, sire. I simply bet him that while he was away from home, his wife would be unfaithful. Nothing more." But eventually the king got the whole story out of him, and then the old sorceress was promptly summoned to the palace. When the old lady had confessed her part in the plot, the king declared that the rich man had to return everything he had won to the other man immediately. As for the wicked old woman, she was tied between the wildest colts in the kingdom and torn to pieces in the dust. Finally the young husband appeared at the palace again.

"Would you know your wife if you were to see her?" asked the king.

"Yes, your majesty. Seeing her, I'm sure I'd know her right away."

The king repeated the question three times, and each time the man assured him that he would certainly recognize his wife.

"I am she," declared the king, much to the poor man's bewilderment. With that, she sent him off to be washed, bathed, and dressed in the finest suit there was. The king and her husband lived on happily together, and I believe they haven't died yet.

Now the tale goes up a bean stalk so the next storyteller can spin us another.

• *38* • *White Onion*

• A LONG, long time ago, White Onion lived on an island in the center of the sea. She vowed one day that she would give a ship full of gold and silver to whoever could go to bed with her and turn toward her side of the bed. He who turned was to marry her, and he who didn't was to pay her the treasure ship. There were many millionaires who thought about this and concluded, "Being in bed with her, how would it be possible not to turn over to her side?"

One morning a very rich man arrived with his loaded ship to take up the bet. As they were tucking themselves in together, White Onion gave him a little glass of refreshment. Immediately he fell into a deep sleep until the next day, when she awoke him. The millionaire remembered with a fright that he had lost his fortune. After taking breakfast with the girl, he delivered her the ship and, penniless, took his leave. Very soon after, he told another millionaire about his encounter with White Onion. His friend was sure that he could certainly turn over in her bed, and loaded his treasure ship to set sail for the island.

"Do you come for the bet, my good gentleman?" she asked as he docked.

"For the bet, White Onion," he said confidently.

When they had agreed on the terms, she invited him to supper and bed. Just as they were getting under the covers, she gave him also the little bedtime nip. He took the drink in one swig and fell into the bed in a profound sleep. When she shook him awake the next morning, the poor man was greatly shocked at having lost all his riches. After breakfast, he headed home as poor as a church mouse.

Eventually he told a third millionaire of his misadventure with the famous White Onion. This one too set out confidently on the voyage. She invited him in for lunch and afterwards took him for a stroll in the garden. The afternoon flew by agreeably and it was soon time for supper and bed. She gave him the same little glass just before bedtime, whereupon he too fell into a groggy slumber and didn't awake the whole night through. The girl roused him for breakfast in the morning, and of course he was heavily burdened with the loss of his fortune. In sheer dejection he nibbled at his breakfast and went trudging home, his pockets turned inside out. He told the tale to yet another millionaire, who tried and failed as the rest had done. She had now four victims to her credit.

Now it so happened that there was a very rich man who had one son. When this man was on his death bed, he warned the boy never to fall in love with White Onion, for he would be left in the street with nothing. After this, the lad used to pass by many vendors selling onions, but he never bought a single one, for he wished to heed his father's advice. One day he passed a scabby old man with two baskets of onions.

"Will you buy some onions, young sir?" asked the vendor.

"I will if they're colored," he answered, "but not any white ones."

"Why on earth not?"

Then the boy told him how his father had warned him never

to fall in love with White Onion. The grubby old fellow burst out laughing and said, "Young gentleman, it's not that at all. What your father said was never to fall in love with the princess White Onion who lives on the sea island and has a bet with all young men who will sleep with her that they can't turn over to her side of the bed."

The boy bought two baskets of onions from the seedy old fellow, and all the way home he wondered how it could possibly be that one could sleep with the princess without turning over. Right away he began to sell all his possessions and load a ship with gold and silver, after which he sailed away to the sea island. As he was getting into bed with White Onion, she gave him the glass of refreshment, and sure enough, he collapsed into a deep sleep until the next morning. He was greatly startled when she awoke him and cheerily served him breakfast. But immediately he asked her to lend him a boat so he could go for another shipload of gold and silver. The boy went straight to his godfather, who was twice as rich as White Onion. This old man knew that his godson had a great deal of wealth and decided that it was safe to lend him the ship for three days time, on the condition that he would claim a pound of flesh from his godson's rump if the boat weren't returned in time. As the boy was approaching White Onion's island for the second time he chanced through the garden near her house. Just at this moment a mangy, ragged old woman under the trees spoke up. "There goes that poor boy to lose another boatload. If only someone could tell him what it is that White Onion gives him."

"Listen, dirty one," said the boy, overhearing the woman's mumbling, "what makes me fall so sound asleep with her? If you'll tell me, I'll make you rich and powerful."

"Then heed me," she croaked. "Take the drink she gives you at bedtime and throw it away secretly under your cape. That way you won't fall asleep."

The boy went inside and undressed to go to bed with White Onion. She passed him the regular glass of refreshment, which he tossed away under his cape, tucking himself snugly under the covers. About midnight, he rolled over to her side of the bed, whereupon White Onion exclaimed, "This man is going to be my husband." The next morning, she sent for priests and bishops to wed the two of them. There was a great celebration, and in the midst of his joy, the young groom forgot completely about returning the boat to his godfather. When he remembered, he thought, "It really doesn't matter anyway. If he gets angry, I'll return two ships to him instead of one."

Once the celebrations were over, he sailed the ship back to hand it over to the old man. But his godfather refused to receive it, saying that he would demand his pound of flesh from the young man's rump. The boy refused and was immediately thrown in jail. As he still had a coin in his pocket, he sent for some paper and wrote a letter to White Onion. Upon receiving the news, she dressed herself as a viceroy and headed for the godfather's house, notifying him beforehand to expect a viceregal visit. White Onion sailed in her boat and went ashore with all the pomp of a true viceroy. She went directly to the jail and began to take declarations from the prisoners. One by one she set them free, until she came to the very last cell and spotted her husband. White Onion recognized him at once, but he had no idea who she was. She asked him for his declaration and got the whole story of his godfather's cruel greed.

"Is this so?" the viceroy asked the godfather sternly.

"It is," he answered.

"Very well, my dear sir. In that case, you shall take your pound of flesh, but all and exactly in one slice. If you cut either too much or too little, you'll have to pay."

The godfather protested that he wanted to take it in little pieces, and when the viceroy insisted on one single chunk, he shouted, "Then let everything be lost. To hell with it!"

With that, the viceroy took the prisoner aboard her boat and set sail. Since her husband was unshaven and disheveled after his days in jail, she dispatched him to clean up and change into some fresh clothes. When he was properly cleaned, he was the very mirror of fashion. The viceroy went to her cabin to change as well, and appeared dressed as a lovely woman.

"Look at me," she commanded her husband. "Do you know your woman now?"

"Maybe so and maybe not," he answered hesitantly, for they had been together only a short time before he was jailed.

"I'm your true wife," she announced joyously.

"No!" he gasped incredulously.

"What marks did your wife have?"

"Why, there were three golden hairs on the left side of her waist."

At that, the woman lifted her skirt. "Are these the ones?"

"By God, so they are!" he cried, opening his arms and hugging his wife to him.

They arrived home in great joy and began the celebrations again without any danger. The young husband was so happy that he went to see the grubby old woman and gave her a furnished house and a shipload of gold and silver. She became rich and powerful, and White Onion and her husband lived happily together on the island.

• *39* • *Quico and Caco*

• THERE WAS in a certain land a king who had an only son. The boy turned out to be such a thief that not even his father could tolerate him. He had nicknamed the lad "Quico." The son kept finding one way or another of robbing his father, until finally the king was fed up and gave him some money to move to another place where nobody would see him any more.

Quico wandered through many parts and always was looking for a companion who would be his equal in the art of robbery. One day he heard that in another kingdom there was a man who was more of a thief than he. The lad traveled in search of this fellow and found out that he was called "Caco." When they finally met, Quico said to Caco, "My friend, I have come to see you, for I hear that you are the finest thief in all these parts."

"That I am," answered Caco proudly. "I believe there's no one equal to me in skill. Why, I can even rob the eagle of eggs without its feeling a thing."

"I'd have to see that to believe it," said Quico skeptically.

They went to a precipice where an eagle was nesting. Caco began to scramble up, with Quico climbing behind. Caco stuck his hand under the eagle, took out the eggs ever so carefully, and put them in his pocket.

"Let's see those eggs," said Quico when they were back to earth. Caco stuck his hand in his pocket and found nothing, for while he had been robbing the eagle, Quico had robbed him.

"You've beat me, friend," he said sheepishly.

"At all events," said Quico, chuckling to himself, "I need you as a partner. The two of us can steal much better together." Right on the spot they vowed that whatever happened to them, neither one would back out of the deal.

That night they decided to initiate their partnership by robbing the king's palace. He had a whole room full of gold locked away as safe and as sound as could be. When the two thieves crept up in the night they looked about for a long while, trying to figure out a foolproof plan. Quico, being the cleverer of the two, suggested that they enter by the roof. So they unnailed a sheet of zinc from the palace roof and swung down inside on a cord. Caco was the first to go in. When he had his sack full of gold, he jerked on the cord and was pulled out by Quico. They sneaked away leaving the sheet of zinc just as it had been before.

The following night, it was Quico's turn. When Caco had pulled him out, they scurried merrily home to bed, thinking that they had left the roof well arranged. But it wasn't so. When the king sent his administrator to take out some money, the man came dashing back frantically with the news of the great robbery. There appeared to be no clues, but the king immediately summoned a wise old counselor, who was blind. If Quico and Caco were thieves, this fellow had been a much greater one in his time and would be sure to have some suggestions in this case. The counselor told the king that the solution was the easiest thing in the world. The guards had merely to put a smudge fire in the treasure room and the smoke would escape wherever the thieves had entered. The men did just as the old fox advised, and sure enough, the smoke began to circle out around the edges of the zinc sheet. After this, the blind counselor instructed them to place a tub full of tar under the loose zinc plate.

That night the two thieves arrived to pull the same trick. It was Caco's turn to go down, so Quico bound him with the cord and lowered him down to the gold heap. By the time poor Caco had realized what the trap was, he was stuck hand and foot in the tar.

"We're done for," he called up. "I don't know how the devil I got into this, but I can't move an inch."

The two partners struggled half the night with the infernal tar bucket, but it was all to no avail. Finally Caco charged Quico to take care of his wife and asked him to cut off his head and bury it with his body, taking care that nobody should ever discover their identity. Quico fixed the cord tight on the roof and lowered himself down to his companion. They bade each other farewell and Quico sliced off his partner's head. This he put in his sack as he slipped away from the palace, nailing down the piece of roof just to get the king's goat. When he got to Caco's house, the poor robber's wife was beside herself with desperation.

"No, ma'm," said Quico, "it's no use crying. These are the vows which I made with my partner."

When the king sent to see how the counselor's plan had worked out, his men found nothing more than the headless body all mucked up in the tar. How in the deuce could they know who he was? The counselor was summoned once again, for they realized that more than one thief was in on this. The old man told them to drag a cow's hide through the streets with Caco's body on it. Then, wherever the thief's family was, they would have to cry. So the king's men went from street to street pulling the body through the dust. The counselor had instructed them to write "Here there were tears" on any house where they saw someone crying. When they passed Caco's house, Quico was in the front yard carving a little stick. With all the commotion, Caco's wife came to the door and, seeing the body of her husband on the dirty old cowhide, couldn't contain her tears.

"What are you sobbing about, foolish woman?" said Quico quickly. "Just because I cut my finger. At least we're going to have something to eat these days."

Quico had shrewdly cut his finger as soon as the woman started to weep, and when the guards came over, he explained that she was just upset about the blood on his hand. But the king's men were in no mood to pay heed to this business, and wrote on the door in heavy ink, "Here they cried." As soon as they left for the palace to give the king the news, Quico darted out to buy some black ink, and followed the guards, writing

"Here they cried" on all the doors in town. He even wrote it on the palace gate. The king ordered his men to go out and take everyone whose house had the sign. Just as the police left the palace, they spotted the first door with the message scribbled on it. But as they went along examining the other doors, they discovered that the same thing was true all over town. Deciding that this was surely a wild goose chase, they returned to report what had happened. The king was enraged, and summoned the counselor to give him a better idea.

"Let's try something else," said the old blind man. "Prepare a banquet and invite the whole countryside to supper. Then you give them all wine with opium. That way we can see which one is the crook."

"But how on earth?" asked the puzzled king.

"It's very easy," replied the counselor, "because once the thief is caught here, even though he's sleeping, he'll be scared out of his wits. Then he whose heart beats fastest has to be the one."

The king accepted the plan and sent invitations to all the people to come to supper under obligation of royal decree. The whole town flocked to the palace, Quico being one of the first to arrive. There were so many people that when the servants brought on the drugged wine the guests began to topple over one on top of the other. As soon as everyone was asleep, the guards felt all the pulses, even that of the counselor, who had also been feasting and was drugged asleep. The guards discovered that Quico's heart was beating faster than anybody else's, and set the sleeping fellow apart from the rest. Then they brought a razor and shaved off one of Quico's eyebrows.

It was very late when Quico, being quite nervous, awoke before the others and began to check on what he had. He passed his hand over his face and found that one eyebrow was missing. Nevertheless, as a man of foresight, he had taken his razor with him to the banquet, and now had only to shave an eyebrow off everybody else in the room. Eventually he came upon the slumbering counselor, whom he knew to be the king's chief advisor. Quico shaved off both of the old man's eyebrows and lay down to sleep again.

In the morning the king came in with his guards where all the drunkards were heaped up in a batch. On examining the crowd, he found that nobody had two eyebrows. The guard who had shaved Quico was quite taken aback before the royal wrath and stammered that he had shaved only one man. But, after all, there was nothing to do but set everybody free, for they could hardly clear up this mess. The king woke the befuddled old counselor and demanded a new and foolproof plan.

"Your Majesty," he said, "send twelve guards to watch over the dead thief's body on that high hill you see in the distance. That way the whole town will know about it. I hear that the dead man's partner wants to bury the head with the body, so I suspect he's likely to show up sooner or later." The old man was just short of being a prophet, he was so sharp.

Twelve royal police were dispatched to watch over Caco's body on the hilltop. The king gave them a lamb so they could have meat to eat in bad weather. Quico was watching from his house when the procession left town with his partner's remains. Right away he dashed off to buy twelve priest's cassocks of Carmelite color with cordons and all the works—even twelve pairs of sandals. Then he loaded a burro with crates as saddlebags and bought a barrel of wine, in which he sprinkled a liberal dose of opium. When he had said his prayers, he set off with this paraphernalia for the hilltop. It was already dark when he rode by the campsite of the guards, and Quico had put on one of the cassocks and begun to pray. The king's men saw the priest riding alone in the night and insisted on inviting him in. At first he played hard to get and told them he was just taking some air and had to get to mass on time in the neighboring town.

"Why don't you stop by for just a minute, father, to say a prayer for the deceased?"

"Very well, very well," answered the priest, "if it's for that. I'll do it so that this soul will be guided on the right road, for after all, he may have died without confession." He bade them all kneel down and cross themselves, and they began to say the rosary together. The priest stood above the body executing certain ceremonies. Then the leader suggested that his men roast the lamb and invite the priest to supper. The priest protested again that he would be late for mass, but the guards prevailed and cut him the choicest piece of roast lamb.

"The only thing missing for the roast is the wine," they mumbled.

"By good fortune, I happen to have a cask on my burro," said the priest. "It's sweet wine that I'm carrying for the Holy Church, but we can all have a nip just to wash down this delicious roast." He unloaded the barrel, which pleased the guards enormously, and very soon they had all drunk themselves to sleep. Then Quico deftly unloaded the cassocks he had bought, took the uniforms off the men, and dressed each of them as a priest, even down to the sandals and the black hat. After this, he snatched up his partner's body, loaded it onto the burro, and rode off for the cemetery at a brisk trot. There he placed the head together with the trunk and buried Caco, while the guards slumbered away on the hilltop.

Up rose the sun the next morning, but the royal police simply snored on into the morning. When the king chanced to look up to the hill, he was put out at not seeing any movement in the camp. The day was well along when the chief guard awoke and saw everybody dressed in the cassocks and sandals. He shook his men out of their beds, and everybody milled about in confusion, not knowing where to turn. Eventually they realized that the body had completely vanished in the night along with their police uniforms. You can imagine how ashamed they were to think of returning to the palace naked save for their cassocks! Once they had gathered their nerve, they shambled with sheepish looks toward the palace to report their disgrace.

"What on earth is going on this morning?" gasped the king as he looked out the window. "Here come twelve friars who look just like the royal guards." Immediately he rang for his trusty counselor.

"It's just that a priest has played them for fools, or at least someone disguised as a priest," said the wise old man. He had a great power to divine, even though his projects never worked out worth a damn.

"Well, counselor, what do you suggest next?" said the king,

chortling all the while to see his men dressed like poor friars without their weapons and handsome uniforms.

"Nothing, except to wait for the next thief to come and rob," replied the old man, shrugging his shoulders in resignation.

But Quico, who by then had stacked away a pretty little pile of money, decided to repent and spend a peaceful life. I think to this very day he's living happily with his partner's wife.

Part V
Tales of Tricksters and Dupes

·40· *The Black Dog*

• THERE LIVED ONCE in a certain land an old couple with three sons named Juan, Francisco, and Manuelito. One day the oldest asked his father for his blessing, for he wished to go roaming and learn something of the world. The old man blessed his son and gave him some provisions, and Juan set out on his journey. When he had traveled some way, he sat down by a river to eat a little flour mixed with water. The fishes called up to him, "Why don't you give us some? We haven't eaten for seven years."

"Why don't you work so you can eat?" he answered. "I can't give you a bite, since there's little enough for me." With that, he picked up his pack and continued down the road.

Later Juan came to the jungle in another realm. There he was met by a lion, a tiger, and a fox. They too came to ask him for food, for they hadn't eaten for seven whole years. But Juan paid no heed to that. As long as *he* was eating, everything was fine.

"You're going to be sorry you didn't share your meal with us," said the three animals as they returned to the forest.

Soon after, the lad approached the palace of a black cat to ask for lodgings.

"I'm going to ask just one little favor of you," said the cat. "Please pass me that plate so I can give you something to eat." But Juan simply asked the cat why she didn't get up herself. He wasn't there to wait on her.

When God had awakened the next day, Juan saddled his horse and asked the cat where he could find work. She told him to ask the plate and it was going to give him the answer. He rode away in a huff, coming to the palace of a king who told the boy that there was plenty of work. He offered to pay him two *almuds* [an old Spanish measure] of silver if he would go to clear the jungle.

"You must go with the black dog," added the king, "and be very careful! If the dog doesn't come home to eat, you can't come either."

The next day, Juan left for the jungle with his hatchet and the black dog, which went along to take care of him. After his day at work he returned to the palace in the afternoon. Now, the king and Juan had taken an oath the day before: the one to get angry first would have his head cut off.

"How's it going, my boy?" asked the king merrily when Juan came in.

"As a matter of fact, your majesty, it's going rather badly. You've had me working all day without eating a bite."

"And did you get angry?" asked the king slyly.

"Why shouldn't I be angry if you keep me all day without food?"

"Do you remember the little oath we made?" asked the king. With that, he sent his Negro to take the youth away to the block and chop off his head.

It happened that Juan and his brothers had at home a little tree which would wither whenever any of them was in trouble. Francisco noticed that the tree was very brown and dry, and asked his father to bless him so that he might go in search of his brother. Francisco met the same misfortune as the first brother. He didn't give food either to the fishes or to the animals in the jungle. The fishes had warned him that his day of reckoning would come, and when the lion, the tiger and the fox asked him for food, he merely scoffed and told them to work for a living.

"You're going to find yourself in the greatest poverty," they told him as they slipped away.

A little further down the road, Francisco came to the cat's palace to ask for lodgings, which she promptly gave him.

"But one thing I'm going to ask of you," purred the pussy, "Pass me that plate so I can give you a little something for supper."

"Why don't *you* get up?" answered Francisco. "I'm no servant of yours."

The following morning, he readied his horse and left, without even asking the cat where he might find work. Soon enough he arrived at the king's palace, and was put to work clearing the jungle. The king had offered the boy three *almuds* of silver for the job and had made the same little bet which he had had with the first brother. Francisco set off for the jungle along with the black dog, and chopped and cut the whole day through. When afternoon came, the dog trotted home to the palace, followed by the boy.

"How did it go, Pancho [nickname for Francisco]?" asked the king.

"Pretty damned badly, your majesty," he answered peevishly. "You kept me there the livelong day without a square meal."

"Don't you remember our vow?" asked the king, tapping his finger on the throne. "The first one to get angry would lose his head." Pancho too was dispatched to the chopping block without further delay.

Meanwhile, Manuelito noticed that the little tree had withered again and asked his father for permission to go out in search of his two older brothers. He took special care to ask the old man for two loads of provisions, one of flour and the other of cooked meat. After a long journey, the boy came to the same river where his brothers had stopped before him. He had sat down to eat some flour when the little fishes spoke up.

"Manuelito, it's been seven years since we last had a meal."

"My poor little fellows," said he. "I was hungry already, and I've just left the house." He took a bag of flour and emptied it all into the water for the hungry fishes. When he had packed his load and headed on, they called him to come back. Thinking they were still hungry, he ran back to the river bank.

"Here I am, little fishies. What did you want?"

"We called you to give you a magic charm," they said, presenting him with a wand with which he could obtain anything he desired. Manuelito thanked them and continued on his travels. As it was getting dark he came upon the same jungle where his brothers had been before, and he sat down on a log to have a snack. The lion, the tiger, and the fox appeared and told him they hadn't eaten in seven years. Immediately Manuelito pulled out half of the cooked meat from his sack and gave a generous chunk to each one. Afterwards, he invited them to a second helping, and the ravenous animals gobbled up everything he could give them.

"My companion," said the lion to the tiger, "I think it's about time we gave this youth a charm." So the lion pulled off a magic ear and presented it to Manuelito. Whatever he asked of the ear would be granted him. Next, the tiger cut off his own tail, which was magic and could also grant any wish. Finally, the fox gave him a satchel which would bring him all that he desired. They told him to remember them whenever he was in trouble, for they would always help and favor the boy.

Manuelito continued on his road and eventually came to seek lodging at the cat's palace.

"A place to sleep?" purred the cat. "With great pleasure. But do me a little favor and pass me that plate so I can give you a bite to eat."

"Of course, my good pussy, I'll pass you a hundred plates if you wish." Then he sent the cat's servants to give food to the animals as well.

When the cat had prepared him some provisions the next day, she said, "I'm not really a cat at all, you know, but really a princess enchanted in this form." She went on to tell him the story of how her stepmother had bewitched her, and added, "Insofar as you go along doing your work, I will be gradually disenchanted. But don't accept anything to eat, for they're going to try to kill you."

The boy promised to follow the cat's advice, and the following day came to the king's palace where his brothers had come before. Naturally, the king made the same vow and sent Manuelito off to work in the jungle, offering to pay him five decaliters of silver. When the boy and the black dog arrived at the work site, Manuelito sat down to take breakfast and then lay down for a little nap. The bitch began to bite and scratch him so he would get to work, but that day he didn't strike even one blow with his axe. In the late afternoon, the black dog trotted home to the palace, with Manuelito following behind.

"How did it go today, Manuelito?" asked the sly king.

"Quite well, as a matter of fact, your majesty."

"Why didn't you come home for lunch?"

"Oh, I can stand it for a year without eating," answered the boy.

"Didn't you get angry when I didn't send you any lunch?" queried the king insistently.

"Not at all, your highness."

"Laugh three times," ordered the king. Manuelito laughed heartily, and the befuddled king exclaimed, "By Jove, I'm done for now."

The following dawn, Manuelito told the dog they were going to set out for the jungle as soon as the birds sang, to get an early start on the day's work. But when the boy arrived he sat down as before for breakfast and a little nap. Once again the dog jumped on him and began biting and mauling.

"Go on with your nonsense, black bitch," he said. "You're not bothering me." But the dog didn't understand and kept on pestering him until Manuelito's great patience ran out. He seized the axe and smacked the creature soundly, killing it on the spot.

"Well, where's the black dog?" asked the king when the boy had returned.

"She came on ahead, your majesty."

"No, she hasn't been here at all," said the king suspiciously.

"I'm going to tell you the whole truth, my king. I was resting when the dog came along and began to bite me. And, you see, I lost my patience and did her in with the axe."

"Ayeee! For God's sake, man, you've killed my mother-in-law!" wailed the king.

"Are you angry, sire?" asked Manuelito calmly.

"No, of course not," stammered the king. "Not at all, my good fellow."

"Laugh three times."

Without the slightest desire, the king managed three hollow laughs and went off disgruntled to take tea. Over tea, his mother told him that they had to do away with the boy by poisoning him. Manuelito was listening to every word.

When the king sent him to supervise the workers in the vineyard the next day, Manuelito told them, "My king said you should tear up the whole vineyard." Later, his majesty arrived to check on things and found only three little stubby vines left in the earth.

"Oh, you boy!" moaned the king, "first you killed my mother-in-law, and now you've torn up the whole vineyard."

"Are you angry, sire?"

"No, no, of course I'm not," mumbled the king in great consternation.

"Then smile five times."

The king grimaced the smiles and thought to himself, "I'm in a bad way. He's gotten me on two counts now."

That evening, the king's mother proposed that they turn her grandson into a parrot in a cage of gold and place him on top of a soaped pole. Then Manuelito was to climb up nude to get it, and when he reached the top, the parrot would peck his eyes out. But all the while, the boy was listening to their scheme.

Sure enough, the next day the king ordered the youth to fetch down the prophetic parrot from the soaped pole. When the bird pecked his hand, Manuelito took out a dagger and cut off its head. Then he carried the cage and the headless parrot into the palace.

"Woe is me, now you've done it!" cried the king. "First you killed my mother-in-law, then you tore up my vineyard, and *now* you've killed my son."

"Are you angry?" asked Manuelito softly.

"Not a bit, fellow, not a bit," stammered the king.

"Laugh seven times."

Without the slightest desire to do so, the king forced seven "ha-ha's" and retired promptly to his room. The queen slipped in and said, "Tomorrow I'm going to turn myself into a cow with golden horns and you are to put me to pasture. Then send the boy in on a skinny horse, and I'll kill him. There's no other way."

The king ordered Manuelito to saddle one of the scrawniest nags in the corral. But there was a beautiful colt there which caught his eye. "I'll have nothing to do with that other bag of bones," thought the boy. So he lassoed the colt and nailed the saddle to its back with long, sharp nails. Then he mounted up and went in search of the cow with the golden horns. The cow became ornery and stubborn when it saw the rider coming and didn't want to budge forwards or backwards. Manuelito quickly leaped down, drew his dagger, and cut off the head with the golden horns.

"Ay, ay, boy, what you've gone and done," groaned the king

when he saw the cow's head. "You drove nails into my father-in-law and now you've just killed my wife!"

"Are you angry, sire?"

"Not a bit, not at all," he affirmed, grinding and clenching his teeth together.

"Laugh twenty times." The king blurted out a few cheerless laughs.

By now, everybody in the palace was getting angry at the king. His mother, the old queen, ordered him to invite Manuelito to tea. The boy accepted the invitation, but refused to eat, for he remembered his promise to the cat, and would eat only after seven years. When this failed, the mother proposed another plan to the king.

"Tonight," she said, "we're going to sleep with the boy, and we'll send three Negroes to heat up the three ovens. When he's asleep, we'll slip him a special potion." Manuelito was listening to everything.

That night he got into bed very early with the king and his mother, and pretended to have fallen asleep right away. The king and the old lady lay down in the same bed and very soon they really dozed off. While they were snoring away, Manuelito slipped the potion to both of them. Then he pushed the old woman toward the edge of the bed, placed the king in the middle, and hid himself in the corner on the very edge of the bed. When the Negroes came to say that the oven was piping hot, Manuelito jabbed the ruler with his elbow to tell him it was time. The king immediately shoved the old woman out of bed and into the fiery ovens. He returned to bed to give Manuelito a big hug and a kiss, thinking all the while that the boy was his mother. At dawn, he awoke to find himself sleeping with the boy, and shrieked, "By the gods, you again! Now see what you've gone and done! You killed my father-in-law, you tore up my vineyard, you killed my wife, and now you've made me burn my own mother."

"Are you angry, your majesty?"

"I'm furious!" roared the red-faced king.

"Does it really enrage you?"

"How can it do anything *but* enrage me?" stormed the king.

"Do you remember our little vow? You're going to lose your head."

"No, my good man," cried the terrified king. "What are you going to do with me?"

" 'No,' you say? Word of honor! You have to die. Now, where are you keeping my brothers whose heads you cut off? If you restore them to life, I'll spare you."

The king led the boy to one of the palace rooms, and there were the two dead brothers stretched out. His majesty promptly restored them to life.

"What can we do with this king?" Manuelito asked them when they had risen from death. They answered that he had to pay the same price he had asked of them, and all three slew the ruler without further ado.

"Now," added Manuelito, "one of you will stay on in the palace as an administrator, and the other as an accountant. I'm going home to see my mother."

But while he was still at the palace, the pussy cat arrived in a golden coach accompanied by a whole regiment, to pay honor to the youngest brother. Then and there, the cat's palace was disenchanted. If Manuelito's palace was beautiful, the cat's was a treasure in comparison. She told him that first he had to marry her, and afterwards he could go for his parents. Manuelito and his cat-princess were wedded, and to this day they're probably still celebrating the happy event.

• 41 • *Pedro Animales Fools His Boss*

• ONE DAY Pedro Animales, finding himself without any money, took work as a hired hand on a ranch. The owner sent him to be a swineherd. Pedro took the pigs a little way off from the house and began thinking of a way to make some business out of these animals. He cut off their tails and stuck them in a swamp. That way it would seem that the pigs themselves were caught there. Then he went on merrily to sell the swine in town. Once the deal was made and he had pocketed the money, he returned to the swamp. Since he was very late in getting back with the animals, the boss had set out on a search and found his new helper without a single pig.

"Well, where are the swine, Pedro?"

"Over there, boss. They got mucked up in that swamp and are sinking under. You can't see anything but their little curly tails!"

"Didn't I tell you not to take them near the swamp?" roared the owner.

"I know, but it just happened, boss."

The rancher began to tug on the tails until they popped out in his hands.

"Man," he called to Pedro, "go to the house and get me three tools; a shovel, a pike, and a crowbar. And don't be long about it. We're going to get these pigs out yet."

Pedro ran off to the house, where the owner's wife and two daughters were waiting in the doorway. He said that the boss had sent orders for the three of them to give themselves to him. Of course the women didn't believe a word of it. Then Pedro held up three fingers and called over to the rancher, "Didn't you say all three?"

"Yes, all three," he shouted back impatiently.

And that was how Pedro Animales did some good business and made fools of the three women. Right after that, he fled from the house.

· 42 · *The Unknown Bird*

· ONCE THERE was a man named Juan Bautista who lived with his wife, Maria Inez. He was so poor and forlorn that one day when he was twenty years old he declared that if the Devil would give him some money, he would make a pact with him until the age of eighty. The time passed, and when he was working in the fields one day, a gentleman appeared before him.

"What was it you promised, Juan Bautista?"

"I promised to speak with the Devil if he gave me some riches."

"What would you give in return?" asked the stranger slyly.

"Myself."

"Very well, I am the Devil. Let's make the contract right here and now."

They agreed that the man would go with the Devil when he was eighty years old. That same night, Juan came home to his little cottage with three loads of silver. He had a bungalow built just like his employer's, and he became richer and richer with ranches and possessions. Finally he realized that he was going to be old with all his money. The longer he lived, the richer he was, but the deadline was drawing near and he was daily weighed down by the knowledge.

"Why are you so downcast, my love?" asked his wife one day. "Before, we were so poor that we didn't have a day's supplies or anything to put on. We were practically nude, and you weren't sad like this. But now you don't eat a bite and you spend the whole day worrying."

"What good will it do to tell you?" he moaned. "You can't do a thing about it."

But, since women are sometimes so stubborn, she kept on pestering him. A month passed and another, and the wife was still nagging her husband to tell her his sorrows.

"Look," he sobbed one day, "how are you going to save me, when I've made a pact with the Devil? That's why we're so rich; and now there are only fifteen days left before he comes for me."

"Is that all it is, my dear?" said his wife. "Why, this is nothing to worry about. Listen to me: you get some hunters to bring you all the birds there are in the world."

Now, how was this man to save himself from the Devil's clutches with a bunch of birds? Nevertheless, he set dozens of hunters to catching birds in all the fields and woods. Meanwhile, his wife was eating as never before to fatten herself up.

"The Devil is coming to get me at noontime tomorrow," announced John one morning.

"My dear," answered his wife, "you must cover me with feathers from all your birds." She stripped down to the skin and covered herself with honey. The rich man and his servants set to plucking feathers from all the different birds they had gathered. Then they stuck them all over the wife until there wasn't a bare inch left.

"Now," she announced in a muffled voice from behind the feathers, "when your friend comes, he's going to say 'Here I have a fine bird.' If he can't guess what bird it is in one minute, he can't take you away. Of course, if he recognizes me, he'll take you and me together, my dear."

When the Devil arrived, he asked for the bird that everyone had been talking about so much. Out strutted the rich man's wife.

"What bird can there be in the world that I don't know?" thought the Devil. He began to study this strange creature with four feet and a round tail, for it had come in rump first. For the life of him, he couldn't recognize it. When the time was up, he shrugged his shoulders and said to the rich man, "All right, take the contract. This must be some woman's work."

The husband kicked the wicked fellow outside, and the Devil exploded on the doorstep. That's how the rich man remained as rich as ever before.

•43• Pedro Urdimale, the Little Fox, and the Mare's Egg

THERE WAS ONCE a shrewd gentleman named Pedro Urdimale. He said to himself one day, "Here I am without a cent in my pocket, and I'm a man who needs money. I'm simply going to have to get it, and that's all there is to it." A bit later he was passing by a farmer's garden and spotted a vine with a beautiful squash the shape and color of an egg. This was just what he needed. He picked the squash with the greatest of care and put it on his shoulder, all the while humming to himself, "I'm going to make a little pile from this. Yes, siree!"

Along the road came a *gringo* [any European or North American] on horseback. He had just arrived from Europe and worked at harvesting, although he didn't really know much about farming.

"What have you there, my friend?" he said upon seeing Pedro with the handsome squash.

"It's a mare's egg, sir."

"What do you mean, a mare's egg?"

"Just that. Listen, this egg is going to hatch a great racing colt."

"Then sell it to me on the double," said the man excitedly.

"But how can I sell it to you when it's about to produce such a fine horse? I couldn't possibly part with it now."

"I *must* have it, at whatever price you ask."

"Well," hedged Pedro, "I'm going to give you a special price, sir. After all, I have to do well by someone like you. Look here, for five thousand *pesos,* the egg is yours."

"It's a deal, man! Take five thousand cash right now."

"But be very, very careful," cautioned Pedro. "Don't let the egg slip, for you'd surely lose the colt."

Pedro tucked away the money and placed the squash on the horse in front of the man. He rode off balancing himself precariously with the mare's egg. Nearby there were some farmers cutting wood. "Hey! That rider has a squash that looks just like my prize one," yelled one of the men. But the foreigner just rode contentedly along with his new acquisition. All of a sudden, his horse stumbled and the squash slipped away and began to roll down the hill. Below there was a *litre* bush which had been uprooted and was lying on the ground. When the squash hit this, it split wide open. Now, what do you suppose! There was a fox sleeping in the shade under the bush. The poor animal was so startled when the squash rolled in upon him that he began to run pell-mell behind the horseman.

"There goes my colt! Stop him! Oh me, what a racing colt it is!" cried the *gringo*.

The poor man galloped away hallooing after the fox, and almost killed himself in the wild pursuit. I believe, Mr. Pino [the editor], that he's still chasing it to this very day.

• ONCE UPON A TIME there lived a gentleman named Pedro. As he could think of no way to earn some money, he set out on the road one day to wander. When he had walked a good bit, he had a need to do his duties, and promptly covered them afterwards with his hat. Just as he was finishing this, two men came along mounted on horseback.

"Good morning," they called to Pedro. "What are you up to there?"

"Good morning," said he politely. "I have a golden partridge and I can't take it out because I'm all alone."

"Really, man?"

"Yes. Why don't you lend me your horse to go for some help?"

One of the riders gladly dismounted and gave Pedro his horse, after which the rogue galloped away, never to return.

"I'm just going to uncover this little bird myself," said the horseman, rubbing his hands in glee and watching Pedro fade from sight over the horizon. He stuck his hand very carefully under the hat and pulled out the treasure. Ugh! He flung it away against a rock and wiped his hand in disgust. [The narrator laughs.]

Meanwhile Pedro had taken the horse to sell in town. With this money he bought clothing and still had some pocket money left over. Now, what should he spot next but a hawthorn bush! He promptly pierced all his coins and hung them on each thorn on the tree. When it was well loaded down, he stretched out on his back to guard it. Very soon two horsemen rode along.

"Isn't that Pedro Urdemales over there?" asked one.

"It sure enough is," answered the other as the two galloped over to the hawthorn bush.

"Hello, boys," said Pedro. "I'm just taking care of this tree until the fruit is ripe enough to pick."

"Humph," responded one, "really?"

"That's right. It's the nicest little money tree anybody could wish."

"Won't you sell it?" asked one of the riders.

"How could you think of such a thing? Not on your life!"

"Oh, come on and sell it to me," urged the other. "I'll give you three hundred *pesos* cash."

"What!" exclaimed Pedro. "For three hundred *pesos* you expect me to sell a tree that I can pick every year? No, sir!"

But the man pestered him so much that Pedro finally gave in. He took the money and hightailed it out of there. The two men lay down beside their tree to watch over it. But the hawthorn bush didn't yield any more. It just stood there without even flowering, the money dangling from the thorns.

"Well, we might as well pick it," said one to the other. "I've got a hunch that something is fishy here." They picked the tree of what there was and set out in pursuit of the vanished Pedro Urdemales. "We're going to nab this scoundrel and make him pay for such a dirty trick!"

In the meantime, Pedro had bought himself a little clay pot and made a hole in the ground. He placed a tin can in the hole, covered it, and lit a fire underneath. Not so long after, the irate horsemen came galloping up on him. When he saw them in the distance, Pedro began whipping the pot and chanting,

> "Boil, little boiling pot,
> I'm going to eat you piping hot.
> Boil, little boiling pot."

It boiled away merrily as the two horsemen rode up at breakneck speed.

"All right," they said, "what the devil are you doing now?"

"Good day, sirs. Why, I'm making some broth to eat, for I've got a wicked appetite."

"How do you think you're going to make broth there, man?" asked one of the riders. "You don't even have a fire."

"Boil, little boiling pot," chanted Pedro again, and away it boiled. He uncovered it and stirred up the broth. The potatoes were well done, so he took it off the hidden fire and sat down to eat lunch.

"Sell me that pot," exclaimed one of the wide-eyed horsemen.

"Now it's the same old story," said Pedro, trying to eat his lunch, "pestering and bothering around so I'll sell you the pot, and afterwards you come chasing me. I won't sell a damned thing."

But the other man insisted and made such a fuss and bother that Pedro finally sold him the pot. The two of them rode home and proudly set the little pot, full of water and potatoes, out on the patio. And how they worked, whipping and beating it!

> "Boil, little boiling pot,
> I'm going to eat you piping hot."

But it was all to no avail. The pot wouldn't even simmer the least little bit.

"Let's move it over to my house to see if it works there," suggested one of them. But it was the same old story: the little pot simply wouldn't boil.

"Now we're really going to catch him and finish him off for good!" they roared, thoroughly enraged with this latest trick.

Pedro had taken the money from the sale of the pot and bought himself a young lamb, which he took home to his wife. Then he slaughtered the animal and filled its intestine with the blood, meanwhile carving himself a little hemlock whistle. Eventually he spotted the two horsemen coming on the double and called to his wife, "Here they come, my dear. I'm just going to drape this intestine around your neck and then stab you there. When the lamb's blood spurts, you'll play dead."

Up came the riders. "Now we've got you on the spot, Urdemales. What a nerve to sell us that fake boiling pot! You'll pay for this."

Pedro turned to his wife and shouted, "You, woman! You're to blame for all my fooling around!" With that, he snatched up his knife and stuck his wife in the back of the neck. The blood gushed out all over, and she fell dead to the floor. Immediately Pedro seized his hemlock whistle and blew: "Pirulí, Pirulí, Pirulí, Pirulí!" Slowly she moved a foot. "Pirulí, Pirulí, Pirulí!" Gradually she moved a hand. "Pirulí, Pirulí!" he blew again. Then and there, his wife came alive and sat up.

"Ay, Lord God, what has happened to me?" she moaned.

"You see?" said Pedro to the two men. "Thanks to you, I had

killed my wife. That's how much you bother me, pestering me the livelong day."

"Sell me the whistle, old chap," burst out one of them.

"No, sir! I'm not selling any whistle."

"But you've got to. Look, I'll give you three hundred *pesos.*"

"Again?" exclaimed Pedro. "For God's sake, how long will this go on? And afterwards you always come back to make my life miserable."

Eventually the men insisted so much and were such a nuisance, that Pedro sold them the whistle and they left, full of contentment. One went home and started strutting about in a rage with his wife.

"You don't do what I tell you," he yelled, and—BOOM!—he stabbed her in the back of the neck with a long, sharp knife. She died, of course. Right away he began to pipe in her ear. "Pirulí, Pirulí, Pirulí!" ("Pirulí," my eye! She was stone dead.)

"I'll take her to my house to see if anything happens there," suggested the other when the husband had about given up. But it was the same story—"Pirulí, Pirulí, Pirulí!"—all over again. The poor woman never got well. They had to bury her.

Now the men were at their wit's end. "We're going to kill this guy for certain. We'll take him to pieces the minute we lay hands on him."

Pedro had already scampered away from his house. The men, however, were not to be put off, and eventually came upon him.

"Now, Urdemales, your game is up. You won't be fooling anybody any more."

"Oh, yes?" he answered. "Well, I suppose you know best."

Nearby there was a tremendous precipice, and down below a river flowed through some meadows where there was a large flock of sheep grazing. The men took Pedro to the edge of the cliff. But then they simply tied him hand and foot to a tree, for it happened to be twelve o'clock and they had to go home for lunch.

"After we have lunch," they said, "we'll be back to throw you into the river."

But what do you suppose happened? A poor old man chanced

by while the others were gone and asked Pedro what he was doing tied to that tree.

"Oh, it's because I'm not capable of eating a tray of *empanadas* [a Chilean meat pastry] and of marrying the king's daughter. They're going to throw me off the cliff, and I'm a married man to boot."

"Well, I'm a bachelor and I want to marry," said the other. So he untied Urdemales from the tree, and Pedro bound the man in his place. After lunch, the two horsemen arrived to finish the job.

"No, no, sirs," begged the old man, "Don't throw me over! I'm going to marry the king's daughter. Don't you see? Listen to me!"

"Ah, you're going to marry the king's daughter, eh? That's a good one." And down he went.

Meanwhile, Pedro had hidden at the bottom of the cliff in the little inlets of the river. The poor old man sunk straight to the bottom like a stone, and out popped Pedro from the water, carrying a long switch.

> "Hey, hey, look at my flock!
> If you'd thrown me a little further down,
> More lambs and sheep I would have found."

"There's that devil again," said the two men, looking down at the river. "And look at that flock he has! Come up here, you."

"There you go again with that foolish pestering," shouted Pedro.

"Are there a lot of sheep down there?"

"Pooh," he answered, "of course there are. I got them, didn't I? If you'd thrown me a little harder, I'd have gotten even more."

They were both so full of envy that they begged Urdemales to tie them up to the same tree and find out what good herdsmen they were. But since it was twelve o'clock again, Pedro merely bound them and left them while he went to take lunch. When he returned, the two men put up a great ruckus. "No, sir, don't throw us over, we're going to marry the king's daughter. Please!"

"Hah!" said Pedro, "the old story about the king's daughter, eh?" And—*poom!*—over and down went both of them forever.

• THERE WERE once upon a time two kings, one rich and the other very poor. One day the poor king went to ask his rich brother how he had made his fortune.

"By getting up early," answered the other. "There's nothing better, because whatever you find on the road is yours."

"But what if they want to take it away from me?" asked the poor king.

"They can't, because you find it thrown away in the road."

The next day the poor brother stole four cows from the rich one and then went over to notify his brother that he had found these animals wandering in the road that morning. The brother told him that the cows surely belonged to the finder, and that he should get up even earlier the next day. That night the poor brother stole a magnificent bull from the other and set it loose in the road. He got up at dawn the following morning and drove the bull into his pasture, trotting off happily to tell his brother of his good luck. He had to ring the bell for some time, for the rich king had no reason to get up early.

"Did you spend a good night?" he asked, finally appearing in his bathrobe at the door.

"Good enough," answered the other, "for I got up with the birds this morning and found a beautiful bull."

"Well, now you have the breeding problem solved," said the rich king. "There's no need to get up early any longer."

But the poor king calculated that he would have to keep up his dawn activities for a couple of days more in order to be rich like his brother. Again that night, he pinched ten cows from the other king's pasture and set them out in the road. After rounding them up in the morning, he decided not to tell his brother this time. "After all, he could surprise me," thought the poor king to himself.

At noontime, the rich brother went out to survey his ranch. Counting the animals, he found that fifteen were missing. "Bah," he grumbled, "that rascal brother of mine is robbing me blind. I'm going to take a little turn over by his pastures." Sure enough, he found his livestock in the other's fields. "If I take them home," he thought, "he's going to raise a ruckus and accuse me of having come to break his fences. I guess I'll have to leave them here, since it was my own fault for giving him that advice."

Arriving home, he told his mother about the other brother's tricks, and decided upon a plan: he would take all of his animals out of the pasture and leave only the fattest cow he had. After that, he headed for the poor king's place.

"Good day, brother," said the rich king. "How does it go with you?"

"Oh, very well these days," answered the other slyly.

"It seems you've recently become very rich. How come you don't get up early any more?"

"Well, tomorrow I plan to get started at dawn again."

"By the way," said the rich king, "how many animals have you found up to now?"

"Only about fifteen, I'd guess," answered the other innocently.

"With those, you're pretty well off. I think it would be a good idea for you not to be up so early any more, because I'm going to run out of animals. That's about all I have to say. So long."

The rich brother stomped off home and took his prize fat cow out into the road. When the other king rose early the following day, he found the animal grazing about in the ditch and took it home for the slaughter. He made a delicious *charqui* [jerked beef] of it. The rich king discovered, just as he expected, that the cow had disappeared in the night.

"Look at that, mama," he snarled. "What did I tell you! My brother came and stole it."

"I don't believe it," said the old lady. "I'd have to see him eating the meat."

"Well, that's the easiest thing in the world, mama. I'll go over to his place tomorrow and tell him that my house is going to be ransacked and that I want him to guard a chest of silver for me. But I'll put you inside so you can clamp down on this boy. I'll bet you that when he finishes eating at night, he'll tell his wife how delicious the meat from his brother's cow was. Maybe that will convince you."

The rich brother loaded his mother into the chest, giving her a teakettle and a *mate* [a gourd for drinking mate] so she could refresh herself from time to time. Then he lugged the chest over to the poor king's house.

"Of course, I'll be glad to keep it for you," said he, rubbing his hands greedily.

"Fine, brother, but the only thing I ask is that you keep it in the kitchen so no one will know about this business. After three days, I'll stop by to give you a little something for the trouble."

Once the rich king was gone, the other brother put on a roast to cook and laughed to his wife, "If he knew we were eating his cow at this moment, do you think he'd come by to leave us chests of silver?" All the while, the old lady was listening from inside the chest.

"So, you're the one who's eating the cow after all," came the muffled voice. The poor brother and his wife were quite startled, but soon they threw open the lid and saw the old woman seated inside calmly sipping her *mate*.

"I'll be damned," he exclaimed, gawking at the sight, "if it isn't my mother! What are you up to here?"

"Why, I just came for the roast, my son."

"Hold on just a minute and we'll invite you." Saying that, he jammed a great chunk of hot meat and a handful of bread into the old lady's mouth. The next morning she lay there dead with the little *mate* up near her mouth. She had tried to take a sip in her haste not to choke to death.

Meanwhile, the rich brother thought it was about time for him to check on how his mother was making out. He went to fetch the chest with his wheelbarrow, and after he had taken it about a quarter of a mile on the road home, he called out, "Mama, did you hear anything last night?" But not a word from the chest. "She's certainly sleeping," he thought. "When I get home, she'll tell me the whole story." At his house he opened the box only to find the poor old woman inside. "Get up, mama," he cried. But she didn't stir. The king began to shake her frantically. "Lord," he thought, "how she must have wanted to drink that *mate* beside her." Then he looked very carefully and saw that she had choked to death on the bread and meat. Immediately he set off for the other brother's to notify him of the death.

"Brother," he cried breathlessly, racing up to the door, "Mama died. It must have been very sudden. I've come to ask you to bury her."

"Do you think I can do it with the little bit I have?" grumbled the other.

"I'll help you with the wake. How much will you need?"

"At least ten thousand *pesos,* because when your mother dies, you have to have a decent funeral so the neighbors won't talk. I'll do the job tomorrow."

The next day, the poor king went alone to a shallow little grave he had dug, and covered his mother with some loose dirt. Then he returned and reported to his brother. "Imagine, old chap. If I had watched over her another night, I wouldn't have had the money. The place was full of people."

"Very well," answered the other. "Tomorrow I'm going to get up early and light a package of candles for her."

That night, the poor brother dug up his mother, slung her over his shoulder, and left her in his brother's doorway with a club in her hand. When the rich king came out at dawn with the candles in his hand, the old woman fell over and clubbed him full on the forehead. He rushed frantically inside, crying to his wife, "Good Lord, my mother was at the door. I'd no sooner opened it than she slugged me with a stick."

"But it's because you owe her a decent burial," answered his wife, trying to calm him down. "That's why she's pursuing you. Now go and tell your brother to take care of her again. This time bury her deep down, and you go, too."

The king was very shaken with his morning misadventure, but he eventually got up the courage to go over and tell his brother of the problem.

"You must owe her something," chuckled the other brother. "That's surely why she follows you. Well, I'll go to get her, and this time we'll bury her so she'll never get out. By the way, there's just one thing. It's going to cost you at least ten thousand *pesos* more."

"Now just stop this nonsense! If you keep on like this, you'll have me in the streets begging."

"What do you mean? This is what you've got money for, isn't it?" asked the poor king, chortling to himself.

The next day they buried her deep. The rich king was satisfied with the job, for he was sure she'd never get out of that pit. But when darkness came, the other one dug her up again. Then he corralled one of his brother's colts and tied her on it with a thicker club than she'd had before. "These whacks are going to count more than the first ones," he laughed.

The rich king set out to look over his ranch the next morning. As he was riding home from the inspection, it occurred to him to head over and check on his prize colt. By a piece of bad luck, the king was mounted on a mare. When the colt saw him coming, it galloped over at full speed, carrying the old lady strapped on its back, and kept trying to mount the mare's buttocks. At every leap of the wild horse, his mother's club came down with a resounding smack on the bewildered and terrified king.

"Mama, for God's sake! What have I done that you should return from the dead to club me like this?" He lit out for home all covered with blood. "My God!" he cried to his wife, "my dear mother is riding on that crazy colt with a cudgel in her hand. You should see how she left my shoulders. She must have slugged me a dozen times."

"Didn't I tell you?" said his wife. "You owe her a decent burial. Now how much is that brother of yours going to ask to put her under this time? There's not a thing left in the house. At this rate, you'll be bankrupt in no time and you'll simply have to sell the rest of the livestock. And be sure to tell him to come and take her off that colt's back. If you go out now, she'll give you the works again."

Resigned, he limped over to his brother's house and said, "Well, mother's out riding on the colt."

"You must be up to something here," replied the poor king. "How is it that she follows you and leaves me alone? This time it'll be thirty thousand *pesos,* because I can't possibly dig the hole in a couple of days." Saying that, he marched off to where his mother was circling in the pasture on the crazy colt, and took her off without any trouble.

"Don't you see, old boy?" he said to his brother, "Mama doesn't lift a finger against me."

Then he took her home and ordered ten men to help him dig

the hole. The rich king had already sold his last livestock to scrape the necessary money together. He had a paltry twenty sheep left straying around his ranch, and the poor brother was busy plotting how he could get these as well. When the burial was finished, the brother who had been so poor said to the other, "If by any chance she gets out again, I won't bury her, because you won't have the dough to pay me."

Sure enough, that night he dug her up another time and left her sitting on the edge of a well near his brother's house. She had an enormous club in one hand. Next, he nabbed his brother's remaining sheep and threw them into the well so it would look like the old lady was guarding them.

Before breakfast, the rich king's wife went out to fetch some water at the well. She spied the old woman with the cudgel, dropped her bucket in the path, and scurried home to her husband, running in fear all the way that the old woman would catch her before she could get through the door.

"Don't you realize?" she gasped to her husband. "The old dame wants to thrash me as well."

"Did you see her?" he asked as his jaw dropped open.

"Sure enough. She's sitting by the well armed with her stick. You can thank God I managed to get away."

"It can't be! I just don't believe it can happen!" he roared, steaming out of the house in a black rage. "For Lord's sake, mama, what's wrong with you? Now you even forbid my woman to draw water." He took great care to keep a good distance between himself and the old woman. "I don't have a cent left to bury you with," he pleaded. "About the only thing that remains is a couple of sheep. If you like I'll get them out of the corral so you can count them and not haunt me any more." But when he went to fetch the sheep, he found the corral empty, with tracks leading toward the well. "Mama," he said, approaching her timidly, "I'll bet you've got the sheep there, haven't you? Why don't you just move back a little bit so I can take a peek? After all, it's about time you were fed up with this business, what with the beatings you've given me. And if you won't move, why don't you at least throw that nasty old stick away?"

The old woman, being of course quite dead, just sat there tight-lipped. The king slipped around behind her and grabbed her hand where she was holding the cudgel. She was stiff as a board! He looked down into the well and saw what was left of his flock baaing and milling around at the bottom.

"It's unbelievable," he groaned, "that a dead woman can run a living man broke. I think I'll just tell my brother to bury me along with her this time. Then I can fix him afterwards and get rich again with all the goods he's cheated me out of." He ran as fast as he could over to his brother's house and announced, "All right, all right. Mother is sitting by the well with all my sheep down inside. I'm thinking that the best thing is for you to bury me with her."

"But how the devil are you going to be buried alive?" laughed the other. "I'll have to make the hole much bigger, because you could get out in a jiffy. I suppose I could put you on the bottom and her on top. With that cudgel in her hand, she'll see to it that you don't go anywhere."

"Good enough," agreed the first king. "You're rich at the moment, but you'll soon be poorer than I am now. Hurry it up with the pit, for I can hardly wait to get my goods back."

"I too think it's the only way you'll ever be rich again," added the other. When he had the hole dug, he asked, "Do you think you'll ever give advice again like that you gave me once? By the way, where do you prefer to be, on top of mama or underneath?"

"I'll take the top," said the first brother. "If I'm under her, she'll start in with that club again."

They loaded the old lady, cudgel in hand, down into the pit, and the rich brother composed himself on top of her. From above, the other king chortled down, "Have a nice time, my friend. Mother's not going to haunt you any more. She's got you nice and close for clubbing any time you do her wrong."

"I'll be up before afternoon," shouted the other. "Mother's going to set in on me in no time." But the other king simply went on tossing in the dirt, placing a great load of sticks and logs on top of the grave.

"I won't take any chances," he thought, "of his coming out to rob me now that I'm rich. It's about time to go home and count my fortune in peace without any more advice from my poor brother who lives in the ground." And until this very day he's a millionaire, and must still be counting his gold.

·46· Pedro Urdimale and the Dead Priests

• ONCE THERE WAS a young girl who was so sanctimonious that she went to mass every single day of the week. In the monastery where the Mass was celebrated lived four priests, three young ones and an old man. The three young priests had their eyes on the girl all the time. As time went by, they went to her house for a visit. She made appointments for each of the three for every other night. When the first priest arrived, she led him into the parlor and killed him on the spot. Two nights later the second one appeared and met the same fate. The third came at his hour and was dispatched with one sound blow. But now that she had the three dead priests on her hands, the girl was distressed over how she was going to get them away from the house and bury them.

One fine morning she was standing in the doorway when Pedro Urdimale chanced by. Seeing this nice young girl, he greeted her politely and in no time had begun to make love to her.

"This is all very well," she blurted between kisses, "as long as you accept the secret I'm going to tell you and never say a word."

"How could you imagine anything else, miss! Whatever enters my heart never comes out."

"Then come along with me to prayer," she said, leading him into the room where one of the bodies lay. "Now, if you will go and dispose of that priest where nobody will see him, I'll marry you."

"It's a deal, miss. Just give me a sack." Pedro grabbed the priest and tucked him in a burlap bag which the girl had brought. Then he hoisted him over his shoulder and headed for the river, where he tossed the bag over the highest cliff. Pedro stood there a minute to see if the priest would float, but he didn't. "Ah, the girl is mine now," he thought happily to himself. But while he was on the way back to the house, she was busily setting up the second priest in the same place.

"What's up?" she asked when Pedro knocked. "Have you thrown him away?"

"Yes, miss, he went over the highest cliff there is."

"Come on in to see something," she said, leading Pedro into the same room.

"Why, that whoreson priest!" he exclaimed, catching sight of the second body. "How in the devil did he get out? Have you got another sack?"

The girl passed him another bag. He packed the priest away, loaded him over his shoulder, and returned to the cliff. This time he put three big rocks in the bag, tied it as tight as he could, and hurled it down into the river. When he saw that there was nothing afloat, he returned at once to the girl.

"Did you get rid of him?" she asked.

"Yes, the job's done."

"Well, just look at this!" she cried. "Come here and see where he is."

Pedro went in to take a look, and gasped, "How did this *padre* ever get out? I threw him in the river with three rocks. Have you got a hatchet, miss?" The girl promptly produced one. "Just lend it to me a minute," he continued. "I've had enough of this tossing into the river." Then he took the hatchet and the priest over his shoulder and went to a lovely little clearing in the woods. He began to chop wood until he had stacked a great pile. Then Pedro heaped it all on top of the poor priest and lit the bonfire, tossing logs on furiously. With his hatchet, he circled all around the fire, just in case the priest should manage to sneak out. Eventually the flames burned down and began to die out, and Pedro was overcome by sleep and was caught up in his dreams.

Meanwhile, the one little old priest who was left in the monastery saddled his horse and went out to look for a cow he had lost. He chanced by that same clearing in the woods, and came upon the bonfire. The old priest rode up and spoke to Pedro, who was sleeping on his back.

"Pedro, my boy, haven't you seen my cow?" he asked. But the

fellow was in such a deep slumber that he didn't hear a word. The priest continued chattering on at such a pace that Urdimale suddenly awoke in a great fright and leaped up, all in a dither, with his hatchet in hand. Blurry-eyed, he stared at the old priest and was sure he was the same one who had been in the fire.

"Father, you whoreson bastard!" he screamed. "I went and burned you, and you got out after all." Pedro lit out behind the terrified old man, almost catching him a dozen times, only to lose him once again. The old priest saved himself by a hair, and frantically bolted himself inside the monastery. Disgruntled, Pedro returned to the ashes of his fire and thought to himself, "How am I ever going to deceive this girl? Sooner or later, the priest is going to visit her house. I might as well go home and forget about her. By the way, I'll just take this axe along in order to pay for my work." And he did just that, to put an end to the tale.

·47· *Pedro Urdimale Makes Exchanges*

• ONE FINE DAY Pedro Urdimale was going along scheming with all his might when he came upon a pea belonging to some ladies who made clothes. As they were busy in their shop, he went over and said, "Ladies, I've come to ask a little favor of you."

"What will it be, friend Pedro?"

"I just want to leave this pea with you. Since there isn't any around here, you can use it for seed."

The woman took the seed and left it on the table. After Pedro had gone on his way, a hen got into the workshop and gobbled up the pea. Very soon Pedro returned and said he had come for his little package.

"Ay!" exclaimed the woman, "my old hen got in here somehow and ate it."

So, in payment for the pea, Urdimale walked away with the hen. "It's beginning to work out," he thought. "From a pea to a chicken is pretty good business."

A little further down the road, he stopped by a house and asked the lady to take care of his hen for a few minutes, for he would return promptly. The woman took the hen and let it loose to scratch in the patio. The foolish bird wandered into a pen of pigs the lady was fattening, and was instantly gobbled up. When the lady dashed out, there was nothing left but a pair of feet. In the midst of her consternation Pedro arrived to reclaim his possession.

"Oh, Pedro, just look what happened. The pig devoured your hen."

"Which one is the pig?" he asked calmly. The lady pointed it out.

Without any further protest, he declared, "The pig is mine. I'll just take it along."

With the animal under his arm, he came to a ranch house where some men were branding livestock. He asked the owner if he might leave his pig there for a few minutes while he did an errand. The gentleman told him it was quite all right, that he could leave it in the corral. As soon as Pedro had wandered off, a heifer gored the pig and sliced it open. Not at all concerned about that, the cowhands sat down to a fine pork dinner. When Pedro calculated that the pig must have changed into something else, he returned to the ranch. Discovering the men licking the last bones of the pork chops, and hearing the story of his pig, he lassoed the heifer in the corral and headed off to new parts.

Eventually he came to the palace of a king and asked if he could leave the animal there a few moments. The heifer was left in a grazing place with the king's consent, and Pedro just slipped around the corner of the castle. At this same time, the princess was strolling back and forth taking some sun on her balcony. Suddenly she was seized with a wild desire to eat a roast from the heifer. The king obeyed her wish and killed the animal. As the princess was sitting down to her roast beef, Pedro came back around the castle and asked for his property.

"What do you know, my good man!" said the king. "We just slaughtered the little creature to make my daughter happy."

"And which one is the lady?" asked Pedro, "for I'm taking her with me."

He produced a great sack, stuffed the princess inside, and trudged away. Soon he came to the house of an old woman and stopped by to leave the bag with her.

"Be very careful," cautioned Pedro, "because I'm carrying some delicate things."

When he had left, the old woman wondered and wondered what could possibly be in the bag. Finally she was unable to contain herself and opened it, whereupon the princess popped out.

"Listen," said the old dame when she had heard the story, "I have a dog which we can toss into the sack, and you can be on your way, my dear."

About an hour later, Pedro came back to get his bundle. When he had hiked with it some distance through the country, he got the idea of having some fun with the princess, but when he untied the bag, there was only a little dog all curled up asleep. In the midst of his confusion, seven bandits rode up in pursuit of him. Pedro immediately jumped into the sack and shouted, "I won't marry the king's daughter, I won't marry the king's daughter!" The puzzled, bandits asked him why in the world he was tied up in that sack in the middle of nowhere.

"It's because I refuse to marry the king's daughter," he answered. "Didn't you hear me shouting?"

"Well, put me in that sack. I'll marry her in a jiffy," said one of the bandits. Pedro tied him in as tight as he could and scurried away.

Soon two more bandits rode up. "What the devil are you doing in there?" they asked the other.

"I'm going to marry the king's daughter," came the muffled voice.

"What makes you think you can do a thing like that?" Laughing at all this nonsense, they hoisted him on their shoulders and threw the sack over a cliff in the desert.

Pedro was far away by this time. "Cursed be my bad luck," he said to himself. "I'm going to tell my story: from a pea, a hen; from a hen, a pig; from a pig, a heifer; from a heifer, a princess; and from the princess, a bitch."

·48· We Ourselves

• LET'S BEGIN TELLING about the three young men who found themselves in need of learning a few manners—polite speech and all that. One day they left their houses, just like brothers who live together in the country, and set out to travel together. They had no idea of the manners of town life, but eventually they came to a pretty little city with a plaza. Two gentlemen were having a friendly stroll and conversation. "For an *almud* [about 10 quarts, dry measure] of salt, we ourselves," said one.

"Now I have some manners," said one of the youths. "That was a nicely put phrase."

A bit further on, they overheard another man say, "It was the three of us." The three peasant boys listened carefully and heard another man say, "Of course." The farm boys repeated the phrases until they had learned them by heart: "For an *almud of* salt, we ourselves," "It was the three of us," and "Of course." On their way back to the country, they came upon a corpse in the road and stood there gawking at it until the police arrived.

"Why did you kill him" asked the officer.

"For an *almud* of salt, we ourselves," answered one.

"And who did it?"

"It was the three of us," said the second.

"You're all going to be taken prisoners," said the officer.

"Of course," answered the third, whereupon the police carried them away to the station. The only words they had to say were their phrases of polite conversation. The judge kept them locked up for a good long time. One day he said, "Go out and get those peasant lads that are in jail and bring them in to me."

When they entered the court room, they had the following things to say: "For an almud of salt, we ourselves," "It was the three of us," "Of course," and not a word more. The judge just stood there staring at them.

"What poor innocent fellows I have as prisoners!" he exclaimed. "Set them free."

The poor farm boys, who still didn't know any manners, were given their liberty.

• ONCE THERE WERE two young friends, good looking and well dressed, who were submerged in the vice of drink. They knew a great deal, for both of them were educated men. One day one said to the other, "A hell of a mess we are in, my friend. Here we are with our educations and all, and miserable because of drink." All they had left were undrinkable dregs in a dirty old can.

"Look, partner," spoke up the second, "I have an idea of how we can get some money and leave this vice of ours. You go over to see the neighboring king and tell him a whopping big lie. Within an hour, I'll come by to confirm your story. This king is very kind and merciful and will surely give us clothing and food if we agree to leave our drinking."

"Agreed," said the other. "Why, thanks to our vice, we haven't even got credit." (And that was the truth of the matter.)

The first boy went off to spin his yarn at the royal palace. Now this king was very generous and friendly when he was told little jokes and stories. He took great delight in them and always began immediately to hand out money, meals, and gifts to those who came to entertain him. When the first lad, who was named Julio, presented himself at the palace gate, he was ushered inside to the throne room.

"Good morning, your majesty," he said, boldly looking the king in the eye, "I have come to ask for a great favor, for I'm a little scant in my stomach and without a thing to put on."

"But surely, my boy," answered the king cordially. Then he beckoned to one of the servants. "Look here, little girl, fix this lad a good breakfast right away with the best we have in the kitchen." As the young fellow sat down to the table, the king hovered about him. "I say, why don't you tell me a little tale, one of those little riddles I like so much. Why, people like you go all over the place, and I always have to stay in the palace; I can't go out at all."

"But, your majesty, the things I'm going to tell you have hardly ever been seen before. I hope you'll pardon me for saying that when I was on the way to your palace, the river was catching on fire."

"Young man, that's an absolute lie."

"Just as you say, sire; but it *was,* after all, burning."

"We'll see about this," grumbled the king. "Get one of the guards," he called. "As for you, trickster, you're going to be locked up until further orders, for I'm not taken in by your lies."

At least the young man had a full stomach and wasn't hungry in his cell. He just sat there thinking about the friend who was going to come and confirm his tale. And sure enough, about an hour later the second fellow arrived at the palace gate. This chap was skillful of tongue and had the vocabulary for speaking to a king. He was well received by the ruler and served with the best in the house.

"Look, my lad," said the king presently, "you fellows who are always footing it around the world must have some little tale to tell. You know I'm always eager to hear stories, riddles, and that sort of thing."

"Certainly, your majesty. I know a few little ones."

"And is it true," said the king anxiously, "I want you to tell me—is the river near the city burning up?"

"Perhaps it's so, your majesty. I don't doubt it, for I just saw a load of wagons with a lot of rubbish around them, and on one of the spokes of a wagon I found two scorched fish. As a matter of fact, sire, I happen to have them right here." The boy had two fish which he had roasted on the way to the palace.

"Very well, my boy, very well. I didn't believe the prisoner, and it's true after all." Immediately the king ordered the other fellow brought from his cell. "Look here," he continued to the second liar, "do you know this man?"

"Yes, I believe I do; but he's not with me, your majesty."

"At all events," said the king, "you two go on now as companions. I'll provide you with clothes and money for your travels."

When they were safely outside the palace, they decided to head for Spain, now that they had a wardrobe and some funds. Disembarking in Spain, they planned the lie they would tell to Alfonso XIII, who was then king of Spain.

"Tell me, young man," said the Spanish king upon receiving the first fellow, "how are things in Chile?"

"They couldn't be better, my king. I've never been to Spain before. It's very rich, yes sir, very, very rich." The boy was well prepared, for he had hidden his good clothing and was wearing the same old rags as before. "Traveling through Spain, your majesty, you'll never guess what I saw. There was an enormous wall with one *adobe* [a brick of mud and straw] made of cheese and another of mud."

"Yes," mused the king absent-mindedly, "Spain is rich, very, very rich."

"Beyond the wall, sire, I heard a great noise of people and a whole herd of mares that were on the threshing floor. But instead of wheat, they were threshing curd, my king, to make cheeses. How could it be said that Spain is not rich!"

"Wait a minute!" roared the king, suddenly realizing what he was hearing. "How are they going to make cheese by threshing curd with mares? Why, you've just come to my palace with a pack of lies."

Once again the boy was locked away until further orders. But soon after, the second swindler arrived.

"Majesty," he said, "I come before you a poor and hungry man who would much appreciate a bite to eat. In Chile, we're badly off. Don't you see how I've arrived, dressed in rags like a poor Chilean *roto* [member of the humblest class]."

"Well, here you'll have plenty," said the king proudly, "for Spain is great and powerful."

"By the way, sire, as I was on my way to the palace, I chanced to see a wall with an *adobe* of cheese and another of mud. A little further on, two Spanish boys were washing some brooms and a round mat, about so big. Everything was scrubbed clean, and there was a whole load of freshly made cheese. I bought a slice, and as I was cutting it, out came a young colt's hoof." With that, he handed the king a tiny little hoof which he had found near some mare that had just given birth to a colt.

"Good Lord!" exclaimed the king, "and here I was calling the other Chilean a liar, when this fellow has brought me the very curd the mares were threshing and a hoof to boot." The king sent for the prisoner and asked the two if they knew each other.

"Yes," answered the second one, "I know he's a Chilean, but we're not partners."

"Good enough," beamed the king. "From now on you're going to travel together. So that you may go in peace, I'll give you each two large *pesetas* [Spanish coins], which, after all, are worth at least five thousand Chilean *pesos.*"

"Let's get moving," whispered one Chilean to the other, "for this king will surely find us out sooner or later if we stick around. We can go to France to tell the emperor a lovely little tall tale."

At the French palace, the first swindler presented himself before the emperor and said that on his way from the port he had stopped outside the city at a tile-roofed house where there was an older woman washing clothes, and a young one with a baby in her arms. Being very dry, he had gone to ask for a drink of water. To his great astonishment, he had seen that the baby had nine arms. That was enough for the emperor who shouted, "Nine arms! How can a woman have a freak like that?"

"But that's the way it was, your royal highness."

"Get inside!" roared the emperor. "You're under arrest until I give further orders. If there's anyone who knows of this, let him come to confirm the tale."

A little behind his companion, the second Chilean arrived to do his dirty work.

"My good emperor," he began, "I've come to ask you a favor, for I have traveled all the way from Chile and am going on an empty stomach."

"Why, of course," said the emperor cheerfully. "Very gladly. But tell me, how are things with the Chileans?"

"Ah, we are so very poor and in great need," moaned the other.

"Tell me what other news you bring, my lad. I just love to be entertained with fortunes, prophecies, and all that."

"Certainly, my emperor. But you must know that there is very little time left for this poor world."

"Why on earth do you say such a thing?" asked the emperor, aghast.

"Yes, sir, that's how it is. There are signs of the end of everything, just as it says in the Bible. Why, when I was on my way here, I went by a tile-roofed house to ask for a drink of water, and I saw a young woman and an older one washing out some clothes. In the middle of all the wash they had spread out there was a tiny little shirt all wound up and entangled. Now what do you suppose? It was for a little baby with nine arms!"

"Oh my God," gasped the emperor, "that was the shirt of the baby the other prisoner saw!"

Now the second Chilean had had a neighboring seamstress make him a little shirt with nine sleeves to it. He brought it to the emperor all fresh and clean, as if it had been worn and just washed.

"Let me see that!" the emperor exclaimed, grabbing the curious little garment. "Quickly, tell the high lord of the court to bring the prisoner here. Are you both Chileans?"

"Yes, your majesty, but I wasn't with this other fellow."

The emperor told them to go along together to keep each other company and gave each one five thousand *pesos*. When they had slipped out of the palace, they sat down in the city square.

"Listen," said one, "we're pretty damned good swindlers, what with this money and a whole suitcase full of clothes. Why don't we invent a real whopper now, just to see who can tell the biggest lie? By the way, partner, do you know the *pampas* [plains] of the north?"

"Sure, all of them, the plains of North America, Africa, just about everywhere, my friend."

"Well, in the middle of Africa a cabbage plant grew which was so big that all the squadrons of the world, including those of Chile, fitted on it. Since Chile is so tiny, our squadron was perched on just one of the leaves, in the shade of the others, along with the whole Chilean people. Don't you see what good plains there are in Africa?"

"My friend, have you heard that they're constructing a boiler so big that it takes the riveters twenty-four hours to receive a rivet on the other side where you put the bolt? The men on that side can't even hear the crash of the rivet until twenty-four hours after it's put in. You can just imagine how thick the plates are."

"Hey, that's just the thing to cook that cabbage head with all the squadrons on it I told you about. It would make a delicious stew!"

Well, if there really were cabbages in Africa, we're all simmering in the boiler right now, steaming along with the two Chilean swindlers who got together just to tell a few tall ones.

Part VI
Cumulative Tales

The Thrush

· ONE NIGHT in the middle of winter there was a very great frost. A little thrush set out to look for food and found the cold so great that it broke one of her claws. "Look here, Frost," she chirped, "you've gone and broken my claw."

"The sun is even worse than I," replied the frost, "for he melts me."

The thrush flew to the sun. "Look here, Sun, why are you so wicked? You melt the frost that breaks my claw."

"The clouds are even worse," boomed the sun, "for they cover me." Right away the thrush flew to the clouds and said, "Clouds, why are you so cruel? You cover the sun that melts the frost that breaks my claw."

"Even worse, far worse," moaned the clouds, "is the wind that blows us away." The thrush flew to where the wind was. "Wind, why are you so bad? You blow away the clouds that cover the sun that melts the frost that breaks my claw." The wind whispered, "Even worse is the wall which holds me in." So the thrush swooped off to the wall. "Wall, why are you so wicked? You tie up the wind that blows away the clouds that cover the sun that melts the frost that breaks my poor little claw."

"But even worse is the rat which gnaws me away," creaked the old wall. Again the thrush flew, this time to say to the rat, "Rat, why are you so nasty as to gnaw the wall that ties up the wind that blows away the clouds that cover the sun that melts the frost that breaks my claw?"

"Listen," squeaked the rat, "don't you realize that the cat chases me?" The little bird flew straight to the cat. "Cat, how can you be so wicked as to chase the rat that gnaws the wall that ties up the wind that blows away the clouds that cover the sun that melts the frost that breaks my claw?"

"But all the worse," purred the cat, "is the dog that always runs after me." The little thrush flew off again. "Dog, how can you be so mean as to run after the cat that chases the rat that gnaws the wall that ties up the wind that blows away the clouds that cover the sun that melts the frost that breaks my claw?"

"The club which beats me is worse than I," whined the dog. The thrush asked the club, "Club, why do you beat the dog that runs after the cat that chases the rat that gnaws the wall that ties up the wind that blows away the clouds that cover the sun that melts the frost that breaks my claw?"

"Ah, but fire," groaned the club, "is the villain who burns me." The thrush went to seek fire. "Fire, why are you so bad as to burn the club that beats the dog that runs after the cat that chases the rat that gnaws the wall that ties up the wind that blows away the clouds that cover the sun that melts the frost that breaks my claw?"

Then the fire crackled, "Water which puts me out is the worst." The thrush swooped away to the water. "Water, why do you put out the fire that burns the club that beats the dog that runs after the cat that chases the rat that gnaws the wall that ties up the wind that blows away the clouds that cover the sun that melts the frost that breaks my tiny little claw?"

Then the water gurgled ever so sadly, "The ox is bad, for he drinks me up." The thrush flew to the fields. "Ox, why do you drink the water that puts out the fire that burns the club that beats the dog that runs after the cat that chases the rat that gnaws the wall that ties up the wind that blows away the clouds that cover the sun that melts the frost that breaks my claw?"

"But mind the knife that kills me," lowed the ox. When the thrush found the knife, she asked, "Knife, how can you be so bad as to kill the ox that drinks the water that puts out the fire that burns the club that beats the dog that runs after the cat that chases the rat that gnaws the wall that ties up the wind that blows away the clouds that cover the sun that melts the frost that breaks my poor little claw?"

"Ah, but terribly worse," screeched the knife, "is the blacksmith that makes and unmakes me." The thrush flew straight to the smith's. "Listen, blacksmith, why are you so evil that you make and unmake the knife?" The smithy looked up at the little thrush and said, "What in the devil is this bird of ill omen that comes to pester me?" Saying that, he struck the thrush and killed her.

Notes
to the Tales

PART I

ANIMAL TALES

· *1* · *The Vixen*

Type 4, *Carrying the Sham-Sick Trickster*. Motif K1241, "Trickster rides dupe horseback." CFCH No. 227, "The Vixen."

Collected in February, 1954 in Olmué, Valparaíso, from Clodomiro Tureo, an illiterate peasant laborer, born in 1884.

This episode of the cycle of the Fox and the Wolf (or Bear) is a variant of Type 4 in an exceptionally independent form. The other Spanish and Indian versions that we know in Spanish America (CFCH III, p. 382) appear in combination with other animal stories and also magic tales (Types 700, *Tom Thumb* and 950, *Rhampsinitus*, I). In the five Chilean versions and in one from the Dominican Republic the wolf is replaced by the vixen as horse and the fox by a monkey, or the two characters become a thumb and a little elf. In this story the vixen appears as the butt of the joke, not the joker.

· *2* · *The Tarbaby*

Type 175, *The Tarbaby and the Rabbit*. Motif K741, "Capture by Tarbaby." CFCH No. 241, "The Tarbaby."

Collected in February, 1952 in Ignao, Valdivia, from basketmaker Juan de Dios Díaz, born in 1891. Another tale from the same narrator is No. 47 in this book.

Aurelio M. Espinosa has studied 318 versions of this story in *Cuentos populares españoles*, II, pp. 163–227. Thompson, in *The Folktale*, p. 225, makes the following summary: "From India it seems clear that this story has reached the Negroes and Indians of America by several paths. It came from India to Africa, where it is a favorite and where it received some characteristic modifications before being taken by slaves to America. Another path was through Europe to the Hispanic peninsula and thence to American colonies. The third, but apparently very unimportant route, was directly across Europe."

A North American version of this type from Louisiana is given by Richard M. Dorson in *Buying the Wind* (Chicago, 1964), under the title "Bouki and the Rabbit and the Well" (pp. 248–49).

In Spanish America, this is one of the most popular stories. Forty-three Spanish versions, along with four Indian ones, have been published either independently or in combination with other tales of animals, magic, and jokes. Story No. 2 corresponds to the original versions in which the protagonists are men. Nevertheless, the motif K1833, "Disguise as ghost," is foreign to those versions.

Although our Chilean version has human characters, this type is classified under "Animal Tales" in the Aarne-Thompson index because most versions contain animal actors.

PART II

WONDER TALES

· 3 · *The Three Stolen Princesses*

Type 301, *The Three Stolen Princesses*. Principal motifs: F92, "Pit entrance to lower world"; R11.1, "Princess (maiden) abducted by monster (ogre)"; R111.1.4, "Rescue of princesses from giant"; R111.2.1, "Princess rescued from lower world"; K1931.2, "Impostors abandon hero in lower world"; K677, "Hero tests the rope on which he is to be pulled to upper world. By placing one stone on the rope he discovers his companions' treacherous plan to cut the rope"; F101.3, "Return from lower world on eagle"; B322.1, "Hero feeds own flesh to helpful animal. The hero is carried on the back of an eagle who demands food. The hero finally feeds part of his own flesh"; N681, "Hero arrives home just as princess is to marry another"; H151.2, "Attention drawn by helpful animal's theft of food from wedding table; recognition follows"; L161, "Lowly hero marries princess." This story contains an introduction contaminated with Type 408, *The Three Oranges,* Motif D211.1, "Transformation: man (woman) to orange." Motif D141, "Transformation: man (giant) to dog," is also foreign to this type of story. CFCH No. 3, "The Three Stolen Princesses."

Collected in February, 1951, in Los Lagos, Valdivia, from an illiterate laborer, Pantaleón Ulloa, born in 1888. Other tales from the same narrator are Nos. 16 and 35 in this volume.

This story is well known in Europe. Thompson and Roberts, *Types of Indic Oral Tales,* p. 46, list one Indic variant; Littmann, *Arabische Märchen aus mündlicher Überlieferung,* p. 136, includes an Arabic version; and Eberhard and Boratov, *Typen türkischer Volksmärchen,* p. 79, list thirty-eight Turkish versions. In Spanish America some versions have also been collected. Those which are known among the American Indians are probably of Spanish origin. An American version from North Carolina is given by Richard Chase under the title "Old Fire Dragaman," tale No. 12 in his *The Jack Tales* (Cambridge, Massachusetts, 1943), pp. 106–13.

·4· *The Mermaid and the Poor Fisherman*

Types 302, *The Ogre's Heart in the Egg,* and 316, *The Nix of the Millpond.* Motifs: S240, "Children unwittingly promised"; F420.1.2, "Waterspirit as woman"; B92, "Hero divides spoil for animals"; B500, "Magic power from animals"; D630, "Transformation and disenchantment at will"; R11.1, "Princess(es) abducted by giant"; E711.1, "Soul in egg"; E713, "Soul hidden in a series of coverings"; R111.1, "Princess rescued from captor"; F420.5.2.2, "Water-spirits (siren) kidnap mortals and keep them under water"; R152, "Wife rescues husband" CFCH No. 7, "The Giant."

Collected in February, 1951 in Ignao, Valdivia, from an illiterate day laborer, Francisco Coronado, born in 1875. Additional tales collected from the same narrator and included in this volume are Nos. 5, 6, 8, 10, 12, 22, 24, 25, 32, 34, 38, and 46.

Thompson, *The Folktale,* p. 35, notes that Type 302, *The Ogre's Heart in the Egg,* had a deserved popularity in the whole area from Ireland to India and that it has been taken several times to Africa and America. On the other hand, the tale of Type 316, *The Nix of the Millpond,* is a European story. Numerous independent or contaminated Irish versions have been listed, with only some scattered versions from the north to the south of Europe. From Eastern Europe Thompson lists one Polish version. This story came to America by way of French and Spanish colonists. It is known in Canada, the French Antilles, Jamaica, the Dominican Republic, and Chile. In the latter country one independent version has been listed besides our combined one. This combination of Types 316 and 302 is not extraordinary. O'Súilleabhain and Christiansen, *The Types of the Irish Folktale,* pp. 73–77 list twenty Irish versions, and Ranke, *Schleswig-Holsteinische Volksmärchen,* II, p. 188, three German ones. The Dominican version (Hansen, *The Types of the Folktale in Cuba, Puerto Rico, the Dominican Republic, and Spanish South America,* p. 48) is an amalgam of Types 316 and 302, contaminated with motifs of Type 400. American versions of the types represented in the following tale are given by Marie Campbell, *Tales from the Cloud Walking Country* (Bloomington, Indiana, 1958); Type 302 under the title "The Weaver's Boy," pp. 85–89, and Type 316 as "The Golden Comb," pp. 40–42.

·5· The Fisherman

Type 303, *The Twins or Blood-Brothers*. Motifs: T512, "Conception from drinking (water in which fish has been washed)"; T589.7.1, "Simultaneous birth of domestic animal and child"; T685.1, "Twin adventurers"; E761.3, "Life token: tree fades"; L161, "Lowly hero marries princess"; G221.1.1, "Witch's hair has power to bind;" K1311.1, "Husband's twin brother mistaken by woman for her husband"; T351, "Sword of chastity"; N342.3, "Jealous and overhasty man kills his rescuing twin brother"; B512, "Medicine shown by animal"; E1, "Person comes to life." CFCH No. 8, "The Fisherman."

Collected in January, 1951 in Ignao, Valdivia, from Francisco Coronado.

This widely spread story has been studied by the eminent folklorist Kurt Ranke, on the basis of 770 versions in *Die zwei Brüder,* and afterwards by Thompson in *The Folktale,* pp. 24–33, and by Liungman in *Die schwedischen Volksmärchen,* pp. 49–53. Our story No. 5 corresponds, with slight variations, to the original form of Type 303 established by Ranke, pp. 341–42, but without the episode of the dragon slayer. In the introduction, the motif of eating fish is expressed by drinking water in which the fish has been washed. The motif of the king of the animals does not appear and that of the fish which speaks is replaced by the voice of an invisible being.

Other versions of this story may be found in *Folktales of Norway* and *Folktales of Germany,* companion volumes in this series.

·6· The Prince of the Sword

Type 314, *The Youth Transformed to a Horse,* II, V, and VI. Motifs: B401, "Helpful horse"; H56, "Recognition by wound" and motif's variants; C615.1, "Forbidden lake"; C912, "Hair turns to gold as punishment in forbidden chamber"; R222, "Unknown knight (three days' tournament)." CFCH No. 21, "The Prince of the Sword."

Collected in February, 1952 in Ignao, Valdivia, from Francisco Coronado.

This story is a variant of Type 314, *The Youth Transformed to a Horse,* which in Germany is known preferably by the name of "Goldener" and in France by the name "Le teigneux." Thompson, *The Folktale,* p. 60, notes that this complicated story appears without much variation over a large area and in many versions. In effect, its dissemination covers Europe, India, Indonesia, Africa, Madagascar, and North and South America. No Spanish versions strictly fitting Type 314 have been listed in the Iberian peninsula, but, without any doubt, the rich Spanish source is responsible for ten Spanish versions and variants of New Mexico and Colorado, three Chilean versions, and one from the Araucanian Indians in Argentina. All these versions, which are characterized by their use of archaisms, belong to widely separated American regions. For other important references, see Delarue, *Le conte populaire français*, pp. 242–43, and Liungman, *Die schwedischen Volksmärchen*, pp. 60–61.

An oriental version of Type 314, in combination with other Types, appears as No. 38, "Fire Boy" in another volume of this series, *Folktales of Japan*.

· 7 · Seven Colors

Type 314A, *The Shepherd and the Three Giants*. Motifs: L113.1.6, "Cowherd as hero"; B557, "Unusual animal as riding horse"; B412, "Helpful sheep"; G512.1.1, "Giant killed with magic knife." Motif D719 "Disenchantment by rough treatment" (casting the frog to the ground), is a contamination with Type 402, *The Frog as Bride*. CFCH No. 78, "Seven Colors."

Collected in February, 1950 in Paihuano, Coquimbo, from a day laborer, Efraín Rodríguez, born in 1910. Other tales from the same narrator are Nos. 9 and 39 in this volume.

This story corresponds to the new Type 314A of the Aarne-Thompson index, which Ranke, I, p. 175, had proposed on the basis of twenty-six German versions. Delarue, p. 254, had proposed, on the other hand, the number 317 for nine French, three French Canadian, and two Basque versions. Aarne and Thompson, p. 110, include nine Lithuanian versions as well. In CFCH II, pp. 9–45, there are four more Chilean versions.

· 8 · The Faithless Sister

Type 315, *The Faithless Sister*. Motifs: B421, "Helpful dog"; D1096, "Magic firearms"; C611.1, "Forbidden door"; K2212.0.2, "Treacherous sister as mistress of giant plots against brother"; H1212, "Quest assigned because of feigned illness"; B524.1.1, "Dog saves life—kills giant"; B515, "Resuscitation by animals"; Q261, "Treachery punished." CFCH No. 4, "The Faithless Sister."

Collected in January, 1951 in Ignao, Valdivia, from Francisco Coronado.

The story of the faithless sister appears generally in combination with Type 300, *The Dragon-Slayer*. Its independent form is very rare in Germany, according to Ranke, I, p. 184. Delarue, p. 268, lists only three French versions. Tale No. 8 is in this sense an exception in Spanish-speaking areas, where the combinations 300 and 315 and 327 (The Children and the Ogre), and 315 are frequent.

·9· *The Lost Prince*

Type 328, *The Boy Steals the Giant's Treasure*. Principal motifs: G610.1, "Stealing from ogre for revenge"; H1151.13.3, "Task: stealing horses from king"; H1172, "Task: bringing a snake to court"; D1470.1.25, "Magic wishing-rod"; H971, "Tasks performed with help of old woman"; G514.1, "Snake trapped in box." CFCH No. 29, "The Lost Prince."

Collected in February, 1950 in Paihuano, Coquimbo, from day laborer Efraín Rodríguez, born in 1910.

This story is scattered throughout all of Europe, Turkey, India, and the American continent from Canada to Argentina and Chile. Up to this date, three versions have been published from Colorado and New Mexico, three from the Dominican Republic, five from Argentina, and five from Chile.

In the Iberian versions, the story is frequently contaminated with Motif K1611, "The ogre kills his own children. Nightcaps changed in bed (places)." This is demonstrated by two Spanish versions, a Portuguese one, one from Catalonia, two North American Spanish versions, two from the Dominican Republic, two from Argentina, and three from Chile.

·10· *The Wandering Soldier*

Type 329, *Hiding from the Devil*. Principal motifs: H321, "Suitor test: hiding from princess. She has magic sight"; D1323, "Magic object gives clairvoyance (field glass)"; H901.1, "Heads placed on stakes for failure in performance of task. Unsuccessful youths are beheaded"; D170, "Transformation: to fish"; L13, "Compassionate man"; H982, "Animals help man perform task." CFCH No. 31, "The Wandering Soldier."

Collected in January, 1951 in Ignao, Valdivia, from Francisco Coronado.

A reduced number of versions of this story have been found from Ireland to Turkey and Russia, and from Catalonia to Finland. No Spanish version is known. On the American continent, it is represented by three Franco-American, one Franco-Antillean, two North American Spanish, one Brazilian, three Argentinian, and two Chilean versions.

In story No. 10, we find the motif of the fox that digs a tunnel as far as the site of the princess. This motif also appears in two Caucasian versions; see Dirr, *Kaukasische Märchen,* tale No. 1, and Bolte and Polívka, *Anmerkungen zu den Kinder- und Hausmärchen der Brüder Grimm,* III, p. 367.

· 11 · Pedro the Blacksmith

Type 330A, *The Smith and the Devil.* Motifs: M211, "Man sells soul to devil"; K1811, "Gods (saints) in disguise visit mortals"; G2071, "Three foolish wishes"; D1413.5, "Bench to which person sticks"; D1413.1.3, "Fig tree from which one cannot descend"; D1413.9.1, "Wallet from which one cannot escape"; Z111.2, "Devils magically bound to tree"; K213, "Devil pounded in knapsack until he releases man"; A661.0.1.2, "Saint Peter as porter of heaven"; Q565, "Man admitted to neither heaven nor hell"; K2371.1, "Heaven entered by a trick." CFCH No. 32, "Peter the Blacksmith."

Collected in February, 1953 in Olmué, Valparaíso, from retired illiterate day laborer Pedro Ponce, born in 1873.

In its total structure, this story shows similarity to the secondary Type 330A of Aarne and Thompson, III A of Espinosa, and with redaction B of Ranke. But it also contains Motif K213, "Devil pounded in knapsack until he releases man," of Type 330B. Actually it corresponds more exactly to redaction B of Ranke. For further references, see Espinosa, III, pp. 140–50; Ranke, I, pp. 245–46; and Delarue, pp. 347–48. Referring to the general Type 330 of Aarne and Thompson, with its secondary Types 330A and 330B, several versions are known in Europe and on the American continent from Canada to Argentina and Chile.

An American version of Type 330 is given by Richard M. Dorson in *Buying the Wind* under the title "Pedro de Ordimalas," pp. 429–34. Another from Virginia, is given by Richard Chase in *Grandfather Tales* (Cambridge, Massachusetts, 1948), pp. 29–39, No. 3, "Wicked John and the Devil."

· 12 · Pedro Urdimale Gets into Heaven

Type 330*, *Heaven Entered by Trick.* Motifs: A661.0.1.2, "Saint Peter as porter of heaven"; K2371.1, "Heaven entered by trick." CFCH No. 246, "Pedro Urdimale."

Collected in January, 1951 in Ignao, Valdivia, from Francisco Coronado.

The Motif K2371.1, "Heaven entered by trick," appears as the new Type 330* with independent development in the second revision of the Aarne and Thompson Index. The tricks can be varied. In story No. 12, the trick consists in the rogue's getting St. Peter to open the gate to heaven a bit so he can enter up to his waist, but St. Peter slams the door and cuts his body in two. Our Lord picks up the part of the body which remained outside and fastens it to the rest. That way the rogue gets into glory alive.

In another Chilean version (CFCH No. 247), the rogue enters glory riding on a nun, for that day corresponded to the entrance of those belonging to orders of chivalry. A similar situation is found in a French story in Paul Sébillot, *Littérature orale de la Haute-Bretagne,* p. 209, and a Swiss one in Bolte and Polívka, II, p. 346.

In our tale here, the famous picaresque character known in Spain as Pedro de Urdemalas and in Spanish America as Pedro Urdemales appears as the protagonist. His name has been altered many times, going through the most varied derivations and corruptions. The Spanish American Pedro Urdemales exceeds the characteristics of the Spanish rogue and takes to himself the role of other popular characters. This name, therefore, does not always indicate a certain reference to definite types of stories. In the Chilean stories he appears in multiple types: 330*, 1000–1090, 1528–1563, and 1650–1655.

· 13 · José Guerné

Type 400, *The Man on a Quest for his Lost Wife.* Motifs: D5, "Enchanted person"; D157, "Transformation: man (wife) to parrot"; Q502.2, "Punishment: wandering till iron shoes are worn out;" H1385.3, "Quest for vanished mistress"; D1361.5, "Magic cap renders invisible"; D1472.1.8, "Magic tablecloth supplies food and drink"; D1520.10, "Magic transportation by boots"; N681, "Husband (lover) arrives home just as wife (mistress) is to marry another"; Z62.1, "The old and the new keys (variant: the golden and the silver keys)." CFCH No. 35, "José Guerné."

Collected in February, 1951 in San Francisco de Mostazal, province of O'Higgins, from illiterate day laborer and rabbit hunter Ambrosio Fuentes, born in 1891.

This story is a variant of Type 400, in which the original motif of the Swan Maiden is completely modified. The princess changed into a parrot is bought by an old man at the store. When the parrot discovers that he is married, she takes flight and flees. After this comes the central episode, *The Man on a Quest for his Lost Wife*. The hero receives three magic objects as a reward from two sisters arguing about their beauty. Then he arrives at the royal palace just at the moment when the princess is going to marry another. The story ends with the modified motif of the old and new keys, which justify the marriage of the old man to the princess.

This story has been widely disseminated and has passed through multiple variations, especially in the following Spanish American versions that have been listed: Colorado and New Mexico, five; Dominican Republic, five; Puerto Rico, nine; and Chile, three. The tale as given here also contains motifs of Types 313, *The Girl as Helper in the Hero's Flight;* 328, *The Boy Steals the Giant's Treasure;* 563, *The Table, the Ass, and the Stick;* and 566, *The Three Magic Objects and the Wonderful Fruits.* For references to its dissemination and discussion, see especially Bolte and Polívka, II, pp. 318–43; Thompson, pp. 90–92; and Liungman, pp. 80–85.

In the oriental version of Type 400, which appears in another volume of this series, *Folktales of Japan,* No. 23, "The Woman Who Came Down from Heaven," the lost wife is a heavenly swan maiden rather than a parrot. In the Mexican version, "The Son of Tata Juan Pescador," (Riley Aiken, "A Pack Load of Mexican Tales" in *Publications of the Texas Folklore Society,* XII [1935], 1–87; 79–86), the lost bride is a fairy. Additional versions may also be found in *Folktales of Norway* and *Folktales of Hungary,* in this series.

·14· *The Little Frog*

Type 402, *The Frog as Bride*. Motifs: H1242, "Youngest brother alone succeeds on quest"; H1306, "Quest for the finest of linen"; H1331.6, "Quest for marvellous dog"; H1301.1, "Quest for the most beautiful bride"; B313, "Helpful animal an enchanted person"; B493.1, "Helpful frog"; D700, "Person disenchanted." CFCH No. 248.

Recorded on tape on April 21, 1962 in Parral, Linares, from an illiterate countrywoman, Amelia Quiroz, born on April 14, 1889. Mrs. Quiroz belongs to a family of good narrators. She and a sister learned stories from one of their grandmothers, and Mrs. Quiroz has transmitted some to a son and a grandson. Other tales of hers presented in this book are Nos. 19, 21, 29, 33, and 44.

This story has been widely spread throughout Europe, from Ireland to Turkey and from Portugal to Scandinavia and Russia. Thompson and Roberts, p. 57, list one version and eight variants from India. It has been listed sporadically in Armenia, North Africa, and the Philippines. A more important path is the one it has followed from France to Canada, and from the Iberian peninsula to Brazil and areas of Spanish-speaking America. The Iberian source has been responsible as well for versions among the Indians of Mexico and Argentina. In Chile, it is one of the most popular stories, with eight published versions.

Espinosa, III, pp. 55–56, studies thirty versions from the Iberian Peninsula, Brazil, and Spanish America. Among these, eleven contain the episode of the banquet at which the enchanted princess keeps the bones on her plate and afterwards casts them down during the dance. They change into flowers, pearls, or gold. The sisters-in-law imitate her, but merely cast junk or some other despicable thing. The development of this episode in the Chilean versions confirms the thesis of Espinosa that its dissemination in such widely separated regions presupposes that it is a case of a characteristic feature which could belong to an original form from the peninsular tradition. The story is found as well in a beautiful Araucanian version in Kössler-Ilg's *Indianermärchen aus den Kordilleren*, No. 65, which also contains archaic elements.

The kind of animal or object into which the princess is enchanted is varied in the European versions, but in those from the Iberian peninsula, and in the Spanish and Portuguese versions in America, the animal is a frog, a toad, or a monkey. There is one exception: a rat appears in a Catalonian version in Amades' *Rondallística*, No. 127.

For more references, see Thompson, p. 107; Ranke, I, pp. 319–20; and Liungman, pp. 86–87.

· 15 · Delgadina and the Snake

This story may be considered as a variant of Type 403, *The Black and the White Bride*. Motifs: B491.1, "Helpful snake"; D1454.2, "Treasure falls from mouth (hands)"; T51, "Wooing by emissary"; S432, "Cast-off wife thrown into water"; B557, "Unusual animal as riding horse"; K1911, "The substituted bride"; Q261, "Treachery punished." CFCH No. 249, "Delgadina and the Snake."

Recorded on tape on September 17, 1961 in Linares, Linares, from Manuel Urrea, a retired army sergeant born in 1891.

The similarity between this story and other previously published Chilean versions is notable. See *Biblioteca de Tradiciones Populares Españolas*, I, p. 137, and Lenz, *Consejas chilenas*, p. 80. The Lenz version is mixed with motifs of Type 707, *The Three Golden Sons*. There is also a similarity between our version and one from Puerto Rico recorded by Rafael Ramírez de Arellano, *Folklore portorriqueño*, No. 71. For Motif K1911, "The substituted bride," see Thompson, *The Folktale*, p. 117; for Motif D1454.2, "Treasure falls from mouth," see Bolte and Polívka, III, p. 91, and Liungman, p. 86.

· 16 · Sleeping Beauty

Type 410, *Sleeping Beauty*, III, IV. Motifs: D1364.17, "Spindle causes magic sleep"; D1960.3, "Sleeping beauty. Magic sleep for definite period (a year)"; N711.2, "Hero finds maiden in castle (house)"; D1978.3, "Waking from magic sleep by removal of enchanting instrument (thorn)." CFCH No. 42, "Sleeping Beauty."

Collected in February, 1951 in Los Lagos, Valdivia, from Pantaleón Ulloa.

The versions of this beautiful story are not numerous. Thompson, *The Folktale*, p. 97, remarks that the tale has never become a real part of oral tradition. The Grimm version (No. 50, "Dornröschen,") and especially the one of Perrault (*Perrault's Popular Tales*, "La belle au bois dormant," pp. 7–19), which has crossed to Canada, are well known. It would be necessary to verify whether or not this same influence has existed in Portugal and Brazil.

Tale No. 16 does not contain the introduction of the prophecy; it ends with the persecution of the heroine and her two children by the mother-in-law, as in the fragmentary story of Grimm No. 215, the versions of Perrault and of Basile (*The Pentamerone of Giambattista Basile*, I, pp. 192–95, "The Eighth Diversion of the Second Day"), the popular Italian versions, Pitrè, No. 58 and the variant, and Gonzenbach, Sicilianische *Märchen*, No. 4, one Portuguese version, Braga, *Contos tradicionaes do povo portuguez*, No. 4, Brazilian one, Câmara Cascudo, *Contos tradicionais do Brasil*, p. 44 and one Spanish one, M. Curiel Merchán, *Cuentos extremeños*, p. 24. It seems that this combination is characteristic of the romance language versions. In this second part of our story No. 16, the motif of the sounding dress is notable. The versions of Basile and of Gonzenbach, the variant of Pitrè, and the version of Curiel Merchán also contain this motif. The same thing can be said of the feature of the consummated or frustrated cannabalism which occurs in the versions of Basile and Curiel Merchán as well as in ours.

There is no consensus of opinion on the origin of this story. Jan de Vries, *Fabula*, II, p. 121, says that its origin is lost in the mists of prehistory. Ranke, II, p. 18, implies that the tale might be of romance language origin.

· 17 · The Little Orphan Girl

Type 432, *The Prince as Bird*. Motifs: D641.1, "Lover as bird visits mistress"; S181, "Wounding by trapping with sharp knives"; H1385.5, "Quest for vanished lover"; H1232.1, "Directions on quest given by peasants"; N452, "Secret remedy overheard in conversation of animals (witches)"; G211.3.2, "Witch in form of duck"; E113, "Resuscitation by blood." CFCH No. 48 "The Little Orphan Girl."

Collected in February, 1951 in San Francisco de Mostazal, province of O'Higgins, from hotel owner María Navarro, born in 1886.

This story is a very complete version of Type 432. The tale of the bird-lover, says Thompson in *The Folktale*, p. 103, appears several times in medieval literature, notably in Marie de France's *Yonec*. Details of the medieval stories vary somewhat from those of the modern folktale, but it seems likely that they belong to the same tradition. The story was probably current in Italy during the Reniassance. It appears in Basile's *Pentamerone*, I, pp. 141–46, "The Second Diversion of the Second Day," and it is especially popular in the Mediterranean countries today. In the Iberian peninsula, Spanish, Catalonian, and Portuguese versions have been listed. In America, there are versions from Canada, New Mexico, and Chile. For further references, see Bolte and Polívka, II, p. 261 ff., and Liungman, p. 99.

· 18 · The Four Little Dwarfs

Type 503, *The Gifts of the Little People*. Motifs: F331.3, "Mortal wins dwarfs' gratitude by joining in their song and completing it by adding the names of the days of the week"; N471, "Foolish attempt of second man to overhear secrets from dwarfs. He is punished." CFCH No. 252, "The Four Little Dwarfs."

Recorded on tape in 1957 in Pomaire, Santiago, from an illiterate day laborer, Abraham Vélez, born in 1889. Mr. Vélez also contributed tales Nos. 26, 27, 43, 48, 49, and 50 in this volume.

The first literary versions of this story appeared in Italy and Ireland in the seventeenth century. It has spread throughout Europe and has been listed sporadically in Turkey, Persia, India, Tibet, Japan, Algeria, Morocco, The Cameroons, and Sudan. Its American versions were brought to Canada, Costa Rica, Brazil, Venezuela, and Chile by French, Spanish, and Portuguese colonists. Ina-Maria Greverus has studied 139 European versions of this story, *Fabula,* I, pp. 263–79. See also Bolte and Polívka, II, pp. 324–29; and Thompson, *The Folktale,* p. 49.

The theme of fairy gifts is a popular one in folktales. Other versions of Type 503 are given in *Folktales of England,* No. 8, "Goblin Combe," and in *Folktales of Japan,* No. 36, "The Old Men Who Had Wens." Lolita H. Pooler presents an interesting New Mexican variant, "Mariano and Abran," in her article "New Mexican Folktales," *Western Folklore,* X (1951), 63–71. In this tale, the dwarfs are replaced by devils.

· 19 · Maria Cinderella

Type 510A, *Cinderella.* Motifs: S31, "Cruel stepmother"; L55, "Stepdaughter heroine"; B411.3, "Helpful calf"; D815.3, "Magic object received from godmother"; D1051.1, "Clothes produced by magic"; D1111.1, "Carriage produced by magic"; N711.4, "Prince sees maiden at church and is enamored"; H36.1, "Slipper test." CFCH No. 254, "Maria Cinderella."

Recorded on tape on April 21, 1962 in Parral, Linares, from Amelia Quiroz.

The story of Cinderella is one of the most widely spread, best known, and most thoroughly studied of all folktales. The old study of M. R. Cox, *Cinderella* (London, 1893), has been revised and completed by the Swedish folklorist Anna Birgitta Rooth, *The Cinderella Cycle* (Lund, 1951). Our story, No. 19, is a complete and pure version of Type 510A in its five parts and fundamental motifs. A Japanese variant of Type 510A is given as No. 38, "Benizara and Kakezara" in a companion volume in this series, *Folktales of Japan.* A Virginia variant from the United States is given as No. 12 "Ashpet," by Richard Chase in his *Grandfather Tales,* pp. 115–23.

From this story comes the expression *"salir con su domingo siete"* (to come out with one's Sunday seven). The expression, which means "to put one's foot in one's mouth," is very common in Chile and other Spanish American countries.

· 20 · The Little Stick Figure

Type 510B, *The Dress of Gold, of Silver, and of Stars.* Motifs:
T411.1, "Lecherous father. Unnatural father wants to marry his
daughter"; N846.2, "Priest as helper"; F821.1.5, "Dress of color of
sun, moon, and stars (sea)"; N711.6, "Prince sees heroine at ball
(Chilean horse race) and is enamored"; R221, "Heroine's three-fold
flight from ball (Chilean horse race)"; H94.2, "Identification by ring
baked in bread"; L161, "Lowly prince marries heroine." CFCH No.
54, "The Little Stick Figure."

Collected in February, 1950 at the San Francisco farm, Los Andes,
Aconcagua, from Augustín Poblete, an illiterate. Another tale from
the same narrator is No. 23 in this book.

Tale No. 20 is the best Chilean version of Type 510B, *The Dress of
Gold, of Silver, and of Stars.* It contains all the fundamental motifs
with which Rooth characterizes Type 510B1 in her study, *The Cinderella Cycle,* pp. 19–20. There is another similar Chilean version;
see CFCH, I, p. 403. In *Folktales of England,* a companion volume in
this series, a modern British version is included as No. 4, "Mossy-
coat." An American version from Kentucky appears in Marie Campbell's *Tales from the Cloud Walking Country* as "The Queen with
Golden Hair," pp. 30–31.

· 21 · Florinda

Type 514, *The Shift of Sex.* Motifs: T411.1, "Lecherous father. Unnatural father wants to marry his daughter"; T311.1, "Flight of
maiden to escape marriage"; K1322, "Girl masked as man wins
princess's love"; H1578.1, "Test of sex of girl masking as man"; D11,
"Transformation: woman to man." CFCH No. 255, "Florinda."

Recorded on tape on April 20, 1962 in Parral, Linares, from Amelia
Quíroz.

This version of Type 514 with its two fundamental motifs, K1837,
"Disguise of woman in man's clothes," and D11, "Transformation:
woman to man," has been found, according to Aarne and Thompson,
p. 182, throughout Europe, especially in Finland, Lithuania, Denmark, Ireland, Poland, Rumania, Greece, and Turkey. It has been
found sporadically in Norway, Scotland, Germany, Austria, Italy,
Russia, Yugoslavia, Indonesia, Canada, and The West Indies (Negro). Hambruch, *Malaiische Märchen,* No. 41, includes a version
from Minahasa, Malaysia. In the Iberian peninsula, two Spanish ver-

sions and a Portuguese one are known. In the Cape Verde Islands, a Portuguese version has been found. Spanish America has produced one Mexican and two Chilean versions.

For references in oriental and classical literature regarding change of sex see Espinosa, III, pp. 101–07, and *Handwörterbuch des deutschen Märchens,* II, p. 570. For popular beliefs on the idea, see *Handwörterbuch des deutschen Aberglaubens,* III, p. 752.

·22· *The Moorish Prince and the Christian Prince*

Type 516, *Faithful John.* Motifs: T11.1, "Love from mere mention"; P273.1, "Faithful foster brother"; B143, "Prophetic bird"; M352, "Prophecy of particular perils to prince on wedding journey"; D991, "Magic hairs"; C961.2, "Transformation to stone for breaking tabu"; H1558, "Test of friendship"; S268, "Child sacrificed to provide blood for cure of friend." CFCH No. 81, "The Moorish Prince and the Christian Prince."

Collected in January, 1951 in Ignao, Valdivia, from Francisco Coronado.

Thompson, *The Folktale,* p. 112, notes that this story is of rather frequent occurrence in all countries from Portugal to India. In Portugal it is notably widespread, with no fewer than ten versions having been published. See Câmara Cascudo, *Estórias,* p. 153. From Portugal it went to the Cape Verde Islands and also to Brazil; see Câmara Cascudo, *Contos,* p. 25; *Estórias,* p. 148; and Almeida, *142 Histórias brasileiras,* No. 5. In Spain, Spanish-speaking areas of the United States, the Dominican Republic, Puerto Rico, and Chile, versions of the complete form of this story have been found.

For discussion of the origin, development, and dissemination of this story, see Rösch, *Der getreue Johannes,* in Krohn, *Übersicht,* pp. 82ff.; Bolte and Polívka I, pp. 46ff.; Thompson, *The Folktale,* p. 112; and Liungman, p. 139. See also the German version and accompanying notes in *Folktales of Germany,* a companion volume in this series.

·23· *The Golden-Haired Beauty*

This story is a conglomerate of motifs in which Type 554, *The Grateful Animals,* plays a principal part in the development. Other motifs enter from Type 302, *The Ogre's Heart in the Egg,* Ia, and Type 531, *Ferdinand the True and Ferdinand the False,* IIb. Motifs: D825, "Magic objects received from maidens"; D1361.5, "Cap renders invisible"; D1470.1.25, "Magic wishing-rod"; D1065.2, "Magic shoes";

B392, "Hero divides spoil for animals"; B350, "Grateful animals"; B571, "Animals perform tasks for man"; H911, "Tasks assigned at suggestion of jealous rivals"; H1151.13.3, "Task: stealing horse from king"; H1091.1, "Task: sorting grains; performed by helpful ants"; H1023.6.1, "Task: washing large heavy quilt covered with ghee and oil (washing large earthen jar covered with unguent)"; H324, "Suitor test: choosing princess from others identically clad"; L161, "Hero marries princess." CFCH No. 61, "The Golden-Haired Beauty."

Collected in February, 1950 at the San Francisco farm, Los Andes, Aconcagua, from Augustín Poblete.

·24· *The Magic Coconut*

Type 560, *The Magic Ring*. Principal motifs: B360, "Animals grateful for rescue from peril of death"; D840, "Magic object found"; D1470.1.6, "Magic wishing-nut"; D1132.1, "Palace produced by magic"; L161, "Lowly Hero marries princess"; D861.4, "Magic object stolen by rival for wife"; D2136.2, "Castle (palace) magically transported"; B548.1, "Animals recover lost wishing ring (nut). Grateful dog compels mouse to steal it from thief"; Q414, "Punishment: burning alive"; Q416, "Punishment: drawing asunder by horses." CFCH No. 63, "The Magic Coconut."

Collected in February, 1951 in Ignao, Valdivia, from Francisco Coronado.

Thompson, *The Folktale*, p. 70, remarks that this story was one of the first to receive exhaustive treatment by the so-called Finnish method, (A. Aarne, "Vergleichende Märchenforschungen," pp. 3–82), and that in regard to its origin, Aarne was sure that it came from Asia, probably from India. The oldest European literary variant is found in Basile's *Pentamerone*, "The First Diversion of the Fourth Day," II, pp. 5–9.

The Tale of the Magic Ring, Type 560, is more popular in eastern than in western Europe. Aarne, and Liungman after him, believed that the eastern European versions were the best. But Espinosa, III, p. 69, soon noticed that there were Iberian versions very faithful to the original form established by Aarne. Among these are three Spanish versions from New Mexico, a Mexican one, and a Portuguese one. Nevertheless, we believe that tale No. 24 as published here can be considered the most complete version in Spanish of Type 560. Among the Araucanian Indians of Argentina and Chile two variants of this type have been found. An Oriental version is to be found in *Folktales of China,* in this series.

·25· *The Foolish Boy*

Types 590, *The Prince and the Arm Bands,* 590A, *The Treacherous Wife,* II, and 675, *The Lazy Boy,* III, IV. Motifs: T513, "Conception from wish"; S146.2, "Abandonment in cave"; F610, "Remarkably strong man"; F628.2.3, "Strongman kills giant"; C611, "Forbidden chamber"; S12.1.1, "Treacherous mother marries ogre (giant) and plots against son"; H1211, "Quest assigned in order to get rid of hero"; S165, "Mutilation: putting out eyes"; N836, "King as helper"; E30, "Resuscitation by arrangement of members"; E106, "Resuscitation by magic apple"; Q261, "Treachery punished"; L162, "Princess marries hero." CFCH No. 70, "The Foolish Boy."

Collected in February, 1951 in Ignao, Valdivia, from Francisco Coronado.

This story develops essentially the theme of the treacherous mother in a combination of Types 590, *The Prince and the Arm Bands,* and 590A, *The Treacherous Wife.* But it has as an introduction Type 675, *The Lazy Boy,* III, IV, and is also contaminated by motifs from Types 650, *Strong John,* and 571, *"All Stick Together."*

Although well-known in Europe, the story of the prince and the arm bands has appeared in the Iberian peninsula in only one Portuguese version, Coelho, *Contos populares portugueses,* No. 60. From there is passed to Brazil; see Roméro, *Contos populares do Brasil,* No. 30. In Spanish America, our own version, another Chilean one, and one from Puerto Rico have been published. On the other hand, the tale has been found numerous times in Canada. For further references, see Bolte and Polívka, I, p. 551; III, p. 1 and Thompson, *The Folktale,* p. 114.

Type 590A has been incorporated in the Aarne-Thompson *Index* in its new revision, taking as basis the Polish versions of J. Krzyżanowski, *Polska Bajka Ludowa w Układzie Systematycznym,* I.

Thompson, *The Folktale,* p. 68, notes that the story of *The Lazy Boy,* Type 675, had been known for a long time, since Straparola's *The Nights* appeared in the sixteenth century. A hundred years later it appeared in Basile's *Pentamerone,* I, pp. 34–42, "The Third Diversion of the First Day." It has been disseminated throughout Europe, even as far as Siberia. It has also been listed in Spain and Portugal, and gone from there with the colonists to Brazil, the United States,

Puerto Rico, Costa Rica, Argentina, and Chile. For the Franco-American, West Indies Negro, and American Indian versions, see Aarne-Thompson's *Index,* and Thompson, p. 68. For other references and versions, see Bolte and Polívka, I, p. 485.

Type 590 appears in companion volumes in this series, in *Folktales of Norway* as No. 75, "The Blue Band," and in *Folktales of Hungary,* as No. 8, "The Story of Gallant Szerus," where it is combined with several other Types.

· 26 · *The Five Brothers*

Type 653, *The Four Skillful Brothers.* Motifs: F660.1, "Brothers acquire extraordinary skill"; F676, "Skillful thief"; F661, "Skillful marksman"; F668.0.1, "Skillful physician"; D1712, "Diviner"; R10.1, "Princess abducted"; T68.1, "Princess offered as prize to rescuer"; R166, "Brothers having extraordinary skill rescue princess"; F662.2, "Skillful tailor (physician) sews together scattered planks in capsizing boat." CFCH No. 259, "The Five Brothers."

Recorded on tape January 25, 1962 in Pomaire, Santiago, from Abraham Vélez.

This story, on the Indic origin of which researchers agree, has a long literary history. Bolte and Polívka, III, p. 51, and Thompson, *The Folktale,* p. 81, refer to the oldest Indic version, which is in the *Vetālanpañcavimçati,* or *Twenty-Five Tales of Vampires.* They also mention the later Mongolian version in the *Siddhi Kür,* the Persian one in the *Tuti-Nameh,* and the Italian ones of Morlini, Straparola, and Basile, II, pp. 139–43, "The Seventh Diversion of the Fifth Day." Its dissemination covers Europe and Asia as far as Japan and China, India, and Indonesia. It has also spread through Africa. On the American continent, it has been found in Canada, the United States (in Spanish), the Dominican Republic, Puerto Rico, and Chile. By way of Portugal, it came to the Cape Verde Islands and Brazil.

Tale No. 26 is a complete version of Type 653, *The Four Skillful Brothers,* with the only variation at the end, where the king orders the five brothers to shoot an arrow. The youngest wins and thus gains the hand of the liberated princess. Then the king gives the other four daughters to the remaining brothers.

· 27 · *The Jewel Stone*

Types 676, *Open Sesame,* and 954, *The Forty Thieves.* Motifs: F721.4, "Underground treasure chambers"; N455.3, "Secret formula for opening treasure mountain overheard from robbers"; N471, "Foolish attempt of second to overhear secrets. He is punished"; K312, "Thieves hidden in oil casks. In one cask is oil; in the others the robbers are hidden. The girl kills them." CFCH No. 90, "The Jewel Stone."

Collected on tape in March, 1961 in El Bollenal, Santiago, from Abraham Vélez.

Tale No. 27 is a good version of the story of Ali Baba and the Forty Thieves, from *The Thousand and One Nights*. It has been known in Europe since the beginning of the eighteenth century through the translation of Galland. The only thing lacking in this Chilean version is the motif of the accusing gold measure. This combination of Type 676, *Open Sesame,* and 954, *The Forty Thieves,* has been listed within the Iberian and Spanish-American oral tradition, in Spain, Catalonia, Portugal, New Mexico, the Dominican Republic, Puerto Rico, and Chile. The independent form of Type 954 is not known to exist. For versions and references, see Bolte and Polívka, III, pp. 137 ff.; Thompson, *The Folktale,* pp. 68, 173; and Liungman, p. 191.

An American variant of Type 954 is given by Emelyn E. Gardner in *Folklore from the Schoharie Hills, New York* (Ann Arbor, 1937), as No. 10, "Ali Baby," pp. 140–46. Another version of Type 954, "The Millman's Daughter," pp. 47–50, is given by Richard M. Dorson in "Polish Wonder Tales of Joe Woods," *Western Folklore,* VIII (1949), 25–52.

· 28 · *Blanca Rosa and the Forty Thieves*

Type 709, *Snow White.* Motifs: D1311.2, "Mirror answers questions"; S31, "Cruel stepmother"; K512.2, "Compassionate executioner: substituted eyes and tongue"; D1364.15, "Pin causes magic sleep"; F852.2, "Golden coffin"; N711, "Prince accidentally finds maiden"; E21.3, "Resuscitation by removal of poisoned comb (pin)"; Q416.2, "Punishment: dragging to death by horse." CFCH No. 98, "Blanca Rosa and the Forty Thieves."

Collected in 1949 by Marino Pizaro in Monte Patria, Coquimbo, from a schoolmistress, Amanda Flores.

This story is well known in Europe, especially from the version of Grimm, No. 53, on which Aarne based his outline of Type 709. Before Grimm, two variations are found in Basile's *Pentamerone,* I, pp. 192–95, "The Eighth Diversion of the Second Day." The old world area of dissemination of this type is from Ireland to Asia Minor and central Africa. In the Iberian peninsula it is well represented by at least eight Spanish versions, seven from Catalonia, and seven from Portugal. In Portuguese- and Spanish-speaking areas of America, it has been listed in Brazil, the United States, Mexico, the Dominican Republic, Puerto Rico, and Chile.

Although the origin of the story does not seem to be very ancient, nothing conclusive can really be said about it. Liungman, p. 200, suggests Italy as a center of dissemination; it has also been suggested that the origin must be sought in a Celtic variant. For further references and versions, see Bolte and Polívka, I, pp. 450 ff.; Thompson, *The Folktale,* p. 124; Liungman, pp. 198–202; Espinosa, II, pp. 431–41; and Ranke, III, pp. 66–67.

· 29 · Juanita

Type 710, *Our Lady's Child.* Principal motifs: V271, "Virgin Mary as foster mother"; C611, "Forbidden chamber"; N711.1, "Prince finds maiden in tree and marries her"; G261, "Witch (Virgin Mary) steals children"; K2116.1.1, "Innocent woman accused of eating her newborn children." CFCH No. 263, "Juanita."

Recorded on tape on April 20, 1962 in Parral, Linares from Amelia Quiroz.

Two versions of Type 710, *Our Lady's Child,* have been distinguished. In the first, the supernatural being is the Virgin Mary; in the second, it is an evil creature, black and enchanted. The first version has seldom been recorded. Liungman, p. 203, assures us that the area of dissemination of this version extends in general from Denmark and Alsace, throughout Scandinavia to Germany, Poland, and the Baltic countries as far as Russia. There is also a mutilated variant from Sicily. The story has also gone to Czechoslovakia, (Jech, *Tschechische Volksmärchen,* No. 30), to Spain, (Espinosa, No. 89), and to Chile (the version recorded here). For further references, see Bolte and Polívka, I, pp. 13–16; Thompson, *The Folktale,* pp. 122–23; Espinosa, II, pp. 346–48; and Liungman, pp. 202–05.

PART III

RELIGIOUS TALES

· 30 · Food for the Crucifix

Type 767, *Food for the Crucifix.* Motif Q172.1, "Child taken to heaven: offers food to crucifix." CFCH No. 109.

Collected in January, 1951 in Ignao, Valdivia, from illiterate country midwife Zoraila Corona, born in 1871. Other tales collected from
the same narrator appear as Nos. 31 and 42 in this volume.

This story, to which the narrator gave no name, is a variant of Type
767, *Food for the Crucifix,* which Boggs, *Index of Spanish Folktales,* lists with that number on the basis of two *"cantigas"* of the
Spanish king, Alfonso X El Sabio (Alphonse the Wise). The type appears in the Aarne-Thompson *Index.* The first Latin literary version
dates from the twelfth century and was followed by various others.
Bolte and Polívka, III, pp. 474–77, in their comments on legend No.
209, "Die himmlische Hochzeit" of Grimm, include medieval literary
versions and contemporary popular ones. The story is internationally
widespread. Important studies of it have been made by Josef Szövérffy, "A Medieval Story and Its Irish Version," in *Studies in Folklore, in Honor of Distinguished Service Professor Stith Thompson,* pp.
55–65; and "Ein Grimm-Märchen in Irland," in *Irisches Erzählgut
im Abendland,* pp. 141–51.

The fact that in Ireland one hundred manuscript variants of this
tale exist, although only three have been published, shows clearly that
this religious legend has spread among the people and continues to
live in the twentieth century, one hundred and fifty years after the
publication of Grimm's version.

Our story No. 30 is the only oral version in the Spanish language
which is known to date. Almost certainly it was brought from the
Iberian peninsula by priests, but it was then modified by the people.
This is proved by the variation of the motif of "The straight road,"
which consists in our story of the correction of the priest's bad con-
duct by advice from the crucifix, resulting in his eventual salvation.

Szövérffy calls attention to the fact that this theme served as the
subject of the Spanish moving picture *"Marcelino pan y vino,"* which
has been shown in many countries.

·31· *The Poor* Compadre

The story is one variant of Type 804, *Peter's Mother Falls from
Heaven,* with the Motifs: A661.0.1.2, "Saint Peter as porter of
heaven"; and F51.1.3, "Stalk as sky-rope." CFCH No. 105, "The Poor
Compadre."

Collected in January, 1951 in Ignao, Valdivia, from Zoraila Corona.

This story contains the motif of the son who goes to heaven and
sees his punished mother hanging from a thread over the fire of hell,
as in Type 804, *Peter's Mother Falls from Heaven.* Aside from that,

however, the story is different. The son returns to earth, does penance, and saves the soul of his mother. He himself goes to heaven in the form of a dove. For the complete versions of Type 804, see Bolte and Polívka, III, pp. 538–42; Thompson, *The Folktale,* p. 150; Espinosa, II, pp. 310–12; Liungman, p. 218; and Ranke, III, p. 131. There is a good Argentinian version in Chertudi's *Juan Soldao,* No. 22.

PART IV

ROMANTIC TALES

· 32 · *The Simple Lad and the Three Little Pigs*

Type 850, *The Birthmarks of the Princess,* I. Motifs: H51.1, "Recognition by birthmark"; H525, "Test: guessing princess's birthmarks"; K1358, "Girl shows herself naked in return for youth's dancing hogs (little pigs)." CFCH No. 111, "The Simple Lad and the Three Little Pigs."

Collected in January, 1951 in Ignao, Valdivia, from Francisco Coronado.

Thompson, *The Folktale,* p. 156, says that this story, which seems to be a concoction of two other stories, is told throughout Europe and has gone as far as Virginia. Aarne and Thompson, in their *Index,* list twenty-four Franco-American versions and two West Indian Negro ones. In the Iberian peninsula, only one Spanish version has been published, *Revista de Dialectología y Tradiciones Populares,* III, p. 89. In the Spanish-speaking regions of America, four versions from the United States, nine from Puerto Rico, one from the Dominican Republic, and two from Chile have been published. See also the version in *Folktales of Germany,* in this series.

Motif H315, "Suitor test: to whom the princess turns," which doesn't appear in our version, is found in an Argentinian version, Chertudi, *Cuentos folklóricos de la Argentina,* No. 41, and in another Chilean version, CFCH, No. 73, both of them in combination with Types 554, *The Grateful Animals,* and 621, *The Louse Skin.*

· 33 · *He Who Has Money Does What He Likes*

Type 854, *The Golden Ram.* Motifs: H344, "Suitor test: entering princess's chamber"; K1341, "Entrance to woman's room in golden ram (golden turkey)." CFCH No. 268, "He Who Has Money Does What He Likes."

Collected on tape on April 21, 1962 in Parral, Linares, from Amelia Quiroz.

Thompson, *The Folktale*, p. 157, says that the story of *The Golden Ram* reminds us of a scene in Shakespeare's "Cymbeline." This story has been listed throughout Europe, especially in Finland, Ireland, and Italy. Eberhard and Boratav, p. 236, list three Turkish versions, and Thompson and Roberts, p. 103, two Indic ones. In the Iberian peninsula one Spanish version is known. In the Spanish-speaking areas of America the following versions have been published: two from the United States, one from Mexico, two from Puerto Rico, one from the Dominican Republic, one from Venezuela, and three from Chile. In Canada nine French versions are known. The story also appears among the American Indians and in the West Indies (Negro).

·34· *Juan, Pedro, and Diego*

Type 870D*, *Magic Mirror Reflects Blemishes*. Motifs: A2721.3.1, "Man tells Jesus he is sowing stones. 'You shall get stones' "; D1451, "Inexhaustible purse (vest) furnishes money"; W11, "Generosity"; H411, "Magic object points out unchaste woman." CFCH No. 122, "Juan, Pedro, and Diego."

Collected in February, 1952 in Ignao, Valdivia, from Francisco Coronado.

The first part of this story, which serves as an introduction, is a variant of the religious legend of goodness rewarded and lack of charity punished. It corresponds to Motif A2721.3.1, "Man tells Jesus he is sowing stones. 'You shall get stones.' " For this legend see Espinosa, III, pp. 94–95. The second part of our version resembles Type 870D*, which Thompson included in the new revision of his *Index*, taking into account number *1621 of Boggs' *Index*. While in the Spanish version it is a mirror which denounces the blemish, in our story No. 34 it is the right hand of the hero which has received the magic power of revealing the chastity or unchastity of the kings' daughters. There is a notable similarity between the second part of this story and the German story included in Zaunert's *Deutsche Märchen seit Grimm*, I, p. 216.

· 35 · King Clarion of the Island of Talagante

Type 873, *The King Discovers His Unknown Son*. Motifs: T11.2, "Love through sight of picture"; T645, "Paramour leaves token with girl to give their son"; H81, "Clandestine lover recognized by tokens"; H94, "Identification by ring"; L161, "King marries heroine." CFCH No. 123, "King Clarion of the Island of Talagante."

Collected in February, 1951 in Los Lagos, Valdivia, from Pantaleón Ulloa.

This story is an extraordinary variant of Type 873, *The King Discovers His Unknown Son*, which Thompson incorporated into Aarne's *Index* in his first revision on the basis of Danish versions. To date, only the following versions are known: thirteen from Denmark, eight from Ireland, one from France, two from Russia, eight from Greece, one from Portugal, one from the Dominican Republic, one from the West Indies, and our story, No. 35, from Chile. The Portuguese text is given in "Contos Populares Portuguezes," by Z. Consiglieri Pedroso, *Revue Hispanique,* XIV (1906), 115–240, the Dominican one in Andrade's *Folklore de la Republica Dominicana,* II, No. 265.

· 36 · The Basil Plant

Types 879, *The Basil Maiden,* I, II, and III, and 875, *The Clever Peasant Girl,* III and IV. Motifs: H705.3, "How many leaves are on the tree? Counter-question: how many stars in the sky?"; J111.4, "Clever peasant girl"; L162, "Lowly heroine marries prince (king)"; J1191, "Reductio ad absurdum of judgment"; J1191.7, "Rice pot on pole, fire far away (variant)"; J1545.4.1, "The besieged woman's dearest possession." CFCH No. 125, "The Basil Plant."

Collected in October, 1953 in Pomaire, Santiago, from illiterate potter Sofía Ahumada.

The first part of this story corresponds to the development of the first three episodes of the new Type 879, *The Basil Maiden,* and the second part to the last episodes of Type 875, *The Clever Peasant Girl.* Seven other Chilean versions have this same characteristic. For references to this combination of types, as well as to the independent Types 875 and 879, see Espinosa, II, pp. 61–78 and 227–29, the episode of the sugar puppet. For Type 875, see De Vries, *Das Märchen von Klugen Rätsellösern;* Bolte and Polívka, II, pp. 349 ff.; and Liungman, pp. 228–31.

A Kentucky variant of Type 875 appears as "The Farmer's Daughter," in *Tales from the Cloud Walking Country* by Marie Campbell, pp. 198–200; and a German one appears in *Folktales of Germany,* in this series.

·37· *The Wager on the Wife's Chastity*

Type 882, *The Wager on the Wife's Chastity.* Principal motifs: N15, "Chastity wager"; K2293, "Treacherous old woman"; K2112.1, "False tokens of woman's unfaithfulness"; K1837, "Disguise of woman in man's clothes"; Q473.2, "Punishment: tying to horse's tail." CFCH No. 128, "The Wager on the Wife's Chastity."

Collected in January, 1951 at the Gjüeimén farm, Ignao, Valdivia, from Escolástica Garrido, a day laborer's wife born in 1885.

Ranke, III, p. 217, cites the essay by Schwewe, "Die 'Wette' eine neu aufgefundene alte Ballade," pp. 176–86, in *Volkskundliche Gaben,* to suggest that the beginnings of this story reach back to the eleventh century. The theme of the bet on the wife's chastity was used numerous times in the Middle Ages; it then appears in Boccaccio's *Decameron,* II, 9, and from there goes to Shakespeare's "Cymbeline," to a story of Timoneda, No. 15, and eventually to the theatrical piece "Eufemia" of Lope de Rueda. It is probable that the written tradition has influenced the oral one. The story is now spread throughout almost all of Europe and into Turkey. Thompson and Roberts, p. 107, list two Indic versions; Littmann, p. 204, includes a modern Arabic version. From Spain the story went to the United States, the Dominican Republic, Argentina, and Chile. From France it has gone to Canada. Compare Gaston Paris, "Le cycle de la gageure," *Romania,* XXXII, 481–551; Liungman, p. 231; Thompson, *The Folktale,* p. 109. See also the version and accompanying notes in *Folktales of Germany,* a volume in this series.

·38· *White Onion*

Type 890, *A Pound of Flesh,* II and IV. Motifs: K1837, "Disguise of woman in man's clothes"; H1385.4, "Quest for vanished husband"; K1825.2, "Woman masks as viceroy and frees her husband"; J1161.2, "Pound of flesh"; H51.1, "Recognition by birthmark." CFCH No. 131, "White Onion."

Collected in January, 1951 in Ignao, Valdivia, from Francisco Coronado.

This story is an extraordinary variant of Type 890, *A Pound of*

Flesh. The oldest literary version appears in the *Dolopathos* of the twelfth century and it is known in our times through Shakespeare's "The Merchant of Venice." Its oral dissemination is limited. Tale No. 38 is the only variant in the Spanish language recorded to date. For discussions of its origin and bibliography see Wesselski, *Märchen des Mittelalters,* pp. 252–54, Taylor, in *Handwörterbuch des deutschen Märchens,* II, pp. 153–54, and Liungman, p. 236.

"White Onion," the name given to the heroine, leads to a play on words which produces confusion and pertains to the traditions of the Iberian peninsula.

· 39 · *Quico and Caco*

Types: 1525H₁, *One Thief Steals Egg from Bird's Nest;* 950, *Rhampsinitus;* compare also 1525G, *The Thief Assumes Disguises,* IV. Motifs: K305.1, "Thieving contest: first steals egg from under bird; second meantime steals first's breeches"; J1143, "Thief detected by building straw fire so that smoke escapes through thief's entrance"; K730, "Victim trapped"; K407.1, "Thief has his companion cut off his head so that he may escape detection"; J1142.4, "Thief's corpse carried through street to see who will weep for him"; K415, "Marked culprit marks everyone else and escapes detection." CFCH No. 157, "Quico and Caco."

Collected in February, 1950 in Paihuano, Coquimbo, from Efraín Rodríguez.

This is a complete version of Type 950, *Rhampsinitus,* but it has as an introduction the secondary Type 1525H₁, *One Thief Steals Egg from Bird's Nest,* and is contaminated with a variation of the secondary Type 1525G, *Theft by Disguising,* Episode IV.

The oldest versions of the story of the treasure house of Rhampsinitus come from Eugammon of Cyrene and Herodotus in the fifth century B.C., but the later literary versions undoubtedly come from Herodotus. Thompson, *The Folktale,* p. 171, says that "it appears not only in the literary collections of the European Middle Ages and Renaissance, but also in the Buddhistic writings of the Early Christian era and in the Ocean of Story from India of the twelfth century." Versions of this story may be found in *Folktales of Israel* and *Folktales of Germany,* volumes in this series.

Published versions of Type 950 from the Spanish oral tradition include combinations of Types 1525A, *Theft of Dog, Horse, Sheet, or Ring;* 1525B, *The Horse stolen;* 1525G, *The Thief Assumes Dis-*

guises (as Priest); and 1525H₁, *One Thief Steals Egg from Bird's Nest.* These versions have been published only in the United States, the Dominican Republic, Puerto Rico, Venezuela, Argentina, and Chile. For the last see CFCH, II, p. 348.

PART V

TALES OF TRICKSTERS AND DUPES

·40· The Black Dog

Types 1000, *Bargain Not to Become Angry*, 1003, *Plowing*, and 1011, *Tearing up the Vineyard.* Compare also Type 303, *The twins or Blood-Brothers*, II. Motifs: E761.3, "Life token: tree (flower) fades"; B422, "Helpful cat"; B313, "Helpful animal an enchanted person (princess)"; K172, "Anger bargain"; K1411, "Plowing the field"; K1416, "Tearing up the vineyard"; D141, "Transformation: Man (woman) to dog"; D157, "Transformation: man to parrot"; D131, "Transformation: man to horse"; D133.1, "Transformation to cow"; G512.3.2.1, "Ogre's wife (queen) burned in her own oven"; D700, "Person disenchanted." CFCH No. 161, "The Black Dog."

Collected in Los Vilos, Coquimbo, on April 2, 1959 from Juan de la Cruz Cáceres, a woodcutter and the owner of a herd of burros, who was over eighty years old at the time of collection.

This story belongs to the cycle 1000–1029, *Labor Contract;* the nexus of this tale is Type 1000, *Bargain Not to Become Angry.* Thompson notes in the second revision of Aarne's *Index* that "Type 1000 is usually combined with one or more types, especially 1000–1029, and also 1060, 1062, 1088, 1115, 1386, 1653, 1725." In the oral tradition of the Iberian peninsula and in Spanish- and Portuguese-speaking areas, these combinations are more numerous. In the Americas, its range includes the United States, Brazil, Guatemala, the Dominican Republic, Puerto Rico, Bolivia, and Chile. See CFCH, III, pp. 349–54. For references to this cycle of stories, see Espinosa, III, pp. 130–40. Types 1000 and 1011 are again combined in the North Carolina variant No. 7, "Big Jack and Little Jack," collected by Richard Chase and published in his *The Jack Tales*, pp. 67–75.

·41· Pedro Animales Fools His Boss

Types 1004, *Hogs in the Mud,* and 1563, *"Both?"* Motifs: K404.1, "Tails in ground" and K1354.1, 'Both?' The youth is sent to a house to get two articles. He meets the two daughters and calls back to the master, 'Both?' "Yes, I said both!" replies the master. The youth has his way with both daughters (variant: the mother and the two daughters). CFCH No. 163, "Pedro Animales."

Collected in July, 1958 in Mamiña, Tarapacá, from traveling salesman Luis Saavedra, born in 1898.

Type 1004, *Hogs in the Mud,* is found from Iceland to India and Indonesia, and in Spanish- and Portuguese-speaking areas from the United States to Argentina and Chile, as well as among the Quechua Indians of Bolivia. On the other hand, Type 1563, *"Both?,"* an anecdote which appears in the *Thousand and One Nights,* has had a very irregular dissemination in Europe. No version has been listed from the Iberian peninsula. Nevertheless, it has spread from Spain and Portugal to America, where two versions from Puerto Rico, three from Chile, and one from the Chane Indians of Bolivia had been published. Thompson, p. 203, says that it appears in the folklore of three Indian tribes of North America and in the Portuguese tradition of Massachusetts. The combination of the two types mentioned above has been found in Brazil, Bolivia, and Chile; see CFCH, III, p. 352.

Type 1563 appears in combination with other types in "Big Jack and Little Jack," No. 7 in Richard Chase's *The Jack Tales,* pp. 67–75. (See notes for tale No. 40 in this volume.)

·*42*· *The Unknown Bird*

Type 1091, *Who Can Bring an Unheard-of Riding Horse.* Motif K216.2, "Bringing the devil an unknown animal." CFCH No. 168, "The Unknown Bird."

Collected in January, 1951 at the Güeimén farm, Ignao, Valdivia, from Zoraila Corona.

Type 1091, *Who Can Bring an Unheard-of Riding Horse,* appears in the jest books of the seventeenth century, as Bolte and Polívka I, p. 411, note 1, inform us. It is frequent in the oral tradition of Europe. In the Iberian peninsula, one independent Galician version and one Spanish version combined with subtype 1091A are known. In Spanish America, one independent version has been published from each of the following countries: the Dominican Republic, Bolivia, and Argentina. Two have been published from Chile. The combined version with the two types has appeared in the following places: one in Argentina, one in Chile, and one among the Araucanian Indians; see CFCH, III, pp. 354–55.

·43· Pedro Urdimale, the Little Fox, and the Mare's Egg

Type 1319, Motif J1772.1, "Pumpkin sold as an ass's egg." CFCH No. 174, "Pedro Urdimale, the Little Fox, and the Mare's Egg."

Collected on tape on December 22, 1962 in Pomaire, Santiago, from Abraham Vélez.

This joke is known throughout Europe as well as in Turkey, Armenia, India, and China. In the Iberian peninsula, a Catalonian version has been collected. It has also spread in North America among the English-speaking inhabitants, the Indians, and the Negroes. Richard M. Dorson, *Negro Tales from Pine Bluff, Arkansas, and Calvin, Michigan,* No. 47, includes one version and cites another; Leonard Roberts gives a Kentucky variant as No. 46 "The Irishman and the Pumpkin," in his collection *South from Hell-fer-Sartin,* p. 121. In Latin America, one Argentinian version and two Chilean ones have been published. The story is well-known in Chile.

·44· Pedro Urdemales Cheats Two Horsemen

Types 1528, *Holding Down the Hat;* 1539, *Cleverness and Gullibility;* and 1535, *The Rich and the Poor Peasant.* Motifs: K1252, "Holding down the hat"; K112.1, "Alleged self-cooking kettle sold"; K113, "Pseudo-magic resuscitating object sold"; K119, "Sale of other pseudo-magic objects"; K842, "Dupe persuaded to take prisoner's place in a sack." CFCH No. 186, "Pedro Urdemales."

Collected on tape on April 21, 1962 in Parral, Linares, from Amelia Quiroz.

Type 1528, *Holding Down the Hat,* is told in Europe, especially in the Scandinavian countries, Lithuania, and Russia. It has not been listed in the Iberian peninsula but, on the other hand, exists in North, Central, and South America. In Spanish or Portuguese areas of America it appears in independent form or in combination with other types or motifs. A British variant is given as No. 69, "The Irishman's Hat" in *Folktales of England,* a companion volume in this series. A variant related in Japanese was told by Austin Bach, a German raised in Japan, to Joseph L. Sutton in 1946. Richard M. Dorson recorded it from Dean Sutton of Indiana University in 1966. An old Korean gentleman tricks a Japanese policeman.

Types 1535, *The Rich and the Poor Peasant,* and 1539, *Cleverness and Gullibility,* are widely dispersed in Latin America. The famous trickster Pedro Urdemales enters the Iberian and American versions

of the three mentioned above. This character is explained in the notes
for story No. 12. For the Spanish and Portuguese versions, see Hansen's *Index;* Espinosa, III, pp. 158–59; CFCH, III, pp. 363–65; and
Pino-Saavedra, *Chilenische Volksmärchen,* pp. 279–80. Riley Aiken
gives two Mexican variants of Type 1535 ("The Two Compadres,"
pp. 29–36, and "Pedro de Urdemalas," pp. 49–55), and one of Type
1539 ("Charge This to the Cap," pp. 41–44), in his collection, "A
Packload of Mexican Tales."

·45· The Miserly Rich Man and the Unlucky Poor Man

Type 1536A, *The Woman in the Chest.* Motif K2321, "Corpse sets out
to frighten people." CFCH No. 195, "The Miserly Rich Man and the
Unlucky Poor man."

Collected in February, 1952 in Vivanco, Valdivia, from a shoemaker, Calixto Carrasco, born 1907.

This story appears throughout Europe. From Spain it went to
America, where versions have been listed in the United States, Argen-
tina, and Chile. It is also known among the Tepecano Indians of
Mexico and Negroes in the West Indies. For references, see Espinosa,
III, pp. 166–80.

Type 1536A is given as No. 8, "Whiteshirt," in *Folktales of Hungary,* and another version appears in *Folktales of Germany;* both volumes are in this series.

·46· Pedro Urdimale and the Dead Priests

Type 1536B, *The Three Hunchback Brothers.* Motif K2322, "The
three hunchback brothers drowned." CFCH No. 197, "Pedro
Urdimale."

Collected in January, 1952 in Ignao, Valdivia, from Francisco
Coronado.

Folklorists agree upon the oriental origins of this story. It is found
in our time as far east as China and in some European countries. Sean
O'Súilleabháin has listed numerous Irish versions in his *Index.* Besides the versions noted in Thompson's *Index,* we should cite two
Polish examples in Krzyzanowski's *Index.* The story also has ramifications in America, where the following versions have been collected:
a French one from Canada, a Spanish one from the United States,
one from Puerto Rico, one from Argentina, and four from Chile. In
the West Indies, four Negro versions are known. Riley Aiken gives a

Mexican variant of Type 1536B in his "A Pack Load of Mexican Tales," as "El Borracho del Bahía," pp. 57–60.

Special studies of this story include those of Pillet, *Les trois bossus ménestrels;* Taylor "Dane Hew, Munk of Leicestre"; *Modern Philology,* XV (1917), 221–46, 223 n.3; and Espinosa, II, pp. 153–59.

· 47 · Pedro Urdimale Makes Exchanges

Type 1655, *The Profitable Exchange.* Motif K251.1, "The eaten grain and the cock as damages." CFCH No. 212, "Pedro Urdimale."

Collected in February, 1952 in Ignao, Valdivia, from Juan de Dios Díaz.

Type 1655, *The Profitable Exchange,* is known especially in France, Ireland, and Turkey. Its area of dissemination extends to India, China, and Africa. From the oral tradition of America, the following versions have been gathered: twelve French versions from Canada, two French versions from the United States, a Portuguese one from Brazil, and Spanish versions from the United States (one), Cuba (one), and Chile (four). It has also been found in the West Indies and among the Zuñi Indians of North America.

· 48 · We Ourselves

Type 1697, *"We Three; For Money."* Motif C495.2.2, " 'We three— For gold—That is right': phrases of foreign language." CFCH No. 213, "We ourselves."

Collected on tape on December 23, 1962 in Pomaire, Santiago, from Abraham Vélez.

The largest number of versions in the oral tradition of Type 1697, *"We Three; For Money,"* is to be found in Finland, France, Holland, and Belgium. Thompson and Roberts, p. 163, list three Indic versions. From the Iberian peninsula three Spanish, one Catalonian, and one Portuguese version have been published; A. Espinosa, Jr., has also collected five unpublished Spanish versions. From France, ramifications of this story have been found in Canada, Louisiana, and Martinique. From Spain, there have been ramifications in the United States, the Dominican Republic, Puerto Rico, and Chile. A modern British variant is No. 70, "The Three Foreigners," appearing in *Folktales of England.* Richard M. Dorson has published another version, "The Three Irishmen Who Couldn't Speak English," in his *Negro Folktales in Michigan* (Cambridge, Massachusetts, 1956) pp. 183–85.

· 49 · The Chilean Swindlers

Types 1920E, *The Greatest Liar Gets his Supper Free;* 1920A, *The First: "The Sea Burns."* The Other: *"Many Fried Fish"* (the first tells of the great cabbage, the other of the kettle to cook it in); 1930, *Schlaraffenland;* and compare types 1960D, *The Great Vegetable,* and 1960F, *The Great Kettle.* Motifs: K455.7, "Greatest liar gets his supper free"; X907.1, "The second liar corroborates his lies"; X908, "Lie: sea has burned up"; X909, "Other stories about liars"; X1423.1, "Lie: the great cabbage"; X1031.1.1, "Lie: the great kettle." CFCH No. 221, "The Chilean Swindlers."

Recorded on tape on January 17, 1962 in Pomaire, Santiago, from Abraham Vélez.

This amalgam of Types 1920E, 1920A, and 1930 is not frequent in the oral tradition. In the Iberian peninsula a Spanish and a Catalonian version of Type 1920A, and a Spanish one of Type 1930, have been collected. Spanish literature, on the other hand, has elaborated motifs of Types 1920A and 1930, for example, in the writings of Juan Ruiz, Pinedo, and Lope de Rueda; see CFCH, III, p. 378. In Chile, I have collected another combined version of Type 1930, *Schlaraffenland.* Type 1920A is told as a true tale in a British variant in *Folktales of England* as No. 91, "Mark Twain in the Fens." A Mexican variant of Type 1920A is given by Riley Aiken in "A Pack Load of Mexican Tales," as "Keeping the Shirt-tail In," pp. 55–57, and Richard M. Dorson presents a Michigan version in "Dialect Stories of the Upper Peninsula: A New Form of American Folklore," *Journal of American Folklore,* LXI (1948), "Big Bagies," 138–39.

PART VI

CUMULATIVE TALES

· 50 · The Thrush

Type 2031, which also constitutes Motif Z42, "Stronger and strongest." CFCH No. 225, "The Thrush."

Collected on tape on January 17, 1962 in Pomaire, Santiago, from Abraham Vélez.

Type 2031, *Stronger and Strongest,* has had only limited dissemination in Europe. The Aarne and Thompson *Index,* p. 530, lists ten versions, one from Spain and one from Catalonia, as well as Turkish, Indic, Indonesian, and African versions. To these we must add three Portuguese ones. In America no fewer than Twenty-two version have been published: a Portuguese one from Brazil, six Spanish versions from the United States, four from Puerto Rico, one from Guatemala, two from Argentina, four from Chile, three from the Araucanian Indians of Chile and Argentina, and one from the Tehuano Indians of North America. For references to the origin and development of this story, see especially Taylor, *JAF*, XLVI (1933) 84; and *Handwörterbuch des deutschen Märchens*, II, pp. 182–84. For the Latin American versions, see CFCH, III, p. 381.

Glossary

adobe A mass of mud mixed with straw and molded in the form of a brick of variable size, generally about 16 inches long, 6 inches wide, and 1½ inches thick. The bricks are dried in the sun and used in the construction of walls.

almud An old Spanish measurement for dry substances, which in Chile corresponds to about ten quarts.

caco A thief who robs with skill. In Chile the use of this term has been extended to include any ordinary thief.

chaicancito A dish made of toasted wheat flour and hot water.

chamanto A kind of poncho.

charqui Meat cut in thin strips and dried in the sun. (Jerked beef.)

chilco The Araucanian name for a Chilean bush with red corollas which is similar to the fuchsia, *Fuchsia magellanica*.

comadre See *compadre.*

compadre A term used to designate reciprocally the godfather and the father of a baptized child. The *compadrazgo* is the relationship between these two men. By extension, the mother and godmother call the godfather *compadre.* The connection established between the parents and the godfather is still very significant in the villages and rural districts. Upon the death of the child's father, the *compadre* is obligated to watch and protect the orphan. The feminine word *comadre* is used in the same way as *compadre,* referring in this case to the relation between the parents and the godmother. By extension, the terms *compadre* and *comadre* are used simply to denote friendship.

cueca A Chilean national dance.

empanada A pastry made by folding dough over a filling of meat and chopped onions. It can be fried or baked in the oven.

gringo A nickname used popularly in Chile to designate Europeans and North Americans; originally it was applied only to Englishmen.

guacha (masculine: *guacho*) An orphan.

lara A popular mythological feminine being.

litre The Araucanian name for *Lithraea caustica,* a tree with very solid wood and poisonous leaves that usually produce skin irritations.

lola A mythological being who robs horsemen and hides in the mountains.

mate Maté, *Ilex paraguayensis.* The term is also used to designate the mixture of leaves from this tree and the cup, either a dry gourd or made of clay, in which the tea made from the leaves is sipped through a tube.

mingaco A community work project at the conclusion of which food and drink are passed out.

mote Cooked and hulled wheat which is prepared as a drink with cold water, or as a hot dish.

nalca The edible stem of the *pangue, Gunnera chilensis.*

paipay A nonsense word.

pampa A great flat plain.

Pancho The familiar diminutive of the name Francisco.

patagua A name of Araucanian origin for *Crimodrendon patagua,* a tree bearing white flowers.

Pedro Animales A corruption of Pedro Urdemales. This protagonist of the comic stories is called Pedro Urdemalas in Spain, the last name having the most diverse derivations in Spanish America.

pellín A name of Araucanian origin for *Nothofagus obliqua,* a tree with very hard wood.

peseta The basic unit of Spanish currency.

peso An old Chilean coin.

peumo A name of Araucanian origin for *Cryptocarya rubra,* an evergreen tree with edible fruits.

pi-pi-pi Onomatopoeic rendering of the cry of the partridge.

pirulí Onomatopoeic rendering of the sound of a whistle.

quico A very skillful thief. In the Chilean stories, the companion of Caco. It is formed an ablaut of caco.

quillay A name of Araucanian origin for an evergreen tree, *Quillaja Saponaria,* the bark of which contains saponin and is used for shampooing hair.

quintal An old Spanish measure equal to one hundred and one pounds avoirdupois.

relvun A perennial herb with meaty red fruits. Its roots are used for dyeing.

roto A member of the humblest class in Chile.

taitita (diminutive of *taita*) An affectionate nickname for the father.

tortillas A hearth bread made of cornmeal.

trara A mythological bird which announces news.

Bibliography

CHILEAN

CFCH. *See* Pino-Saavedra.

GUZMÁN MATURANA, MANUEL. "Cuentos tradicionales en Chile," *Anales de la Universidad de Chile,* Year XCII, Nos. 14–15 (1934), 34–81; 5–78.

LAVAL, RAMÓN A. *Cuentos populares en Chile.* Santiago de Chile, 1923.

———. *Tradiciones, leyendas y cuentos populares.* Santiago de Chile, 1920.

———. "Cuentos de Pedro Urdemales," *Revista de Folklore Chileno,* VI (1925), 147–203. 2d ed. 1943.

———. "Cuentos chilenos de nunca acabar," *Revista de Folklore Chileno,* I, 2a (1910), 3–44; also *Anales de la Universidad de Chile,* CXXV (1909), 955–96.

LENZ, RODOLFO. "Consejas chilenas," *Revista de Folklore Chileno,* III (1912), 3–152.

———. "Cuentos de adivinanzas en Chile," *Revista de Folklore Chileno,* II (1912), 337–83.

MONTENEGRO, ERNESTO. *Cuentos de mi tío Ventura.* 3d ed. Santiago de Chile, 1963.

PINO-SAAVEDRA, YOLANDO. *Cuentos Folklóricos de Chile.* 3 vols. Santiago de Chile, 1960–63. (=CFCH.)

———. *Chilenische Volksmärchen,* trans. Ingeborg Wilcke-Brubacher. Düsseldorf and Cologne, 1964.

SAUNIÈRE, S. DE. "Cuentos populares chilenos y araucanos," *Revista de Folklore Chileno,* VII (1918), 3–282.

GENERAL

AARNE, ANTTI. "Vergleichende Märchen-Forschungen," *Memoires de la Société Finno-Ougrienne,* XXV (1908).
——. and STITH THOMPSON. *The Types of the Folktale: A Classification and Bibliography* ("Folklore Fellows Communications," No. 184). Helsinki, 1961.
AIKEN, RILEY. "A Pack Load of Mexican Tales," *Publications of the Texas Folklore Society,* XII (1935), 1–87.
ALMEIDA, ALUÍSIO DE. *142 Histórias brasileiras.* São Paulo, 1951.
AMADES, JOAN. *Rondallística.* Barcelona, 1950.
ANDRADE, MANUEL JOSÉ. *Folklore de la República Dominicana.* 2 vols. Santo Domingo, 1948.
BASILE, G. *The Pentamerone of Giambattista Basile.* London, 1932.
Bibliotica de las tradiciones Populares Españolas. Seville, 1883.
BOGGS, RALPH STEELE. *Index of Spanish Folktales.* ("Folklore Fellows Communications," No. 90). Helsinki, 1930.
BOLTE, JOHANNES, and POLÍVKA, GEORG. *Anmerkungen zu den Kinder- und Hausmärchen der Brüder Grimm.* 5 vols. Leipzig, 1913–31.
BRAGA, T. *Contos tradicionaes do povo portuguez.* Oporto, 1883.
CAMARA CASCUDO, LUÍS DA. *Contos Tradicionais do Brasil.* Rio de Janeiro, 1946.
——. *Trinta Estórias Brasileiras.* Lisbon, 1955.
CAMPBELL, MARIE. *Tales from the Cloud Walking Country.* Bloomington, Indiana, 1958.
CHASE, RICHARD. *The Jack Tales.* Cambridge, Massachusetts, 1943.
——. *Grandfather Tales.* Cambridge, Massachusetts, 1948.
CHERTUDI, SUSANA. *Cuentos folklóricos de la Argentina.* Buenos Aires, 1960.
——. *Juan Soldao. Cuentos folklóricos de la Argentina.* Buenos Aires, 1962.
COELHO, F. ADOLPHE. *Contos populares portugueses.* Lisbon, 1879.
COX, MARIAN. *Cinderella.* London, 1893.
CURIEL MERCHÁN, MARCIANO. *Cuentos extremeños.* Madrid, 1944.
DELARUE, PAUL. *Le conte populaire français.* Vol. I. Paris, 1957.

DIRR, A. *Kaukasische Märchen*. Jena, 1922.

DORSON, RICHARD M. *Buying the Wind*. Chicago, 1964.

———. "Dialect Stories of the Upper Peninsula: A New Form of American Folklore," *Journal of American Folklore*, LXI (1948), 113–50.

———. *Negro Folktales in Michigan*. Cambridge, Massachusetts, 1956.

———. *Negro Tales from Pine Bluff, Arkansas and Calvin, Michigan* ("Indiana University Folklore Series," No. 12). Bloomington, Indiana, 1958.

———. "Polish Wonder Tales of Joe Woods," *Western Folklore*, VIII (1949), 25–52.

EBERHARD, WOLFRAM, and BORATAV, PERTEV N. *Typen türkischer Volksmärchen*. Wiesbaden, 1953.

ESPINOSA, AURELIO M. *Cuentos populares españoles*. 3 vols. Madrid, 1946–47.

GONZENBACH, LAURA. *Sicilianische Märchen*. 2 vols. Leipzig, 1870.

GREVERUS, INA-MARIA. "Die Geschenke des kleinen Volkes," *Fabula*, I (1958), 263–79.

HAMBRUCH, PAUL, ed. *Malaiische Märchen aus Madagascar und Insulinde*. Jena, 1922.

HANSEN, TERRENCE LESLIE. *The Types of the Folktale in Cuba, Puerto Rico, the Dominican Republic, and Spanish South America*. Berkeley and Los Angeles, 1957.

HOFFMANN-KRAYER, E. and BÄCHTOLD-STÄUBLI, H., eds. *Handwörterbuch des deutschen Aberglaubens*. Berlin and Leipzig, 1927–42.

JECH, JAROMIR. *Tschechische Volksmärchen*. Berlin, 1961.

KÖSSLER-ILG, BERTHA. *Indianermärchen aus den Kordilleren (Märchen der Araukaner)*. Düsseldorf and Cologne, 1956.

KROHN, KAARLE. *Übersicht über einige Resultate der Märchenforschung* ("Folklore Fellows Communications," No. 96). Helsinki, 1931.

KRZYZANOWSKI, JULIAN. *Polska Bajka Ludowa w Ukladzie Systematyeznym*. 2 vols. Warsaw, 1947.

LITTMAN, ENNO. *Arabische Märchen aus mündlicher Überlieferung*. Leipzig, 1957.

LIUNGMAN, WALDEMAR. *Die schwedischen Volksmärchen*. Berlin, 1961.

MACKENSEN, L., ed. *Handwörterbuch des deutschen Märchens*. Vols. I and II. Berlin and Leipzig, 1930–33.

O'SÚILLEABHÁIN, SEAN, and CHRISTIANSEN, REIDAR TH. *The Types of the Irish Folktale* ("Folklore Fellows Communications," No. 188). Helsinki, 1963.

PARIS, GASTON. "Le cycle de la gageure," *Romania*, XXXII (1903), 481–551.

PEDROSO, Z. CONSIGLIERI. "Contos Populares Portuguezes," *Revue Hispanique*, XIV (1906), 115–240.

PERRAULT, CHARLES. *Perrault's Popular Tales*, ed. Andrew Lang. Oxford, 1888.

PITRÈ, GIUSEPPE. *Opere Complete*. Rome, 1940–57.

POOLER, LOLITA. "New Mexican Folktales," *Western Folklore*, X (1951), 63–71.

RAMIREZ DE ARELLANO, RAFAEL. *Folklore portorriqueño*. Madrid, 1926.

RANKE, KURT. *Schleswig-Holsteinische Volksmärchen*. Vols. I, II, and III. Kiel, 1955–62.

———. *Die zwei Brüder* ("Folklore Fellows Communications," No. 114). Helsinki, 1934.

ROBERTS, LEONARD. *South from Hell-fer-Sartin*. Lexington, Kentucky, 1955.

ROMÉRO, SYLVIO. *Contos populares do Brasil*. 2d ed. Rio de Janeiro and São Paulo, 1897.

ROOTH, ANNA BIRGITTA. *The Cinderella Cycle*. Lund, 1951.

RÖSCH, E. *Der getreue Johannes* ("Folklore Fellows Communications," No. 77). Helsinki, 1928.

SCHEWE, HARRY. "Die 'Wette' eine neu aufgefundene alte Ballade," in *Volkskundliche Gaben*, ed. Erich Seemann. Berlin, 1934, pp. 176–86.

SZÖVÉRFFY, JOSEF. *Irisches Erzahlgut im Abendland*. Berlin, 1957.

———. "A Medieval Story and Its Irish Version," in *Studies in Folklore in Honor of Distinguished Service Professor Stith Thompson*, ed. W. Edson Richmond ("Indiana University Publications. Folklore Series," No. 9). Bloomington, Indiana, pp. 55–65.

TAYLOR, ARCHER. "A Classification of Formula Tales," *Journal of American Folklore*, XLVI (1933), 77–88.

———. "Dane Hew, Munk of Leicestre," *Modern Philology*, XV (1917), 221–46.

THOMPSON, STITH. *The Folktale*. New York, 1946.

———. *Motif-Index of Folk-Literature*. 6 vols. Rev. ed. Copenhagen and Bloomington, Indiana, 1955–58.

THOMPSON, STITH, and ROBERTS, WARREN E. *Types of Indic Oral Tales* ("Folklore Fellows Communications," No. 180). Helsinki, 1960.

VRIES, JAN DE. *Das Märchen von klugen Rätsellösern* ("Folklore Fellows Communications," No. 73). Helsinki, 1928.

———. "Dornröschen," *Fabula*, II (1959), 110–21.

WESSELSKI, ALBERT. *Märchen des Mittelalters*. Berlin, 1925.

ZAUNERT, PAUL. *Deutsche Märchen seit Grimm*. 2 vols. Jena, 1922–23.

Index of Motifs

(Motif numbers are from Stith Thompson, *Motif-Index of Folk-Literature* [6 vols.; Copenhagen and Bloomington, Ind., 1955-58].)

A. MYTHOLOGICAL MOTIFS

Motif No.		Tale No.
A661.0.1.2	St. Peter as porter of heaven	11, 12, 31
A2721.3.1	Man tells Jesus he is sowing stones. 'You shall get stones'	34

B. ANIMALS

B92	Hero divides spoil for animals	4
B143	Prophetic bird	22
B313	Helpful animal an enchanted person	14, 40
B322.1	Hero feeds own flesh to helpful animal	3
B350	Grateful animals	23
B360	Animal grateful for rescue from peril of death	23, 24
B392	Hero divides spoil for animals	23
B401	Helpful horse	6
B411.3	Helpful calf	19
B412	Helpful sheep	7
B421	Helpful dog	8, 24
B422	Helpful cat	24, 40
B491.1	Helpful snake	15
B500	Magic power from animals	4
B512	Medicine shown by animal	5
B515	Resuscitation by animals	8
B524.1.1	Dog saves life—kills giant	8
B548.1	Animals recover lost wishing ring (nut). Grateful dog compels mouse to steal it from thief	24
B557	Unusual animal as riding horse	7, 15
B571	Animals perform tasks for man	23

C. TABU

D. MAGIC

G. OGRES

H. TESTS

L. REVERSAL OF FORTUNE

M. ORDAINING THE FUTURE

N. CHANCE AND FATE

P. SOCIETY

Q. REWARDS AND PUNISHMENTS

R. CAPTIVES AND FUGITIVES

S. UNNATURAL CRUELTY

T. SEX

V. RELIGION

W. TRAITS OF CHARACTER

X. HUMOR

Z. MISCELLANEOUS GROUPS OF MOTIFS

Index of Tale Types

(Type numbers are from Antti Aarne and Stith Thompson, *The Types of the Folktale* [Helsinki, 1961].)

I. ANIMAL TALES (1–299)

II. ORDINARY FOLKTALES

A. Tales of Magic (300–749)

IV. Cumulative Tales (2000–2075)

General Index

41634